Acknowledgements

PART I: Naked Cowboys 5
Chapter one 6
Chapter two 14
Chapter three 20
Chapter four.. 25
Chapter five.. 28
Chapter six 30
Chapter seven 34
Chapter eight.. 39

PART II: The Yellow Tram.......................... 43
Chapter nine 44
Chapter ten 55
Chapter eleven.. 62
Chapter twelve 67
Chapter thirteen 73
Chapter fourteen 80
Chapter fifteen 87
Chapter sixteen.. 96
Chapter seventeen 102
Chapter eighteen 107
Chapter nineteen 114
Chapter twenty..118
Chapter twenty-one 122
Chapter twenty-two 125
Chapter twenty-three 127
Chapter twenty-four....................................129
Chapter twenty-five......................................133
Chapter twenty-six 138
Chapter twenty-seven 145
Chapter twenty-eight....................................154

PART III: The Art Of War 159
Chapter twenty-nine 160
Chapter thirty..167
Chapter thirty-one 172

Chapter thirty-two 178
Chapter thirty-three 182
Chapter thirty-four 185
Chapter thirty-five 190
Chapter thirty-six 193
Chapter thirty-seven 198
Chapter thirty-eight 201
Chapter thirty-nine 207
Chapter forty 215
Chapter forty-one 218
Chapter forty-two 224
Chapter forty-three 227
Chapter forty-four 235
Chapter forty-five 241
Chapter forty-six 245
Chapter forty-seven 249
Chapter forty-eight 256
Chapter forty-nine 261

PART IV: The Crock Of Gold 267
Chapter fifty 268

BLACK BOAT DANCING

By

GERARD CAPPA

Copyright © 2014 by Gerard Cappa. All rights reserved.

Black Boat Dancing is a work of fiction. Certain incidents described in the book are based on actual recent and historical events, but other than well-known public figures referred to by name, all the characters are products of the author's imagination and are not construed as real, and any resemblance to actual persons living or dead is entirely coincidental. Neither the publisher nor author can be held liable for any third-party material referenced in the book.

No part of this book may be reproduced, or stored in a retrieval system, or transmitted in any form or by any means, electronic, mechanical, photocopying, recording, or otherwise, without express written permission of the publisher.

In Acknowledgement:

A novel doesn't write itself. I owe a huge debt of gratitude to Cassiana Teodoro in Brazil, Paula Santos, Luis Portas and Nuno Peralta in Portugal, and Patrick Murphy in the USA for their advice and support. Of course, all mistakes are of my own making!

Book Design and Production:

Cover concept, design and illustration, overall book design, typography and layout by Davy McDonald Creative: davymac.com

BLACK BOAT DANCING

Authority is the source of knowledge, but the reason of mankind is the norm by which all authority is judged.

Johannes Scotus Eriugena
(Eoin, the Irish-born Gael)

(815 - 877)

PART I:
NAKED COWBOYS

I fear the Greeks, even when they bring gifts

Virgil (70 BC – 19 BC)

CHAPTER ONE

January 13th

Blind Mary's Bar, Hell's Kitchen, New York City.

It was the tip of her shoe I saw first. A cream leather brogue tapping the tiled floor. She was here, scrummed by the defeated with their shallow kinship and piss stained sneakers. They were here to celebrate the Manchester soccer game but Cora was here for me, and her cool presence neutered their grim swagger so they looked and didn't look, then looked away. I retreated into the back room and breathed again.

I hunkered down and wiped my hands on the edge of the dust sheet covering the tables and chairs, tagged my footprint painted across a cracked white floor tile. Cagney's spattered smirk peeped from the shelf. Careless, needed to shake my act together, time to snap out of this fog.
It had been over a year, the Fredericksburg 150th, time to move on.

Shadows mustered on the other side of the smoked glass. I burrowed further into the dust sheets. The door tilted towards me, wedged a red purple prism of rainbow across the black and white floor.

'Hi, Mr Maknazpy,' Cora said, 'May I come in?'

She splashed through the rainbow, clicked the door closed against the shadows behind her. I saw the red sparkles on her cream brogues.

'How have you been, Con? Is everything still okay?'

'Sure Cora, everything is just fine. You can tell them they have nothing to worry about, we know the drill, there are no leaks this end.'

Cora moved closer, floating in a bubble of fresh air and perfume, whipped back the dust sheet and scraped the chair against the tiles, fizzed my nerves.

'We know we can rely on you, Con. You have proved that. You saved many American lives and the people of the United States owe you their deep gratitude. It won't be forgotten, be assured.'

'But they're still worried we'll start mouthing off about it, aren't they? Afraid me and Ferdia will spoil the party?'

She pulled another chair out, offered it to me, accidentally grazed her fingers against my cheek. Except Cora never did anything accidentally.

'And how is Ferdia McErlane? Is he coping?' Her voice was steady; knew what she wanted, knew she would get it, stamped my inferiority with her deference.

'Those are the same shoes,' I said.

Cora stalled, a phantom wrinkle cracked out from the delicate corner of her left eye until she stroked it smooth. She leant forward slightly and lifted her right foot at the same time to inspect the cream soft leather brogue. I could see the eyes working, slipping away from her script.
Her hair was longer now, and more blond, tied back behind her ears.

'The same shoes?' Cora prompted.

Her dark eyebrows contoured the delicious burnished black eyes, waiting for me. And I didn't care that I was staring, close enough now to notice the miniscule grains of mascara shimmer on the long lashes. And the sheer gloss of the metallic crimson lips. Jewelry too. Chic and expensive ruby red rings draped each ear, a blood red beaded necklace against her tanned neck. Still a tan, in January, a hint of sun red on the high arched cheek bones. Maybe skiing. She hadn't worn make-up before; no jewelry, no lipstick, just that same troubling perfume. And the shoes.

'When you triggered his brains to red mist. The same shoes,' I said.

'He was going to kill you,' she said, neutral, back on track, barely missed a beat.

'You wiped those shoes on him', I said. 'You nutted him point blank, then wiped the blood off those shoes.'

She tossed her head back, stroked the longer, blonder hair with her right hand, almost smiling.

'He would have killed you, Con.'

I moved closer still, looked into her eyes, noses almost touching, breathed her breath.

'It isn't easy to get blood off shoes like that, is it?'

The eyes pulsed, just once, but she gripped her composure, always ready to stare me out.

'These are different shoes, Maknazpy. Those were black, these are cream. He would have killed you. Your memory is playing tricks again.'

Maybe, and that would always be their trump card. Con Maknazpy's memory played tricks. I sat back, linked my paint fingers behind my head. The moment passed.

'You're working for Gallogly now?' she scanned my handiwork.

'Yeah, sort of,' I said, easy now, just an ordinary pass the time of day conversation. 'He calls me sometimes when he needs something done. A bit of painting in here, gutting out that old warehouse on 44th Street, pulling security on his entertainment venues. Just casual stuff, nothing special.'

'Nice color scheme,' she said. 'You picked it?'

Rustic Flame red on the main wall, Sahara Evening on the others.

'I like it, a big improvement.' Cora stretched her long legs but then quickly tucked the cream brogues back under the seat. The sly bitch knew I didn't pick it. 'And how is your wife right now, Con?'

She must have known Rose was living with Gallogly.

'Yeah, that's fine. We're sorting things out, it'll be fine,' I said.

Something deep rippled under the dark fluid eyes but the voice gave nothing away; a slight nod, satisfied, maybe on a professional level. I wondered about the personal.

'So, Ferdia McErlane is doing fine?' she sighed, as if it was hardly worth the mention.

'Looks like it to me,' I echoed her sigh. 'The past doesn't exist for him, he's not that sort of guy, only looks ahead, what's happening tomorrow.'

Cora nodded, like she already knew what sort of guy Ferdy was. 'It's just we've heard he is mixing with borderline people.' Conjured concern in her voice. 'You know, like he is missing the excitement?' Just her voice, not her eyes.

I caught the Cagney picture again, made a mental note to clean it when she was gone.

'It's like you said,' She had rehearsed this. 'We have an arrangement. It is really in no-one's interest to look back, dwell on that version of the past. But the past can be a parasite, Con, sucking away on all those bad memories of yours, re-inventing itself until there is no present. You understand what I'm saying here, right?'

She was saying what she had been sent here to say. She was saying that Ferdia and I had been up to our necks in a treacherous game, bought the luck to come out the other side, but with blood on our hands, the sort of blood that we couldn't expect to be pardoned. But this time ours weren't the only bloody fingerprints, and the others weren't expendable; the continued sanctity of the United States needed these others to be left unimpeded. So, keep your mouth shut and live, is what she was saying.

'I understand,' I said. 'You're saying these are different shoes. It was all a trick of my memory.'

Cora smiled and stretched her legs again, held the cream brogues out for my inspection. 'Exactly, Mr Maknazpy, that is exactly what I'm saying. And Ferdia McErlane is still hearing the message? Because there are people who want to make sure all those loose ends are tied up now, once and for all.'

I let her see I was staring at the shadows on the other side of the frosted glass. Two of them, maybe three.

'Those people had better mind their business, Cora,' I said. 'Making threats doesn't work around here, you should know that.'

She drew her legs in, straightened up, clamped those black eyes on me.

'Don't get excited, Con,' she squeezed my wrist. 'Nobody wants trouble, but it is still a take it or leave it offer. Any doubts about you, either of you, and the arrangement could be terminated, just like that.' She snapped her fingers, clicked her tongue and lips.

Yeah, I knew it.

'We are all on the same team, aren't we?' Leaning too close to me now, her perfume smoking all over me. 'We are still talking about the security of the United States here, you can't allow your friend to jeopardise that, right?'

Yeah, right, I was still on that team.

She relaxed, the shadows outside seemed to know it and drained away from the door. She kept her hand on my wrist, I waited.

'Okay, McErlane needs to be monitored,' she said. 'He needs to know he has been making people nervous. That has to stop. You will speak to him, Con, right?'

'What about me, Cora?' I said. 'Anybody nervous about me?'

She moved away, her hand trailed off my wrist.

'Not nervous, Con, no.' Her black eyes were just too earnest, too persuasive. 'Your record as a soldier and servant of the United States are exemplary, no one could doubt your loyalty.'

'So what's the problem?' I said. 'Still doubt my sanity?'

'Not a problem,' she said. 'An opportunity, look at it that way. You aren't an ordinary man, Con, we know that. Your war record said so even before that thing happened.'

Sounded almost like a compliment, but I knew that's how she would smooch a death sentence.

'So, you were sent for therapy, Con.' A shrug, forget it. 'No wonder, after all you were put through. No big deal. Most people just wouldn't have come through at all.' Cora was getting excited, and that prickled a stab of excitement in me now. 'And maybe it was easier to label you with some sort of mental health problem related to stress. But what if that's not what it is?'

They had spent a long, long time convincing me it was a mental health problem, and some of the things I had done could only be filed away by that tag, so I wasn't sure right then that I wanted to revise that whole set-up. Those red tinged ghosts were always there, ever ready to creep back into my brain, and accepting the victim of trauma ticket was still my only alternative to looking straight into the vacuum of my ugly heart. One day at a time. Let sleeping dogs lie.

'What if it is the physical structure of your brain that gives you that edge on ordinary people?' Cora said. 'I mean, we have all seen what you can do, and that's fine if it is controlled and channelled appropriately. But you know it becomes a problem when you can't switch it off and on at the right time.' She switched on the full force of her dark eyes and bright mouth. 'What if we could identify what it really is, and help you control it?'

I was the one getting nervous now. 'I don't need to control anything, Cora, I won't be getting into those situations again. Lead a quiet life, isn't that our new arrangement?'

'Of course, but none of us can be sure that your past isn't going to spark up again someday, can we?' Sympathetic, caring, interested. 'You are just too unpredictable, Con. Maybe that's why your wife and son aren't living with you right now.'

'What do you people want from me here?' I said. 'Look what happened the last time.'

'Not therapy, Con, at least not what you mean.' Gentle, reassuring, comforting.

'What then?' I said. 'A miracle cure?'

She hesitated; genuinely, I thought, not the usual manipulation.

'I really think it would be good for you. One of the leading neuroscientists in America is working with us. He has seen other cases like yours. Men who have done things which they really shouldn't have been able to do.'

'Oh yeah? So I'm Superman now?' I laughed. 'That's not what you were all saying the last time!'

A little spark ignited and fizzled in her eye. She didn't like being laughed at, wasn't used to it.

'How were you able to do all the things you did, Con? Kill all those people, in Iraq, and those other places we won't ever mention, and yet it didn't exist in your conscious memory. Never happened, right?' She was pushing hard. 'Did you think you were a superman, Superman Con Maknazpy, when you were slaughtering those people?'

'How did you feel when you were wiping his blood off your shoes?' I countered.

Her eyes matched her voice now; cold, ready to fight.

'I felt something, Con,' Cora said. 'That's the difference, I knew what I had done and I felt something. What did you ever feel?'

I wasn't going there this time.

'What's this Frankenstein of yours got in his locker?' I asked.

She settled back, still smouldering.

'Just go see him,' she said. 'You don't have to commit to anything.' Maybe a smile. 'Just see him. If it works, great. If it doesn't, then so what? You're still ahead, aren't you?'

Movement outside, the shadows swayed across the glass, voices spilling out from the bar, Cora pulled her cellphone and read a message.

'I have to go right now,' she said, still reading and tapping the screen.

'Well, Cora, just let me know the next time you need to check me out, I'll be right here.'

'And you will consider the neuroscientist?' she said.

I shrugged it off with a laugh, made for the door and yanked it open. The shadows were two heavy guys; about my age, in their thirties, older than her, hard polished faces, arrogant: they jerked to attention when she appeared behind me.

'That'll be fine,' she directed over my shoulder. 'Just wait outside.'

'Miss Oneale?'

Cora didn't answer, just a curt nod, they looked me up and down, then trooped out without looking back.

She stood against me; I could feel her coolness, she must have sensed my heat. I waited.

'One more thing,' she said. 'Did you know a guy called George Oliver back in Yonkers?'

Never heard of him, but Yonkers is a big place.

She shrugged, as if it didn't matter, but everything mattered – she wouldn't have mentioned it otherwise.

'Just somebody we are interested in,' she fingered the red beads of the necklace. 'I thought you might have known him when you were growing up. He's about your age, lived not far from you.' She looked hopeful.

'I'll ask Ferdy and Gallogly, maybe they know him,' I said. 'What about it if they do? Who is he?'

She slipped past, her perfume doping me, the hand on my wrist again. Pulled an envelope out, a photo inside.

'Here, George Oliver, thirty five years old, native of Yonkers, most recently living in Brooklyn Heights.'

Dark guy, well groomed, ordinary looking, but torment locked inside. I recognised that much.

Cora braced me with her eyes, knew I couldn't hide from her now.

'Keep the photo, ask around. Maybe somebody has seen him.'

'And? What if they have?'

'I'll be in touch,' she said, a promise, a squeeze of my wrist again before she turned away and made for the street.

Ferdia McErlane and Jack Gallogly were at the end of the bar now, on the fringes of the soccer mad Irish guys in front of the TV.

'Hey Cora honey! Here I am! Get over here! Why don't you ever take me in the back room?' Ferdy's hoarse drunk whoop roused the other drinkers.

Cora ignored them, half turned to fire a question shrug at me. I nodded, I would take care of it. Ferdy started to lurch towards her but she walked off before he got near her, as if she was in an empty room, as if all those eyes on her didn't exist.

Cora was outside when the crowd erupted in cheers, she probably thought it was for her. 'ROON-EY! ROON-EY! ROON-EY!' She dipped into a silver Honda sedan with the two gundogs at her heels. The windshield reflected the light away from the driver's face so that I couldn't see his features; just a shadow, a wide flat head tapering to a tight jaw and sharp chin, shaped like an old-fashioned anvil. A head forged at the altar to righteous duty and collateral damage. Cora reported back with her hand over her mouth. He tilted his head to listen, then slipped the Honda into the 10th Avenue flow. Gallogly was at my shoulder now.

'Trouble, Con?'

'Hope not,' I said. 'Maybe just a reminder to keep our mouths shut.'

Ferdy was in the middle of the soccer fans now, still chanting 'ROON-EY! ROON-EY!' even though the rest had stopped.

'Who is that Rooney guy, Jack?' I said. 'An American?'

'Don't think so,' Gallogy said, looking back at his drinking customers. 'Must be Irish, I guess.'

'Keep an eye on Ferdy, Jack, will you? I don't need Cora coming to visit again.'

Gallogly started a wisecrack, but snipped it. He had developed a PC sensitivity since my wife had gone to live with him. I showed him the photo.

'Ever hear of this guy? George Oliver, supposed to be from Yonkers?' I asked.

Gallogly glanced at the photo, then at the space where the Honda had been.

'That's why she was here?' he said.

I studied George's sad face. Thousands of guys in Yonkers had a face like that.

'When was Cora Oneale in the back room, Jack?' I asked.

'Cora? She has never been in here before, not that I know of,' he said. 'Definitely not there in the back room, no way she could have ever been back there without me knowing. Why? What makes you think she was?'

I crumpled George's face into a tight ball.

'No trouble, Con, right?' Gallogly buzzed. 'You know it's not good to get those guys nervous.'

'Not this time, Jack,' I said. 'I'm keeping out of their business. I don't care how many times they send Cora, I'm out and I'm staying out.'

'ROON-EY! ROON-EY!'

Gallogly looked back at the rocking Ferdia, I flipped the photo ball in the air and booted it on the way down, it skimmed across the soccer fans and bounced off the TV screen.

'ROON-EY! ROON-EY! ROON-EY!'

Cream soft leather brogues, splashed with a man's blood.

CHAPTER TWO

Ferdia didn't want to know what Cora had said. At least he didn't ask and I didn't volunteer. Gallogly had work for us all that week, tearing the guts out of his old red brick warehouse on West 44th Street, so we hammered and hauled and sweated, and spoke about everything and anything else. Just not about Cora. We were free as long as we kept our mouths shut, he knew that as well as I did. I just wasn't sure if he cared anymore.

But it turned out Ferdy must have been waiting all week for the right time to say what was playing on his own mind.

'Gallogly asked me if you wanted to take young Con to his judo fight tomorrow,' Ferdia breezed it, forced it normal.

'Did Con say he wanted me to?' I pretended not to care.

'Yeah, sure, the kid wants you to be there.' Ferdy was a strange safety valve in this mess. 'Thought I might come too. I'll drive if you want?'

I was already waiting outside my apartment when he came rolling up McLean Avenue. Gallogly had lent us his shiny Merc SUV, a nice gesture, but neither of us would spill Gallogly's name into this, still too delicate, just get through the day. He knew I wasn't in the mood for talk now, so he boosted the volume on Avicii's 'Wake Me Up' and crooned away the slow miles, singing half the lyric in Irish, half in English.

I wasn't in the mood for singing either, just rolled the ticker tape snippets of dialogue I should play with Rose and Gallogly. The civilized pearls of wisdom I knew I should say to make young Con's situation easier. The killer shards of bile I really wanted to spit in their faces. But it was a long way from Yonkers to Gallogly's other house in Hampton Bays, and my see-saw jabber looped around my skull like Ferdy's music until he left the Sunrise Highway and pulled up at a coffee shop.

'You want to talk it through before we get there?' he said.

No, I had nothing to talk through. We were collecting my son and taking him to his first judo contest, what was there to talk about? Not that he had been in my life for fifteen years but now suddenly disappears because it suits Rose. Not that Rose was only using all that shit about my stress as an excuse. Not that I really should have cracked Gallogly's thick Irish neck. No, I was fine, don't worry about me.

'Just play it cool, brother,' Ferdy advised. 'Just for Con's sake. It will get easier for all of you, but you've got to think of him first, okay?'

'Did she tell you to say that?' I asked.

'Fuck you!' Ferdy blasted the music on again and thundered back on to the road, revved it until we spun to a stop outside the house.

I knew this used to be Gallogly's holiday retreat, where he would escape the frantic city and finger his cash. It was a ranch style beach cottage, maybe built in the 1960's, circled by trees and close enough to Tiana Bay. His wife had found the place even before they had first started to rake serious money, and she had caressed it into this magical hideaway of her dreams. Nobody mentioned her anymore, and I hadn't seen much of her in recent years, but I remembered her as a good looking girl, the woman who tolerated Gallogly when he was young and reckless, dragged him out of the gutter and kept him out of gaol. Now my Rose had taken her special space after Gallogly decided he had outgrown the good looking girl who had nurtured him to manhood and who was satisfied with what she had. I was on the outside now, like Gallogly's wife, just waiting.

And I was sitting there a long time before young Con bounced into the back seat as if this was the way it had always been. I was the absent father, just come now to do my weekend duty, no big deal. I guessed Ferdy must have been reassuring Rose and Gallogly, took a few minutes to follow young Con down the red paved driveway.

'Okay, next stop Brighton Beach,' Ferdy laughed. 'Let's go kick some Russky ass!'

Ferdy kept his banter stoked, no embarrassing silences, joked and provoked young Con the whole way back. Con was a little pale but played along with Ferdy's chaffing, just like the old days. I pitched in where I could, a big effort, held it together, young Con didn't notice. And I was grateful. Ferdy made it easier for both of us but it still bit into me. It didn't feel right, I shouldn't need him to help me talk to my own son. I would take him out on my own the next free day, invest some quality time.

'You look a little nervous there, son,' I said. 'Just relax, try getting your breathing going. You have nothing to worry about, this is going to be fun.'

Con rummaged about in his sports bag, checking Rose had put everything in there. He sat back for a minute, then opened the bag and went through the same ritual again.

'I'm not nervous,' he said. 'Why do you always put me down?'

Ferdy sneaked a sideways smirk at me. 'No problem, Con,' he said. 'Your dad is just more nervous than you are right now, isn't that so?' He leant over and played a couple of soft slaps on my cheek.

'You'll do good, son, don't worry,' I said.

Ferdy darted another sideways glance at me. He knew I was a little worried, and maybe he was too. I thought we were worried about the same thing.

★★★

We eventually found the sports hall in Brighton Beach after trailing up and down all those Russian streets. Plenty of money still around here, nice automobiles and classy restaurants. Snow neatly groomed in cute geometry along the sidewalks. Young Con jumped out and ran to the hall before Ferdy had parked the Merc. No goodbyes or see you later, he just skinned through the smoking fathers crammed outside the door and didn't even look back.

'Shit, I've got a bad feeling about this,' I said.

'Don't start that crap again!' Ferdy gripped my shoulder and I felt his breath on my cheek. 'No fucking way are you pulling one of your red death frenzies here! There's nothing for you to get worked up about, okay? If you're starting to lose it again, you had better stay out here, hear me?'

He was right, I knew it, but that pulsing murmur of alarm was ebbing around my nerves, I couldn't ignore it. Ferdy skipped out, carefree whistling and posing, but I knew he was working it through his own mind. He knew, more than anyone, more than me, what could happen if I slipped under that crimson cloud. He patted my shoulder and steered me into the hall, kept buzzing in my ear, kept me rolling.

It was a small arena, and it looked like there were maybe two hundred judo kids from all over Brooklyn straining the place at its seams, as many girls as boys, all bubbling with hope or jangling with nerves. Cold in here, fist sized balloons of breath steam, red noses and rubbing hands. Young Con was over with his pals getting changed into his judo uniform, taking last minute tips from their coach. Ferdy and I found a space on a bench behind the judges' table, squeezed past a line of judo moms and restless younger siblings. A kid was selling programs for a dollar; Con was in the Juvenile B category, under sixty kilograms, 140 pounds.

The girl sitting next to Ferdy was a woman, maybe in her forties, maybe fifty, but a real high value client of a grateful cosmetic surgeon. Ferdia bounced his chat with her, dearly wanted to hear about her son and all the great training the kid had put in for this, bent over real close to read her program. Her friends lapped it up, sniggered behind their programs, nudged elbows, rolled eyes, arched eyebrows. Ferdy's new lady friend played up to her audience, still got it, jangled her gold and beamed her best smile. Ferdy knew it but didn't care. A guy with a smooth head like a heavy round boulder hovered at the end of our row. He did care.

The first contests were starting on two separate mats. No-one in our row noticed the two scrawny kids feinting and dodging, gripping and pulling. The real fancy footwork was going down right here beside me. The crowd cheered and screamed their support for the tiny judokas down there, so I couldn't hear what Ferdy was telling her, but all of us knew what he hoped she was hearing. Her cellphone came out, exchanging details, maybe she was tweeting her catch right back to Moscow. Because these were Russian ladies, proud and rich, and Brighton Beach was their playground. The rock head glared as hard as he could, like his eyeballs were about to explode, but the Brighton Czarina ignored him and he transferred his poison stare to me, ready to bite my head off and string my guts out with his teeth. Wasting his time. I was nobody's chaperone.

Soon it was young Con's fight, I dug Ferdy with my elbow, he swung around to whistle for Con, his right arm draped neatly around her waist. But she was screaming too, pushed Ferdy away so she could stand on the bench and screech and jump like the cheerleader she could have been. The rest followed her, so me and Ferdy were drowned by an irresistible Russian mother wave of gene love and protection. Even Con looked up, must have registered that his feeble support was wiped out by this other kid's fanbase. He breathed in deeply, tried to fill out his suit, he was on his own out there, that's already the way his life was shaping up.

They started off like two circling tigers, pawing at each other's cuff and collar, testing for a weakness, probing and teasing. The stone head appeared down at the end of the row with two other slate skulls. Young Con dived in, a sweet move, feet skimming over the mat. The Russian chorus froze, but just for a second, because their kid was just as quick, he levered young Con over his hip, kept spinning, Con's ankles arcing up and over. Slap! Con back flopped to the mat. The other kid skipped a little dance going back to his side of the mat, the judo moms erupted, Con lay still, Ferdy and I slouched back to the bench.

'Too bad,' Ferdy said. 'He'll be better next time, he's got the moves. Just didn't work out this time.'

The girls chanted some Russian song. The three hard heads smirked their glee at me and Ferdy. I was about to get in the moron's face when Ferdy stood up and grabbed my wrist.

'Con, get down there quick!'

Young Con's face was twisted into a hard knot, frothing at the mouth, one eye squeezed shut, the other like a red beacon blazing out hate.

His body coiled and stretched, the heavy cotton judo suit strained. We both started to move, almost knocked the gray haired official over his table, had to get a hold of Con before he exploded. Too late. The Russian kid waltzed back to Con to shake hands. He was about three feet away when Con dived, planted his forehead straight into the kid's nose, bursting a cloud of blood and mucus over their gleaming white suits. The referee grabbed Con's wrist, tried to yank him away, but fell to his knees when Con buried his knee into the old guy's groin.

The place erupted, Russian moms screaming, officials and coaches swarming across the mat, me and Ferdy dragging Con off the Russian kid, Con still stamping and kicking at the red spattered face. Stone heads between us and the exit, I pushed Ferdia ahead and wrapped Con under my left arm, funnelled our way through the excitement, ignored the angry salvo from Con's coach, just get him outside.

We almost clipped Con's red-faced coach, punching the Merc back out of the parking space, Ferdy spinning through the traffic and shoppers, a bottle smashing off the roof, but we were out of there. I held Con down on the back seat, he was still gulping air and straining hard against me. I had lost some weight, still must have carried one ninety pounds, but he heaved and twisted me as if I were fifty pounds lighter.

'He's convulsing here, Ferdy!' I yelled. 'Get us to the nearest Emergency Room!' I couldn't breathe, felt paralyzed, just panic and fear. 'He is going to die on me, Ferdy, I'm fucking going to lose him! Do something, you fucking prick, do something!'

Ferdy looked back at us, slowed down, pulled over. I couldn't believe it, he stopped, I'd tear his fucking head off, he stopped.

'It's okay, Con,' Ferdy soothed. 'He will be okay, just let him rest a while, he will come through this soon.'

I heard him but couldn't understand, it was like he was speaking a foreign language.

'What the fuck you talking about!' My fear cramped into a high pitch squeal that was like somebody else's voice. 'How would you know it's fucking okay? Move or I'll fucking kill you, man!'

Ferdy reached over to hold my hand, everything slowed down, the tension snapped out of young Con's body.

'That's how it always happens,' Ferdy said quietly. 'He will calm down, then he'll be okay. That's just what happens.'

Young Con had these seizures before and they all knew about it? Him, Rose, Gallogly? And they all hid it from me?

'Not him, Con,' he said. 'It's you, that's the way it always happens with you. He's the same as you, he'll be okay. That's just the way you are.'

A vise scalloped my temples between white noise and red light, my eyes diamond splintered out of my skull, a hot claw nailed my lungs.

'Keep breathing, Con!' Ferdy roared at me. 'Keep it together for fuck's sake! I can't handle both of you!'

I could only see his eyes, but kept breathing, in and out, deep and slow, in, hold it, out, slower, steady. Young Con was asleep or unconscious, I propped his head on my chest, held him, smelt his hair, caressed his pale cheeks.

'That's it, Con,' Ferdy eased me. 'You're in control, don't let it slip now, keep it going, hang in there.'

Fear, anger, now guilt, and then fear again.

'That's the way it happens with me?'

Ferdy half shrugged.

'He's the same as me,' I said. 'The same as my father.'

We both knew what that meant. An outlier. Pain and isolation for him. Extreme and random. A life of heart break and loss for anyone who ever loved him.

'Rose knows, right?'

'I don't know.' Ferdy was weary now. 'I thought maybe that's why she went with Gallogly. Maybe she thought she could protect him, you know? But she hasn't said anything about it.'

That made sense now. Why else would she leave me for that prick Gallogly? Con nuzzled his head into my lap. Soft, easy breathing, holding my hand.

'What do you want to do now, Con?' Ferdy was my rock.

Young Con turned over, stirred a little, jerked his head and a shower of steaming vomit flushed across the back of Gallogly's car. Ferdy handed me moist tissues to wipe his mouth and face. He settled down, safely asleep on my lap.

'I'm going to see Cora,' I said. 'I'm going to see her Frankenstein.'

CHAPTER THREE

The same Honda sedan skewed a perfect symmetry of black Woodlawn slush over my shoes. I knew she would come sniffing around before too long. On her own this time, no backup required.

'I heard about the incident with your son,' Cora said.

No need for role playing today. Get the deal done and get out of there.

'Yeah, right,' I said. 'It was an incident, I guess.'

She looked me over, measured my mood, no diversions.

'Have you thought about our proposition?'

I had thought about almost nothing else since young Con turned Diablo in my arms, but I still didn't know what the proposition was.

'Dr Blake will see you. He'll recommend a strategy for coping with your situation.' It sounded like a drab status update she would reel off over coffee to her work group. 'He is the pre-eminent authority in the United States, Con. This is a once in a lifetime opportunity for you. For your son.'

No need to persuade me now, no sincere eyes, no warm hand on my wrist. Con's 'incident' guaranteed my meek surrender.

'Okay,' I said. 'So what happens now?'

Cora stretched for her bag on the back seat, her left hand used my left shoulder as support, heavier than she looked. No make-up this time, no jewelry. Less tanned, less blond. She pulled out a typed page and offered it to me. I skimmed over it; directions, date, time, name, number.

'Who told you about my son?' I said.

She made to start the engine, we were finished.

'Your wife must be very worried,' she said.

Yeah, Cora, but I knew Rose would screw a stiletto in your lovely ear before she would ask you the time of day.

'I know Rose didn't speak to you.' I forced it neutral. 'Who told you about it? Ferdy? Gallogly?'

Cora lent right across my lap to open my door. We were finished here. Fine by me. Half out the door, right foot cracked the ice wafer glazing the pot-hole, felt the hand on my wrist again.

'How about George Oliver?' she said, softer now.

Took me a second to recall the name.

'Sorry Cora,' I said. 'Nobody ever heard of him.'

Squeezed a little harder.

'You sure about that, Con?' she said. 'Not even Jack Gallogly? He doesn't know George Oliver?'

That's what Gallogly had told me, if he had told me anything. I couldn't remember exactly what he had said, more important things on my mind. But Cora wasn't on a phishing trip, wasn't her style.

'Just tell me straight what the deal is with George Oliver, Cora,' I said. 'Because I don't have time to play second-guess games right now. Had an 'incident' with my son, you know?'

Cora clicked her fingers and pointed at the door.

'Let's go some place,' she said. 'We need to talk about the George Oliver deal.'

George Oliver was a real lucky guy. In his mid-thirties, like me. Grew up in blue collar Yonkers, like me. Had issues with authority when he was younger, like me. So he ought to have limped along the tight path that was our sure inheritance. Should have accepted that ambition was the birthright of more deserving kids. But Yonkers George was lucky, something sparked him, wouldn't be grateful for what was on offer, wanted more. And then he was real lucky, because he had a gift to back up that selfish streak. George Oliver was a genius.

'He's really a charming guy,' Cora mused. 'The problem is he has discovered he can be anyone he wants to be.'

It was Prime Rib Night in the River's Edge Sunday and Monday, Parmigiana Night Tuesday and Wednesday. Rocco talked me out of the Mixed Irish Grill, said I would prefer the Veal Sorrentino. Cora had coffee, 'The Best on Bronx River Road'. She gazed into her espresso, stirred it with intent, the spoon never clinking the sides. She was quiet and thoughtful, her silky voice toned with regret. George was a lucky guy, I was jealous.

'But he can't do this to us.' Her work voice resurrected. 'I need to get him back. We will get him back.'

No sugar, just lots of stirring, that was Cora.

'And that 'we' has got something to do with me, right?' I said.

She mocked a dry smile, shook her hair back and purred a sigh.

'Well, you do owe me, Maknazpy.' Called me Maknazpy every time she levered her authority. 'I kept you out of trouble, didn't I? Where do you think you and Ferdia McErlane would be right now if I hadn't stuck my neck out for you, huh?'

And I thought we were protected because the big people had to be protected.

'Yeah, well we can always talk to the Washington Post and the Times about that, can't we?' I said. 'In fact, maybe we have statements ready to be opened if anything ever happens to us. Your friends should consider that before they send you down here to bust our balls.'

'That's not your style, Maknazpy,' she giggled. 'Wouldn't make any difference anyway. Two fantasists like you and McErlane? That would be no problem, believe me.'

That was too candid, I didn't like it when she didn't pretend I was important, and she knew it. She recovered almost immediately, took my hand, not just my wrist this time, but took my right hand in both of hers, stroked it.

'I'm sorry Con.' She lowered her voice. 'I really didn't mean it to sound like that, I wasn't demeaning you.'

Demeaning? Yeah, I guess that was the right word.

'This is a delicate situation,' she said. 'Very important to the United States, but very delicate. And sometimes better outcomes can be achieved by doing things quietly, without official zealots getting all fired up about it, you know?'

Her eyes and mouth were close, her hands felt good, her voice said she needed me. This was dangerous, but I let the thrill flutter up my spine, forgot about demeaning.

'George Oliver is a genius,' she said. 'We need that genius to come back to work for us.'

'Tony the chef here is a genius too,' I said. 'But if he leaves today then Dom and Rocco will get another genius tomorrow. What's so special about your George?'

'Bottom line?' Cora said. 'We can't let him go work for the opposition.'

She turned away when my veal arrived, Rocco gave me the look, winked at the back of Cora's blond head. Scalopinne with razor thin eggplant and prosciutto, flavor boosted with super-charged melted mozzarella. No more Irish Grill for me.

'And what am I supposed to do this time?' I said.

Cora sat bolt upright in her seat, elegant like a ballet dancer; this was it.

'George Oliver travelled to Portugal for the Christmas vacation, was supposed to be visiting family out there.' No emotion, straight reporting. 'He hasn't returned, and we want him back. No way is anyone else going to profit from the skills and experience he has acquired whilst working for the United States. That's it, Con; simple, no big mystery. He can't walk out on us, that just doesn't happen.'

'Why me, Cora?' I said. 'Things got way out of control the last time, why would your bosses want me involved again? Or is this really about you? Is it because George walked out on you?'

She almost blushed, tried to frost her ice queen front, but I saw it, I knew.

'Don't be ridiculous, Maknazpy!' she said. 'It's like I told you, sometimes a more effective solution can be found outside official channels. That's what we're here to do, after all, achieve the best possible outcome for the United States.'

She was struggling now, and that thrilled me a little as well.

'We just want you to do a very routine, mundane task,' she said. 'And hey, it's really no big deal, you know? If you aren't up to taking the opportunity we'll just make other arrangements, no problem.'

I savored the veal and mozzarella, let Cora stew for a moment, see if she still giggled, still thought it was smart to 'demean' me. But that was a mistake, gave her time to rally, and the bitch was way smarter than me.

'You know, Maknazpy, I think it would be a great pity if you decided Doctor Blake couldn't help you,' Cora said. 'And your son, of course. Young Con will never get an opportunity like this again, will he? I mean, I know Jack Gallogly is quite wealthy, comparatively, but this is out of even his league, don't you think?'

Even his league? What, like I was somewhere down in the gutter? Rocco passed by, asked if I was happy. Yeah, Rocco, the veal was fantastic, but this fucker had pissed on my appetite.

'You know you are a nasty dirty piece of shit, don't you, Cora?' I said.

She bowed slightly. 'As long as we understand each other, Con, that's the main thing.' She gloated. 'We can work out the details later, but I assume I can report back that you will do this small duty for the United States? Ferdia McErlane is already on board.' Cora straightened her skirt as she stood up. 'We will be in touch to make arrangements.' A quick scan to see who had noticed her. 'Thanks for the coffee, Maknazpy. And Faugh a Ballagh.'

Cora moved as if she had capsules of air under her heels, only seemed to work forward and upward, never downward. Maybe she had been a ballet dancer, maybe a gymnast. Four younger women at the table nearest the door cut their chatter to check her out as she drifted past. Looked her up and down shamelessly, sour expressions exchanged to insist that they weren't impressed, this one wasn't as special as she thought she was. Cora ignored them, made her exit without looking back. No applause this time, because I hated Cora right then, really hated her, and the thought of her cranked that dark energy misting around my skull.

I had known something was going to happen, and I told Ferdy as much that day in Brighton Beach. He laughed in my face but then had signed up for this without telling me. Sometimes he was a real shithead, he took me for granted, like they all did. But the Belle Aires still doo wopped 'I wanna be loved', my veal regained its flavour, and a tingle of provocative excitement zipped through my veins. It was starting again, I knew it, and I really did hate Cora right then, but, more than that, I knew that this George Oliver was a real lucky guy, and I had every reason to be jealous. Angry with her, jealous of him.

CHAPTER FOUR

'Why not? What else are you doing here?' Ferdy laughed it off. 'Painting Gallogly's bar, is that the best you can do?'

He was already in my apartment, steak and fries in the microwave, a beer in his hand, feet up on the table.

'Because we don't fucking know what she's getting us into, for one thing,' I said. 'Because you should have fucking talked to me about it before you let Cora twist you around her finger.'

Sometimes he was my rock, most times he was a millstone.

'Yeah, I hear you brother,' he said. 'But I knew you wouldn't listen to me, Cora knows how to work you.' He did that irritating tuneless singing of his, 'Oh, Cora baby, I love you, I'll do anything you want me to, oh Cora baby'.

I knocked his feet off the table, pulled the dish out of the microwave and spun it across to him. He spilt a mouthful of beer over the mat, rubbed it in with his shoe.

'Hey, we're going to Lisbon, what's not to like?' he said. 'Get some sunshine on our bones again, get away from this fucking place. Pick up this guy Georgie boy and bring him home to Cora. $5,000 each. How long would we be humping for Gallogly to get that money?'

I turned the television on, Tom Hanks in that old movie where he tries to fix a house up. Young Con almost wet himself one time, laughing at it so much. Ignored Ferdy, gave him the silent treatment, he wasn't my rock now. He laughed at the movie through a mouthful of steak and fries, sounded a lot like young Con.

'Where did you get the balls to agree to it without asking me first?' Too riled to keep the silent thing going. 'When did you see her, anyway?'

'A couple of days before she came in to see you in Blind Mary's that time,' he said.

'Well fuck you, Ferdy!'

He tried to shrug it away, but I wasn't letting him off the hook yet.

'And what if I say I'm not in?' I said. 'What happens then?'

He shrugged one shoulder, set his beer on the table, wiped his hands and mouth.

'Nothing happens,' he said. 'We forget it. But then we forget that doctor Cora has lined up for you and young Con too.'

'Oh right!' I said. 'Use young Con against me, just like her, that's great!'

'Like who?' Ferdy said. 'Like Rose?'

'Like fucking Cora, you asshole!'

'Sorry about all that, Con,' he said, and planted a hard slap on my thigh. 'But you are going to do this thing with me, aren't you?'

He knew we were going to do it, but I didn't like the idea that they could gang up behind my back, conspiring their sly tricks to force my hand. So okay, we were going to do it, and Ferdy already knew most of it, seemed Cora had more trust in the prick than she had let me think.

'Here's Cora's file on gorgeous George.' He dumped a neat red folder on my lap. 'Shouldn't be a problem, this guy won't be trouble.'

I threw the folder over my head towards the hall, the neatly printed sheets scattered over the floor or landed on Ferdy's steak and fries.

'I might read that some time,' I said. 'Some day after Cora's doctor has done something useful for young Con. Until then, you can forget it. You're on your own on this one, just you and Cora, okay?'

Ferdy plucked the sheet off his meal. It was smeared with grease and gravy, he wiped it over the table, cutting a brown trail across the varnished beech, then skimmed it to the floor with the rest.

'Whatever you say, brother,' Ferdy said. 'I'm just trying to help out here. For you and young Con, that's all, so whatever you say.'

That was real big of him, always pinning whatever shit we got into on me, never his doing.

'Yeah?' I said. 'I guess you were trying to help down at Brighton Beach too, right? When that Moscow whore's goons were lined up to jump us? Who were they? The husband's bodyguards? Fuck you, Ferdy! You are always number one, the rest of us are just your excuse, so don't embarrass yourself with that 'just trying to help' shit, okay?'

He stood up from the table, made a big deal of scraping his dinner into the bin. Silence, except for the rasping scrape of cutlery on the plate.

'Odessa,' Ferdy said then, as he put the dinner things in the sink.

'What?'

'She was from Ukraine,' he said. 'Those girls were from Odessa, not Moscow. And she didn't know those guys. I asked her who they were. She didn't know them.'

I didn't answer, forced a flashback to the scene, Ferdy all over the woman, the stone head glaring at me.

'She did say they were Russians, though. She hadn't seen them before, but she knew they were Russians okay,' he said. 'The 'fucking Russian mafia are here' that's what she said.'

CHAPTER FIVE

Ferdy was gone when I woke the next day. Cora's folder on George was put back together and lay on the table. A message from Gallogly, wanted me to work today, cash collections over in Brooklyn. A message from Cora, Dr Blake was expecting my call. A message from Rose, young Con had been in trouble at school, more or less said that was my fault. I deleted Gallogly's message and dumped Cora's folder under that pile of papers Rose had left for me to sort out. No coffee left, how much could that selfish bastard have used? And there was a smell in here, even I noticed it. The garbage hadn't been put out for a couple of days, Ferdy's dirty dishes were stacked for me to wash, a big rusty roach scuttled down his beer bottle, thought I powdered the place good with boric acid last week. My head throbbed. Fuck this, fuck all of them.

Jorge Eduardo da Silva Oliveira hadn't been a good student. Teachers had difficulty recalling the prickly loner who dropped out, just another failure like all the rest of us. He malingered through a series of jobs where he couldn't avoid people, until he surrendered to the panic and his parents helped him shrink away in his bedroom.

Was this the same guy I was supposed to be jealous of? This nondescript weed? No sign of the genius on these pages, no charm either, so maybe Cora was the weird one.

But the luck was only on sleep mode, the net shock was coming to kick it into life. That's when the genius inside started ticking, chipping away at the shell that choked it, spreading like the black mold on his bedroom wall, injecting the loser with the steam to key a new avatar of himself; still virtual, and still confined to the squalid bedroom, but a hero in that grim space. Then hundreds of hours perched in front of a cracked screen combined to purge his stain of cocooned inferiority. For the first time in his miserable, underachieving life something worked for him. Hundreds of screen hours became thousands until blind routine and frustration evaporated, Jorginho's hardwired intuition blossomed, and George the Genius Oliver emerged, like a snake in a new skin.

Invisible through the nineties, by 2001 Jorge had become George had become Zumbi, the blackhat sensei hacker consuming the respect and admiration of the lone wolf ninjas of the cyber underworld. This was the golden age of CarderPlanet, Shadowcrew and DarkMarket. Skimming, carding and drive-by downloads. Black knights waging gamer war against 'The Man'. Phishing and pharming, victimless crimes by remote netpunks.

By 2003, Zumbi George had the teeth to take the genius pedestal, driven first by the revenge he thirsted, but then acclaimed by his cyber dark peers. His Einstein gift was as a bot herder, corralling swathes of virgin computers with his zombie infections so that he could direct his heavy duty processing power at his paralyzed targets. He liked to show off too, and soon hosts of hackers and crackers were hitting him for solutions, his reputation keeping pace with his blooming ego.

By 2005, that reputation had spread beyond the twilight world of chat rooms and internet cafes and stretched out to a welcome host. Organized crime are the earliest adopters, true American entrepreneurs, greedy to test market forces, boom and boom the only option. So Zumbi George was flattered when an alliance of Princes anointed him to drive their new business model.

They wanted an early win to start with, so George wrangled his botnets to pump target share prices through the roof, letting the guzzling bandits cream it as they dumped the fool's gold before bankruptcy slapped some reality into the market. George rolled his loaded dice into the Big Board and NASDAQ, learnt his trade and then really hit the jackpot with penny stocks on the Pink Sheets and London's Alternative Investment Market. The perfect logic of pure capitalism, red in tooth and claw. Each time bigger and better, always a queue of grasping cut throats smelling blood, until they tongued it and, too late, tasted their own.

This was an ice cold results world and, just like any business meritocracy, George's champions spotted their winner and pushed the limits of his power and responsibility. His new punch bridged the skimming markets of eastern Europe and Turkey, harvesting dumps and fulls; cards with their three digit numbers and security pins. A cyber harvest of Black AmEx prestige pumping cash and an effective tax rate of 0%. Scareware and phantom payroll schemes oiled like Swiss clockwork, smishing and pharming on an industrial scale. By 2007, this George was untouchable.

But then the file stopped, nothing here after August 2007. I looked under the table, maybe Ferdy had missed some pages when he reassembled the folder my bad temper had scattered. No, no more pages anywhere. Cora's file on George Oliver stopped dead when he was still the Zumbi warlord of the dark cyberworld. Six and a half years missing. Somehow, George's luck had twisted his virtual genius with Cora's duty and honor gig in that time, but she didn't need us to know about it right now. Just needed us to make it right again. Like wiping a man's brains and blood off her soft cream brogues. I slammed the folder down on the table, felt the cockroach crunch and crack under my fist.

CHAPTER SIX
· · · · · · · · · · · · · · · · · ·

My call went straight to the man, no PA or diary secretary to negotiate, and the surprise tangled my script for a second. Doctor Blake sounded as if he was smiling at his end, just a regular guy, an easy velour voice. Sure, meet him for lunch, no problem, the Oyster Bar, Grand Central, look forward to it.

Blake had already been served when I came jogging through the crowds in Grand Central Station. I stumbled into a waiter at the door, all eyes pinned me as an awkward jerk. I apologized for being late, Blake apologized for not waiting, but his apology had the comfortable good grace of the socialite, mine sounded like a lazy excuse.

'Naked Cowboys,' he said. 'Long Island Oysters. Would you care to try one while you are waiting?'

Looked older than he sounded; mid-sixties, still perfect teeth, healthy bloom to his cheek. Expensive but understated linen jacket and tie combo, classy links on the cuffs. Thick black hair swept back from the high tanned brow. Intense dark eyes behind stout black frames. And a stark red crescent scar gouged two inches below his right eye.

'No thank you, Doctor Blake. Please don't let me disturb your meal.' I hoped that didn't sound as fake to his ears as it felt on my lips.

The truth was that I had always wanted to eat in the Oyster Bar but had never made it. The cloister of marble columns and vaulted ceiling was my idea of where I should have been eating, with Rose and young Con, instead of burger joints and bars like Blind Mary's, surrounded by guys with tattoos and ear-rings. I guess that was what Rose had hoped for as well. But, now that I was here, I was too intimidated by Blake's easy sophistication to even read the menu properly. Croaked out the first thing I could see, New England Clam Chowder. And a Michelob Ultra beer, had the stupid idea that would impress him because it was low carb. Shit, get a grip, this was what Rose meant when she said I was an asshole.

'So, Mr Maknazpy, I'm told you are interested in participating in our research project,' Blake said. 'Would you like to tell me what your expectations would be?' I needed a prompt. 'You know, have you thought what would make this a successful enterprise, in your eyes?' he said. My blank stare unsettled him, I had to regroup quickly.

'I'm sorry, Dr Blake,' I said. 'I guess I just want to know what sort of life my son can expect. I mean, is he going to end up like me, or can you help him?'

Blake sipped his Saratoga water, bubbles fizzed as he sat the glass down.

'That's a difficult one, I'm afraid,' he said. 'I guess we would all like to know how to make life better for our children, wouldn't we?' Seemed like a fragment of regret in his voice.

'He's only fifteen years old,' I said. 'He's beginning to have the same problem as me, starting to get in to trouble. Can you help him?'

Blake had good eyes, made him appear intelligent and sympathetic at the same time.

'Like you, and your father before you?' he said.

That knocked me. Like my father? What did he know about my old man?

'I apologize, Mr Maknazpy,' he said. 'I should have explained that our interest in you is precisely because there are similarities in the displayed behavior of your father and yourself. If your own son also displays the same pattern of behavior that obviously increases my interest.'

'So what is your interest, exactly,' I said. Sharper than I meant to be, but Blake didn't react, let it slide over.

'Well, we can't really discuss the full details here, Mr Maknazpy,' he said. 'Of course, if you decide to proceed I will be as open and transparent as possible when we get to the lab. For now, I guess all I can say is that I am interested in the flight or fight response. Especially in individuals who have a history of an exaggerated or extreme response.'

Exaggerated, extreme, sounded like Rose again.

'And you can help my son to control it, so it won't be extreme?'

'I'm afraid I can't guarantee anything just now, Mr Maknazpy,' he said. 'I can say that there may be a range of pharmological or behaviorial supports that may be appropriate, and these may go some way to assisting your son to achieve the quality of life that you obviously want for him, as any good father would.'

Yeah, a good father, he really sounded like Rose now.

'Okay, Dr Blake,' I said. 'I'm in. What happens now?'

'Call me on that same number,' Blake said. 'Don't call the center or speak to anyone else. Strictly you and I, okay?'

He wiped his hands with the napkin, then pulled a large linen handkerchief from his jacket and dabbed around his lips.

'And I think we should report to Miss Oneale that our friends there have been over interested in our little chat.'

The Doc had good eyes okay, his glance directed me to the table across the room. Two heavy guys, dodging their faces now behind the marble column. Stone head's two pals from the judo hall.

'The one on my right seems to have some sort of recording device directed at us,' Blake said, eyeing over the dessert menu.

'You know these two? Seen them before?' I asked, keeping them on the tip of my peripheral vision.

'I think so,' he said. 'Either these two or others like them. Been hanging around since your George Oliver went AWOL.'

'You fucking know about Oliver?' I wheezed.

'A participant in our research,' he nodded. 'Quite interesting mental capabilities. Extraordinary potential, like all our participants. Like yourself, I think.'

The Russians stood up, one flicked some notes on the table, and they made for the exit. No hurry, no excitement. Didn't look over at us, just swaggered through the other tables to the door, even stood aside to let a girl pass to the rest room.

'Your research isn't going to cost me anything, right?' I said. Blake shook his head in confirmation. 'Do you mind paying for lunch, Doc? I have to go right now.' The Doc nodded.

I stopped at the door to pick up the leather jackets, they were behind a knot of Japanese tourists heading up the ramp. I let three women in swaying black robes file in front of me. Each had a shopping trolley in tow, and two dark men in expensive American suits quickly elbowed between me and the trolleys. Okay, I could keep my distance here, the Russians were coasting behind the Japanese, just take it easy.

The American suits were agitated, deep guttural tongues, some sort of Arabic. Funny how you know when somebody is talking about you even when it is a foreign language, they must have sensed I was trouble. The older one, maybe the father, turned to face me and barked a command to the women. They half turned, but the woman in front dismissed him with an impatient retort and a flick of the wrist. He cursed then, maybe at the women, his authority wasted. I brushed past him without catching his eye, he spit an insult, the younger one laughed. The Russians didn't notice, didn't turn around anyway. I had to keep moving, kill any attention, no fuss. The three women stopped now and turned to the men. Sounded angry to my ears but you can't always tell. I kept my head down, kept going, stepped around the shopping trolleys. One woman turned and bumped into me. Beautiful black eyes flashed above the silk veil, chic make-up, perfume like Cora's. Not shy and demure either, but a bold appraising blaze. The man barked louder, the women laughed, this one's eyes smiled behind her veil, cracked something smart to the sisters. I had to keep moving, keep my distance from the Russians but avoid the angry man behind me as well.

The main concourse was just ahead now, the Japanese blocked the exit, caught by the drama of the sky ceiling, the Russians filtered behind them, I had nowhere to go.

'Is there a problem here, man?' a Russian turned and said to me, in the thickest Brooklyn accent.

I kept going, pushed my way through the tourists, out into the concourse, speeded up, over to the clock. The Brooklynovs took their position against the wall, made like they were tourists themselves, panned the glory of the ceiling with their cellphones. Okay, but they weren't getting out of there without me. I pulled my cellphone and called Ferdy. No answer. Called Gallogly. 'Jack, I've got a problem right now. I need a couple of good guys over here at Grand Central. I'm at the clock.' Maybe ten minutes before Gallogly would get organized, maybe fifteen.

The Russians split up, meandered through the bustle to the opposite staircases, still playing the tourist. I picked the one who hadn't spoken, headed straight for him. He saw me coming and skipped through the crowds, headed for 42nd Street, looked over his shoulder, bumping tourists and commuters out of his way, cleared a path for me to follow. I looked back for the other one but he had disappeared, I had one chance to nail this shit in front of me, couldn't wait on Gallogly.

Out to 42nd Street, he didn't hesitate, turned towards Times Square, broke into a trot, knew I was behind him. I called Gallogly, he was in the Bronx but an automobile would be coming out of the Kitchen towards me any minute. The Russian quickened, started to attract attention from people standing aside on the sidewalk. Past the library now, he darted up the steps into Bryant Park, slowed down by spectators bunched around the ice rink, a winter wonderland, two cops in the corner, we kept going, headed across to West 40th Street. Felt my ankle a little, panted hot breath, cold air stinging my nostrils, but he was still right there in front of me, slowing down now, rounding a dumpster, I had him. But I was on my back before I saw them, the three heavy Russians squeezing my face against the icy sidewalk.

'You think you can fucking follow us, Maknazpy?' a Russian growl through my head. 'We follow you, you prick!' This one a real Russian, not Brooklyn. 'We get George Oliver first, understand?' A stone face with a bear's red eyes. 'You tell the fat fuck Gallogly! I get Oliver or else I get your kid! I eat the liver, it is good, yes? Eat the liver and tear the head from the neck! Tell Gallogly, he knows!' They all laughed. 'Either Oliver or the boy, Gallogly decides, okay?'

A boot knifed my kidneys, my skull clanged off the dumpster, and they were gone. Walking off slowly, laughing, no problem.

CHAPTER SEVEN

They left me waiting in the back room for a long, long time. The picture of Cagney was back up there on the wall, still had my paint spatters across his wise guy leer. A pumping lump like a polished cobblestone throbbed on the back of my head, ribs on fire, a scab of blood crusted down my neck. One of the guys poked his head in to say Gallogly was on his way, wouldn't be long. Ferdy's cellphone was switched off, Gallogly let my calls run to his voicemail. Maybe not such a bad idea, they knew me well enough to let the steam fury ease its pressure inside my skull, but I knew they were avoiding me and that just wired my nerves, like a starved rat gnawing out of a trap.

I was still convulsing the hyper hell around my head when Ferdy appeared. Casual, in his studied way, he slapped his arm around my shoulders, checked the dressing on the back of my head. He stroked my hair and clapped his hands over mine.

'Take it easy, brother,' he said. 'Gallogly is on our side so don't start busting his balls here. He's doing his best, believe me. He's under a lot of pressure right now but he'll always be there for us. You know that, Con, he is one of us. Just cut the poor prick some slack, okay?'

Ferdy was the only one left that could sweat out my demons when he wanted to, he could work me, anchored me back in the real world now, called Gallogly in.

'Look, Con, before you start, I had nothing to do with that,' Gallogly blurted. 'I didn't know they were going to nail you, you brought that on yourself, so don't think you can start your shit with me!'

Gallogly was vivid purple behind his brutish black beard. Globlets of white froth speckled the stray bristles. His flaccid yellow tongue bloated out of the empty hole of his mouth. I killed the image of Rose that flickered through my mind.

'I'm not starting anything, Jack,' I said. Ferdy kneaded my hands. 'But we need to work out what's happening here, and how we are going to make it right. You, me and Ferdy, we need to pull together on this one, okay?'

Gallogly glanced at Ferdy for comfort, rubbed his fat salami finger stubs through the beard. Flakes of dead skin powdered the table. 'You can rely on me, Con,' Gallogly said. 'You know that. I'm there for you, all the way.' He swept the skin snow off the table, scumming a white layer on his thick blue-jeaned thigh.

'Okay, okay, let's see what we've got here,' Ferdy said, looking me over, keeping it moving.

'Well, we've got a problem with this George Oliver, that's for sure,' I said. 'And you all have been keeping me in the dark, we've got that too.'

Gallogly shifted his broad butt, one cheek hanging over the chair. Ferdy rubbed my shoulder, gave Gallogly the look.

'Okay, okay, for fuck's sake!' Gallogly said through the flaky fingers. 'I knew him when he was J orge Oliveira. Fucking Jorginho! How was I supposed to know he was George pissing Oliver as well?' Hurt, aggrieved, indignant.

'Well, now you do,' I said. 'So who was he? How are you tied into this pile of crap?'

Gallogly's blood gorged eyes shifted from me to Ferdy, Ferdy to me, me to Ferdy.

'He was a useful guy. I wasn't the only one. Opportunities like that don't come along every day of the week, you know!' Gallogly worked it through his head. 'You guys were in Iraq at the time. You left me here on my own. There was a lot happening in this city those days, you know, and I was on my own. What was I supposed to do? Turn the opportunity down so some other schmuck could take advantage?'

I leant over and gripped Gallogly's right wrist, squeezed until he settled, he flicked the slug slimy tongue around the hacked lips.

'He used to be just a nerd back in Yonkers.' Gallogly was steadier now. 'His mom worked in that Portuguese restaurant on Palisade my wife liked.' Glanced at me, carried on. 'I don't know. He came out of nowhere all of a sudden. Had credit cards, good ones, pin numbers and security codes. I knew people who were interested. The fucking guy had a bottomless pit, as many as you wanted. I made arrangements, everybody was happy. Then Jorginho just disappeared a while back. End of story. That's all I know.'

Ferdy just watched, but he had read Cora's file on George, just like I had.

'So he disappeared when? Like 2007?' I said. 'But he came back, didn't he, Jack? All of a sudden, our George is back and he's bringing an opportunity with him, right?'

Gallogly twisted it around his brain, the cracked lips squeezed tightly together like a black liver pumped with bile.

'Yeah, he came back,' he said. 'Last year, when you two dickheads were goofing around on that last little adventure. You know, the one you needed me to save your balls on?'

Ferdy gave an encouraging nod, I had an image of Rose with Gallogly while I was away.

'Well, he came back anyway,' Gallogly carried on. 'But he was different now, you know. He was like you two, like all you guys. Full of shit, all big talk and letting everybody know how important he was. Like he knew all the answers and I was small time compared to him. Like he was doing me a favor just speaking to me.'

Gallogly needed no prompting now, the hurt was bursting out.

'Jorginho walked in here one day, right out of the blue,' he said. 'Sat right there where you are sitting now, Con. He was all, like, 'I've got this deal, Jack, maybe it is too big for you but I just thought I would give you a chance. Maybe you could raise some cash.' The pisshead! I remember him when he was a pathetic geek in Yonkers, now he walks in here and talks to me like that?'

Gallogly's face was plumping purple again, the beard and unreliable skin pummelled into surrender.

'I thought he was just blowing the breeze,' he said. 'Had this thing going down, like millions, he said, crazy numbers, a string of zeros. Needed backup to make it happen, he said, but he said he would clear fifty million, easy.'

'And you passed that up?' Ferdy quizzed.

'Fuck that! Too right I passed it up,' Gallogly said. 'The prick was full of this shit about swiping it from under the government's nose. Fifty million dollars, and the government wouldn't miss it? Yeah, thanks, and no thanks, dickhead!'

'So what did you do, Jack?' I said. 'My Russian friend is pretty pissed off, and he sure as hell thinks your fingerprints are all over this.'

Gallogly stamped his tan Timberland boots on the tiles, as if his circulation needed a kickstart.

'The guys he used to do business with aren't there anymore.' He pistolled his right thumb and index finger. 'Like the Sopranos, know what I mean? So, I put him in touch with some new guys, over in Brooklyn.'

'You mean like Brighton Beach, right?' I said.

Gallogly squirmed in the seat like a child.

'Yeah, Brighton Beach, maybe' he said. 'I just made the connection and took a finder's fee, like any normal business. The rest is up to them, it's not my problem.'

I still had hold of his wrist with my right hand, tugged him off balance and cracked him with a short left. He took the table with him as he went down, Ferdy jumped and clamped his arms around my biceps, Gallogly's head and chest were under the table, I kicked it out of the way.

'Maybe that's not your problem either, you piece of shit!' I screamed, lifted Ferdy's 200 pounds off the floor, light as a feather in my rage.

'Hold it! Hold it!' Ferdy shouted in my ear. 'Calm down, Con, fucking calm down! This isn't helping!'

Gallogly prised himself up on one hand, grabbed the table away with the other.

'It's fucking helping me!' I roared.

Ferdy spun off my back and hit the floor with his legs straddled around Gallogly's neck. The door burst open, four of Gallogly's guys were on top of me, pinned me to the corner, somebody stuck a pepper spray in my face. 'Don't fucking set that off in here!' Gallogly ordered from the floor. Ferdy was up and pulling the guys off my back, Gallogly struggled up behind him, I breathed deeply, slowed everything down, start again.

'These hoods are threatening my son, Jack, and you think it isn't a problem?' Controlled now. Head clear.

Gallogly's guys backed away to the door, he waved them out.

'I didn't mean it like that, Con!' he said. 'You know I would die for that kid! That wasn't what I meant!'

'Okay, we all want to protect young Con,' Ferdy was the peacemaker. Usually a danger magnet but now he was the peacemaker. 'Like, you two beating shit out of each other isn't going to help, is it?'

Gallogly's beard stemmed a plug of blood from his left nostril. I held out my hand.

'I'm sorry, Jack,' I said. 'Over-reacted. It won't happen again. I'm sorry.'

Gallogly was getting used to this high moral ground, would love spinning the tale to Rose, and she would ratchet up my weakness, use this to fool herself she had made the right choice. We shook without a grudge, Ferdy clapped our backs, a good grip on our collars, guided us to the door, shouted into the bar for a drink, steered us back to our chairs, replaced the table.

'Okay, now we have cleared the air,' Ferdy said. 'What the fuck are we going to do about this? I mean, like, constructively?'

Gallogly worked his jaw with the meat hammer fist, I could feel the sympathy welling up in Rose already.

'I'll take Rose and young Con away,' Gallogly said. 'Somewhere safe, nobody will know. That'll leave the way clear for you two to sort it out.'

He spoke with a quiet dignity; just his way of making himself look mature and wise, supposed to make me out to be a pathetic loser. A deep nugget of my core still wanted to tear his head off, but I had to respect this jerk. Rose wasn't such a bad judge of character, just hadn't come down to character when she fell in my lap.

'Okay, Con, what do we do?' Ferdy asked. 'Kicking some Russian ass is one thing, but Cora's people? That's another level. We can't just drop some muscle on them. They've got you and me by the balls on this one, brother.'

I knew I would make better sense of this later on, when my head had cleared and these two weren't in my face, demanding a quick answer. The Russians were a business deal gone wrong. Gallogly had his snout in that trough, maybe more than he was telling us, and the Russians knew young Con was the only lever they needed to push. But Cora's people could pull the plug on me and Ferdy at any time. They had us cold for that trouble last year, and would hesitate before burning us about as much as I had hesitated before smashing that cockroach.

'We can't fight two fronts at the same time,' I said. 'I guess if Jack can take Rose and Con to a safe place, you and me can fix Cora's problem.' I reached across and took Gallogly's heavy paw in my hand. 'That might get the Russians off our backs anyway, if we are lucky. If it doesn't, at least it will free us up to take care of them when we get back, without worrying about what Cora has planned for us.'

Ferdy perked up, something to feed his adrenaline habit. Gallogly fingered the swab of blood from his nose and smeared it across the wall I had painted last week. He greased the delicate Sahara Evening with coarse blood and nose scum, then squinted closer to inspect it. And Rose left me for him? Shit, what did that say?

'You got somewhere real safe to take them, right Jack?' I said.

'Trust me on this one,' Gallogly said. 'I've never let you down before, have I?'

No, I guess he hadn't, I was the only one here who ever let his people down, I knew that, we all knew that. I would work something out later, on my own, but that was enough for the moment. Gallogly would keep young Con safe for me, and Rose too. Ferdy and I would nail George Oliver, then see where we stood with Cora and the Russians. Either way, that stone headed Russian bastard would be going down, the death frame was already squirming behind my eyes. And that should give Dr Blake some meat to work on, that and the other red purges that still ghosted through my skull, all those glory kills that I pretended I didn't remember. That nobody knew about except Ferdy. And Rose, yeah, I guess she had always known.

CHAPTER EIGHT

I knew Blake would be punctual. I skated over the ice to get to the junction of McLean and Kimball Avenue for 7 a.m. and barely had time to thaw my shaking fingers with a polystyrene cup of coffee before he pulled up outside the Kozy Korner Diner. It was still night dark but those good eyes of his somehow picked me out even though the truck abandoned outside the Shamrock Gift Shop should have blocked his view.

He cranked his stern attention to the road ahead like I wasn't there, like the appointment had started already and he was working some sort of professional code that meant I was reduced to a piece of meat and he needed to pretend I didn't exist. Suited me anyway, I was having major second thoughts about the whole deal and didn't need oily small-talk: the odor of clinical disinfectant pulsing from deep in the car upholstery was almost enough to choke me already. Fleetwood Mac playing Go your Own Way. I swiped through his iPod, boosted Cantaloupe Island through his cool Bose speakers, made Blake snort and twitch his clipped eyebrows like I had over-stepped some mark, some code of conduct that he had created inside the bubble of his car. We played straight through to Art Blakey and the Jazz Messengers before he gave me a sideways look.

'Our work here is confidential,' he said. 'None of my staff need to know your business so just leave the talking to me, okay?'

Sure, that would always be more than okay with me. Blake twisted into his parking space with a little more torque than was necessary, and breezed past the security guy like he wasn't there. He punched the entrance code and strode across the lobby like he owned the place and the receptionists should avoid his eye in case he was having a bad day and felt the itch to fire someone. A stooped cleaning lady joined us in the escalator on the second floor but realized her mistake and escaped on the third. We continued in silence to the sixth floor; Blake peering into the little mirror above the buttons and I knew he would have preened himself some more if I hadn't been there.

'Is Cora aware you are here?' Blake said.

That sounded like a pretty loaded question. I waited until he had keyed us into his too white office.

'She knew I would be here sometime,' I said. 'Why? Is there a problem?'

'Of course not! I was just wondering how involved you are with your Miss Oneale. I apologize if I was out of line.'

'My Miss Oneale? And here was me thinking she was yours!'

His computer pitched a blue light against the wall until the screen saver buzzed back to life; a white wolf against a crisp blue sky. He pulled two paper cups, filled them with steaming jasmine tea, and toed open the door to the adjoining room. The lights flickered on and my guts warped into a steel knot. It was a tight room with a narrow aisle of red carpet pinched between a jumble of chrome and black scientific equipment on either side. The machine throbbed in white splendor at the end of the red runway; an over-sized laundry machine, a waste incinerator, a crematorium – he wasn't getting me in that thing.

'I am still quite uncertain who our Miss Cora belongs to,' he said. A lilting, humorous tone, time to turn the small-talk switch. 'I mean, I literally can't keep up with all their empire building acronyms and shiny new badges! What can they all be doing?'

He clamped the black skull-cap to my head and laced the wires like he was untangling last year's Christmas tree lights.

'I keep myself far removed from all that absurdity,' he babbled in my ear. 'I jumped through the hoops for security clearance, of course, no other option for my line of work, from a purely practical viewpoint.'

I lay down on the conveyor, like I was about to ship off on the International Space Station. Blake swivelled back to the desktop to adjust the headset of glasses and ear-piece.

'Have you any idea of how that industry has mushroomed since 9/11?' he said. 'It really is incredible! Something like 3,000 organizations out there to look after our security. Almost a million folks with top-secret security clearance. How come we don't feel any more secure, eh?' He dredged up a dry laugh from his gut, doing his best to put me at ease. 'So many of them are private operations, too. I guess that's where you fit in with Cora, right?'

All I could think of was how I was supposed to fit into this fucking steel tube in front of me. Satisfied with the head-set, he lurched over me to slip it over my eyes, a metallic click like the safety on a Carbine, and it started. Music first, soft and warm, like Blake thought he should thaw me out. An Irish lament for the emigrant, starved and scraped off the green landscape.

Oh Erin Grá mo Chroí, you're the dear old land to me
You're the fairest that my eyes did e'er behold
The land St. Patrick blessed, the bright star of the west
You're that dear little isle so far away

Then the blinding flash and head splitting thunder of an explosion, the scenes from a soldier's head-cam, one of our soldiers, running in panic down a long dusty road towards a Humvee, other boots and legs in scrambled focus around him.

At the setting of the sun, when my long day's work was done
I rambled down the seashore for a walk
And being all alone I sat down upon a stone
For to gaze upon the scenes of New York

Getting closer, black smoke, screams of merciless pain and terror, shell casings scattered thick in the dust, a red pool in the sand, the running soldier praying and cursing and praying until he reached his comrade.

And Blake had it rigged up pretty good with sight and sound so I could nearly put my hand out and touch the red corpse, smell the burning flesh, taste the fear drowning the comrades. But it didn't work. If he thought he could spark an eruption in my own head he had me figured wrong, big time, because these were just images that reeled away in front of me, like I was in a floating capsule and this was all just random shit happening to some nobody in Blake's simulated fabric of imagination. This was never real, nothing was happening in my head, I didn't even have to try to hide it.

On the cold moonlit night when the turf fire burns so bright
And the snow does fall so gently to the window pane
When St. Patrick's Day is near we'll wear the Shamrock green
In our own native land far away

But where to fuck did he get that recording of McErlane's father? It was his favorite song, and I had heard it a thousand times at birthdays, weddings and wakes, but nobody had ever recorded him. But it was no big deal, merely a curiosity, Blake was way off the mark, and that stabbed a little thrill of glee up my spine; he wasn't getting the better of me, even here in his magic cave.

The guy's head was red pulp; no helmet, no Kevlar, taken by surprise. One of them turned away to vomit, the rest just stood over the shredded body like they hoped somebody else would happen along and do something about it. Then shouts from behind the Humvee, they shuffled around there, three more sacrificial lambs; two with their heads ripped off and thrown in the sand, steaming shit in their eyes and mouths, the third with his pants around his ankles and ripped open right up to his chest. Still nothing, maybe Blake was proving that all that red fury shit was an illusion, I was already free, it was all over.

Then a couple of guys dragged a wounded insurgent into view, found him lying under the Humvee with his leg broken. They went berserk, the helmet-cam rocking like they were in an earthquake, deep-throated shrieks and howls like wolves squirming over a kill until one figure kicked and pushed them all back; the leader of the pack, forcing their submission, drawing their venom for himself. He circled the prisoner, twice, three times, stoking up the kill fever bursting out of their hearts. The helmet-cam was knocked over, bounced back in time to catch him lift his knife high into the blue sky above them, the pack moaning their blood lust – then it went dead, Blake pulled me back out of the tunnel and lifted the head-set off my eyes.

'So, how was that for you?' he said. 'Not too uncomfortable, I hope?'

I rubbed my fists over my skull and gouged my eyes back to focus.

'Head-set was a bit tight but no problem,' I said. 'Pity I couldn't get myself worked up for you, Doctor. I hope that wasn't a waste of your time.'

'It was fine,' he said. 'I am very satisfied.'

He turned his back on me to scribble something quickly, like he was about to dish me out some man-flu paracetamol, paused to think and rattled his pen between his teeth, then scraped a final flourish before slapping the file closed. It was a battered brown folder clasping together more pages than it was designed for, with my name printed in bold letters across the front.

'Of course, that tape from the soldier's helmet-cam will remain classified,' he said.

He reached across to his jacket and pulled out a large linen handkerchief, just about large enough to absorb the tears swelling on my cheeks.

'Don't worry about it, no-one else will ever see it,' he said. 'You can safely forget about that unfortunate incident. The rest of the world already has. It never happened. It never happened and we have all forgotten it.'

PART II:
THE YELLOW TRAM
....

To feel today what one felt yesterday isn't to feel – it's to remember today what was felt yesterday, to be today's living corpse of what yesterday was lived and lost.

Fernando Pessoa (1888 – 1935)

CHAPTER NINE

February 2nd

Lisbon, Portugal

We touched down in Lisbon at 6.30 a.m. on a Sunday morning. Ferdy had made a big deal over the hassle he took when making the flight booking; whinged about the on-line system crashing, cribbed at the lack of support from Cora, sulked because I left him to it. Then the jerk almost missed the plane, came waltzing into Newark as the shout went out: 'Passenger Ferdia McErlane. Last call for passenger McErlane, flight now departing for Lisbon'.

Cora was already out here somewhere but she would contact us, no way was she risking a trail back to her. Ferdy had the address for a holiday rental scribbled, the driver nodded but looked like he hadn't a clue. I sat in back, in somebody else's hands, let them work it out.

The tourist glossy on the plane said this was the 'City of Light' but this Lisbon was still dark and cold under its winter shroud; sleety rain drilled the windscreen, the driver had been smoking shit cigarettes, the aircon didn't work. It wasn't how I figured southern Europe would be, this was more Cape Cod winter than Santa Monica summer. Trucks and buses muscled us to the wrong lane until the driver horned and cursed his way to victory, swung off the carriageway, too fast through city streets, too close to scooters and pedestrians, pulled into a warp of needle-thin lanes spiking through the oblique stack that knitted a neighborhood.

'Alfama,' he announced.

A narrow terrace house, a torrent gouging through the broken gutter, a solid street door beneath grafitti, cute blue tiles framing the window, something religious. This was it, should be somebody here to let us in. The taxi vanished into a hole between two houses, brake lights bounced off the oil rainbowed cobblestones. We looked up and down, huddled under a dead street light, Ferdy getting uptight: somebody was supposed to be here. Hailstones smacked off my red ears, Ferdy fumbled for the phone number, couldn't get the local code right. We were on our own.
I wondered where Gallogly had taken Rose and young Con.

A door shuddered across the street, a brown skull crested with a film of silver stubble, bright blue eyes, a few twisted teeth.

'Americano?' he said, his bright voice ringing through the rain.

Luis had a key, said the stupid hag that looked after the place was getting too old and forgetful, this always happened. He had a key, he had been a good neighbor to the old couple who died there. He didn't know why their son hadn't asked him to look after the place. The young man was in Brazil, a big engineer, but he shouldn't have left that old hag in charge, Luis had been his father's friend since before the cub was born.

It was darker and colder in here, Luis would have left the heating on if only someone had told him American tourists were expected. He showed us how the heating worked, switches to turn, buttons to push. An electric cooker. Satellite TV, we would have to work that out for ourselves. He dismissed the burglar alarm with weary contempt. The streets had changed; the people never locked their doors in the old days, back when he knew all his neighbors. Now strangers screwed profit from their old homes, holiday rentals with burglar alarms ringing night and day, disturbing his sleep. And no-one ever came to investigate the ringing anyway. He had complained to the council many times and still no-one ever came. I left Ferdy to shuffle Luis back out the door, found a bed, ignored the dampness clinging to the duvet, and buried myself. Almost 9 a.m. here, it was 4 a.m. at home, I needed sleep.

Luis shook me at noon, his old claw hand still strong and tough. 'Come, filho, eat. It is hot.'

Ferdy was already at the table, bare feet and chest, washing the jet sleep away in a cloud of fierce coffee and SG cigarettes. Luis blinked at the shrapnel scars swathed purple around Ferdy's neck and torso, caught my cloned mark of Cain before I could pull my sweater up. He mouthed some small curse to himself in Portuguese, then pulled a cardboard box with custard tarts and four small rolls wrapped around beef and pork steaks.

'I live in America long ago,' Luis said. 'I work the boats in Bristol, Rhode Island. I was a young man one time. Long ago. Fifty years.' The sad eyes of an old man, no way back to those sweet days, to relive that joy or make amends. The claw hand had a faint tremor when he offered my coffee. 'You here for vacation?' Kept eye contact, as if he hadn't noticed our scars.

'Yeah, that's right,' Ferdy was cool. 'We are travelling Europe, a Portuguese friend of ours told us we couldn't come to Europe and not visit Lisbon.'

Ferdy was cool, but old Luis could smell a lie.

'Turns out our friend is in town right now,' Ferdy kept it going. 'Sorta hoped we could touch base with him.'

Luis nodded his interest, but stroked the white shadow around his tight lips and chin, wouldn't make it easy.

'Maybe you know our friend?' Ferdy was bright and open. 'His name is Jorge de Oliveira. His friends call him Jorginho,' Ferdy said. 'In the United States, he is called George Oliver. Maybe you have heard of him?'

A light flashed in his eyes but Luis shook his head and rubbed the back of his neck. His knuckles were too big for the wrinkled skin, still the hands of a boatman, pulling ropes in his dreams, hauling nets.
He coughed from his gut and spat a yellow pellet towards the radiator, where a fireplace had been replaced.

'He is a good friend of ours,' Ferdy kept trying. 'We are from Yonkers, he knows us.' Nothing doing. 'He works for the United States government, like us.'

Luis couldn't hold down his eyebrows, his shoulders heaved a shrug, he nodded, but Ferdy was getting nowhere. I went into the bedroom and came back with a wad of dollars, flipped $50 under Luis's cigarette lighter. He thumbed a quick count, then held his hand out for more. $100.

'This is the name of many people in Lisbon,' Luis said. 'Like John Smith.' He plucked a ten dollar bill in his left hand and neatly folded the rest in his right, before stashing it in a hip pocket. We waited, like he wanted, let him make his story worthwhile, an old man dispensing his wisdom.

'But the neighbors say a young boy came from America,' he said. 'I remember this, before Christmas. The old man up there in São Vicente died, and a boy came from New York. Too late for the funeral, but he came anyway.'

Ferdy stood up and came around the table to stand behind Luis. He rested a reassuring hand on the old man's shoulder. Luis coughed some more, suddenly short of breath.

'Up there in São Vicente, they know your American Jorge,' he said. 'You will not say my name? Please? I live here for long time. Never any trouble when I come from Rhode Island.'

Ferdy took out another $100 and palmed it to Luis. 'Don't worry, Luis. There will be no trouble. And we won't say a word, okay?'

Luis shoved the notes into his pocket and anchored his big hands on the table to hoist himself to his feet, Ferdy caught his elbow and eased him from the table.

'But be careful,' Luis said. 'The old man was crazy. I do not know this young man, but...'

'You mean he was dangerous?' Ferdy said.

'Yes, dangerous, yes,' Luis said. 'But like an animal, not like a man. Be careful with those people, and do not tell my name. Please, I am old man now. When I was young like you, in Rhode Island, I fear no man. But that is over for me now, and one day it will all be over for you.'

Ferdy yakked some more to Luis as he steered him to the door, I pulled a map from the heap of tourist guides piled on a shelf beside the TV. Shit. Like all these European city maps, these streets were too small and twisted together like Rocco's spaghetti. I couldn't see where we were, never mind find São Vicente.

'Let's get over there and nail old George boy right now,' Ferdy chimed. 'Didn't I fucking tell you, Con? Didn't I? Would you rather be at home eating Gallogly's shit or lifting ten grand for this piece of piss?'

I folded the map and drained my coffee.

'Yeah, it's so easy that the Russians couldn't find him,' I said. 'And so easy that Cora needs two dopes like us to come pick him up. What does that tell you?'

Ferdy sneered from the bathroom, started his stupid singing again, 'Oh Cora baby! I'll do anything you want me to, Cora baby!'

★★★

The streets looked even tighter in daylight. Not wide enough for two cars to pass, splitting off at random into alleyways that would squeeze a scooter, like somebody had decided to build the houses first and then thought about the streets afterwards. The rain had mellowed to a misty drizzle and the choked sun still didn't stretch into these narrow ravines but the bleached walls and baked cobbles leaked their ingrained luster, the City of Light releasing its hoarded sunshine to keep the winter darkness at bay. We came out on to Rua das Escolas Gerais now, São Vicente was to our north and not too distant, as far as I could tell. We were working out which way to go when a bell clanged behind us, a yellow tram just like the ones they have in San Francisco. It passed and stopped just in front of us so that made our minds up, we ran down and jumped on. Ferdy struggled to find the correct coins, I went down back and grabbed seats beside two fat French tourists who insisted on standing. Ferdy slid in beside me and we clinked off, swaying around impossible corners and missing parked automobiles by inches. The French guys held on to the handrails, just the right height to smother Ferdy with their sweaty armpits. His sour face twisted more when I started 'Oh Cora Baby' in his ear.

We followed everyone else off at a street near the castle, then asked directions from a few people until we found it. Rua São Vicente was pretty neat; room for two cars, mostly, three or four storey houses opening right on to the street, no fences or steps to the doors. All painted a creamy beige color, or tiled with small decorative brown tiles, black metal grilles over the windows and around the balconies on the higher floors. Washing hanging to dry above our heads, sprayed graffiti on a boarded up shop, the smell and noise of lunch cooking, it was just a regular street, but we weren't seeing it like tourists.

There was a bar ahead, but not like a bar in the United States, this was just a door into a house that was used as a bar. I went in first, the clutch of men stopped their talk and let the bartender receive us. Two beers. A regular neighborhood bar, sport on TV, a fruit machine, middle aged men drinking their lunch, soccer pictures and souvenirs, some old men playing a card game in the corner. Ferdy got talking to the two standing beside us at the end of the bar. He grew up with me as a Yankees fanatic but he had spent enough time in Ireland as a teen with his folks to be fully conversant in the language universal to all these places – soccerese.

In here, they were split between Sporting and Benfica, but the bar owner was a Sportinguista, so the green and white scarf of Sporting Clube de Portugal draped the centerpiece clock above the bar. Of course they knew about Manchester United, so Ferdy started to stoke it up, the late greats; George Best and Eusébio, El Beatle and the Black Panther. Everybody had something to say, opinions and definitive statements on the good, better and best. And language didn't seem to matter, we made ourselves understood the way sportsmen do in bars anywhere.

So Ferdy bought a few drinks, the guys warmed to us. I bought drinks, we were old friends. Ferdy kept it going, regaled them with tales of Yankee Stadium, one guy set his drink on the counter and made for the rest room. I followed, found him sighing his relief in front of the overflowing urinal, carried on our soccer laughing until I took my chance.

'A good friend of ours lives around here,' I said. 'He came over for the funeral, before Christmas. We would really like to meet up with him.' Going well, he was attentive, though struggling to understand the non-sport language.

'Jorge de Oliveira,' I said. 'From New York, he was here for the funeral.'

He froze. 'No Jorge here, no Jorge here.' No laughing now, just concentrated on his zipper, a perfunctory rinse of hands, and he was gone. He was spinning it into his pal's ear when I got back in there, both of them removed from the fun circle now. Ferdy noticed, called for more drinks, these two refused graciously, they had somewhere to go. A few minutes more and another one had to piss, followed him, same routine at the urinal. 'No Jorge, no Americano.' He left, but before I could follow, one of the old card players came in.

'You ask for Jorginho?' he said.

I dealt the same spiel, our friend, said we would meet up, lost his address.

'You want make gamble?' he said.

Gamble? I nearly said no, hesitated, maybe I did. Jorginho and gambling? Very likely. Could he bring me to Jorginho?

'No, we not need that bastard,' he said. 'I work with Chinese, we are like that.' He linked his two crooked yellow index fingers together. 'I am best friend with Chinese. Forget Jorgingho, he is loser.'

I nodded, needed to keep this creep sweet, play him along, let him think he was playing me.

'How much you want play?' he said.

'How much can you handle?'

He shrugged that 'no problem' shrug that said he was big time, big time enough for any American.

'Ten thousand dollars?' I said. 'You can handle that? Good. But what if Jorginho finds out? He will make trouble.'

An even more expressive shrug. 'Fuck him!' he said. 'Jorginho is a nobody in this city. And nobody make trouble for Chinese. Not even Americanos!' He snarled a vicious laugh, had to force a shadow laugh out of my mouth before I lost it and punched the scuzzed little shit.

'You come here tonight,' he said. 'Stand outside. I come for you in car. Take you to game, okay? How much you play? Ten thousand? And your friend, he play ten thousand also? Dollar, not Euro?'

Yeah, yeah, I had to get out of there, he was starting to crowd me and the stinking urinal was choking me. He hung on my shoulder as we got back to the bar, Ferdy still in full flow. I clapped his back, time to go. The boys gave us a send off like we had just won the Champions League for Sporting, I dragged Ferdy out behind me.

'We've hit the jackpot,' I said. 'How much cash can we rustle up for tonight?'

★★★

Luis told us he was seventy nine years old. He must always have been small and wiry, but now arthritis twisted his limbs into a daily sweat of brittle defiance and warped his spine into a painful husk forcing his head to be jibbed back when he stretched to spy out his dirty window.

He saw it was me tapping his door and shuffled out in threadbare slippers. We needed him, and I guessed no-one had dignified his soul like that for a long time. He pretended to protest, at first, but let us bend him into joining us for a meal.

He quickly changed into something that looked a lot like what he had already been wearing, and led us through a dark alleyway, maybe four feet wide, that opened into another steep lane running parallel with our street until it split in three. Up some steps and we were in a small square with a rigging of festive lights blinking through the black branches. A gaggle of kids honked and bobbed around our ankles, heavy matriarchs and light girls fell silent for a second before giggling a catcall after Luis.

'Don't give these whores your ears!' he said. 'I knew their mothers and their mothers' mothers!' He shouted something cruel at them, the women sulked, the kids whooped. The attention grew him a little taller, a little younger.

There was a crumbling low wall at one corner of the square, and a ledge of cracked pavement tendered just enough space for three small tables to be wedged between the erupted roots of a tree. Luis flourished a grand ship steward's gesture and pulled out two seats for us, called into the doorway of the tight little bar and cranked himself as straight as his failing bones would allow. Looked like Luis wanted to sit out in the cold. A young dark man came out to take our order, toed the cats from under the table and clipped a cheeky kid's ear. Luis babbled our order, no need to ask us, and flipped his seat backward so he could swing his legs astride it, his taut chin supported by the big gnarled hands gripping the backrest, his ghost jade eyes rocking like he was on speed.

'We need a bit of advice, Luis,' I said. 'Do you know anything about the gambling scene here? Is George Oliver involved, or the old man that died, you know, the crazy old man?'

'Ahh, that is it,' Luis nodded. He was the tribal sage preparing the young bucks for the outside world. 'You are here for gambling. Yes, I knew it was no vacation, men like you do not vacation.' He winked towards Ferdy's neck scars.

'Something like that, Luis,' Ferdy said. 'We are going to meet people tonight. Chinese people. Is there a Chinatown in Lisbon?'

Luis closed his eyes, pursed his lips and rubbed the back of his neck, then sat back as the young man skipped out with three beers, a foamy splash in each glass and the bottles stomped on the table. Sagres Bohemia, the label said, a strong red beer. Luis sucked the foam through the gaps left by missing teeth, then set the glass down with an exaggerated air of solemnity.

'The Chinese,' he said. 'You know, I left my mother when I was fourteen years. Went to sea with my uncles. I was sixteen years when I first saw Macau.'

Ferdy gave me the look, nodded at Luis like he was a rambling waste of our time. I shook my head and lent closer to Luis.

'You know about Macau?' Luis said.

'It's a sort of parrot, isn't it?' Ferdy said.

Luis rocked back in his seat, slapped his thigh, bared his gums in a croaking laugh.

'It is China. Portuguese China,' Luis wheezed through his laughter. 'The Portuguese Empire, before there was an American Empire. Before there was America!'

Ferdy sipped his beer, I felt a cat rack against my ankles, flicked my toe out, the mangy thing probably covered in fleas.

'But you are right, sir,' Luis said. 'Many fine birds there, very many. Imagine what I saw then in Macau when I was sixteen years, over sixty years ago!'

'What Portuguese Empire?' Ferdy said.

Luis swivelled as much as his spine would allow and collected his thick throatspit before whistling it over the wall.

'What Empire?' Luis said. 'What language do they speak in Brazil, do you think?'

'They're Latinos,' Ferdy said. 'They all speak Spanish down there.'

'Ahh!' Luis sighed a mournful breath. 'And my woman left me so that our children could have an American education!'

The dark man bounced out of the bar with our three plated meals arrayed along his left arm, a basket of bread and a bowl of fries on his right. We sat back to let him scoop it to the table. Luis wasn't satisfied and reeled off demands into the guy's ear. The young dark man called into the doorway and a young dark woman emerged carrying a heaped salad and a little basket with sauces and mustard and relish in chipped glass bottles and cracked jars. Each plate had four long thick sardines, heads and tails intact, grilled in crisp silver, black and blue rings. The fish were framed by grilled red potatoes and yellow and green peppers, and then fringed by fried onions and tomatoes. Luis knocked back his beer and held up his glass to the young man, before deftly skewering the head off the sardine with a quick swish of his knife.

'You have heard of the South China Sea, haven't you?' Luis said. 'Hong

Hong? Guangzhou? Shanghai? These were the places I got education, before I was twenty years, before I ever hear of Rhode Island.'

He slipped a sliver of sardine between his gums, left the white fish skeleton suspended between fork and knife.

'Macau was ours. Portugal. But it was rough,' he said. 'Rough for us sailors. Opium dens, whorehouses, pimps, cut-throats. And gambling. An education before I was twenty.'

Illicit sex, proscribed narcotics, illegal gambling; the quicksilver thrill of those addictions never change. The underworld never changes. This contorted old man was describing a life of debauchery on the other side of the world, a lifetime ago, but I sensed George Oliver was living those thrills now, and not far away.

'So what? There is a Chinatown here in Lisbon or isn't there? Where is George Oliver hiding?' I said, close up to Luis's hairy ear.

'I pulled a girl out of the harbor one night. Her throat was cut,' he said, and lent over to stab the head off my fish.

I held his old fragile arm in my fist.

'Luis. Where is he hiding?' I said.

He took his beer in his left hand and turned his head away from me to drink.

'I don't know your Jorge de Oliveira,' he said. 'But if he is with the Chinese, then you must forget him and go home. He is in a different world that you do not understand, with your American education. No passport can take you there, just go home to what you know.'

Ferdy lent over from his side and took his left arm.

'Where is he, Luis? Where is Chinatown?' Ferdy said.

Luis laughed his sour old breath of beer and sardines in my face.

'Chinatown?' he laughed. 'It is still back there in Macau.' He squeezed my thigh with his old rope hand. 'We gave Macau back to the Chinese. But we did not give back all the Chinese.'

The dark young man and woman watched us from the doorway.

'They made a license for a grand casino in Lisbon,' he said. 'Very rich. Very nice. But it is legal, not like the place I was educated.'

The woman was inside now, but I could see her speaking into a cellphone.

'Jorginho is not there,' he said. 'Not in the nice casino with the license.' He sank the rest of the beer. 'If he is with the Chinese, he is at the waterfront. That is like old Macau. Bacara ponto e banca and Mah

Jong. Money, whores and drugs, you don't get these things with a nice license.'

I stroked the old guy's shoulder.

'You know where this joint is, Luis?' I said. 'This place on the waterfront?'

His eyes danced and his voice was stronger. 'I know these things. I was in Macau when I was sixteen years,' he said. 'I know these things. I put my knife in a man's back there, a poor man from Brazil. They made me do it because of a woman. I finished him and we threw him in the water. That was the way it was done.' Two strong beers were too much for his worn out liver. 'But now they are in Lisbon. They bring Macau to Lisbon. You should go home now, you do not have the education!'

The dark man brought out a third beer, I steered him away but Luis started shouting all over the square. 'Give me that beer! There will be no more when I am dead! These sons of bitches hunt Jorginho but keep my beer from me!' Cold shadows shivered around the edges of the square, two young guys looked out from the bar. I gave Luis his beer.

'Who runs this place on the waterfront, Luis?' I said. 'Are they gangs? From Macau?'

The old man laughed, with tears frosting his squeezed tight eyes and no sound from his lips, just a deep wheezing in his chest. I smelt piss, either him or the mangy cats.

'Yes! Yes! But they are Portuguese now!' he laughed. 'They were permitted to marry Portuguese whores. So now they are welcomed as citizens of Portugal! They are as Portuguese as I am. The Triads are Portuguese now, citizens of Europe!'

Luis grabbed at the young woman but she swerved him without looking. Ferdy and I picked through the sardine bones and sipped our beers. Luis spilt his beer and his heart through his song -Barco Negro. He gripped my hand as if the words were too painful, as if he needed an anchor before the song could be let free. 'The sun entered my heart,' the young woman translated. 'A cross stuck on a rock, and your black sailboat dancing in the light'. We had lost him, he was twenty years old again, back in the opium dens of old Macau, losing his mind, stabbing his friend. They had made him do it because of a woman. It was time for Ferdy and me to go meet the Chinese. A plump middle-aged woman appeared from the shadows and grabbed Luis by the loose skin at the back of his neck. She shouted at the young woman and hauled Luis off the chair and dragged him back across the square, back to the dark alleyway. The daughter of his wife's sister, the young woman said, she had come to take him home. The young woman said he was not used to alcohol, he was not allowed to drink beer. It made him crazy, it made him sing his old songs and tell lies about all the things he had never done when he was young, like all old men. She said he had never been to Macau, he had never been anywhere, just these narrow lanes. He was a liar, she said, like all men.

CHAPTER TEN

We were late. Almost 9.30 p.m., I said we would be there at 9 p.m. No-one here, just the warm glow from inside the bar and a couple of hungry dogs pawing and pissing over the garbage outside.

'What if he doesn't show up?' Ferdy said.

'How many illegal gambling joints can there be in this town?' I said. 'We'll find it ourselves if we have to. But he'll show. He probably gets a commission for every American he brings through the door.'

It was cold here, not as cold as New York, but there was nowhere to hide from the wind snapping through the thin streets. A dog sniffed the air and shot a quick piss against the wall. Headlights carved around the corner, the taxi stopped in front of us. No shiny black limo for this casino, just a small hatchback taxi with a broken meter.

He rolled the taxi down through the spider's web of Alfama and then across a wide carriageway, cursed at traffic lights, then we were cruising along the waterfront.

'How much dollar you play?' Scuzzball said.

'Enough,' I said. 'Will Jorginho be here?'

'Jorginho, Jorginho. Forget this shit!' he said. 'You go to good place now. Nice girls, very friendly. You enjoy.'

He drove carefully, as if he was short-sighted and had to feel his way along. The lights on a container ship marked the deep water of the Tejo river to our right, a rail track seamed the road to our left. We passed docks and parking lots behind high wire fences and then cruised past a row of vacant buildings. This wasn't tourist Lisbon; these streets were deserted except for a band of drinkers huddled together for safety and warmth around a fire on the rough ground they called home. He pulled up at a security gate stretched between two old red brick walls, a red light flickered on a camera and, after a few seconds, the gate scraped into life and parted slowly before us.

More security lights and cameras were mounted above the entrance to a windowless black-bricked warehouse. A black man in a white tuxedo held open a heavy metal door, which led us into a small rectangular reception area, with another security door on the opposite side of a narrow archway. The tuxedo guy eyed us up and down, working out what our thrills might be, what we would be worth tonight. He said something in Portuguese to our driver, something funny, because they both sniggered. The driver palmed a brown envelope from Tuxedo and swaggered back out to the car. We watched the driver's image on the security monitor mounted above our heads.

'Cabrão!' Tuxedo spat his distaste.

He engaged the dropbolts on the outer door before leading us to the inner door.

'Enhoy', he said, before ushering us into the promised land.

It was a long, dark 'T' shaped hall, split into different sections. To our left was a bar, mostly under dim lights except for the end corner, where spotlights picked out the five or six girls who looked like they really didn't want to be there. Along the right wall, a row of drinking cubicles offered the privacy that some patrons needed. Fruit machines spun against the wall behind us, beside the door we came in. In between the bar and the cubicles there were maybe fifteen tables arranged around a small dancing podium in the middle of the floor. A tall skinny girl was up there, defying gravity on a silver pole that reached to the low ceiling. Beyond the podium, at the far end, the cross stroke of the 'T' held the gaming tables; nine or ten, from what I could see. A cloud of smoke wafted above head height, and swirled around the lights. Dino crooning 'Everybody Loves Somebody' through speakers that nobody heard.

The Tuxedo stood behind us for a moment, waiting for our eyes to acclimatize to the smoky darkness, then called out to a woman at the bar. She saw us, and took her time to sidle over, but then purred towards us like a cat on heat. A tall dark woman in a long emerald Chinese kimono, she shimmered across the floor as if the lights had been choreographed to flaunt her catwalk strut, just so the first thing the customers would see would be her doing that walk towards them.

'Good evening, Gentlemen!' A strong feminine voice. 'A little champagne before playing the tables?'

Not really a question, maybe a suggestion – no, not that either - from her, this was a command.

She half turned towards the corner of the bar.

'What sort of girls you like?'

The tired girls knew they were being auditioned.

'Any sort,' Ferdy shrugged.

She clicked the fibreglass castanets between thumb and index finger and two girls rolled off their bar stools and linked an arm each to direct us to a vacant cubicle. Mine was a young black girl with a close cropped thicket of hair and a face that beamed with naive energy. Ferdy's must have been beautiful one time but now in her mid-twenties she was dyed blonde with a fake orange tan and vacant eyes.

The emerald kimono disappeared. My girl said she liked Americans, Ferdy's was too pissed off to talk. Mine said she had always wanted to live in America, would do anything to get there. Ferdy's girl had given up long ago. I wondered where Gallogly had taken Rose and young Con.

The champagne arrived; two bottles, four glasses. 'Champange Don Perignom – Made In Franc' the peeling label said. And it really was piss water, even Ferdy gagged on the first mouthful. But the waiter was a star – he spilt a mouthful of bubbles into a glass for each girl and watched it fizz to the lip of the plastic glow-in-the-dark flutes, flicked a wrist and Ferdy and I were tanked to the top, no fizz, no waste. I wasn't drinking this shit, and the girls weren't expected to, so we stalled for a few minutes until the same waiter returned with the clear plastic tabs hidden in his fist – White Dragon, or so he said. It didn't matter what it was because now the girls giggled, even Ferdy's, and we were in business. But it was hard work, sounded like they really had never seen nor heard of our Jorginho, the flash Americans were all going to the legitimate casino. 'Ask Yasmin,' Ferdy's girl said. 'She see all these rich men. We only get poor men.'

Yasmin was working the bar area, keeping the girls moving and the champagne flowing. She didn't notice me behind her and only turned to me when the bar tender gave her the nod. In her heels, she was almost my height, just about six feet of lithe movement under the kimono sheen. Her dark shoulder length hair was brushed back from her face, and I thought I noticed a smudge of hair dye behind her right ear. Wide, black eyes –almost oriental, unless that was a make-up effect. A wide mouth too. Thick lips, almost bulbous in a permanent pout, accentuated in this twilight by the crimson lip gloss. She had extraordinarily white teeth; an un-natural ultra white, but I decided they must be natural. Too many teeth, maybe, and some a bit crooked, but striking. Her skin was dark, more African than European, and patches of her cheeks were orange pitted underneath her make-up. She let me stare, she didn't care.

'I'd like to buy you a drink,' I said.

She inclined her head to listen, then shook a little shrug.

'You have girl already,' she said. 'Buy a drink for her.'

Just business-like, not really a rejection, no emotional response.

'I want to buy you a drink,' I insisted.

She turned to the bar tender, he shrugged, then nodded.

'Two hundred dollar,' she said. 'One hundred for the girl you already have, then one hundred to drink with me.'

That rocked me.

'I'm just talking about a drink here,' I said.

'Yes.' Still business. 'Just a drink. $200. What you think you pay for?'

Her eyes flashed, she winked at the bar tender, they were having fun with me. Okay, but Cora better be good for the expenses.

'Is there any real alcohol?' I said. 'Not that piss champagne.'

'You want American whisky?' she asked. 'Okay. Still $200.'

The bar tender rattled some ice and Kentucky bourbon into our glasses, and she led me away from the other girls, down to the gaming tables, placed me next to a table spread with dice and weird scrabble tiles.

'You like to play?' she said.

There was a glint in her eye but I figured it was permanent, and I was definitely just a mark, and I'd better not forget it.

'What's the game?' I said.

'This table is Hong Hong Mahjong. You know it?'

I shook my head, she edged me along to the next huddle. Dino asking Ain't that a Kick in the Head? The smoke down here even thicker, catching in my chest, like Luis's Macau opium dens of long ago. They had made him kill a man because of a woman. This game looked like craps, dice crashing over the green baize, the players a heartbeat from riches or despair.

About ten people around this table, maybe fifty playing the tables in total. All Europeans, no Chinese that I could see, not even the staff. Then I noticed a worried looking fat man tip-toe over to the side. There was a room there behind smoked glass mirrors. A mirror slid open to reveal a teller behind a security grille; just his hands, counting cash and dumping out the gambling chips. I hunkered down to get a better look, saw a Chinese man, aged about fifty, dealing with the fat man, saw another Chinese man, maybe older, counting rolls of cash in the background.

'You play this one? Banca Francesa?' she said. 'You Americanos all like this one.'

'Let's watch,' I said. She glanced at her wristwatch, setting her deadline so she wouldn't waste her time. How much of her time was worth $200? I'd better get down to it.

'You have many Americans come in here?' I asked.

She lent closer to hear me, her ear almost against my lips, then pulled away again.

'Many people from everywhere,' she said. 'This more fun than the licensed casino, that place is for bores!'

I had pretended to snort the White Dragon but the smoke in here was laced heavy with some sort of shit, and I was getting light-headed.

'Yeah, this is way more fun,' I said. 'So how do I get to have some fun with you, Yasmin? Just you and me?'

She levered me back with her elbow, but kept the business voice.

'We have drink together,' she said. 'That is fun. You see the other girls if you want more. She is very fun, that little one waiting for you, with your champagne.'

'I don't like her. I don't like any of them,' I said. 'But my friend comes here. He told me to ask for you. Yasmin is the best, he told me. I want to have some fun with you.'

That made her think. Her frown rucked up some wrinkles across her forehead that I hadn't noticed.

'Ten years ago, a man might say this thing.' She sounded wistful, I guessed she was about my age. 'But not now. Never. Who is this American friend who tells you lies?'

'You know who it was,' I said, taking hold of her wrist. 'Jorge de Oliveira. Jorginho. George Fucking Oliver.'

Yasmin froze at the first syllable of his name, the blood drained from her face, and she dropped a couple of inches.

'You have seen him?' she said. 'Jorge is safe?'

Shit, wrong answer, Yasmin. And it was pretty clear that Cora wasn't the only woman worried about the gorgeous geek. But I had made a big mistake, I had put my hands on her without paying. Before I could figure what to say next, the White Tuxedo came out of nowhere and was working an armlock around my neck. He almost had me cold, but I stamped down hard on his shin and spun my elbow into his ribs. Yasmin tried to cool it but Tuxedo still had one arm around my neck, and he was one strong bastard. I stabbed three fingers into his throat and twisted anti-clockwise, taking him off balance, I dodged low and twisted again, came up this time with his arm cranked backwards, just about to lock him good when he took my wrist and yanked me off my feet. I landed heavily against the fucking craps table and cracked my skull. The fucker had me now, wedged his knee in the back of my neck and forced that wristlock right up my back. Three bouncers appeared from behind the mirrors. Tuxedo stood back and one of them stuck with me a cattle prod, or some fucking thing that creased me into a ball. They waited until I stopped convulsing, then dragged me across the floor to the secret room. Where the fuck was Ferdy McErlane?

They trailed me in past the teller and dumped me in a small bare room. Two of them held me down until the older Chinese guy came in, still a wad of cash in his hand. He gave an order, in Chinese or Portuguese, and they held me down so Tuxedo could search me. He pulled out $1,100 and 900 in Euro currency, offered it to the Chinese boss with a bow, then turned back and kicked me in the ribs. That was it, I chucked the piss alcohol and sardines sideways over Tuxedo's shoes. He jumped back and then screamed at the other three to get me out of there. Two minutes later, I was lying in a heap on the street outside the security gates. The street drinkers stopped to watch, laugh, then carried on with their own business.

I was still lying there, waiting for the shivers to stop, when the gate creaked open again.

'Fuck's sake, Con,' Ferdy said. 'You've messed up big time now! I had to give them fifty bucks to get out of the fucking place! Why did you start a fight? You should have just apologized to the guy and everything would have been sweet.'

'Thanks for your support,' I said.

I was still shaking from the taser, or whatever to fuck it was, and my legs couldn't hold me. He lifted me, draped my left arm around his shoulders and hiked me back down the street, past the rough drinkers, past the derelict buildings and past the docks. We eventually pulled a taxi outside the train station. I was back to normal when we pulled up, normal now but shaking with fury. Ferdy went in to the house to get the taxi fare, I grabbed the money off him and jumped back in the cab. I was going back down there, this time they wouldn't catch me cold.

'Con, don't do this, brother!' Ferdy whinged at me. 'This isn't the way, man. We have a job to do here, you can go look for your revenge later, okay?'

Fuck him. I would do this on my own. I told the taxi driver to take me back down there. The driver didn't know what was happening, but knew it wasn't good, and he didn't want any trouble, and especially not down there. He shouted at Ferdy to get me out of his cab, I shouted at him to move it unless he wanted a big problem.

A light came on in Luis' hallway, the old guy stuck his head out the door, then shuffled over to the cab. He pressed his parchment skull into my face and took my hand.

'They made me kill my friend because of a woman,' he whispered. 'We found her body in the harbor. It was his woman, she loved him, so they cut her throat. We took her out, so they made me kill my friend and put his poor body in the water instead. I do not understand why I did it. I was twenty years old. But I did it because they made me. You are American. You do not understand. Stay here with me.'

Tears flushed the deep wrinkles strafing his cheeks. He kissed my head and gently lifted my hand to his face. I got out of the taxi and Luis walked me into the house. Ferdy shut the door behind us and the three of us sat at the table.

'Okay, okay, I'm sorry,' I said. 'I messed up. But he was down there, Ferdy. She knows him. That's where the answer is, we have to go back.'

Ferdy pulled out a bottle from under his jacket. Ramos Pinto, vintage port from the Douro Valley, 1983. Luis almost had a stroke when he saw the bottle, never had anything like it. Did we know how rare this was, how expensive?

'Don't worry, Luis. Drink up and enjoy. Didn't cost me a cent,' Ferdy said. He winked at the old man. 'While my friend here was letting us down in that joint, I liberated this fine potion by way of reparations. Two hundred bucks for that piss they call champagne? Let's see what this tastes like, for free!'

Luis sipped the thick red port like he had been waiting all his seventy nine years for this delight. Ferdy toasted bread made with sausage – Bola de Carne – and sliced some cheese with pickles and tomatoes. Old Luis could eat like three young men.

'We will still have to go back some time,' I said. 'It may as well have been now.'

Ferdy tore off a hunk of bread and swiped up some pickles.

'You think you are the only one on the job, Con, don't you?' he said. 'That's what you always think, that it all comes down to you.'

'Oh yeah?' I waited, knew he had pulled something more than the port.

'Yasmin told me all about it. While you were in there getting your ass burnt off,' he said. 'She gave me her number. She is worried about poor Jorginho. I'm going to call her in the morning, when she is finished work.'

My fingers still tingled some from that electric shock, the port shivered in the glass as I tipped it to my lips. Ferdy had done real good tonight. An expensive vintage port. A lead to George's latest girlfriend. Tasty bread and cheese. And George was close, I could taste him, like the blood red port that trembled in my fingers.

CHAPTER ELEVEN

The port took the ragged edge off my purple bruises but I had to angle myself slowly into bed before I was comfortable. We shouldn't have let Luis drink so much, but Ferdy liked his old seadog tales, didn't much care if they were fact or fiction. I pulled a pillow over my head to smother their singing. Luis' Clandestino, and Ferdy's The Flower of Magherally, then Fado Toninho and Úr-Chill an Chreagaín, Cumha an Fhile and Verde Gaio - the Portuguese and Irish swallowed as one by my American ear. The last I heard was a duet, Little Ole Wine Drinker Me, as Ferdy half carried Luis back across the road, before I tripped into my shaking dreams. Cora with George, Jorginho with Yasmin, Rose with Gallogly. My dreams, and yet I wasn't in there, just a spectator while real life floated by. There was something wrong with all this. I couldn't pin it down when I was awake but now, in my sleep, my brain bounced images and sounds, snapped faces and voices, teased with meanings and contorted truths.

I heard it. I was fighting back, clawing up to the light of consciousness, when I heard it. A bang on the door, a heavy fist, three times. Pause. Three thunder bolts. A shout in Portuguese, footsteps skinning the cobblestones, then the echo, either real or just in my anchored brain. But Ferdy heard it too, made for the door as I stumbled after him. He yanked it open and a hollow shadow slumped at our feet. I swear I heard Ferdy scream 'Luis!' before he even opened the door. A short knife disappeared between the old man's sharp shoulder blades. A blood red ten dollar bill quivered under the knife, a grotesque plaster pinned to his spine. Ferdy eased the old head up off the cold tiles. His eyes were open but glazed into empty shells. His mouth moved, but he wasn't a man now, looked like a sun lizard trapped under a stone, his jaws cracking together, the death rattle, an involuntary pre-human reflex.

'Phone 911, Con! Phone 911!' Ferdy screamed in my face.

I lifted the cellphone. Stuffed it back in my pocket.

'The number is 112 here,' I said. 'But we can't do it, Ferdy. I can't phone.'

Ferdy had Luis propped against his lap now, bent over him, wishing it had never happened, the blood greasy ten dollar bill stuck to the doorstep.

'Fuck!' He screamed in red-faced fury. 'What are you talking about? Phone the fucking number right now, you asshole!'

'We need to get out of here, and quick,' I said. 'We can't get involved, we need to get out of here before anyone comes.'

'Involved? Fucking involved?' Ferdy shouted. 'We got this old man killed! They nailed our money to his back! How much more fucking involved you wanna get?'

I stepped over Luis and levered his legs inside the doorway, the light from our open door glistened on the dark swathe of slicked blood that was the old sailor's red carpet into the darkness.

'We are being set up, brother,' I said. 'The cops trace his movements and he was with us. He was drinking with the two foreigners, we get into a fight, we kill him. We have to go right now or not at all.'

Ferdy sighed deeply and rolled his head against the wall behind him. Luis stared up at him, dead eyes and gaping gums. Ferdy tilted the head and closed the mouth, ran his finger over the lips that had been kissing the songs and vintage port just a moment ago.

'That's life, I guess,' Ferdy said. 'Our shitty life anyway. But this isn't real life, Con, so don't ever let them shit us that it is, right?'

We carried Luis to his own house, laid him on his own cold bed. A bare room crusted with an old man's life. A yellowed postcard, 'Greetings from Atlantic Beach, R.I.' At least somebody had thought of him, one time, somebody far away in his past, far away in his Rhode Island memory. Maybe his wife's sister's daughter would let them know he was dead now but she would tell them he had kept that postcard thought beside his bed to the end.

Ferdy whispered a quick prayer and we left Luis behind us; his dark sailboat dancing under the light, the sun in his heart, and his cold eyes staring into the empty silence.

★★★

About three hours until daylight. The butchers had slaughtered old Luis in a public execution but the neighborhood wasn't ready yet to be outraged. I kept watch at the corner while Ferdy threw some things into a bag, but these antique streets broke off into too many forks and nooks and twists, I was keeping watch in the darkness but I didn't know where I was supposed to be looking – the Policia could have knotted the noose around us already. Ferdy whistled, I flashed my cellphone and he jogged over.

'Which way?' Ferdy said.

We had no way. We were on our own, Cora hadn't made contact, the American Embassy probably didn't know we existed, and wouldn't help even if they did.

'Keep under cover until daylight,' I said. 'Then track down Yasmin.'

'What happens when we find her?' Ferdy said. 'It's no good without the big plan. How is Cora supposed to reach us now?'

The thought crossed my mind that Cora had never planned on reaching us. Somebody was perched somewhere on an ivory tower that would always be susceptible to the shakes as long as Ferdy and I were tumbling along like the dice on that table. They made it clear that we were only grudged our freedom that last time because a lot of people got their hands dirty on that one, and no way were they risking due process exposing that squalid web of guilt and disloyalty. And it would be a pretty neat solution; we flush out George Oliver, Cora's people pick him up, we're left behind. Have our backs? Some old guy in Lisbon that nobody would ever hear of? Or conjure 'an action to defend America'? How long would they need to deliberate on that moral conundrum? About as long as it took for one of their slimy frat handshakes. We weren't in that club, never would be, so the code was different, always variable and appropriate to the 'best interests of the nation'.

'Let's see what Yasmin has to say first, then we will worry about Cora,' I said.

Ferdy led through the tight alleyway that Luis had used to take us for our sardines. He stumbled over garbage piled in the darkness, I caught his elbow and steadied him, caught a glint in his eye that disturbed me. Just a fleeting thought, maybe a reflex more than a thought, but Ferdy had been in this with Cora before they told me about it, knew about George Oliver before I did. He knew about the Russians, he took me to Brighton Beach. I blanked the image; Ferdia McErlane had saved my life more than once, he had saved young Con's life when I was a helpless spectator. If even Ferdia McErlane felt he had to betray me, well, then I should just call it quits on this piss life right now.

'Shit!' I said.

'What? What's wrong, Con?' Ferdy said.

'Nothing. Don't worry about it,' I said.

Don't worry about it, I repeated to myself, I guess that's just the way your brain works in the dark hours before dawn, when you have let an old man die on his own, when you are being hunted and you are in a strange city in a strange country that isn't the United States, and when life has let you down too often.

'Yeah, I know,' Ferdy said. 'I hope that old guy forgives us, wherever he is now.'

Like he could hear the voice in my own brain, didn't need me to form the words. That's why I had to wise up, thinking Ferdia McErlane could betray me was like thinking I could betray myself. But there was something different in this voice in the darkness, or something I just didn't hear before. Just keep going I told myself, blank those crazy ideas, get a grip.

A police siren spiralled around the rooftops, down below us somewhere, and not far away, but it was impossible to pinpoint its position. We quickened our pace, keeping to alleyways, avoided two street cleaners who were catching the heat from a bakery during their smoke break, just keep moving, look as if we had somewhere to go.

But I couldn't help myself. There was a time when I knew every thought in Rose's head, just like Ferdy and I could read each other now. So how could that jerk Gallogly suddenly take my place like I was dead? And then what? Like I don't know her anymore? Like the real Rose is dead and just lives in my memory? Or maybe this is a different Rose, a different Gallogly? Doctor Blake had said something like that, said even he couldn't guarantee how anybody would react anytime in the future merely on the basis of how they had reacted before. He said he knew he himself was a different person today than he had been thirty years ago, ten years ago, one year ago, but he couldn't remember now what each of those different Blake selves had been like. He said he would be a different person in five years than he was today. He guessed he might be a different person each and every day. And then other people had different ideas of who he was too, different versions of the same Blake walking around in the same Blake shoes, so who could say who was right? He said he guessed there really was no 'himself', not like I might understand it, anyway.

'Are you okay?' Ferdy said. 'You've got that look on your face, like you're about to lose it.'

He was the one who was always telling me about how I would lose it. And what was that shit supposed to mean anyway? We were in almost absolute darkness here, so just what did he see?

'I'm good,' I said. 'How about you? You look a bit weird yourself there, brother.'

Ferdy stepped up into a doorway, tripped a security light, a tomcat hissed at us for blowing its cover and a dog barked inside the hallway. We walked on quickly, without looking back, nowhere to go and just passing through, no time for conscience to settle and take root. We had learnt that much from our betters. A woman wearing a nurse uniform under an anorak came around the corner, we parted to let her pass on the narrow sidewalk. She kept her head down but we hid our faces anyway. We stopped at the corner, the street narrowed even further, pressed tight up against the twenty foot walls of Castelo de São Jorge. A blue light strobed somewhere below us, pushed us on.

'Look, Con,' Ferdy said. 'It's low enough to get over.'

Where it looked like the street could narrow no more without vanishing, somebody had decided to wedge a line of houses up against the castle wall. The end house had grown a lean-to shed with a corrugated iron roof. Ferdy went first, hoisted on my shoulder, pulled me after him. The rusty roof buckled and cringed under our weight, but held firm enough to get us to the roof of the house.

Same routine, I hoisted Ferdy up to the terracotta platform, he dragged me up. These roof tiles looked about as old as the castle that propped up the houses; held together by a skin of moss and smoke, no mortar, no cement. I started up on hands and knees and it was like crawling up a sand dune, rough and broken tiles slipping under my fingers, fragments tumbling and rolling. Ferdy slid back, and had to grapple with the minor landslide to regain momentum and scuffle his way to the top. Half a dozen tiles exploded like grenades on the cobbled street below. Dogs barked. A woman shouted through the hole in her roof, an old woman with little air in her lungs.

Ferdy chinned up to the edge of the castle lip, I pushed his feet from below until my own feet started another avalanche. He was up, swivelled on his chest and held both hands down to hook me off the roof. There was nothing beneath my feet now, just his strong hands keeping me afloat, reeling me in to safety. I was almost there, but still at his mercy, when I searched his eye for that stranger look. 'Hurry up, for fuck's sake!' he groaned. But it was just Ferdy, the way he had always been, taking the strain, pulling me up, pushing me on. I was laughing when I fell over the wall on top of him.

'I'm glad you see a funny side' he said. 'It's not like you, you're usually a sour kick in the balls these days.'

'I know it. Sorry. Just mixed up stuff in my head,' I said. 'Sometimes you forget you are alive, you know?'

He grabbed the bag and started to jog along the castle battlement. I smacked the red dust off my pants and followed him into the darkness, away from the barking dogs and the shouting old woman with a hole in her roof.

CHAPTER TWELVE

Castelo de São Jorge is the cherry on the Lisbon tourist cake. The 'You are Here' board said some sort of military had drilled their presence into this rock since at least the 6th Century, but Romans, Moors and Crusaders had all flipped their style on it before moving on. From up here, it looked like more than one castle, with wings and walls layered and looped to stump any knight or dragon. About the same footprint as Yankee Stadium, maybe bigger, and the same sweeping grandeur engineered to intimidate the enemy.

We settled in a nook overlooking the city and the showboat river. Freezing up here, almost 8 a.m. and the sun inked through the fractured streets far below. A forest of TV aerials sprouted through the carpet of red roof tiles, pierced a rustic spine of hieroglyphs across the Lisbon sky, receding into the distance of half light and history. The great gates would open at 9 a.m. for the tourist siege, and we could hear the cheery early staff whistle and laugh down in the shadows. Just an hour or so and we would mingle our way out of Luis' Alfama neighborhood.

'So? When are you going to tell me all about it?' I said.

'Don't start that 'another fine mess' crap, Con,' Ferdy said. 'This isn't the time.'

He was lying flat out, eyes closed, using the bag as a pillow, didn't seem to feel the cold. I was shivering.

'Come on, Ferdy. She is making a fool out of me. You both are. You don't have to make it easier for her.'

He sat up. 'She who? Rose?'

'Fucking Cora!' I said. 'You and fucking Cora!'

He sprung up to the balls of his feet, bounced up and down, rubbing his face as if he was washing something away.

'I don't know much more than you,' he said. 'Truth is, I don't think Cora knows much more either.'

He wasn't getting off that easily.

'Yeah, right!' I said. 'So Cora and the CIA, or whoever the fuck she really works for, has sent two arm's length freelancers half way across the world to pick up gorgeous George because he owes gambling money to the fucking Russians in Brighton Beach! Try harder!'

'Okay, okay,' Ferdy said. 'But we don't need to understand what it's about anyway. That's one reason for sending us, we know fuck all about it!'

I kicked the bag, scattered our crap along the battlement.

'Shit! Cool down,' he said. 'The last thing I need right now is one of your fucking blow-outs!' He stuffed the bag full again. 'Okay. Here it is as far as I know. Not that it makes any difference, so I don't see why you always need to get so uptight.' He dropped the bag and used it as a cushion, his back against the wall.

'George Oliver is some kind of genius, right?' he said. 'Some trick of nature says his brain is wired differently, means all that computer shit is just second nature to him. Maybe first nature. Other guys, the real smart college educated guys, spend years trying to work that shit out. George just sees the pattern, no problem.'

A worker banged open a door nearby, wheeled some sort of catering cart up the rough stones, disappeared in another door, lights flickered on in the rooftop cafe.

'So they use him,' he said. 'Of course they do. First it was that hacking shit, credit card scams, all that. Poacher turned gamekeeper. They closed down six big time scams. And George loved it, he was the big guy. But then they realized George was even smarter than they thought.'

'And Cora realizes you are even dumber than she thought, so here we are,' I said.

'Why not? She's a good looking girl, in case you didn't notice,' Ferdy said. 'Oh, but that's right, you did notice. But you were too mixed up in your head to do anything about it. Too bad, you had your chance, didn't take it. So don't be jealous, and for fuck's sake don't tell her I said anything about it!'

'Yeah, yeah, I think I'll survive,' I said. 'So what about George?'

'Well, I don't really understand it,' he said. 'But you heard of Stuxnet, didn't you? Flame? That cyber warfare shit that Bush started, Obama kept rolling? Took out thousands of Iranian nuclear centrifuges, whatever to fuck a centrifuge is! Anyway, turns out our George had a genius for a part of that project. Just a tiny part, but that's how this thing works. Teams of egghead scientists, whole armies of nerd wargamer geeks putting all that shit together, but there was some tiny piece of coding that nobody could do better than our Jorginho. From what Cora said I guess they had George stir up that Arab Spring shit somehow. I don't know how, she didn't say, but it was something to do with Syria and Libya and all that democracy crap.'

George, with his sad Yonkers face, and the big time. An important man, respected, mom and dad proud; that should have been enough, more than he could have imagined. And then Cora, and Yasmin, more money than he could spend. But there is no enough when your brain is wired that good. Dr Blake isn't interested in brains that settle for 'enough'.

'So what's he doing in Lisbon?' I said. 'It's hardly the centre of the cyber warfare universe, is it?'

'He thinks it's safer than Brooklyn right now,' Ferdy said. 'The prick couldn't resist rolling with our Russian friends. But I'll tell you one thing. George isn't going anywhere with all our cyber shit in his head. And especially not if he's going to start mouthing off about stuff we were doing in Syria and wherever. That's why we are here, brother. Unoffical and unattached. You know the bottom line, don't you, Con?'

I knew. The bottom line always amounted to the same thing. George was either coming home with us Yonkers boys or he would be feeding Luis' sardines out there in that big river.

'And what about us? You think you can trust Cora to get us home afterwards?' I said. 'Or are we collateral damage?'

He stood up and leant over the battlement, rubbing his hands and singing, 'Oh Cora baby, when you gonna bring your sweet man on home? You praised me once but I'm distraught without you. Oh Cora darling, I'd prefer you to all the wheat in Ireland!' He wasn't funny, but I couldn't help laughing at the goof.

'I knew you were holding out on me, you know' I said. 'I could see it in your face, smart guy.'

'Yeah, Con. I knew that you knew,' he smirked. 'I could see it in your eyes. I heard it in your voice. That sort of means I wasn't really holding out, doesn't it? Knowing that you knew I was?'

I walloped him with the bag. 'Fuck off, McErlane!' He jumped up on top of the battlement and did his Tarzan chest thumping. The lady from the cafe heard him and pounced on us. She didn't speak much English but we managed to convince her that we had been locked in here since the previous evening. That scared her, two American tourists left to freeze overnight meant somebody would be in trouble with the boss. She hustled us in to her cozy kitchen and loaded the table with coffee and those little custard tarts that Luis liked. Maria was a happy worker, and set about working up a hot breakfast for the poor cold American boys.

'She's another one who will describe us,' I said.

'What you gonna do? Throw her over the wall?' Ferdy said.

'I'm just saying.'

'We'll be long gone before anybody describes anything,' he said. 'Eat your breakfast and keep her smiling.'

Maria kept us topped up with hot coffee and smiles until the castle opened for the daily intake of tourists. At 9.15 a family group of four adults and five lively kids came in and grabbed her attention. The blond Danish giants towered over little Maria, we slipped out unnoticed, Ferdy left ten Euros on the table.

We made our way downstream through the sightseers hurrying to be first to the top of the castle. Nice and easy, like any regular American tourists, no reason for anybody to notice us. We even stopped at a vantage point to survey the sights below. Their Golden Gate bridge bursting through the fog blanket to span the Tejo. Their Rio Christ on a pedestal above the city souls. A fine sight. Even better, no sign down there of a manhunt for murderers on the run. We kept going, out the gate and then downhill, hopped the yellow tram, grabbed seats at separate ends of the carriage.

We rattled down Rua Escolais Gerais, getting close to Luis' street, heart pumping, stomach churning. Police ticker tape holding back a clutch of kids and women. Just one police car outside his door, with a young cop rocking on his heels. Then we were gone, zipping along to immunity in our antique tram, leaving the blue light pulsing behind us.

A couple of minutes later, and the tram started to climb up from Alfama, the streets widened, heavy traffic and Lisboetas about their normal hum-drum business. We skipped off at a busy triangle where three roads converged. A handful of shoppers and workers waited in the small yellow bus shelters, or smoked against the trees that would fringe the diamond with shade when summer came again. Taxi drivers drank coffee from paper cups and ribbed an old guy shaving in his cab. Just another normal day rolling around; no problem, and life trips along no matter who dies in the night.

Into a cafe behind the taxis, Pastelaria Estrela Da Graça. Pastries and savoury foods on display behind the glass counter running the length of the building. Women and men lined up to gossip and taste. Five busy tables along the opposite wall, but only an old man sitting at the middle one. A chatty woman behind the counter recognized our foreign reserve, and breezed out to usher the old man along and offer us seats. We edged in, apologized to the old guy, ordered coffee. And custard tarts – Pastéis de Belém.

The old man was about Luis' age, they must have crossed paths sometime in the narrow streets. But the dice said it was Luis would cross our path, and now he was dead. This one didn't know his luck; lonely and bitter, had that unfulfilled bristle of an old man seething with regrets and anger, his wife despised him, his children abandoned him, his neighbors persecuted him. Ferdy looked the crab face over, then started to lilt Luis's Barco Negro; quietly at first, but then he filled his lungs and plundered down into the deep heart of humanity that he liked to keep tightly chained. The old man's face bloomed, and he started to croak the words, so Ferdy held his old man's shaky hand as he scratched out the song, until a tear greased his gray cheek. I guess we all had our own readymade excuses for tears, and we would never think of Luis again.

When the queue at the counter cleared, I squeezed over to the chatty woman and asked for the public telephone, told her I was phoning the United States and slipped twenty Euros across the counter.

It was just after 5 a.m. in New York but Dr Blake answered his cellphone almost immediately. He sounded as if he was already awake, and not really surprised to hear my voice. Sure, he had a contact for Cora Oneale, he would call her straight away.

'And what about the elusive George Oliver?' he said. 'Have you managed to find him yet, Mr Maknazpy?'

'We're working on it, Doc,' I said. 'We're working on it.'

I waited a long fifteen minutes before the woman made a big deal about clearing the counter so that I could take Cora's call.

'Cora? You have left us hanging,' I said. 'So now we've run into a problem, you better have a back-up plan to get us out of here.'

Cora paused, I pictured her rehearsing our conversation before she engaged.

'Have you traced our man yet, Maknazpy?'

'Not exactly,' I said. 'But we've a pretty good lead. That shouldn't be a problem. Getting us out of here will be the problem. What arrangements have you made?'

She hesitated again, something wrong.

'Have you had any contact from your wife, Maknazpy? Or Jack Gallogly?'

The cafe people melted, the hubbub faded away in my brain swirl, all I could hear was my own breathing into the phone mouthpiece, all I could see was the phone gripped in my fingers.

'Why? What's happened Cora? Where are they?'

'Maybe nothing,' she said. 'Maybe a bluff.'

'What fucking bluff! What is it!'

The cafe noise really did stop now, all eyes swivelled to the angry American. Ferdy was beside me, ear close to the phone.

'There was a message for you. Sent to Gallogly's bar,' Cora spoke slowly but clearly, keeping control. 'They said they have them. They have Gallogly, Rose and your son.'

'Who! Who fucking has them!'

'It may be a bluff! Calm down. They know Gallogly has taken them into hiding, so maybe it is just a bluff.' She was lying.

'Cora! Who fucking has them!'

I heard her sigh and then suck the breath deep into her lungs.

'The Russians,' she said. 'The fucking Russians took them.'

CHAPTER THIRTEEN

Yasmin wanted to meet later, before she would start work in the evening. Ferdy knew my fuse was lit so he told her we had to meet straight away, to see us somewhere we could get to on foot by 11 a.m. Okay, she said she would see us in the Terreiro do Paço. The only problem was she didn't tell us it had a different name on all the maps – Praça do Comércio.

She was still there anyway, whatever it was called, when we entered through the archway at 11.20. The archway itself was one of those grandstand European statements, like the ones in Paris and Berlin, concocted so their armies can march back and forward through them in glory. It was pretty impressive, though, the way only old imperial Europe can be, and opened up to the rectangular pedestrian area of the Praça, which was maybe the size of four of our football fields. The rectangle was bordered by the road along the Tejo waterfront on the side opposite us, and the other three sides were formed by primrose colored classical buildings with cloistered alcoves skirting the perimeter.

Yasmin was pacing around a statue of some big shot on his horse, which must have been at least 50 feet high. She wore a heavily padded orange ski jacket which reached to her knees, and wrapped a plain red woollen scarf around her head and face. The outsize sunglasses confirmed her camouflage, like one of those 'Z' lister celebs spitting outrage when the paparazzi they've tipped off turn up. I didn't like it. I was still shaking, my head sparking between fear and anger, but even I could see we were exposed here, no way out if we were being set up.

'Hi Yasmin,' I said. 'Keep walking and talking.' I linked her arm in mine and tugged her towards the corner where Ferdy was waiting. She didn't look around for her minders so I figured she might be on the level. We reached the cloister on the northern side of the Praça, Ferdy could see anybody getting too close from any direction. I pressed her into a doorway, held her elbows against her sides.

'Keep it simple and keep it short,' I said. 'Where is Jorge de Oliveira now?'

'You think you can scare me?' Yasmin said. 'Seu leite azedo!'

I didn't know what that was but she pronounced it with enough bile and contempt, so I got the general idea. I kept a tight grip on her right arm and took her sunglasses off. Her black eyes were strong and fearless.

'We are the CIA. We are here to bring him home.'

She snorted a laugh in my face. 'Yes, yes. And the mighty CIA need my help?'

'He needs our help, Yasmin,' I said. 'That's why we are here. You are worried about him. That's why you are here.'

'I am worried, yes,' she said. 'But how do I know you do not make it worse for him?'

'There is nobody else out there for him, Yasmin. We are all he has.'

She nodded, then lowered her head. I let go of her arm, but before I could react she threw her weight behind a solid punch into my ribs.

'Keep your dirty hands off me!' she snapped. 'I am not at work now, understand?'

She caught me cold, and it hurt, but I wasn't going to let her see it. She didn't know what was burning inside me right then, and how easy it would have been for me to crush her throat, but I couldn't let myself slide into that selfish redemption. I had to see this through.

'Don't make a scene,' I said. 'Let's all calm down, okay? We just need you to tell us where he is and we will do the rest. Then you won't have to worry anymore.'

'Okay, okay! We walk, we talk,' she said. 'But if you hurt him you will be sorry! I promise you this thing!'

She spun around and marched across the cloister to a street branching off the north-east corner of the Praça, settled the sunglasses on her nose and pulled the scarf to cover the rest of her face. Ferdy caught up and mimed her punch to my gut with a grin stretched across his stupid face, we quick stepped after her, along Martinho da Arcada and down Rua Alfandega until the streets widened again into a square where buses and trams picked and dropped. Cars filled the parking spaces, and then some. Yasmin scooted under some palm trees and we lost sight of her for a second. We sprinted and caught her just as the orange jacket was sliding into a red Seat Ibiza. Yasmin saw the panic on our faces and even the scarf couldn't hide her glee.

'Hurry, assholes!'

Ferdy jumped in the back, I took the passenger seat, she revved into reverse before I slammed the door.

'You have heard of Sintra?' she said.

'No, but I've heard of Sinatra!' Ferdy cracked. She ignored him. I buried the reflex to thump him.

'Sintra, up in the mountains, we go west and north, towards the Atlantic. There is a house there, sometimes parties, you know?

Important visitors, big parties, sometimes they bring girls from the club. Jorginho was a guest. He was important guest, with his own room.'

'And that's where George is now?' I said.

She frowned and shrugged over the steering wheel.

'The last time I see him, this is where he was,' she said. 'But I was with the big boss there two weeks ago, and now no Jorginho. I ask guards and they scream in my face. We are not permitted to say his name.'

We circled Praça De Comércio and headed east along the carriageway that follows the Tejo to the Atlantic. A policia vehicle came speeding from the opposite direction, on the other carriageway. She noticed how Ferdy and me sunk a little deeper into our seats as it passed.

'So Yasmin, why are you helping us, really?' I said. 'Are you making money from this?'

She looked at me and then muttered something abusive in Portuguese.

'What?' I said. 'It's such a strange question? A girl like you?'

She smacked the steering wheel and threw the sunglasses at me.

'Yes! I hear you!' she stormed. 'A girl like me! Hah! This girl is a woman! You understand? A real woman! I am thirty six years old and have survived this shithole to mother two children! But still I am only a girl to buy and sell to you!'

McErlane stifled a snigger in the back seat.

'A girl like me! Hah! What do you know about a girl like me, seu grosseiro!'

'Okay, okay,' I said. 'Just watch the road. So you are really a nun and that's a convent you work in, right? Okay, now why are you helping us?'

She stamped her foot on the gas and the car lunged forward, nearly whacked the bus in front.

'Vai se foder, viado! You know shit, so keep your white mouth closed!' She was purple in the face, white knuckles clenched around the wheel. 'You know a girl like me? You know I was in second year at medical school in Brasil before they trick me to this hell? You know that, huh? Keep your fucking stupid ignorant mouth shut, seu tosco!'

Ferdy reached over to nudge my shoulder, gestured behind us. That cop car had 'U' turned on the carriageway and was coming up behind us, no siren yet, but it was catching fast. The traffic ahead was slowing down. A road block.

'Have you been sent to set us up, Yasmin?' I gripped the back of her neck. 'Because I'll smash your face through this windshield in a heartbeat. See how long they keep you in your convent then.'

Yasmin tensed up, maybe because of the cops, maybe because of me. She breathed deeply to quell her nerves, slowed down, nice and smooth. Five cars and the bus between us and the cop car slung across the carriageway in front, the policia behind us nudged two wheels on to the hard shoulder and skimmed past, stopped beside the waiting roadblock.

'Take it easy, Con. They haven't made us yet,' Ferdy said.

No way we could turn around now, we were hemmed in by a truck on one side and the carriageway barrier on the other. There were two cops standing beside the roadblock car. One was a tall, lean machine scrutinizing the passing drivers, the other was a middle aged gutbucket gassing with the cops who had just passed us. The young one halted the car three spaces ahead, asked for papers, looked impatient and aching for some action. The older one scratched the back of his head and slapped the roof of the other cop car as it trundled on its way.

'I know this one,' Yasmin said. 'The fat pig, he come to the club when his woman thinks he go to football.'

I knew which one would stick his head in our window.

'Are they looking for us?' I said. 'Was there anything on the news about an old man, are they searching for us?'

That spooked her, she shirked her neck away from my hand.

'What old man?' she said. 'What did you do to him?'

'Never mind, just get us through this. Talk nicely to your friend. Tell him we are from Denmark; no English, no Portuguese, just Danish. We are important guests of your boss.'

We inched along until it was our turn. The young cop eyed Yasmin, then bent low to assess her passengers. He saw me first, then did a quick take of Ferdy in the back, reacted straight away, shot his hand out. Halt. The mean machine motioned for her to lower her window, kept his eyes on me. 'Get the fat one over here,' I told her. She was good, had enough brass neck to sweep the young guy away with her big smile and wave to the fat one. The older one saw her, but hesitated at first. Maybe didn't recognize her, probably didn't want the young one to see that she certainly recognized him. She lent half out the window and called him, 'Fofucho! Focfucho!' He dipped his face down low and was about to turn away when the young one laughed and made some sort of crack to him. The fat cop was uncomfortable now but had no option – the stupid bitch wasn't going to shut up – so he plastered his own big smile and sauntered over. He stuck his head in the window and she awarded him an affectionate stroke under his fat chin. He was warming up now, giving her bullshit lines since he was here anyway, we didn't exist.

Ferdy tapped my shoulder. The young one had stepped behind the Seat, had his eyes on us as he spoke into his radio. He pressed his ear to the radio and snapped something urgent to fatso, but the older guy was good too, didn't react much, just kept the tease with Yasmin going, like everything was cool. I undid my seatbelt and made as if I was reaching for something under my seat. His fat face jolted back, he screamed something and pulled his pistol. The young one followed, took up the firing position, pointed at Ferdy's head. Both screaming some shit at us, getting more hysterical when me and Ferdy just stayed where we were. Yasmin squirmed away from the pointed pistol, but we sat tight, just looked them straight in the eye and shook our heads. Tourists. No understand. Denmark.

'Don't move, Yasmin,' I said. 'No-one will get hurt here, just sit back and let us handle it.'

They decided to drag us out. Wrong choice, should have waited on back-up. Fat cop came around to my door, young cop posed beside Ferdy. Fatso called it and they yanked both doors open. We still didn't move, just let them wave the Glock 19's in our faces. Fat boy grabbed my collar with his left hand and twisted his body to haul me out, I went with him, put my right foot on the tarmac and stabbed my left heel through his left knee, caught his right wrist and twisted anticlockwise. The Glock clattered across the car roof, he was off balance now but threw a punch with his left, I ducked it and bounced back with a real nutcracker knee to his fat groin. He staggered back, but I caught his head in both my hands before he fell and threw a crunching head butt into his face. He slapped out star shaped on his back. Ferdy already had the young cop pinned against the carriageway barrier, pistol wedged into the hollow below his left ear, right arm locked up his back.

'Take the belts, Con!' Ferdy shouted.

I had fat cop's Glock, but it would have been too much hassle to whip the belt off his heavy carcass so I pulled his keys and handcuffs and snapped one end around his thick wrist before trailing him over beside the other one. I pulled the cuffs through the support that held the carriageway barrier and clicked the second cuff to the young one. Ferdy kept the armlock on him until I ripped his duty belt off, and we were good to go.

Yasmin was still behind the wheel, shook up but holding it together pretty good for a civilian. The vehicles behind and beside us scrambled to get away, scraping through the gap left by the patrol car. Traffic coming from the opposite direction slowed down to rubber-neck, then accelerated out of the zone. The polícia car that had just passed through the road block would be back here any second, our trained instinct was to get away first, then work out the next step.

I grabbed Yasmin by her left bicep and pulled her out, we were taking the police car. That was too much for the workmen in a mini-bus just behind us. Five guys jumped out, armed with hammers and chisels, they were going to take us on, guns or not. Ferdy jumped square in front of them and fired off three rounds above their heads. The workmen froze, I had Yasmin in the patrol car and swung it around for Ferdy to jump in. He jumped in on top of her in the back and I rammed through a gap in the barrier, spinning across the carriageway and forcing a truck to burn rubber as it squealed to avoid the police car.

I gunned it hard through the traffic, found the light and siren, smacked a couple of slow movers as we slammed our way back into Lisbon center.

'You are crazy sons of bitches!' Yasmin screamed. 'This is Portugal, we will not escape! They will send me home!'

No sirens coming after us yet, and the traffic pulling out of our way in panic. I saw the exit late, and tore across two lanes to make it, the car almost turning over as I squeezed past a beer truck.

'Faugh a Ballagh, Con!' Ferdy whooped. 'Faugh a Ballagh, brother!'

I floored it through red lights and turned up a hill, vehicles parked outside shops and businesses leaving me a narrow funnel to navigate, then turned again, a filling station ahead. I scraped to a halt beside a Mercedes cargo van and jumped out. The driver was still pumping it with diesel when I shoved the Glock in his face. No problem, it wasn't his van, he was just a driver. I helped Ferdy wrestle Yasmin into the back of the Merc van and we were away again.

'You bastard!' she screamed. 'They will take my children! They will take my children!'

The streets were tight here, easy to get boxed in, I turned into a wider street, saw a delivery van pull up outside an office block. Same routine, white works van, driver annoyed but not losing much more than his dignity, we transferred Yasmin into this one, then swung back the way we had come. We passed the street where we had dumped the police car before two patrol cars came racing past us. I helpfully pulled over to let them pass, then rolled back down to the carriageway.

'What are you doing?' Yasmin screeched in my ear. 'You are crazy! They will see us for sure!' A couple of minutes later we were sailing past the fat cop, he was standing beside an emergency vehicle, getting the blood washed off his fat face and neck. The young one was hunkered down on his heels, head in his hands, looking pissed off.

Yasmin wailed, 'They will take my children and send me back to Brasil!'

I flicked the radio on, Santamaria, a Portuguese Eurodance project thumping the tinny speakers, full volume.

'How far is this Sintra place, Yasmin?'

CHAPTER FOURTEEN

Sintra was one weird place. A set for Transylvanian vampires and Disney fairies, each screwball pile outdoing the next, one precipice after another annexed so a trophy palace could bathe in public homage. High cone chimneys like nightmare klan headgear, decorated cake towers that tin soldiers should guard, rooftops straight out of the Forbidden City. No wonder the sign said it was a World Heritage Site.

Five tour coaches waited their turn to twist up the forest paths, even at this time of year. Traffic in the small town slowed to the walking pace of the crowds that couldn't fit on the sidewalk. Sharp mountains draped black with tight forest. Summer retreats for Portuguese royalty and bought flashness of Lisbon rich. This was a cool place to hide.

Yasmin had calmed down after a while, quite a while, and directed me off the main road and through the winter countryside. No police, no roadblocks. The target was on the other side of the mountain, a Lisbon port wine merchant's summer residence built in the 19th century. We worked our way through the town, a couple of cops directing traffic but no interest in us, a white van making a delivery. Climbing high up into the moss green forest, this road snaked to escape the peasants and reward the worthy, a rarified atmosphere too rich for the working poor. Past the Pena National Palace, the road ribboned between a black crag of jagged rock above and the blue splash of a swimming pool down below.

'It is this one,' Yasmin said.

Up above us, hidden by trees, just the red roof and tall chimney stacks visible. I drove past the security gates, found a track into the forest above half a mile further on, pulled the van into the darkness as far as it would go. We walked back through the trees, keeping parallel with the road, ducked down once when a vehicle came chugging up the mountain.

'What sort of security do they have?' Ferdy asked her.

'The usual. Guards. Cameras. Alarms,' Yasmin said.

'Any dogs?'

'There were big dogs before but not now. No, the new guards do not like dogs.'

'What new guards?' I said.

'Chinese guards now. They always used a few boys from the club before, Brasilian or Portuguese, if there was a party,' she said. 'But the new Chinese guards came at Christmas and they stay here all the time.

So no dogs.'

Shit. George was in here okay, but behind a crew of full-time muscle. We needed to think this through before busting in there to kick ass.

'Who are they, Yasmin?' I said. 'Triads? Chinese gangsters?'

She tripped over a branch and grabbed hold of Ferdy to save herself. We stopped while she wiped the moss sludge from her jacket.

'I do not know,' she said. 'They might be gangsters, but they do not look like the ones that come to the club, or the ones that drive the big boss.'

'Well, what the fuck do they look like?' Ferdy said.

She shrugged, smacked her lips and twitched her nose.

'They look like you. They look like soldiers. But Chinese soldiers, with those little black machine guns.'

We waited until 6.30 p.m. before going over the wall. Dark, and all the coach tours gone. Yasmin knocked my hand away and levered herself up and over. The house was about fifty meters up a steep incline, and the forest gave cover for all but the last twenty meters or so. Ferdy stooped low and advanced to get a look at the set-up, I held back with Yasmin. Bringing her with us wasn't ideal, but she was starting to get frantic about her kids, so we couldn't risk leaving her behind. Anyway, Yasmin did know her way around the house, and she might be useful when it came to getting George to play ball.

'They will come for my children when they know,' Yasmin said. 'Then I will kill you. Believe me, big man, I will kill you and your funny friend if my children are hurt.'

She was staring ahead into the darkness but there was enough light to bounce off her clenched jaw. She reached out and gripped my arm. 'Believe me,' she said. I did believe her, and a picture of Rose and young Con being abused flashed before my eyes.

'They will be fine, Yasmin,' I said. 'We will talk to the right people, they will take you to the United States. You will be safe there, your kids will be happy and safe.'

She raked her talons across the back of my hand.

'Liar! You only give shit about you. You will take what you want and go back to your nice comfortable house in north America. It is permitted for my children to be in danger but never yours, that is the truth you should say!'

I was too close to breaking point myself, Yasmin didn't know how close, and I was about to put her straight when Ferdy came scuttling back through the undergrowth.

'It's chow time,' Ferdy said. 'Two of them cooking up some shit in the kitchen. Lights on upstairs at the back, don't see anyone else moving.'

He led the way, I put Yasmin in the middle, and we edged around to the low wall that separated the back yard from the forest. No sign of any motion sensors, and the two guards in the kitchen were heads down throwing their meal together. Lights on in two rooms upstairs, Yasmin said one was George's bedroom, the other a sitting room.

'Try to focus, Yasmin,' I said. 'How many guards did you see the last time?'

Three, maybe four, maybe five, she didn't recall.

'You're good, aren't you, Con?' Ferdy said. 'Remember we just want to take George out of there, so no need for a bloodbath, right?'

'Christ's sake!' I said. 'I'm good! I'm good! Let's just do it!'

Ferdy went over the wall first and skirted to the right of the kitchen door, I went left, kept Yasmin close. The kitchen was tiny for such a big house. A small steamed up window. The skewed rectangle of light staked the limit of our dead space. I blacked myself out into the combat groove, choked back the white noise of shit yourself fear, tuned it to the discrete buzz of sweet spot victory. Ferdy was still on the other side, straining like a hound on nervous overkill; I stalled him, ten seconds to breathe, expel any stains of self-doubt. Wait, breathe, I would give the signal.

Ready, only the kitchen chatter and Yasmin panting, I started to raise my hand just as the door opened and a basin of slops arced into the blackness. Ferdy had the big guy's head pinned against the floor before he knew it, the Glock like a skewer in the back of his neck. I jumped over them and rolled into the kitchen, the other one speared a heavy cleaver past my head, I levelled and fired twice, caught him square in the chest, crashed him back over the table. I swivelled around in the firing position. Ferdy was down, the big guy on top of him, but Yasmin was in my line of sight. Ferdy was hurt, the hair parted where the cleaver had gouged through his skull. The guard had him in a chokehold. I screamed at Yasmin to move, but she didn't flinch, she just swung the cleaver and buried it in the big guy's neck.

Shouts and heavy boots upstairs, Ferdy was bad but they were coming for us, two in the guard's back to make sure, then I ducked into the hallway as another one appeared around the turn of the stairs. I fired before I could see him, and three quick shots from nowhere will freak out anyone. I kept moving, could see his legs and a MP5, three more rounds, he tumbled. I got close to the stairwell and pumped two more into the writhing body.

More Chinese shouting upstairs, a panicked screaming, but at least one more up there. Blood pulsed through my temples like thunder but that was the only sensation in my numb body; no fear, no shakes, just maybe a secret thrill. The screaming was muffled now, behind a door somewhere. The stair guy had the MP5 wedged under his right arm. I prised it out, he gasped, still alive. I mercy killed him, another Glock round, should have four rounds left in this clip, but couldn't be sure what the standard issue was for Portuguese cops. And this wasn't even a real H&K MP5; a clone stamped with red Chinese characters. I hoped the piece of shit worked.

Up the stairs quickly; no stealth, just pure aggression from here on in. The landing was wide, six doors and an archway leading to another corridor. George's room was the one in the corner, the next door must be the living room. All quiet now, waiting for me, the lucky draw - see who walks out of this. I went in the sitting room first, booted the door hard, crashed through ready to spray the MP5, momentum made me stumble, but hit the floor and came up on point. Nobody in here, but the yelling started again, from George's bedroom. Smashed through that door, kept my balance, feet planted, ready. Three of them huddled in a nest of computer screens and wires. A middle aged Chinese man; fit for his age but no way was he muscle. A young Chinese guy; skinny, looked like a school kid. And the sad dark face of Yonkers George the Genius.

'Is Cora here?' George asked.

The older Chinese man shielded the young guy from me like I was a devil. Maybe it was his son, maybe I was the devil.

'Who are these two?' I said.

George shrugged a lazy, couldn't give a shit attitude.

'Just two guys,' he said. 'Forget it, they aren't anybody, forget about them. But I fucking asked you a question there, good buddy! I said is Cora down there?'

It surprised me that he had a Yonkers accent stronger than my own, but just for a second, then I skipped forward and kicked him in the gut, he folded and the Chinese duet shuffled further into the corner.

'No, Cora isn't here!' I shouted in his face. 'But your Russian good buddies have got my family, good buddy!' I kicked his butt. 'You are my ticket to get them back, good buddy!' Kicked the soft tissue on his right thigh. 'So you can forget all about Cora, good buddy!' Kicked his right bicep. 'And I am the one asking the questions here! Okay, good buddy?' Kicked his liver, he was crying and wheezing and squirming into a ball. Gorgeous George wasn't the whiz kid now, he was back to the nerd jerk too pathetic to leave his mom's apartment. The Chinese didn't move to help him, didn't seem to have any empathy for old George at all, that told me something. I grabbed George by the hair and hauled him off the floor, pointed the MP5 at the Chinese.

'I asked you who are these two?' I said.

'Zheng and Liu,' he whimpered. 'Zheng is a computer guy, Liu is the translator. They aren't dangerous.'

That figured; the translator looked as if he was about sixteen, the computer guy was like any academic.

I pushed George out the door and motioned Liu and Zheng to follow. George froze at the top of the stairs, I had nailed the guard at close range and the Glock had ripped his insides out. The older man, Zheng, took in the scene, swallowed hard, then eyed me with a look of distaste that our relative positions didn't really entitle him to. Liu the kid translator pushed forward to see for himself, then stepped back with a mixture of horror and fascination. I rammed the MP5 into Zheng's back, and he staggered against the Liu kid and George. I shouldered them forward, they tip toed over the sprawled body and steaming gore, kept them moving into the kitchen.

Two bodies mangled across the tiled floor. Zheng kept his emotions in check, but I could read him. These two had come down to make the evening meal, laughing and joking, doing their duty, then this fucking gweilo sneaks in from the night to butcher them. Yeah, I could read Zheng, but I didn't care what he thought right then because Ferdy was in a bad way; his blood seeped across the tiles and bulged against the flow from the big guard's wounds, before they merged and trickled away under the door. Yasmin had pulled lumps of ice from the freezer and clamped it against his head with a red sodden kitchen towel. She looked up, and her face collapsed in relief when she saw George but the gifted one blanked her, as if he had never set eyes on her before. Yasmin's mouth opened to plead with him, but she froze, dropped her eyes, and turned her face back to Ferdy.

This was all just too much for Gorgeous George, he tramped over the bodies to plunge his head into the sink and pumped his stomach over the dirty dishes. The young translator was transfixed; he said something to Zheng, the academic answered, some sort of explanation, rationalization of the western barbarity they should have expected.

'You will have to go and get the van, Yasmin,' I said. 'I can't keep these three covered and carry Ferdy that far on my own.'

'These three?' She looked up in surprise. 'Jorginho? You have to keep Jorginho covered?'

'Just go get the van, Yasmin,' I said. 'Let me worry about Jorginho, okay?'

Ferdy was conscious now, said he was fine, told her to go, told me to just get him to fuck out of there before anybody else turned up.

'It wasn't supposed to get so rough, Con,' Ferdy said. 'Better take these Chinese guys with us in case we need insurance to get home, know what I mean?'

I propped him up and he tamped the cloth against the gaping hole in his head. He still had a set of cop handcuffs, I made George link Zheng and Liu together.

'Now, George, a wrong move and I'll blow your fucking head off! Understand?'

I pushed George into the corner, and forced Zheng and Liu to their knees on the blood sticky floor. I pressed the Glock into the kid translator's throat.

'Translate for your computer friend here,' I said. 'Tell him you two are coming with me for a little trip. Tell him to forget that Red 'Hero of the People' shit. Either one of you gives me any trouble and I'll nut both of you! Translate that, okay?'

The kid looked scared and confused. Zheng looked up to George. George sniggered from his corner.

'You're a regular military blockhead, Maknazpy, aren't you?'

He already knew my name?

'Zheng is the kid, he's the computer friend,' George said. 'Liu is the older guy, you need to tell him to translate, you asshole.'

I did a second take. Zheng looked like he was sixteen, couldn't have been anymore than eighteen, maybe twenty at a big push. Liu the translator guy kept his mouth shut until I prodded him with the pistol, then he said something quietly to Zheng the kid, a lot more than I had said.

I went over to George, he quit his smirking and cowered back into his shell. I took a handful of his hair and shoved the Glock into his nostrils.

'How do you know my name, Jorginho? Who told you I was coming?'

'Nobody told me nothing!' He whined like a cranky teen. 'I saw your file, Maknazpy. Like, I was one of Pavlov's dogs too, you know? You hang out in those places and you hear things.'

I tapped his head off the wall.

'Fuck you, man!' he squawked. 'I heard Blake and Cora talking about you. Your file was on his desk.'

I let go of him and stepped back, felt like he had just smacked me. Liu the translator looked at his feet, pretended not to listen.

'Just don't go off on one of those freaky psycho trips of yours, Maknazpy, okay?' George said. 'Anyway, if that mad bastard Moscow Alex has your wife as hostage, then I guess you better make sure I'm buttoned up good, hear what I'm saying? That's if you ever want to see your bitch's ass in one piece again, that is.'

CHAPTER FIFTEEN

Yasmin was cool behind the wheel, nice and smooth down the mountain, slowly through Sintra, back to the Lisbon highway. I was in back, with Ferdy stretched along the floor and the other three kneeling at his feet. No sign of any back-up, no rescue party, no police. Liu the translator didn't know anything, he was just a translator. Didn't know why they were there, didn't know what George was doing, didn't know who gave the orders. Pretty smart guy, for a translator.

'Where are we going?' Yasmin half turned her head to call back to me. I didn't know. We had to get out of that house, that was for sure, and Cora had told me to contact her as soon as we had picked up George, but I needed time to think this through.

'Take us somewhere safe, Yasmin,' I said.

She cursed and slapped the steering wheel again, the whites of her eyes magnified in the dark, she hit the gas a little too hard.

'You said you would take my children to a safe place!' she screamed. 'You don't even have safe place for yourself!'

George chipped in with a crack to her. I thought I just couldn't hear him properly at first, over the van rattle, then realized he was speaking in Portuguese, but with such a heavy Yonkers accent that it was hard to tell. I leant over and slapped his ear.

'You take us somewhere safe now, Yasmin' I said. 'I'll look after it afterwards. Just leave it with me.'

She knew a place; out on the Atlantic coast, a holiday home for some Lisbon big shot that liked to summer party out of town. Yasmin had been coming here for years, bringing girls from the club, entertaining the VIP's, being discreet. The house was sculpted below the rim of a jagged sea cliff, remote and very private in its own grounds. She tapped the security pin to open the gates, parked up close to the side, and retrieved the keys from inside a large, vacant, dog kennel. I waited until she was inside and had disarmed the alarm system, then hustled Liu and Zheng into the hallway, fixed them up with the cuffs knitted through the sweeping mahogany banister, and had George help me carry Ferdy inside.

Blood still seeped from his wound, and he tilted between being fully alert and slipping into a daze. He needed a doctor, but we couldn't risk it, not yet.

'You were at medical school in Brazil, weren't you, Yasmin?' I said.

'No! Do not ask me!' Fear in her voice for the first time. 'That was another life, another world. Take him to a doctor. I can do nothing.'

Ferdy rolled his head and vomited over the end of the sofa. His eyes were fired up like he was high, his skin was yellow, and he was shaking like a junkie.

'He is in shock,' Yasmin said. 'He has lost too much blood, and he is in shock. Get him to a hospital. I can do nothing.'

'We go anywhere near a hospital and the cops will nail us,' I said. 'Then the authorities will take your kids, or the friends of our friends here will take them.'

Yasmin buried her face in her long fingers, muttered something, a prayer or a curse, then stamped off to the kitchen area. I sent George upstairs to look for a comforter, let him see me pull the telephone wires out of the wall before he went. Yasmin marched back in with a heavy staple gun, a bowl of water, clean towels and a bottle of vodka. She cleaned around the wound with the towel, dabbed it with vodka, then pressed the staple gun against the tear in his scalp and fired four staples into his head. Ferdy cursed and swung at her, but she dodged back, motioned to me to hold him, then finished off dousing him with the vodka.

'Your old training coming back to you, huh?' I said.

'My new training,' she said. 'Sometimes this happens in the club when customers get naughty.'

Ferdy took the bottle off her and slugged the vodka straight. Yasmin started to pull it off him but I ushered her away. 'Let him be,' I said. 'He has come through worse than that scratch.' George came back with the comforter, I packed it around Ferdy.

'Now what happens? What big plans do you have?' Yasmin spoke to me but looked at George.

'Now I'm going to get us out of this shit,' I said. 'I'm going to get you and your kids out of here. You should go home to your own people in Brazil, but the United States if you want.'

George fixed his hardest scowl over his soft olive face. He looked the part. Baptized into the Yonkers street hierarchy, ricocheted from cyber lowlife to mob elite, ripened by Russian hoods and burnished by Cora's spooks – George sure knew how to look mean. A crisp jab into his solar plexus crumpled him. I slammed the basement door behind me and pushed him into the corner.

'Just you and me, George,' I said. 'Yasmin won't hear you scream from down here. And I don't think she would try to save you anymore, even if she could.'

The light buzzed and flickered on and off, like it threatened to quit, George blinked each time it faltered. I stretched my left hand to grip his throat and hoist him up on his toes, he wrapped his fingers around my wrist but had no fight in him. I hadn't noticed before that George was almost six feet tall, about my height, but he just seemed smaller, as if he was so mean he had to fold in on himself.

'You're way out of your league, Maknazpy! You can't even begin to imagine what you've bulled into here! None of them know, not even Cora or her so-called superiors so why don't you just cut the crap and get Cora out here, like a good boy, okay?'

I flexed his windpipe a little more; still no physical fight, just the wise-ass mouthing he had picked up along the way. His smooth face started to darken.

'You might never see Cora again, George.' Jerked his head off the wall. 'I might hand you straight over to the Russians.' I tightened my grip, he clawed my fingers.

'Won't happen!' he snorted. 'Way over your head, way more than your fucked up brain can handle, but you're happy to be such an ignorant asshole, right?'

'Right now, George? I'd just be happy to break your neck.'

I rapped my knuckles off his nose, a gurgle sluiced deep in his throat.

'Okay! Okay! For fuck's sake!' he whimpered. 'Moscow Alex doesn't mean shit!'

I cranked my forearm up under his chin, levered his head further up the wall so he was looking up at the dark ceiling.

'Keep going!' I ordered. 'What's the deal with the Russians and what the fuck are you doing here with the fucking Chinese?'

'It was just a deal, that's all. I needed a mule, that pimp Alex was just so greedy it made it easy. He thought he was the real thing, the fucking Mr Russian Bigtime!' I eased the pressure on his throat, let his head slip back down the wall. 'He isn't even a fucking real Russian! His old man maybe defected from the KGB back in the Seventies, but Alex was born on the Upper East Side, went to a fucking $30,000 a year school!'

The slate head that scraped my face into the sidewalk?

'Sure, he riffs a Russian accent when he's acting the tough guy – but you wanna hear him at a cocktail party up there on Museum Mile, he sounds just like any other prick prep boy.'

'Keep going,' I said.

'Even a blockhead like you has heard of the Arab Spring shit, right?' George said. 'Turning the screw on Syria? Putting the choke on Iran's economy? How do you think that all works?'

I had no idea how it worked, never needed to know, it just worked. I took a step back and lent against a heavy old wood and iron gizmo that looked like it had been down here since the house was built. George cleared his throat and spun his torso to spit into the corner shadows.

'They need banks, right? Every government needs the banks. Sovereign Bonds, credit default swaps, all that high finance shit, can't do it without the banks,' he said. 'And we were working on it, long before any of that crap in Syria and Iran hit the news.'

'Oh yeah? Who is we, George? You and Russian gangsters?'

'No, asshole! American patriots, like you and me!' he sneered. 'Our guys knew all that crap was coming, we were already in there long before the other side even got started.'

I had known people like George all my life; lying was as easy as not lying, bespoke spiel to stay ahead, truth a movable feast.

'Another crew thought they took the cream when they hit the Iranian nuclear sites,' George said. 'Swaggering around as if they were something special? Pricks! That was no more than an inconvenience to the Mullahs. A fly in their Jihad ointment. My crew went about our business like fucking ninjas! Hit them where it really hurt! We had fucking Syria turned inside out before anybody Stateside ever heard of the dump!'

And George wouldn't know if he was telling a lie. He was a persuader, tales blossomed under his self styled logic, if you believed him then it was true.

'Where do you think all the Syrian money was stashed?' he said. 'Where do you think Hezbollah launder their drug dollars? Who do you think fucking sponsors them in the first place?'

He was excited now, got a kick from affirming his own importance, George the Genius.

'Beirut city? Lebanon? You think it's all car bombs and kidnapping, right Maknazpy?'

George spoke to me like I was an imbecile, like my hand hadn't been around his throat a minute ago.

'Wrong! Big time wrong! Beirut is Arab Sin City, fucking financial center for all those Arab petrol dollars! That's where the Syrian cash goes. And that's how Iran fucking thought they would dance around our sanctions. And maybe they would have, if my crew hadn't screwed them over!'

A special type of glee trilled in his throat, his eyes jived and he licked his lips, reliving his ecstasy.

'I led that crew,' he said. 'Not one of the rich boys that spent years at college. It was me, and they all know it, the jealous bastards!'

'Sounds great George,' I said. 'What did you do?'

'What? Like you don't believe me? Think it's only frat boys can do something that big?' George was defiant, back to his wise-ass street routine.

'So, the best cyber security brains in the world found four of our codes – SP, SPE, FL and IP. FL is called Flame now, okay? Big deal. They nearly pissed themselves because they eventually found traces of our codes, right? Found them on systems in Iran and Syria, and a bunch of other places like Sudan and other shitholes. Know why they found them? Because I fucking wanted them to, that's why!'

The door to the basement cracked open. Yasmin's voice echoed in the darkness. 'How long are you staying there? I must speak with my children! We need food! I will not stay here waiting all night!' George didn't hear her, didn't react, didn't care. I told her to back off, I would be up in a minute, skipped up the steps to slam the door closed on her. Back down the steps, George hunkered down with his butt weighed against the wall.

'We let them find it because we wanted the enemy to know we had been there. We had been right there in their banking systems. We stole their files. Recorded their keystrokes. We knew exactly who was doing what in those fucking Beirut banks. Where the cash came from, where it went. We had it all tied up. You know we could even switch on the mikes in their machines and listen in real time to the fuckers?'

I hunkered down beside him, looked him over in case he had stashed a weapon when I was distracted by Yasmin. He was clean.

'Yeah! The best security brains in the world. They even found our Red Protocol! Thought they were real smart. Assholes!' George was bitter. 'What they don't know is that there is a fifth code. The one I developed. The one they will never find!'

He transformed into something else. The sad eyes in his photograph were gone, replaced now with an animal energy, a force of nature.

'What does this fifth code do, George?' I asked.

'Do? What I fucking tell it to do!' he snapped. 'Like open those bank accounts as easy as I open my fucking zipper! Like ship that blood money to fuck out of there! You think the UN or any of those do-gooders were ever really going to wrap up chemical weapons in Syria? No chance! But me and my boys can do anything we want in there. That's what my fifth code does, Maknazpy, and nobody but me can do anything about it!'

Even a dedicated liar spills droplets of truth sometimes, and George squawked it out with such a zealous conviction that I guessed some shreds of it must be true. And Dr Blake had said George had an extraordinary mind. Some of this wasn't bullshit.

'That's where Moscow fucking Alex comes in,' he said. 'I needed a mule to offload some of the cash to. The greedy fuck thought I was bringing him a Christmas present! Piss artist! I laid a trail from Beirut to Hong Kong to Brazil and then around half of Europe. The trail finishes in three of Alex's bank accounts in Ukraine, but that's not where the money is now!

'How much are we talking about here?' I said.

'Oh, you're interested now, Maknazpy?' he gloated. 'I screwed them on the large side of fifty million dollars. I sacrificed some to lay dead end trails, but I've stashed twenty million they'll never trace, give or take. What's that do for you, kid? Still feel like smacking me around?'

I thought about it for a second before ramming my left elbow into his chest. He wheezed, but recovered quickly, the adrenalin buzz strong in his head.

'Yeah Maknazpy, so you're a real tough guy. I saw your file, remember,' George taunted me. 'But hey, I'm what's called an 'Express Critical' package. A lot of people are going to be very pissed off if anything bad ever happens to me, you know? Like, you say Alex has your wife? Yeah, you should really be nice to me, pal, if you want her back.'

I sprung to my feet and scooped George's ankles into the air. His head popped a hollow thud off the wall, his arms floundered as I dragged him across the floor. The gizmo I had been leaning on earlier was some sort of ancient machine for pressing the grapes. An iron handle on top screwed the heavy oak lid down to squeeze the juice out of anything that was in the bucket. I punched George in the gut before trailing him by the hair and wedging his head into the gap between the bucket and the lid, I pulled a quarter turn on the handle and his neck bulged red over the bucket rim.

'You read my file, George,' I shouted. 'You know I'll spin this handle until your head explodes like a grape.' I slapped the handle a little tighter, George's squeals were amplified by the oak bucket. 'You are going to contact Moscow Alex and give him whatever he wants.

I don't care if it is $20 million or $50 million or a fucking trillion million! You give him what he wants and he frees my wife and son, get me?' Another stab at the handle. George screamed and banged the sides of the wooden bucket. I left him hanging long enough for his panic to be subsumed by the terror that comes with the vision of your own sure death. Then I left him a little longer. He slumped to the floor like he was dead when I released the handle, I thought maybe I had left him too long. I kicked him on his right thigh, he squawked back to life.

'Okay! Okay!' George said. 'Take it fucking easy, willya? I'll try. Just back to fuck off and I'll try!'

Try? I mustn't have made myself clear. This wasn't a 'do your best' deal, George would do whatever it needed to set Rose and young Con free. I kicked him on his left thigh. He rolled over, clutching his leg.

'It's not that easy!' he squealed. 'It isn't fucking Treasure Island, you know. 'X' marks the spot and dig a hole in the frigging ground!'

'You said you were The Man!' I said. 'You said you could do whatever you wanted. You telling me now that isn't so?' I kicked his right thigh again.

'It's just not that easy!' he blubbed. 'There are other people involved here, not just the Russians! I can't tell them what to do. It just doesn't work like that!'

I guessed the 'Other People' were our Chinese guests now cuffed to the stair banister.

'You mean to say you sold out the United States to the Chinese?' I said, kicked him a little harder.

'I didn't sell out to nobody,' he yelped. 'It's not like that, I'm not interested in the money, that's not what it's all about!'

I grabbed George by the neck and started to haul him up to the grape presser again.

'No! I fucking said I would try! What more can I do, for fuck's sake?'

'Well, what is it about then, George?' I said.

George gripped the top of his head with both hands and sobbed into his forearms. I pushed him away from me and he curled up in the corner.

'You should know, Maknazpy. I saw your file, you're a lot like me. Why don't you leave all that citizen's duty shit to the boring cretins that know nothing better.'

I would really have to get a look at this file, see what Blake had me marked down as. I moved towards George and he wrapped himself into a tight ball in his corner.

'It's not about the money, Maknazpy,' he said. 'It's about doing something big! Being bigger than anyone has been before! It's about pushing the boundaries, for fuck's sake! It's what you can't do in the United States anymore!'

'And what? China is the home of the free now?' I said.

'At least they recognize talent and give you anything you need to make it flourish, how about that?' he said. 'See that kid Zheng upstairs? He's a genius, maybe even more than me. He was born into a piss poor family, survived on a dollar a day, still living in the eighteenth century. But guess what? The Chinese authorities recognised his genius when he was eight years old and sent him away to be nurtured. Now he is somebody. Now he can use his genius. You wanna know how I was treated when I was a kid?'
I already knew, we were all treated like that, so what?

'Sure sounds like you sold us out there, George,' I said.

'Sold what out?' he said. 'Like you believe all that shit about America being the savior of the free world? When we sell our souls to the corporations that spend two billion dollars to elect a fucking President? What is this, the best democracy money can buy?'

'So what was all that crap you just gave me about attacking banks in Beirut?' I said. 'You are just a low-life con artist who hit it lucky, aren't you George?'

'Yeah, well maybe I am at that, Maknazpy,' he said. 'And you know what? At least the Lebanese banks didn't screw their own people with fucking sub-prime loans and loaded mortgage bonds. The Lebanese never had a Lehman Brothers. No Fannie Mae or Freddy Mac. The Lebanese looked after their people and didn't fuck them over. You know why? Because they aren't fucking corrupt pigs choking on their own vomit in the trough, that's why!'

'But you fucked them, George,' I said. 'With your Red Protocol and your fifth code. You fucked those people, and you got off on it. Still makes you a low-life con artist, boy!'
George bent over, his nose almost touching the ground, shaking his head, like it would make me disappear, like he wouldn't have to hear me.

'You don't get it, Maknazpy,' he said. 'You don't get it, but you should! You, of all people, you should get it!'

'Get what, asshole?'

He looked up at me then, all fear and tension washed away.

He had the sad look from his photograph again. Sad, looked like he pitied me as a lost cause.

'All their shit ordinary rules don't apply to people like us, Maknazpy. You, me, Zheng - we are different, we are special, we are the outliers. Their rules were never meant for us, never extraordinary people like us.'

CHAPTER SIXTEEN

Yasmin was in my face almost before I stepped out of the basement.

'He must go to hospital!' she barked. 'I am going to my children. Now!'

Ferdy was asleep or unconscious – it was hard to say which. He was stretched the length of the couch; his face pursed pale and beatific, his right hand cradling the empty vodka bottle. I arched over him, held my cheek close to his as if my kindred presence would divine his life force and spark him into the light. His breathing was shallow but regular, until a raw rasp in his throat would startle his core and he twitched and panted as if in night terror until it passed and his breathing calmed and softened again.

'Cerebral edema,' the voice behind me said. It was Liu. Liu the translator said it. I was half crouched over Ferdy, my torso twisted backwards to look at where the voice came from. Yasmin nuzzled her face behind her long sleek fingers. Liu said it again, 'Cerebral edema. His brain swells. He will die if you do not take him to hospital.'

'How the fuck would you know?' I said it sharply, as if Liu's status as my prisoner defined that he could not know anything, could not tell me anything I didn't already know. He pitched an easy gaze into my eyes; neither challenging nor defiant, but not bowed or submissive either.

'I have witnessed this before,' he said, and shrugged one shoulder as if he was indifferent; I could believe him or not, it made no difference to him. I pinned him with a stare but he held his perfectly neutral composure until I had to concede and look away. And I had witnessed it before as well, when we were young and invincible. The defiant young man cracked on the skull with a baseball bat. He was a fighter, a tough guy from the south Bronx, and climbed back to his feet and swayed along with the expected bravado. We heard later that he had internal bleeding and his body fluids had silently steamed around his head until the pressure could only escape by spitting his brain stem out of the bottom of his skull. His mother brought him his breakfast to bed the next morning as usual, only to find him cold dead in his neat bedroom.

'It is not too late,' Liu tossed it off casually. 'You can save him, or you can let him die.' Another careless shrug. 'Live or die. It is your decision.'

I reached over and took Ferdy's right hand in both of mine. He still wore his dead father's wedding ring on the third finger of his right hand. It was too small for his finger, and the flesh was nipped pink around the gold.

'Where is the nearest hospital, Yasmin?' I said.

'Cascais, I think,' she said. 'To the south, on the coast. Forty kilometers, maybe fifty.'

Take all of them with me or leave them here? George snaked his way behind me – not the rescued hostage anymore, but a prisoner now, like Zheng and Liu, and dangerous. I had to call it. I pulled the Glock as I vaulted the couch and screwed it under George's sculpted chin.

'Back to the basement, George!' I said. 'You can keep your Chinese buddies company down there until we get back.'

I opened the basement door and rammed him down the steps. George stumbled in the darkness and cursed as he smacked the floor. I tossed the handcuff keys to Yasmin, then kept the pistol centered on Liu's forehead as I shaped my way above them on the stairs. Yasmin stepped forward to unlock the cuffs, Liu lent forward to whisper in Zheng's ear before I could grab his hair and yank his head back. I nodded at Yasmin to keep going, scrunched the Glock into the muscle below Liu's right ear and anchored his skull against the banister. The kid Zheng kept his head down, like he couldn't look her in the eye, and Yasmin whipped his wrist up so she could work the key.

Then they sprung. The metallic click was their starter button; Liu arched up and backwards against me, Zheng shouldered Yasmin down the stairs and scrambled over her for the door. Liu threw his arms back and circled my knees, wedged me against the stairs. I still had the Glock tight to the crazy bastard's head but he didn't even try to save himself, just figured on buying the kid a few seconds escape time. I had him, I could have blown his head away as easily as spitting gum on the sidewalk. This time I didn't.

I didn't because Yasmin bounced better than the kid and scythed him with a flying tackle before he made the door. She flipped Zheng over on his back and tugged her skirt up to sit astride him, rocked her knees hard into his shoulders, plunged a middle finger into each side of his mouth and stretched his cheeks until it looked like her talons would shred the red balloon of the squealing kid's face right off his skull. Liu released his grip on me and sagged into surrender.

'Finish,' he said, softly.

★★★

Yasmin's foot was heavy on the gas; she tossed and winged the van around the corners, Ferdy's head jerked and bounced, I gripped the back of the driver's seat.

'Slow down, for fuck's sake!' I bent forward to shout in her ear.

She tossed her hair back, looked like she was laughing, gunned it faster until the road straightened up and then rattled along with one hand on the wheel, half turned to look back in at us.

'The doctor said your friend is dying,' she said. 'So you want me to take it easy? Slow down? It is no problem for me if you wish, big man with the gun.'

'Whaddya mean doctor?' I said. 'Liu? The translator?'

Shook her head again, eyed me in the mirror.

'I was at medical school,' she said. 'I know a doctor when I see one.'

Maybe he was, but what a waste, nursemaiding that kid Zheng when he should be doctoring at home? But who knows, maybe they only have real doctors in red China for the Communist Party elite, don't need doctors for ordinary people, the rice paddy peasants have to make it on feng shui and all that herbal shit. Yeah, well try your feng shui out now, pal, handcuffed to that pulping machine back there in the basement. I propped Yasmin's padded jacket back under Ferdy's head to keep it still, she told me to keep his torso raised to encourage the fluid to drain from his skull.

'How come you left medical school Yasmin?' I said. 'How come you ended up here, working in a club like that?'

She didn't answer, dismissed me with a shrug of her shoulders and a sighed curse, slinked low in the driver's seat, and scalped her hair up high with her right hand. A delicate earring jingled in her right ear, two jade tear drops dripping off a fine golden thread. Matched that emerald kimono. Enough light from outside dappled across her lap to glaze a sheen from her sleek brown legs, bare between the mid-length black boots and the hoisted black skirt. Her knees were red raw and wrestle burnt; she had sure terrified that little nerd Zheng, but at least it was something he could look back on for a thrill when he got old. If he made it to old.

'What happens at the medical center, Mister Big Shot CIA?' she taunted.

I didn't like it when she spoke to me like that, like she was talking to shit. I pulled the Glock and pressed close to her, so she could feel my breath behind her jade ear, slowly stroked the barrel across the soft skin of her neck, along the taut line of her jawbone, let it linger against her lower lip, before playing it across her ear, tipping the jade tear drops in a muted jangle. And she giggled at me. Yasmin had seen me take down the fat cop, nail the Chinese soldier guards, and beat the crap out of George. But she laughed at me now, as if I was another nerd kid like Zheng.

'Okay, Mister Big Shot CIA, with the big hard gun in your hand!' she laughed. 'What happens now?'

What was the word Cora had used that time in the River's Edge Restaurant? Demeaned? She demeaned me? Yeah, that was it. And Cora could demean me anytime she wanted, because we both understood that she called all the shots, no problem. But Yasmin? She felt free to demean me too? She thought she could do that, with no consequences, after all she had seen? The red pressure pulsed a little harder against my temples, darkness bubbled around my eyes, my chest and arms coiled and tightened. All the markers Blake was interested in. But I snapped out of it.

'I'll take care of it, Yasmin. Like I said I would.'

I slipped the pistol under the passenger seat and bent over Ferdy, put my ear to his mouth, the breathing ragged now, and the toxic vodka fumes. Maybe he was just drunk on the Jewel of Russia, a self medicated anaesthetic. I looked up to check Yasmin couldn't see me stroking his cheek and kissing his forehead, then I scuttled as far back in the van as I could.

It rang five times before she answered.

'We've got the package,' I said.

'Is it safe?' Cora's emotion free zone as usual. 'Where are you now?'

I let her hang for ten seconds.

'Right now, I'm taking a good friend of ours to a medical center. Not the package. A good friend of mine. You are going to see he is okay. You are going to see he gets home, with nobody sticking their nose into our business. Understand?' I said.

I could nearly feel her screwing the cellphone to her ear as she worked it out.

'A good friend from home?' she said. 'What happened? Is it serious?'

'I don't know. Could be his brain is swelling. Could be cerebral edema, I don't fucking know.'

The cellphone crackled but I could hear muffled voices, as if she was clasping it tight to her chest.

'Did he experience head trauma?' A man's voice. 'What are the symptoms?' A man's voice. Doctor fucking Blake's voice.

'What are you doing here?' I said.

Yasmin scoped her head sideways to listen in. Silence at the other end, but I sensed the confusion, the panic when meticulous planning bums out.

'Blake? What the fuck are you doing here?' I shouted.

'No names! No names!' Blake shouted back. 'I'm here to help. What are his symptoms?'

Right now it looked like the symptoms were that he had emptied a bottle of 80 proof vodka down his neck, but I didn't tell Blake that.

'He got hit on the head; real hard, maybe three, four hours ago. Bleeding for quite a while but we fixed that. He was groggy but then said he was fine. Now he is passed out, won't wake up.'

'Okay, okay.' Blake said. 'And where are you taking him to? A hospital? Okay. That is fine. We will speak to the right people, he will be fine, don't worry about anything else, okay?' That was his Doctor Blake voice, then he switched on a different voice, a different Blake. 'And you have the package with you? He will be at the hospital also?' Smooth, suave, like he was ordering Nude Cowboys at the Oyster Bar.

'The package is safe,' I said. 'For now, it is safe. It will be delivered when we agree terms. That means you do what I fucking say or you will never see the package this side of the China fucking Sea. Okay? Is that fine also?'

A rustle again, quick words between them.

'What are your terms, sir?' Blake said. 'We understood everything had already been agreed, everything was satisfactory?'

'I'll let you know as soon as I drop off at the hospital. I'll call this number to tell you where the hospital is,' I said. 'And it isn't Lisbon, so don't waste your time setting a trap, get me? Just make sure you speak to the right people and make sure they look after our friend. Then you get him home, ASAP. I'll tell you what we are going to do with the other package after I've left the hospital. Put our lady friend back on the phone.'

'Okay, sir,' the doctor Blake said. 'But, first, what made you say it was a cerebral edema, is there a trained medical practitioner with you?'

'Yeah, he could be,' I said. 'Either that or a fucking herb doctor, rhino horns and shark's fins, know what I mean?'

He drew his breath, I heard him gasp and come back as the other, different Blake.

'He is there also?' other Blake said. 'He is with you?'

I flicked the cellphone off and took the battery out again. Yasmin hit the brakes, the van swerved, the back end shook, I dived forward to cradle Ferdy, keep his head still until we shuddered to a halt.

'You did not tell them about me!' Her voice echoed around the van like a gunshot. 'You will not help me! You will leave me here with my children when you get what you want! You fucked me and you will leave me to be punished for what you did!' She was a dark tornado, a warrior queen, a screaming scary witch.

'It's just one of those things, Yasmin,' I said. 'And you'll just have to trust me here, okay? Because you're right. You have no other choice. You know that. You and your children? They'll make you suffer, big time. Your boss will do it, or Liu's boss or somebody's fucking boss. So right now? All you've got is me. Get that straight in your head and we will be fine, okay? But do it quick, because I'm not here to persuade you, you know?'

Yasmin calmed down, chewed her lip, clasped her hands over her ears. But she still had that killer look in her eyes.

'Hear me, Yasmin?' I said. 'You in or out?'

She didn't answer, slumped back in front of the wheel and trundled the van back onto the road. I pulled the cellphone I had wrenched from George's fist, slipped the battery back in and flicked through until I found the number he said was safe. A few moments before it started to ring, then ringing forever, before he answered. A sophisticated voice, at home in his Upper East Side condo. Sounded like he went through a $30,000 a year school. Sounded like he would be comfortable sipping cocktails along museum mile.

'I've got him,' I said. 'You want him back, you bring my wife and son home. You do that and I might, I just might, let you live a few days longer.'

'They are very safe, I assure you,' Moscow Alex said. 'I'm sure we can do business. They are safe, and I will make you a wealthy man. Where are you?'

'We'll do business. Tell your guys from me that I'm going to kill every man that has laid a finger on them, but you will do business with me after that. Stay by your phone, wait for my call.'

Yasmin kept her hands on the wheel, didn't twist her long body to snoop this time, left me wondering what was going on behind her eyes right then. My own head was spinning with scenarios and possibilities; what to do, what to expect, sequences, timing, trip-wires. I would have one shot at getting the string of decisions right, no second chances, it was all or nothing. No time to be distracted. But I couldn't help wondering what she was thinking, here with me now, and Ferdy maybe dying at my side, driving through the dark night. I knew what I had to do - steamroll over that sympathy shit and drill it into my head that it really didn't matter what she thought. I had been caught like that before and it never worked out good, so, sorry Yasmin, it wouldn't ever matter what you thought. Not this time, baby, not any time.

CHAPTER SEVENTEEN

The guy in the suit was asking too many questions. He had Yasmin's elbow and tried to steer her into the hospital building as the white coats transferred Ferdy to a trolley. I was in the shadows, the Chinese MP-5 under my jacket, straining to catch the first twitch of betrayal. Her voice started to rise, must be spilling the story I prepped her with; she had found this man on the road, she did not know who he was, she did not know anything. The suit wasn't satisfied, started to signal to the security man who was sheltering inside reception, scratching his soft ass. His arm was around her shoulders now, working her back to the door, held open by security. I marched forward as the trolley was wheeled in, kissed Ferdy's gray face and whispered 'Faugh a Ballagh, brother', before lurching in between Yasmin and the suit, heaving her towards the van and him back against the wall. The security guy was back inside scratching his ass before I scrambled her into the van in front of me.

'You did good, Yasmin, you did real good.'

I hopped into the back and slid the battery into the cellphone. Cora answered straight away, noted the name and address of the hospital and said it was under control, no problems.

'So you are bringing the package in now, Maknazpy, right?' Cora said.

A blue light and siren scattered the darkness behind us. Yasmin looked for me in the mirror – okay, just an ambulance.

'Not yet, Cora,' I said. 'Couple of things I want in place first.'

I could feel the frost on Cora's breath.

'First of all, remember you said me and Ferdy would be dismissed as fantasists? Nobody would believe our story?' I said. 'Well, you go arrange for Gallogly's attorney to take a sworn statement saying we have an absolute amnesty for anything that happened last year.'

'Wait! Wait! Maknazpy,' Cora laughed. 'You can't be serious! How do you think I can arrange that? And who's going to make that statement? Who do you think has that authority, for Christ's sake!'

'I dunno, that's up to you, Cora,' I said. 'But Gallogly's attorney is that old guy Ward, he's a real old school attorney, if he is satisfied then so will I be.'

'You are unbelievable, Maknazpy. I don't believe I'm hearing this.'

'Oh, you hear it, Cora. You hear it good,' I said. 'And I want two witnesses along with old man Ward. NYPD Detectives Ed Dart and Mike McAnespie.'

'Shit, Maknazpy! Those two scumbags are no friends of yours! Why are you dragging them back into this thing?'

'Because they might be wondering if somebody is ever going to drop that shit on their plates. Same as I wonder.'

Silence, then whispers in the background. Blake was there, maybe others.

'Maknazpy, look,' Cora said. 'Ward's office will be closed back home at this time. Everybody's office will be closed. You bring in the package tonight, we'll arrange all that stuff tomorrow. You have my word. And it's too dangerous out there, Con. You need to come in where we can keep you safe.'

I laughed out loud, Yasmin turned to give me the eye.

'And another thing,' I said. 'There will be extra passengers going home. A lady and two children. They will be staying in the United States. You can get Ward to witness that guarantee as well.'

'Christ, Maknazpy!' Cora said. 'That's impossible! Completely unrealistic!'

'You remember last year, don't you, Cora?' I said. 'That other lady that got hurt because of me? Because of what you made me do? Book their seats, Cora, you are taking them home with you. I'll call back in two hours. If everything is sweet, I'll bring him in.'

I popped the battery out and climbed in beside Yasmin.

'Happy now?' I said.

Yasmin didn't speak, replied with a one shoulder shrug and a pout of lips and wrinkled nose. She kept driving; a little rough on the gear lever, twiddling her hair between finger and thumb, clearing her throat, deep sighs, no words.

'What?' I said.

A shrug, eyes wide under straight eyebrows.

'My brother,' she said. 'I will not go without my little brother.'

Shit. Like I was going to tell Cora it was happy families now? My turn not to say anything, half turned from her and watched the dark countryside passing by.

'You want to know why I left medical school, no?' she said.

My turn to shrug.

'So, my father died when I was a little girl in Manguinhos favela in Rio,' she said. 'Just me and my mamma. She was weak, she could not live like that. She took me in her bed and we cried to sleep every night.'

She slowed down and did the hair behind her head thing.

'She started to drink. A man who said he was my father's friend brought cachaça, Brasilian rum. He was not a friend, this one was a pig. But my mother could not see; only drinking, drinking every night. Soon he was in my father's bed, and then my little brother was born.'

Yasmin smiled at the thought, despite herself.

'I hated the smell and eyes of my mother's pig,' she said. 'The first time I saw him, I knew to be afraid. Later, he would come to my bed when my mother was drinking. My little brother was there, and it frightened him, so he wet his bed. I was little too, but I knew I had to keep quiet so my brother would not be so frightened.'

No smile now. Tears massed in her eyes until they exploded down her cheeks in quick flowing rivulets. Remarkable heavy globes of tears, not insignificant miserly spatters.

'Then my mother was drinking his cachaça every night, and every night he came to me, and every night my brother wet the bed.'

She scooped the tears with the palm of her hand and smeared them back across her cheeks, into her hair.

'Every morning, my mother was angry at my brother for wetting the bed. Angry at me for not stopping him. That is what she pretended.'

'Didn't your mother know what he was doing to you?' I said.

'Hah! You think it is simple. You think I deserved it because I didn't stop it. That is what she pretended too.'

I didn't mean that, reached over to her, surprised when she took my hand and squeezed it to her lap.

'My father's parents took me away. No one ever said why. My grandfather had a shop in Itabira, in Minas Gerais. The first day he took me to school in Itabira the children laughed at me and I thought I was too stupid to ever open my mouth again. But my grandfather said I was only stupid because I did not know how smart I was! He made me believe it, and soon I was first in my class. I studied even more and passed the exam to go to medical school in UFMG, Belo Horizonte. I was top of my class there also. My beautiful horizon, no?'

'So what happened, Yasmin? What went wrong?'

'Ahh, ya ya ya! My mother went wrong!' she laughed without humor. 'Her drinking went wrong. Her liver went wrong. I had to go and help her, but the pig was there. I thought he would be afraid of me now, an important medical student! Ha! He raped me when my mother was dying in the next room. The pig raped me and beat me and raped me again. That is what went wrong!'

'I'm sorry, Yasmin.'

'Yes, sorry, sorry,' she said. 'Everyone is sorry but no one stops these men, it is normal for them. So, my little brother stopped him. Thiago cut the pig's heart out on Rua Leopoldo, that stopped him.'

I squeezed her hand some more, she squeezed back, and it felt good.

'I had to get away. Some guys in the favela said I could get a job here, in Lisbon, working in a hospital. I come, told Thiago I would soon send money for his ticket to follow. So, I come. But no hospital. No work. No food. Just these gangs to beat and rape here also. So you work and get food, they stop the beating, you work more and get some little money. Then it is normal. Then it is life.' She paused, then choked the self pity in her voice and roared back with a fighter's pride. 'So men like you know what a girl like me is like, no? A girl like me in your California graduates as a doctor, a girl like me in my favela graduates as a whore. Hah! I will be what I will be, and Thiago is here. I will not leave him.'

Yasmin lent sideways to smudge away the tears that bubbled around my eyes; too snarled up in her own misery to allow that the gringo beside her might curdle in his own cesspit of hurt and shame.

'Okay,' I said. 'I'll fix it. Here, use Jorginho's cellphone. Tell your brother to get your kids ready. We will pick them up tonight. Where is he now, Lisbon?'

'Yes, of course Lisbon,' she said. 'Where you saw him.'

The confusion in my eyes sparked a dazzling white smile across her tear blurred face.

'When he kicked your ass in the club.'

The white tuxedo? He was the little brother I was sticking my neck out for? I was crying for that prick?

'The Chinese will come for you soon,' she said. 'More of them. You need help. You need Thiago. He is a strong guy now. A real man! He was Brasilian Ju Jitsu champion in Rio. He kicked your ass easy, no?'

She snuggled my hand deeper into her lap, left it there as she babbled loudly to Thiago, then reached to wipe more tears from my cheeks with her wet fingers, smudged our tears together across my face, and ruffled my hair like the sister I never had.

'All you big men,' she said. 'You are always little boys, with the weeping and tears, always little brothers, no? And what is this Va A Balla you say to your friend? A prayer?'

'Yeah, I guess it is a sort of prayer. It means he will be strong, it means I will come back for him. A New York Irish prayer. You know that song about the little dark boat dancing in the light, Yasmin?'

Yasmin tilted her head to the side and started to whisper the words, and Luis's Barco Negro bobbed in front of my eyes again. She warmed up by the second verse and really let it go – the hairs prickled on my neck and arms, her voice layered a dense turmoil of pain and joy, hurt and delight, unrefined sweetness and bitter guilt. The ripe globes of her tears spiralled as she sang but I pinned my sobs deep down in my gut. And I didn't picture old Luis; I wept for all the little brothers, all the little boys, everywhere.

CHAPTER EIGHTEEN

It was wrong. Yasmin keyed in the security pin and the gates rolled back. Our headlights snaked up the white face of the house as we edged up the driveway. Everything looked just as we had left it. But the dead center of my head burned and twisted. This was all wrong.

'Kill the lights, Yasmin,' I said. 'Stay in the van. If anything happens, drive like hell out of here and wait for me at that first T junction.'

I stowed both Glocks in my belt and checked the MP-5. She squeezed my thigh and pulled my face close to kiss me on the ear. Her mouth was hot and wet. I slipped away from her into a buckshot volley of hailstones and salt rain raging over the house from the cliffs. I crouched behind the front fender. Told myself I was assessing the situation. True, but an excuse. On my own, without Ferdy at my side, the creeping tide of fear wouldn't stay locked down this time, for the first time. This was what it must be like for normal people. Fear palming a choice that was no choice.

Three long deep breaths then I sprinted to the door. Inside quietly, no movement, the basement door still closed. Perfect silence in here, so still I could taste it. Then steps crashing behind me, Yasmin out of the van and running to the house. If she was setting me up I would kill her without hesitation.

'Someone is out there!' She clasped her arms around my middle, I moved her hands away from the pistols. 'I saw them going over the wall, at the back of the house!'

I put two fingers to her lips, then positioned her in front of me and moved her to the basement door. She smelt it before I did; the hanging essence of a fresh kill, the balsamed transfer from one state to the next; ambiguous but real in the stifled basement. I flicked the light switch and there he was. Jorge. Jorginho. Gorgeous George. Propped upright against the pulping machine, but his head hanging loose, hinged upside down, posed as an occult doll.

Yasmin shuddered, and looked away. I held her hair and pulled her face to my neck. Stroked her back as I looked over her shoulder at the pulping machine. It should have been impossible, but Liu and Zheng had ripped that cast iron machine apart, left their blood sprayed over the rough floor. How to fuck could they have done that? I knew how those cuffs bite into fighting flesh. Like the trap we found up on the Shawangunk Ridge one time, the gnawed stump of a fox's leg sacrificed as the trapper's booby prize. So just how desperate were these two, the computer geek and the translator doctor?

'How many did you see out there, Yasmin?' I said.

She stepped back from me and knelt down beside Jorginho.

'I do not know,' she said. 'They were just shapes in the darkness. I could not tell if they were people, just dark shapes.'

'What is there behind that wall? Where does it go?'

She used both hands to straighten his head. The sadness hadn't completely faded from George's glassy eyes, but even I could see that his torment had been released, so now he looked like a different man to the smart assed punk with attitude that Cora had sent me after. Some sort of purging, an absolution, or an escape, had left him looking fulfilled and calm. Maybe that was the Jorginho Yasmin thought she had seen all along.

'It is a path down the cliff. It leads to the beach, then maybe two kilometers to the next path to get back to the road,' she said.

'I'm sorry about George, Yasmin,' I said. 'But he wasn't the man you thought he was.'

'I knew this Jorginho,' she said. 'He was a special person. He could have been happy. And I would have helped him. But he did not permit happiness, and now it is over.'

Yeah, George, you were so fucking special that you threw it all away. I was glad now that the little shit had blanked Yasmin when I had dragged him into that kitchen, when he froze her out with his indifference. Maybe that was your plan, George, huh? Save Yasmin from herself by cutting her off? No, I didn't think so, you self centered prick, your head was too far up your own ass to even notice the woman who could have saved your worthless life.

I left her at his side and ran up the steps, pulled out George's cellphone and tapped Cora's number.

'Cora? What do they say about Ferdy?'

'We don't know yet, Con, but he is in good hands,' Cora said. 'So where are you now?'

'Have you made those arrangements yet? With old man Ward and the extra passengers?'

She paused, I could picture her grimacing at Blake and whoever else was at her side.

'I'm on it, Con, but be realistic here!' she said. 'I'm working on it but it's going to take time to get that all figured out. You need to come in right now, before you become a problem again, you know? Remember what I said about our teamwork? About the people who thought you were too much of a risk?'

I laughed softly into Cora's ear.

'And remember I fucking told you your threats didn't work around here?' I said. 'So now I've got George, and I've got Liu and Zheng also. Maybe all three of these guys would really prefer to be in red China right now. And Cora? Don't tell me you don't know who those two are, okay?'

A muffled silence again. Panic stations. Then Blake.

'Mr Maknazpy?' Blake said. Not the doctor Blake. 'Listen to me carefully, please. You are in a very dangerous situation and we are concerned for your safety. Liu is a Colonel in the Chinese People's Liberation Army. He is currently attached to the Military Intelligence Department, the Seventh Bureau.' This other Blake intoned with all the necessary seriousness. 'Now, Con, you know that I, more than anyone, appreciate your extraordinary capabilities, and I have absolutely no doubt of your loyalty to the United States, but you really need to tell us where you are right now. Colonel Liu is an extraordinary man also, and it is beyond credibility that a Chinese military unit is not on their way to rescue him. Where are you, son? We're here to help.'

'How come you seem to know all about this guy all of a sudden?' I said.

'Look, Con,' Blake said. 'I know Liu. Liu and I go way back. You know this scar below my eye that you homed in on when we first met? Liu gave that to me twenty years ago. I know him, he is dangerous, you need to let us go help you.'

'And nobody thought to tell us about him before me and Ferdy fucking walked in there?' I said.

Another pause, getting their story straight, nodding heads.

'Ferdia McErlane was aware that Colonel Liu could be with George Oliver,' Blake said. 'There may have been operational reasons that prevented Ferdy from informing you, I can't really say.'

I snapped the phone off, hoped the bastards were trying to trace it: George had it rigged so any trace ended up somewhere outside Helsinki, wherever that was. Switched it on again, hit the other number.

'Alex? You've got people in Lisbon, right?' I said.

'Yes, we have associates, contacts, friends. Reciprocal arrangements can be made. Where are you?' Moscow Alex said.

'Send my wife and son home with Gallogly now, Alex. I'll hand Jorginho over to your associates tonight, after I confirm they are home safe. Tell your people in Lisbon to be ready. I'll contact you. And

Alex, just make sure your contacts aren't Chinese, get me? Make your reciprocal arrangements only with Russians, no Chinese, understand?'

'Of course, Maknazpy,' Alex laughed. 'My friend Yakov will be happy to help. Only Russians? Do you think I would even dream of anything else?'

Turned the smirking bastard off.

'Time to go, Yasmin!'

She skipped up the steps, her face strong and resolute, ready to move on, keep going, indomitable, a survivor.

'You know this place, Yasmin. I need you to lead the way. You okay with that?'

She closed the door to the basement behind her, wiped the dust from the rough floor off her red knees, and stroked my face as she passed me.

'You are another Jorginho,' Yasmin said. 'You are too special to permit happiness.'

The storm gods were angry: they roared and thundered to pluck Yasmin over the edge, I caught her ass and hoisted her up the wall, then scrambled after her, and it unleashed; the maelstrom punished our provocation, erupting an Atlantic seizure of screaming gales and spiking rain, demanding human submission before the one true daemon. I couldn't see, or, at least, couldn't see and move and breathe and think all at the same time under its omnipotent frenzy. But yet my hunter's blood tingled and palped with the acute promise of the delicious, tantalising prey. And Yasmin was wrapped around me: it felt good to be a live primitive in this scourged soup of black hell and fury, until the blue touchscreen of my cellphone flickered and glimmered a path ahead, and she lead me into the dark.

Yasmin knew the whipped edge of the cliff was close, but invisible, and she carefully retraced her steps to find the path that had led to those summer parties of wild abandon and reckless self-indulgence on the beach far below. She found the rough hewn slabs that corkscrewed down the rockface; narrow, twisted and treacherous with a carpet of wet green slime. Liu and Zheng wouldn't be far ahead, touching their way down here in cuffed single file, no idea where they were going but feeling my panting hot teeth on their necks, with their MP-5 baby cradled in my arms.

 I yelled in Yasmin's ear to ask how much further. My mouth was close enough to tongue the jade earring but she couldn't hear my voice under the storm, so squeezed my hand as a substitute answer. The sea convulsed and injected its trembling power through the cracked rocks under our feet. Half way down, the path slabs became loose and unstable, I slipped, thrashing blindly for balance, the MP-5 arced and vanished into the black like a ghost, Yasmin cat reflexed to anchor my numb fingers, and slowed down for me, and we kept going until her mid-length black boots sank into the lashed sand of the beach.

To our right, the sand drowned under the umbilical clash of wave and cliff. To the left, it narrowed to a skewed sliver of maybe two meters wide along the base of the cliff, although even that soon disappeared in the darkness, so I couldn't say whether Colonel Liu was waiting in ambush just ahead or had already escaped into the night.

I took the lead now, feeling my way along the precarious aisle, speeding up as my senses absorbed this new world, Yasmin behind with a tight grip on my jacket. The sand path widened and we broke into a jog, agreeing our rhythm and running faster now, until the black sea ruptured into spitting white ribbons just ahead, where it whooshed and slurped the flotsam sand and pebbles before smashing back each time harder and higher up the cliff. She looked over her shoulder at where we had come from: just the swirling black tide behind us now, the path to retreat swallowed and lost. We had to keep going, looked like there was higher sand beyond this sea trap, had to time our run, a few seconds grace between the void ahead and the abyss behind. We watched the wall of sea spout and spume its anger between us and safety, until the meagre plinth of drifting sand beneath our feet shrivelled around our ankles.

Then we ran, I screamed in the face of the ocean's bluster, gripped Yasmin's hand, and we ran as hard and as strong as we could. Our legs splashed through the backtide, up to our knees now, nearly there, she stumbled but I rolled her along and up by her thick black hair until she was upright and moving, nearly there, but a breaker sucker swiped us at an angle and scooped us up and apart and slapped us against the sheer rockface. I lost touch with her, my own life tumbling and tossing in the whirlpool, out of control and swallowing gasps of icy saltwater. It gnawed and sucked and chewed me, then spat me out like a foul taboo, left me clinging by my dirty fingertips to the cleft of rock that had been forming here for millions of years just to save me tonight. But Yasmin was gone, somewhere in there in that tumult of spiteful foam and riptide, she was gone and it had taken her from me and it had interceded to fucking smite me down. Too late now, but Ferdy's lament sizzled through my numb skull –'You praised me once, I am distraught, I'd prefer you to all the wheat in Ireland'. Too late, but I knew I could never have killed her, even if she had set me up.

My elbows levered me further up the rock, and I hung there like the ham I was until my strength chimed with the next lull and let me break through to the sandy height and safety. I flopped down on my back, a smear of ocean detritus deafened by the unremitting roar, dwarfed by the rocking cliffs above. I lay there in the black vacuum; not thinking, not scheming, just existing, just floating. Then I had one of my bright visions; the mind tricks that allowed Cora to bust my balls, the fucking freak fest that Ferdy loved to nail me with.

I dreamt I saw her rise up out of the water; swaying towards me in the emerald silk kimono, the club spotlights choreographed to project her above the waves, with her hair high on her head and the jade earring tear kissing the nape of her smooth brown neck: and she was singing Barca Negro, sweetly and true, her voice killing the fury of the wind and storm, thrilling her death scene back to the shimmering sensuous mirage of her summer pleasures.

'Maknazpy!' The mirage slapped my face. 'Hey! Seu branquelo!' She yanked my hair. 'Fucking tosco!' She kicked me hard in the ribs. I rolled over and plumed a spray of salt water and vomit bile across the sand. Yasmin screwed up her nose, but she was standing there above me; her black hair plastered like seaweed across her face, her saturated skirt torn to shreds, one mid-length black boot missing. But she was there, with the jade earring dangling in front of my eyes.

I floundered to pull her tight to me: to atone for losing her and to affirm to myself that I would never lose her again.

'Calma filho!' She recoiled from my mouth. 'You stink of sick!'

She dragged and pushed me further away from the crashing waves, up the sandbank, until we collapsed against the cliff. She took off her boot to drain the sea water against the rock and we huddled coldly together, panting and shivering, rubbing some life into our numb fingers and legs.

'The Chinese will come. You have lost your guns,' she said. 'Now what big plan do you have?'

There only was one plan - lock down Liu and Zheng. I just needed to adapt the tactics, and I would do that on the move, but right now we had to get to shelter and suck some heat back into our bones. This ribbon of sand was our only hope of salvation, as long as it wasn't sluiced from under our feet, so I pulled her up and we started over again. George's cellphone was dead, so we had no torch to squint our way ahead, just squirmed along the base of the cliff, stumbling and slipping over rocks and boulders.

If Liu and Zheng had made it this far, they wouldn't be much ahead of us, and, if they were ahead, I would catch them - but I really needed this cellphone to dry out and kick back into life, or else my plan was going nowhere past this cliff.

Yasmin kicked off her boot and forced her legs to trot ahead of me. I caught her and we pounded our rhythm into the wet sand, hand in hand, urging each other on, fighting through the Atlantic gale, blanking out the paralyzing cold and pain, just keep going until it is over, survival impulse on pilot. And she did keep me going, until the sliver of sand widened in front of us and the cliff cracked open above us: she knew where we were now and sprinted in front, could see the single light high overhead. She knew the stairs to the parking lot were close. I was too exhausted to scream above the storm, and too weak to hold on to her, so I let her go again and sank to my knees, saw her bare brown legs disappearing up the stone steps; an extra spring in her step, a lead weight on mine.

The storm shrieked around my head in this crucible cut into the cliff as I dragged myself after her like an old man, using my hands to take my weight, limping upwards like an old arthritic dog. There must have been a hundred steps before the polished stone faded into a rough gravel path, with the single light rocking and swaying on its slim metal post in the wind and rain. No sign of Yasmin, just the exaggerated shadows jiving and twisting to keep in step with the lamplight. I clambered up the path. This gravel must have pierced even her numb bare feet, but where to fuck was she?

A swinging door strained against its hinges. The crazy light flashing and winking. A wooden hut beyond the light stanchion, a sanctuary for ripped beach guards during the summer hunting season. And it was wrong. I knew it before this even started; had told Ferdy it was wrong when we got here, felt it when I arrived back at the house with Yasmin. And I told myself now again. I should have kept hold of her but I was too weak. She was there, inside the hut, the door swinging back and forward wildly like a saloon door in a movie ghost town. Yasmin was there, in between Liu and Zheng, in between the flashing winking blades they held to her smooth brown neck.

CHAPTER NINETEEN

They couldn't make me do it. Liu mouthed his order but it was swallowed by the storm. Yasmin whimpered her fear and pain. The kid Zheng bared his teeth and his crazy eyes. I could have melted into the night and never have seen any of them again. Or I could have hid in the darkness until they made their move, take them in the dark and put them down in about five seconds, knives or no knives, because a shackled Liu would really be no problem. I could have saved myself first and that's what I would have done in the old days, but the kid had lost it, he frothed his adrenaline overload, and his shaking hand prised that knife tight against her neck. I hoisted my hands above my head and walked in.

The wooden hut was an empty low rectangular box about fifteen feet by ten. Liu circled me and had me kneel on my hands in the middle of the floor, kicked my ankles until I edged back to where the light blurted through the door. They scuffled a clumsy dance around me to position Zheng so he could frisk me with his free hand. Yasmin gurgled a cry of pain, Zheng frisked. He patted my pockets down, took the cellphone, poked the tips of his fingers into my trouser pockets, nothing there.

'The keys to the cuffs are in the Atlantic,' I said. 'The only way you are getting out of those handcuffs is when the Portuguese police get here.'

Liu barked at Zheng, the kid wrestled his fist into my wet trouser pockets. Failure, sounded like he apologized to Liu. Colonel Liu snapped a kick to the base of my spine, I fell forward but stuck my hand out in time to save my nose from splatting the floor.

'The Portuguese police will not come,' Liu said. 'Our comrades will be here soon.'

'Oh, that's good,' I said. 'Because you two are as wet and cold as I am. Somebody's going to get hypothermia around here if your comrade guys don't hurry to fuck up.'

He kicked me again but I was braced for it and didn't move. It was more painful the second time but I didn't move, and it was worth it to test him out, see what his limits were, what patterns I could map. He had the upper hand for now but he knew I had only gifted it to him for as long as I was prepared to put her life first. He knew Zheng would be a handicap, and not only because the kid was pumped, so Liu had to calculate how far he could push me before I would snap.

And maybe I hadn't played that Mah Jong shit but I was pretty good at reading people like him. He was the big guy, the Colonel in the

Seventh Bureau, but I already knew all about him. He was just like all of them, American or Chinese or whatever color doll uniform you liked to dress them up in. He had that authority thing, the divine grace that set him apart, that meant you really should obey him because he really was your superior, that meant you were lucky to have such a remarkable human being like him to deliver you from your own ignoble shithole of squalor and shame. And he wasn't superior because he was an officer - oh no, that was just padding to make the serfs feel more comfortable - he was an officer because he was superior. Yeah, I knew all about him, and I knew how to push his shiny officer buttons, had been doing that all my life.

'So how do you figure on getting out of here, Colonel?' I said.

Silence. Spinning in his head. How did the imperialist running dog know he was a colonel? Strike one.

'They will come,' Liu said.

Bullshit! If his cavalry had tagged him, it could only have been back to Yasmin's party house. None of us even knew where we were now, so no way his rescue party could know. Strike two.

'Careless of you to lose poor George back there, wasn't it?' I said. 'I guess the secret of the Red Protocol and his Fifth Code died with him. You flunked out on that one, Colonel, didn't you? Bet your comrade bosses won't be pleased.'

They shuffled behind me; Yasmin's knees pressed down on my ankles, her weight anchored to my legs, her forehead nestled against the back of my neck. Liu probed the knife around my carotid artery. I had drawn him in, close enough to take him, now let him settle and think he was in control. Maybe I'd have to take some damage, but he was shackled to Zheng, and Yasmin was an obstruction to him as much as to me. Strike three and you're out, Liu.

'You are not what I expected, Sergeant Maknazpy,' Liu said. 'You are not like your father.'

A shiver jack-knifed up my spine. I was freezing cold and wet but this was another species of shiver altogether: triggered by the panic dormant since childhood, the ghost bottled in the dark shadows of my blood. They moved back; trailing Yasmin off me, smacking her hands away from me. This was Liu's big trick, reasserting his authority, knocking the wind out of me. And I had rolled over too easily, now he knew I was weak, knew there would be other holes in my armor he could lance and shank. But how did he know about my old man? It could only have been that prick Jorginho! George had seen my file in Blake's office, must have spilled his guts to Liu in the basement, thought he was buying his way out. It was just more of Liu's bullshit,

I knew that, but it had hit me like a kick in the balls. And he was smart about it: this fucker knew which knife to pull and how best to twist it.

'A boat is coming from Lisbon,' Liu said. 'It will be here soon.'

A boat? More bullshit! Sure, Yasmin's boss could organise a boat, probably had his own luxury cruising yacht to play with, but the one thing I didn't have to worry about tonight was any sort of a launch scudding through that rough raked ocean.

'Then what?' I said. 'You think I'll be as easy as George Oliver was? Think I'll let your red comrades get anywhere near that door? Before I snap your head off your neck?'

'That will be unnecessary,' Liu said. 'There will be no more killing. We are not savages after all, Sergeant Maknazpy. We are civilized men, are we not?'

'George Oliver wasn't a savage. George Oliver was civilized,' I said.

Colonel Liu was directly behind me in the darkness. He pulled a different voice now; quiet, intimate, maybe even regretful. The doctor translator, not the Colonel in Military Intelligence.

'George made the choice,' Liu said. 'He knew he must die, by my hand or by yours. He knew, and made the choice.'

What did that mean? Nothing cubed by zilch, just Liu with his mind games again.

'What about my father, Liu?' I said. 'You figure he was a civilized man, or a savage like me?'

'I think your father's son will grow to understand what we mean by civilization,' Liu said. 'That is enough for any civilized man, any civilized father.'

Christ! If Chinese Military Intelligence had a Bullshit Bureau, then Liu should have been a five star General in it.

'So what happens in this Seventh Bureau of yours, Colonel?' I said. 'Is that where they promote the hot shot guys who speak good English? More fun than pulling the North Korea duty, huh?'

Liu and Zheng babbled a quick rally back and forward. I dropped my left shoulder and caught the shapes in the corner of my eye. Yasmin on her knees between them. Liu above her, knife still pricking her neck. Zheng folded at the waist, one hand clamped over his eyes, the other hoisted above his head, linked to Liu's cuffed wrist. The kid was coming down from his adrenaline high, this was all too much for him, Liu was losing him. More dice in my favour.

'The woman is cold,' Liu said. 'We will go back to the house.'

Liu was risking high stakes in a rigged game, like those jerks back at the Mah Jong table, and he must have known I was only biding my time before making my own big play. The cellphone was still in Zheng's pocket. That would be my Powerball if it buzzed back to life when we got inside. Either way, Liu was the one who had to gamble right now. Stick or twist, with me aching to strike him down as the biggest loser in the house.

CHAPTER TWENTY

The gravel track stumbled us away from the wooden hut and back to where Yasmin said the road to the party house should be. The storm was desperate to keep us pinned down, and the super-heavyweight breakers still punched the rocks far below, but the track squeezed us away from the Atlantic onslaught and we crouched to shelter behind the low stone wall as we drudged along.

When Liu accidentally stood on Yasmin's bare toes he ordered Zheng to give her his water-logged sneakers, but she waved him away, until Liu persisted and she squatted down to crush her feet into them. He had told us he would slice her neck like the surgeon he had once been if I were to make any trouble, so he gave her Zheng's shoes and rasped the knife against her throat to reinforce the promise as she pulled and pushed them on.

Now, I may be an oddball, but if there was ever the remotest chance that I would be cutting some woman's throat, I sure wouldn't be fussing over the comfort of her feet. If it was me, I would have been keeping that woman at my longest arm's length. I would probably avoid her eyes, maybe rough her up a little so that she would avoid my eyes, kick her like a dog, make like she didn't really exist as a living person with feelings and emotions that I would recognize, maybe sometimes share. Basically, I would have inoculated some semblance of my own humanity by denying hers, by stripping her of whatever that flimsy aura of humanity is that somehow ringfences us from the other animals. And that wouldn't only be a cheap move to preserve my own sanity – it would really be an act of compassion to the woman, because how could you let her see that you acknowledged her humanity, through a small random kindness like giving her Zheng's shoes, say, but then tell her that you are going to kill her anyway? How would that go? Something like, 'Yeah, I see your pain and suffering and I know you are capable of joy and love. Sure, I truly do acknowledge that you exist. But that's not enough, baby, this other thing is more important and the world can survive without you.' At least if you treat them like shit in the first place they can fool themselves into clinging on to their dignity. It wasn't them, it was you. I sure as fuck wouldn't be insisting she protected her bare feet anyway. Not that it looked like Liu saw any contradiction between her comfort now and execution later. And this bastard was somehow disappointed in my grasp of what "civilization" was?

Liu wouldn't move until he was satisfied Yasmin had tied the sneakers up properly, but her fingers were so numb that fine motor skills were impossible. He stood her up again and tugged my sleeve down. I felt my way down her legs to find her feet in the dark, couldn't work my fingers either, but wasn't going to let him know that, so clumsily tucked the laces down the sides of the sneakers. Yasmin stood there like a dead statue, as if my hands weren't on her legs, and I thought I maybe whiffed urine off her, though that could have come from any one of us.

I was close enough to Liu to take him. Zheng I could forget – the geek was already a zombie. But Yasmin was in trouble, going downhill fast, we had to get to shelter quickly. And Liu was tough, seemed to be fighting back hypothermia better than I was, so I would wait until I could get some feeling back into my bones.

Yasmin said it should be another kilometer, that's, like, half a mile. Sure enough, the track soon fizzled out near an abandoned roofless farmhouse, and there was the road to the house on the other side of a broken down fence. Liu bundled her over the fence. I waited, and let another chance to strike pass by.

'You people are weak,' Liu shouted into my ear. 'Your corrupt society has made you all weak.'

Zheng didn't seem to be so strong either right then, but I was too intent on reaching the shelter of the house to debate the point.

'My grandfather was with Mao Zedong on The Long March of the Red Army in 1934,' he shouted against the wind. 'Your imperialist army pursued the Nez Perce natives for three thousand kilometers on their long march before you massacred them. Your great imperialist Napoleon lost half a million men on his long march of three thousand kilometers from Moscow to Paris. Ha! Such weakness! Do you know how far my grandfather marched?'

No, how would I know anything about his grandfather except that he was probably as much a nut as his fruitcake grandson?

'Twelve thousand and five hundred kilometers!' he beamed.

Very impressive, he should tell me about it sometime, maybe when we got back to the house, just before I got to break his neck.

'You do not see how imperialism has corrupted your own people!' Liu was on a roll now. 'I know your history. You are corrupt, you are weak, and one kilometer in cold weather is too much for you!'

Zheng was only still upright because Liu dragged him along by the handcuffs.

'You are not what I expected, Sergeant Maknazpy!' Liu gloated in my numb ear. 'Who do you say you are? What sort of man stands in front of me tonight?'

Well, tonight I was a man who had been just been tossed up on the shore after being flipped around in a whirlpool icy sea. A man who hadn't eaten since that custard bun in Pastelaria Estrela Da Graca. I needed shelter and food, so I wasn't really any particular sort of man at that exact point, just a man who knew he could die of exposure if he didn't keep putting one foot in front of the other. But I still had enough wit to realize that Liu was a manipulative bastard scheming to assert his psychological advantage. I also knew that Liu was about in as bad a condition as I was, he must have been, but he had something, some sort of edge, that let him hold it together enough to still be on my case with that expectation and disappointment crap. And he knew more about the history books than I did. Napoleon? Okay, I could see how they would study Napoleon in military strategy classes, that made sense. But Chief Joseph and the Nez Perce? Didn't the Reds have their own indigenous peoples that they had wiped out, without worrying about ours?

'They have made you weak, Maknazpy!' Again in my dead ear. 'You should be strong like your father!'

My head buzzed. But not the purple renegade pulse of blood purging destroyer – this was confusion, frustration, perhaps even a little shame.

★★★

Liu still had the strength to heave Yasmin and Zheng through the gates: I was just strong enough to push the storm out of my face. The light was still on in the hallway, pulsing a guiding beacon through the stained green and blue window arching over the doorway. I hadn't noticed that before; Almeida Terrace etched in a gothic red crescent leaking through the vivid green and blue. How come my eye pinpointed that artisan flourish now, when my legs were fighting lock down and I should have been wired to reach the door? Funny the way your brain works when the physical you folds under desperation, as if the third eye suddenly steps up, hot for the release from mundane appetites and screwed self-delusion. Maybe that's the brain, or whatever to Christ's hell Blake said it was, preening itself in anticipation of the inevitable escape from the primitive mechanical cage, straining to let go all the grinding hurts and humiliations that you guarded tight to your chest. But maybe I shouldn't have been so far up my own ass right there – then I might have seen them.

Because we were almost on the steps to the doorway when the automobile's high beam ignited in our faces, cutting through the slanting hail-rain like a scalpel, pinning us like rabbits. I twisted to meet Liu's eyes, saw he was as dazed as I was but he recovered in an instant to shield Zheng behind him and thrust Yasmin in front. I froze, like I didn't know what to do, like my body had forgotten how to react, needed an instruction. A steel paw clamped my shoulder from behind and scrunched a pistol into my right ear. He dragged me backwards up the steps, I felt the shadows cloaking around us, and we bundled in a heap inside the door. Liu and Zheng scrambled on top of me, our limbs tangled as we sprawled across the mat, penned together by a thicket of legs and guns.

But Yasmin wasn't on the floor with me, wasn't beat down with shouts and boots, wasn't slapped around with strong hands and pistol butts. No, I could see her brown legs in the Chinese sneakers, standing tall and remote. She was crying from pain and cold and exhaustion and fear, and she wept her relief and joy at cradling him in her arms again. Thiago – the little brother – had come for her.

CHAPTER TWENTY-ONE

Liu was one cool bastard. He was cuffed to me now, bumping along in the mini-bus, a big Brazilian with a sawed off shotgun sitting opposite us. Yasmin sat up front between Thiago and the driver. Thiago figured we should split up, so Zheng and three more Brazilians were in the other van, tagging behind us.

Liu snapped his cuffed wrist up so he could fold his arms. He jerked it hard; to probe me some more, to defy me, one of those little markers that confirm rank and make it easier the next time. I covered my wrist with my free hand and whipped the cuffs back hard enough to nearly break his hand off. He couldn't hide his wince, but then let me see his condescending smirk as if he had won, as if that was the reaction he had wanted to spark. I yanked the cuffs again, harder, stared him out, told him if he tried that one again I would break his fucking arm the next time. Liu forced a chuckle and turned his head to peer through the blacked out window, squinting into the dark night, seeing only his own face reflected at an angle in the black space, with me and the big Brazilian like ghosts on his shoulder. The big guy with the shotgun winked at me; I nodded, Liu was no problem.

Yasmin was quiet now, with her head nestled against Thiago's shoulder as if she was sleeping. She had bounced around the house earlier like a crack fiend in rehab; worked herself into a frenzy, stomping up and down stairs, screaming Brazilian shit in my face, pulling her hair and slapping Thiago around the head. He took it all like a little brother; let her dump her hysteria on him, on me, on Liu. Then he listened, when she had calmed down, bending his mouth close to her face, rubbing her shoulders, stroking her hands. Yasmin skipped out to the van then and took the cuff keys from where I had left them. The big guy in front of me now had taken Zheng out of the cuffs, and Thiago asked me to take care of Liu. Yasmin had pulled me close to her and wrapped my head in her arms before branding my cheek with a kiss. We were going to pick up her children and then I was taking her to the United States. I squeezed her back with my free arm and kissed the jade tear against her ear until Thiago got edgy about it and told her to move it.

Now we bumped along, and I guessed it would take about an hour to reach Lisbon again, an hour for me to work out my next move; I didn't need any distractions from Liu and his bullshit mindgames.

'You are afraid to lose, Sergeant Maknazpy,' Liu's face shrank from the black window and swivelled towards me, like a turtle rimming its head around its crusted shell. 'You are afraid to lose face. This is very selfish.'

More of his crap. 'You're the only loser I see right now, Colonel,' I shrugged in his face.

'How do you know what is winning and what is losing?' he said. 'How do you judge these things?'

'Well, you're my prisoner right now,' I said. 'I guess that's one way of judging.'

He grinned. No problem, I knew he had nothing to grin about, and noticed he had a wide gap in the top right row of teeth where two or three were missing.

'Is that all? I am your prisoner, you are my prisoner, I am your prisoner again? These are only temporary states. They are insignificant,' he said. 'This is how an animal lives. Eat now, drink now, procreate now, sleep now. Are you an animal, Sergeant? Have you submitted so much to your masters?'

Yasmin's head rumbled against Thiago's shoulder; a ribbon of her shiny black hair hung over the seat and I could have reached forward to stroke it if I hadn't been cuff-anchored to Liu.

'So what's the story with Doctor Blake?' I said. 'How come you two know each other?'

Liu juggled a spitting husk of a laugh around the raw gap in his teeth and cranked his turtle neck to look back out into the black nothing; as if I wasn't there, I didn't exist, as if I was nothing, I was less than nothing. The red throb in my temples triggered a ripping elbow hard into his ribs, Liu jolted like a snake forked by a high voltage probe and he exploded a storm cloud of his ice dry breath deep into my mouth and nostrils; and then I saw him, I caught a glimpse of what he really was.

I could smell it off him, taste it deep in my gut, feel it creeping over my skin. Liu was an imperious ruthless son of a bitch and I was just shit under his feet, but I knew that much already. But what unsettled me now, sucked up some primal dread of the dark and unknown, wasn't that he was a blood-thirsty cruel killer. No, that was no problem to me, that much I could understand and match blow for blow. But looking into Liu's eyes, tasting the sick juice from his guts, I knew now it was like looking into the eyes of a different species. Or like looking into eyes that saw me as a different species; the way he would see a locust pinned under a microscope, or a lab rat on a wheel, an ape pumped full of cancer. Liu looked at me as if I wasn't a human being at all, and that bounced back in the distance between us to make him into something other than human to me. And that was bad news for Liu because the first rule of survival, my first rule, had always been "if you don't recognize it, kill it quick before it kills you".

I braced myself to stare deep into Liu's lizard eyes, hoping he couldn't strip away the revulsion that masked my fear, and I knew I had seen eyes like this before, been shadowed by cold evil like this before. Yes, I was looking at Liu now but seeing Blake; the Doctor Blake, the spy Blake, the Cora's pimp Blake, all the Blakes, each one of them taking their cue depending on which hand they meant to shake next or which identity it was that needed to be logged into or which lie needed to be lived that day.

And I guess I could just about have hung in there if that had been all there was to it but even that ghosted deception didn't wrap it up. No, my brain throbbed and pumped like a broken heart while Blake's face faded in and out of the plasma veil that burnt into my eyes; but, in my soul, or in some diseased shrivelled sponge where they said my soul should have been, it wasn't Blake's face gouging an imprint, nor even Liu's. It was my father's face, and it was my own.

CHAPTER TWENTY-TWO

Nearly there, 'Bem Vindo a LISBOA' surfed past the window, Liu twisted away from me to check out if Zheng was still following us. The geek kid was close okay, Thiago's guys tagged along behind us then pulled alongside when we hit a red light. Thiago signalled to the other driver to wind down his window and gave instructions, like he had forgotten to tell him something earlier.

Liu strained forward to hear what Thiago was saying so I yanked the cuffs back and shouldered him tight against the window. The words were a jangle of bum notes to me but Liu cranked his head like a pigeon and looked as if he had heard and understood enough to be interested. No problem, Liu sure wasn't going anywhere so I didn't need to get too uptight about it, just wanted to ram it down his throat that we were in control here and there was nothing he could do about it. I slapped him around the ear. It must have stung but he didn't react, still trying to convince himself I didn't exist.

The light turned green and Thiago called something out to Beto, the big guy beside me. Beto smiled and winked at me, as if I knew what Thiago had said, sharing our joke at Liu's expense. I winked back at him, started to psych myself up for the final play.

Things had turned around pretty quickly, like they always do, and I hadn't it all nailed down yet but I guessed the rest would work itself out just fine. Ferdia would be home soon, his Irish skin was indestructible and I knew I would have sensed it by now if he wasn't going to pull through. Maybe I hadn't managed to bring Gorgeous George back with me but I reckoned Cora would be satisfied that Liu and the People's Liberation Army weren't getting George either. Anyway, I was delivering the Zheng kid and he might turn out to be even more valuable to them than Jorginho. Then there was the obviously unfinished business between Liu and Blake, and I didn't care much either way but the Colonel from the Seventh Bureau should be worth a few points on my account. All in all, and compared to a couple of hours ago, things were looking up.

Okay, so I still had to take care of Moscow Alex but the way the game was fixed now I knew I could lever some help on that score from Cora and Blake if I played it smart. We pulled a sharp right and Yasmin pitched a shaded glance to me when Thiago was looking the other way. Beto caught it though, and winked a comrade's nod to me. The big man's amiable eyes betrayed his hostile cosmetics. The fading hairline danced around the red and black demons sewn into his skull, scars old and new on chin and brow didn't distract from the black hand inked in a grip around his throat. All the same, something about this tattoo warrior reminded me of Ferdy; maybe it was his ease in his own tough skin, or an unspoken 'brothers in arms' bond forged by a common crisis. Anyway, it was like Ferdy always said anytime I was down and wanted to quit - the big wheel of the world keeps right on turning, you just have to keep yourself in the game until it decides to spin again and you find yourself on top. I wasn't quite on top yet, but the buzz in my veins said I was getting there.

We slowed before jerking a sharp turn into a tight street. Three women in long heels and short skirts linked elbows to firewalk across the ruptured road right in front of us, the driver screamed and slapped the wheel as he hit the brake, the conclave of men smoking outside Club Exotic Los Vegas whistled and whooped. Thiago stroked the driver's shoulder and said something like take it easy, then turned his face to give the big guy the nod. The inkhead slid over and eased into the seat behind Liu, flattened his nose against the window to see who was out there. The driver bumped forward again, Beto cradled the sawed off shotgun in the angle of his left elbow and nudged it against the back of Liu's skull. Liu made as if he was dozing off, as if we didn't have him hand-cuffed and with a shotgun wedged against his neck.

We turned again into a lane with no streetlights and squeezed past the cars parked with two wheels on the thin sidewalk, the van carrying Zheng inched along behind us. I strained forward to see where we were, the headlights bounced back off the high wall that sealed the end of the lane. A gate opened in front of us and we stopped inside a wide empty yard. Liu stirred from his pretend slumber and barked an order. Beto turned. The shotgun was hard against my head.

'Do not let shame consume you, this is merely a temporary state,' Liu said. 'Trust me, Sergeant Maknazpy, and you will find your peace. Let your poison be your cure.'

The headlights from the van behind us lit up Yasmin's stony face. She wanted to speak but Thiago crossed his hand over her mouth and tugged her out of the minibus. The door slid open and three more on the muscle payroll pressed their pistols into my face and gut; they rolled me on the floor, released me from Liu and cuffed my wrists behind my back before dragging me out and forcing me to my knees on the wet tarmac. An arm as thick as a thigh braced my neck and forced my head down, so I could only see the hand crafted black leather shoes marching towards me.

'What about Ferdy?' I croaked. 'Is he okay?'

'Ferdia McErlane will be just fine,' Blake said. 'You probably saved his life by getting him to the hospital but he will be fine, don't worry about him. Don't worry about a thing, Mr Maknazpy, everything is going to be fine from here on in.'

CHAPTER TWENTY-THREE

Beto's tickled eyes were the last thing I saw before he noosed the rough cloth bag over my head. He twitched his wink at me and yanked the sack over my face, then wreathed a rope around my neck, an atheist abbot waterboarding a raptured novice. The ruffled hemp erupted in a cloud of dust and fibers to explode in my throat and chest so that I wheezed and rasped like a runt pup being drowned in a bucket. Beto cracked a line and they all laughed, he thumped my back to clear my lungs but only pummelled the last pocket of air out of my throat. Cough and splutter, I couldn't move but two of them hooked my armpits like a couple of hungry dockers ghosting a juicy carcass and hoisted me across the tarmac.

They quickstepped me through icy puddles and sharp rubble until we stalled at a door. Still Beto clowning and jockeying behind me, somebody loosened their grip to negotiate the door, I lunged to my right with a spinning head butt – shit! - missed him, but walloped the heavy door, sparked fizzbomb stars under my hood. They all pissed themselves with cackles and hoots, maybe six of them, maybe a woman's laugh gliding high and clear above their base pack chorus. Was she here, and laughing at me with all the rest? What did Yasmin's laugh sound like anyway? Had I actually ever heard her laugh, or even seen her smile, before I had conjured our happy ending, the fairytale couple ever after in the Bronx or Brooklyn? No wonder she was amused, I should have cracked a rib myself if it wasn't for that fucking hood.

★★★

They planted me down with the cuffs twined through the back slats of a solid wooden chair, slammed the door on their way out. A silent pause, then the rattle and scrape of a key turning the lock, voices and footsteps fading away. The pulse in my head pumped and raged, I strained to hold my breath and block the floating hemp fibers as much as I could but had to submit at ever decreasing intervals to gasp whatever air I could. Just a couple of minutes and the door opened again.

'No problem! You not get whacked!' Beto beamed as he untied the rope and dragged the hood above my eyes. 'Forget this woman, the whore brings pain! Forget the bitch!'

I rolled my head back to fill my lungs, he patted my face twice with a friendly clap, winked his sympathetic nod and slid stepped backwards out the door, stopping to bob his head back in. 'Forget Yasmin, go home to your USA and forget her.' Then he knocked off the light and was gone, and I was on my own.

Go home to my USA. Forget the bitch. Good advice, well intentioned. No problem, and what was she to me anyway? A look in her eye? A tone in her voice? Beto knew the score, mano a mano. There was no look, no tone, except for whatever half-assed meaning I had dreamt up for myself and pinned on that space in front of me that she happened to occupy just at that moment – a decoration, another stopgap affectation, as cheap as her jade ear-ring. No light at all in this crypt, not even a pale shimmer from where the door should be. Silent too, like death, until a freezer tripped into life and the hum of its motor somehow soothed my nerves. I was forgetting her already. Yasmin who? No problem.

Scaly claws scratched across the floor behind me. Sharp teeth scraping and gnawing at wood, or maybe stiff cardboard. I stamped my feet, the gnawing stopped. Silence again for a few seconds, then the scraping again. I stamped my feet harder in the dark. The scraping got louder; more urgent, more intense. I was just a spectator, no problem, more scuttling claws and the gnawing buzzed through the fabric of my black space. Still, there was something. Down there on the beach when she hauled me out of the tide, and then in the hut with Liu's knife at her throat, there was something. Maybe not now, and maybe it could only ever exist in that creeping half light where death was closer than life, but there was something. I knew it, even if she screwed up the strength to convince herself, I knew it. But Beto was right. Forget the bitch.

CHAPTER TWENTY-FOUR

Like Yasmin, the vermin casually blanked me out to scrape and scratch their dirty musak in the dark. I stomped hard on the bare concrete floor every couple of minutes to keep them away but they must have known I was no threat and ignored me, kept on chomping and tearing their way through the seams of our black hole so I tuned them out and gave myself up to the empty darkness that swilled around my head. The big rats would be back soon, and I wasn't going to make life easy for them when they came for me but, for now, it was enough that I was on my own; with no compulsion to look, listen, smell, speak to or feel for any other living person. And maybe they wouldn't come back, maybe they would leave me there in my black cell, me and my rats, with the chewing and scraping, and me just drifting in a dark cloud of nothing. That really wouldn't have been so bad.

It felt like an hour, was probably less, before a thin spill of light bounced and stumbled into life to fill the gap between door and floor. Then the beat and echo of music muffled behind closed doors. Nice time for a party. Beto had said that I wasn't getting whacked. Big of them, but he had spouted it with a mixture of surprise and regret, as if I had been gifted a last minute pardon even after he had psyched himself up to be the triggerman. I got him, nothing personal, all that adrenaline has to be dumped somewhere on somebody.

And somebody was out there. The sip of light under the door pulsed and wavered. I felt their presence, pressing an ear to the door, wondering what I would do, calculating their next move. The rodents sensed them too and fell silent, so now there was just the rise and fall of the music to match the throbbing pulse in my head and the gentle hum of the refrigerator unit. And somebody outside, until the shadows shuffled across the span of the doorway, and then faded away. The boom and beat of the music stepped up a level, maybe escaped through an opened door, then retreated into a muffled pod, like a door closed again.

The sharp-teethed gnawing crept back to its steady rhythm until the odor of burnt cooking fat seeped through the darkness and spiked them into a new high of frenzied scratching and scraping. Cooking fat that had been burnt and re-burnt twenty times. The acrid scent of burnt onions first, then fish. Like Luis's blue and silver sardines, with their glassy eyes and taut skin, presented on a plate to be devoured so that only the fragile head and long backbone and tail remained to be discarded into the garbage. Beto said I wasn't to be whacked after all but I was still hooked here like the prize catch of the day. The music bounced up a level, the smell of sizzled fish filled a bubble cloud around my head, a phantom scuffled to the other side of the door. My stomach rumbled. The door opened.

'Well Sir! You sure like to make life complicated for folks, don't you?' Blake's spectacles flashed as the bare light fitting above my head flickered into life. 'Your friend McErlane was meticulously briefed to ensure there would be no casualties. But I guess that propensity to exacerbate collateral damage just about comes wrapped up in Mr Maknazpy's collective baggage. That should have been no real surprise, Colonel Liu, should it?'

Liu didn't answer but drifted past Blake to stand behind me, more or less the same position he had taken back in the beach hut.

'How is he?' I asked.

'Ferdia McErlane?' Blake said. "He is fine, he will be fine. He was very fortunate to have Colonel Liu present. The outcome would certainly not have been so positive otherwise. Not if your comrade had been solely reliant on your exercise of your duty of care.'

'Ferdy is still in hospital?' I prompted.

'He is in good hands,' Blake said. 'Our immediate concern is to conclude our business here with no further unfortunate distractions.'

'Suits me,' I said. 'You guys free my hands and I'll be on my way. I won't be distracting nobody.'

Blake pretended to smile. He plucked the spectacles off his nose to let the clinically manicured thumb and forefinger pinch a fold of skin between his eyes. He blinked and yawned. The red scar on his cheek contracted into a ball before stretching like a long purple finger. Thin wrinkles spidered under his eyes but didn't break the red lipped bubble of damaged tissue. I couldn't work out which one was the boss but guessed it must be Liu.

'We're working here to accommodate you, Mr Maknazpy,' Blake intoned his Doctor voice. 'But you are a volatile personality, displaying unpredictable behavioral patterns. We can't possibly consider discharging you from our care just yet.' A nod to Liu. 'For your own safety, you understand, and the safety of others.'

'Discharge me from your care?' I said. 'What's that mean? You're going to have me whacked after all?'

Blake swallowed but held the stone face pose pretty well otherwise. Not a sound out of Liu but I could taste the tension in the air between them. Yes, I guessed Liu was the bossman here.

'Ditch the melodrama,' Blake said. 'You are here because you are here but what happens next is up to you, we have no intention of coercing you against your will.'

'What about Cora?' I asked. 'Is she under your care as well?'

Liu cleared his throat behind me; a long rough heave and rumble from deep in his chest, a spinning ball of spit hit the floor in front of my feet, dust and dirt sprayed along the edge of the refrigerator unit.

'Let's just say Miss Cora Oneale is beyond our span of influence,' Blake said. 'A lady of deep conviction and idealism, undoubtedly, but those ideals have been spawned from a rather narrow and spurious worldview. No, I'm afraid poor Cora is a product of indoctrination and manipulation, so she prefers to set herself beyond reason.'

Like I wasn't? Like I could give a shit about 'worldview' and 'reason'?

'How about George Oliver?' I said. 'Wasn't he under your care back in your nice plush office? You trying to say Jorginho had any ideals that weren't about money? How come our friend here twisted his head off his shoulders like a corkscrew?'

I expected a slap from behind but Liu didn't move. I expected it because I owed Liu a few slaps and that's what I would have done if I had been him. Blake crossed his hands behind his back and rocked on his heels. He tilted his head back slightly and stared at the light bulb above my head, as if he was considering some difficult thing beyond my comprehension. I guessed he pictured himself as strong and powerful but his posing exposed the tangle of silver hairs sprouting up his nostrils. He didn't know why I was smirking now and mustered his authority into an intimidating scowl that probably had the freshmen medics under his tutelage shitting themselves. His stern face sparked my smirk into a cackle I didn't try to suppress. I sensed Liu had made a gesture behind my back by the acknowledgement Blake nodded before uncrossing his hands and sidling around behind me to join the Colonel. I didn't turn my head, just picked a point on the doorframe where a chink of wood had been dislodged. That would be my focus from now on.

A strangled whisper between them before Blake gripped the chair with his left hand to take his weight as he bent his mouth forward to my right ear. He had used some sort of astringent clinical mouthwash recently but not enough to kill the spicy tang in his gut. Not the Oyster Bar's naked cowboys this time, probably some shit like curried shrimp or krill paste.

'You surprise me, Mr Maknazpy,' he breathed over me. 'You have asked about Ferdia McErlane, Cora Oneale and George Oliver. But not a word about your wife and son.'

That hit me like a kick in the balls. Blake's turn to smirk now. Liu scoured his lungs to produce another mouthful of phlegm but juggled it between tongue and throat until he reached and opened the door, then turned to blowdart it between my feet. Blake moved to join him. 'Cora is an attractive girl of course,' Blake turned the screw. 'Even this Brazilian courtesan, or whatever she is. But I am surprised at you, Maknazpy, really I am.'

Blake stepped out and Liu knocked the light off before pulling the door closed behind them. My focus spot on the doorframe disappeared.

CHAPTER TWENTY-FIVE

Alone in the dark again. One of Liu's mindgames, taunt me with guilt about Rose and young Con and let me stew in here on my own, spinning my sins on a loop through my head. So what, I had let them down. Rose had scraped it into my soul with her hurt many times. I didn't need Liu's stagecraft to give me my lines. And Moscow Alex was too smart to jeopardise his investment. Rose and young Con would be okay – I just needed to get myself out of here, 'discharge' myself from the care Blake and Liu had mapped out for me. Then we would see how far Blake's urbane veneer could stretch before he cracked open under my fists.

Shit! The rat scuttled against my ankle, I kicked out with both feet and a yell burst out of me. Somebody told me once, don't remember who, that rats will avoid you like the plague, (yeah, that was his joke), as long as you act normal but, once they sense a weakness, they have no fear of humans. And they can taste your fear or despair or whatever it is that is taking you down. They twitch those fucking whiskers and they smell it off you. Before you even realise it yourself, before you can articulate to yourself that you are a loser and you can't get back up there without somebody's help but nobody is there that is ever going to help you. Maybe you never had anybody or maybe you did one time but you pissed them off so much that you forced them to move on without you. Either way, it makes no difference to the rats – they just know when you are fucked whether you have allowed yourself to see it or you are still clinging to the fantasy that made you a loser in the first place. Only this rat was way off beam. I was never made to be a loser, even if Rose and Cora and Blake and Liu and all the other shitheads called it that way. That was their problem, not mine, because I was getting out of this hole and that rat wasn't as smart as he thought he was.

The music cranked up a notch, somebody had opened that door down the corridor. Dino again, 'Everybody Loves Somebody'. Ten tense seconds before the light outside blinked into life and the door in front of me started to creak open. I plugged the breath in my nose and throat. The light from the corridor wavered across the floor to my left but the door was only open a fraction. Whoever was out there was freeze framed, playing it out in their head or in blind panic. It sure wasn't Liu or Blake, their superiority was too deep grooved to allow self doubt. Maybe it was Beto and he needed to psyche himself up after all, a trembling finger on the trigger. I blew the air out of my lungs and drew in a long, slow draught of breath. The light switch flicked on and a hand snapped back behind the door. A strong hand at the end of a thick wrist swathed in black tattoo ink. Dino still crooning, "There's no telling where love may appear – Something in my heart keeps saying – My someplace is here"

The door swung open and she was there, in that long emerald green sheath of a dress and the jade earrings. Yasmin brought a tray of food, hoisted it up almost level with her chin as if it was an offering.

'Remember what I tell you, man,' Beto lilted into the room before pulling the door closed behind him from the other side.

She squatted down low on her heels in front of me, sat the tray on the floor. Four plump sardines hanging over the edge of a blue and white striped dish. Two bread rolls swimming in a bath of oily red sauce.

'What did this fat boy tell you?' Her eyebrows pouted a sharp crease across her forehead and a web of purple threads leaked out from the lip of her left eye. 'He has much hate of me, this one. Much hate, do not believe what he tells you.' She glanced down behind me to my left. 'Unless his lies make easy truth for you.' She nipped the dress against her hips and peeled it up just enough to let her kneel in front of me. Right in front of me, I could have kicked her face in. She knew I wouldn't. 'You want this food or no?' she juggled a steaming sliver of fish to my mouth. The flesh melted like warm milk on my tongue.

'Nobody hates anybody without a reason,' I said. 'What did you do to fat Beto? Make a fool of him? Make him think one thing when you were always thinking something else?'

She jabbed a chunk of sardine at me, made sure the fork stabbed against my lower lip.

'You hate the Chinese men you killed? What did they do to you?' she said.

I swallowed the fish without chewing, had forgotten how hungry I was.

'Men like to trick their minds to believe the lies they make for themselves.' Her tone was sharp and vicious. 'They do not need me for this, not even poor Bebeto.'

'What about Jorgingho?' I said. 'Did he trick himself?'

Yasmin tore a strip of bread apart and splashed it into the red sauce before plugging it between my teeth. She pressed the bread roughly against my mouth, forced my head back as I chewed the thick crust but her fingers felt soft and tender against my lips.

An extra thrust of her palm against my chin. 'And does your wife trick herself?'

Too late, Yasmin – Liu and Blake had already hit me with the Rose guilt trip.

'I was taking you to the United States, Yasmin. You and your kids, and even your hero shit-for-brains brother. You think your kids will have a better life? Living here? Like this?'

She plucked a wad of bread and surfed it through the red juices before firing it high over my head and into the dark shadows. A flurry of squeak and scuffle behind me triggered a shiver up my spine.

'So I go to New York, yes? And then? You are my savior? I tell my children they must please you always or maybe you send us away?' She sponged the roll over the sardine, caught a smear of the red sauce on her little finger and daubed it across her flicking tongue before offering the bread to my mouth. 'You think I will please you always? Obrigada my hero, yes? So, I go with you to be your prisoner for ever?'

'There are no prisoners in America, Yasmin,' I said. 'People are free to do whatever they want. You would have been free in a free country, with or without me.'

She rocked back in laughter, her long black hair tumbled off her strong shoulders and flared down her back like a flag in the breeze.

'Ah ya ya! You believe that?' She scoffed in my face. 'That real people like us are free to do what we please? So, it pleased me to be a medical student in Belo Horizonte but I believed what another savior told me and so I am a prisoner here in Lisbon. But my children have friends, I have people to protect them here. Who do I have in your United States? You? And what will happen to my children when I do not please you?'

A thick vein pulsed and contoured down her neck until it slipped under her emerald silk. Her fingers shook and her nostrils flared. The fury should have sparked her to punch or slap me but she gripped the dish and looked away from my face.

'Nobody said anything about pleasing me,' I said. 'And maybe your kids would learn how to be free, without needing a savior, without needing protection. Just because you have allowed yourself to be trapped in this shit life doesn't mean you have the right to deny your kids their right to a better chance.'

That was too much, she dashed the rest of the fishy stew around my ankles then sprang to her feet to punch me hard in the mouth. Beto heard the ruckus from outside and skipped in to drag her off me. He dived across the floor a lot quicker than a man his size should be able to and folded a bear hug around her from behind. Yasmin was still crying and shrieking her hurt on me as he lifted her clean off her feet and backed out the door, stopped just to turn sideways and tip a wink at me, saying he had told me so, she was bad news, forget the bitch.

The room still echoed with her Brazilian curses when they were far down the corridor. Dino screwed it a little louder as I placed Beto opening the door down the corridor before dumping her inside and closing that door behind them. The big clown probably felt pretty pleased with himself. Hadn't he told me to forget the bitch and now look what had happened. He handled her pretty roughly too, maybe that gave him a buzz. Whatever, he should have kept his mind on the job because his macho swagger made him careless. He was so busy making a big deal about trailing her away he had forgotten to turn the light off in my cell. No problema, Beto might say. But he had been so juiced up about hauling her silk sheathed ass over his shoulder that he hadn't locked my door and that was definitely a grande problema, and all I needed.

The cuffs were tight on my wrists and my arms were clamped behind me through the struts of a simple wooden chair. I stood up and lifted the chair behind me like a snail humping its shell, only this snail launched itself against the wall to smash and splinter the wooden shell to pieces. Five or six crashes and most of the rest of the chair disintegrated around my feet but the back piece held tight. No sound outside, I edged a look into the corridor. A narrow corridor with one door about twenty paces away to the left, that's where the waft of music and cooking was coming from. Another door at the end of the corridor to my right, about ten paces, looked like it was a door to outside and freedom. I angled the back of the chair against the door frame and threw myself backwards, three or four times, the struts started to crack and I twisted and wrestled my arms until the rest of the chair disintegrated. I waited and listened for a couple of seconds, nobody coming. Sat on my ass and wriggled my cuffed hands down the back of my legs. The daddy rat was nosing the fish stew where Yasmin had fired it over the floor. I lifted my feet over the cuffs and stood up with my hands still trussed but in front now. The handcuffs had burnt and cut my wrists and a plump tear of blood slipped away and splashed at my feet. The rat looked me over then sidled off into the dark corner.

Behind one door, Dino's tired Napoli spiel, 'When the moon hits your eye like a big pizza pie, that's amore'. I gripped a leg of the chair as a weapon and crouched forward to listen at the outer door. Nothing. I tried the handle, creaked the door open, the damp night air splashed over my face. Dark, only a single street light peeping over the wall near the gates. The vehicles were still here so Thiago's soldiers probably were too. No movement anywhere, keep close to the wall and get over the gate, if I made it to the streets they wouldn't get me back.

I glided low, tight to the wall, silent – then wham! They steamed into me, six or seven of them; punching, kicking, grabbing, tearing. I axed the chair leg and caught one square on his right temple, he hung in the air for a second before collapsing under the tangle of fists and boots. One down, but I was shipping heavy damage here, had to keep moving back along the wall, protecting myself from their kicks and striking out when I could. One of them swung a thick leather belt embossed with a clunking buckle, caught me across my right arm a couple of times, hurt like hell, like getting nailed by a rattler. The pain kicked in – and the red throbbing cloud hissed and sparked through my skull and burned in my eyes. I knew what it was, the demon that lurked under my skin, that I pledged was tamed and banished every time, until the next time it was unleashed and spawned an explosion of froth-mouthed animal blood-lust. Another one went down, the rest saw it in me now, a specter they had never seen before but recognized from some deep untaught knowledge that lies dormant in all of us, that was first seeded in our veins when we made the leap from howling blood-drinking animals to the illusion we now like to call 'mankind'. And just as their awareness of the real presence of my evil seeped through their numbed heads, my own brain retreated into self-defense mode, as if the real Con Maknazpy couldn't exist or function while this ancient imposter usurped my skin. I held on for a few seconds this time before the blackout was complete, and even lapped the buzz of guilt-free savage power until the invader surged ahead to reap its inevitable climax.

The real me, the shared me, was still bouncing out of my skull when it finished – a fragment of my mind clicked Thiago standing over my quaking body, that taser in his hand, my devil spasm fusing with his electric gun to convulse me into a paroxysm of shrieking red frenzy. But neither human body nor animal brain can sustain such a supernova for more than a few high octane moments, so I was already spent when Blake bent to plunge the needle deep into my red hot flesh. 'Very good!' Liu's voice chimed in a far off chasm. 'Very interesting!' His chest rumbled to harvest the phlegm. 'At last we may commence our project.' His crackled spit sailed over my head into the darkness, and I was gone before it hit the ground.

CHAPTER TWENTY-SIX

I trickled back into their world through a mesh of spinning headache and disconnected shapes, bound to a table and with their vicious light drilling diamonds into my eyes. The sick reflex jerked through my body but I could only skew my head sideways to retch. Nothing came up, just the empty gesture.

'Welcome back, Sergeant Maknazpy.' Blake's even tones swirled in my head. 'Do not be alarmed. You are safe. We are here to support you.'

In that twilight stupor I could only receive the random words, couldn't jig them into any sense, couldn't hang any meaning to the noise from his mouth.

'We are very lucky to have Colonel Liu with us,' Blake buzzed on. 'It is a great honor for me, personally, and an unequalled opportunity for you.'

I was surprised to find I could lift my hands to my face. Not handcuffs, but surgical dressings over the ruptured skin on my wrists. Used my right elbow to pivot on my side. And I wasn't strapped to the table, except by the paralysis that was slowly subsiding now. And it wasn't a table but a padded leather couch, the sort I had burrowed into when being dissected by eager shrinks in the past.

'Do you know why you are here, Cornelius?' Dr Blake soothed. 'Can you tell me where you are? What can you remember?'

I couldn't tell him anything, couldn't remember how to make my mouth work, how to make the sort of sounds he was floating around me.

He loomed over me and used his left hand under my neck to tilt my head forward. 'Would you like a drink, Con?' The iced water gurgled down my throat like pebbles rattling through a tin drum. I couldn't control my swallow and started to choke, coughed and spluttered down my chin and torso.

'Easy does it, Con, easy does it.' The doctor Blake placed a paper towel in my hand, I rubbed my face and mouth, my eyes and neck. My skin was smooth, somebody had shaved me. How long had I been away?

Liu had different ideas on bedside manner, he grabbed my left shoulder and slapped me across my face. His hand was hard, like getting smacked with a marble floor tile. Two, three slaps, each echo whipped around the bare room to collide and bounce off the corners.

'Time wasted!' Liu barked. 'Wake! Wake!'

The slapping agitated the cotton wool casing my skull to disintegrate and churn behind my eyes like the aimless filaments of a safe snow storm. He rocked my snow globe head with more slaps until my eyes went offline from my brain, then clawed his steel fingers over my mouth and cheeks and thrust his forehead against mine so that his bloodshot eyes nailed through me. He held me there until the gyro in my head ran out of steam, the ceiling stopped spinning and I could taste the brown phlegm on his breath.

'He is ready,' Liu pronounced. 'No more waiting. It is time.'

Blake wasn't used to having his ego stomped down so he mimed the apologetic shrug just enough without squandering his stored pride too cheaply.

'So, Con,' Blake started his parley. 'What options would you like to examine?'

My brain was ticking into gear now, all the faces and voices slipping back into their filed slots. Jorginho, Yasmin, the kid Zheng, Moscow Alex, Thiago and Beto. And old Luis with his Barco Negro. All jumbled together as I looked back along the pathway, all pinned to the straight time sequenced intersections of chance and choice that had dumped me here.

'What makes you think I'm going to give you two bastards any options at all?' I said.

Blake sucked back his smug grin. Liu snorted, I thought he was about to drag up an oily spit.

'I really don't think it is helpful for any of us to adopt a negative attitude, Con,' Blake reassured me. 'I think you will find we all have options before us. My best hope is that we identify and progress those options which will accommodate the greater good.'

Yeah? Like what option had I given old Luis, with a knife in his back, left to die in a cold empty room with only his Rhode Island memory to fade on the walls around him? That was the whole problem with all that option shit, it only looked like you had a choice if you gouged yourself the luxury to stop and look back. In realtime there are no choices. You do it and it is done, then it doesn't exist anymore except for the bullshit we fake together afterwards to make ourselves feel good.

'The greater good, huh? Friends of mine have laid down their lives for America, Blake,' I said. 'Others have given arms and legs and wished they were dead. You think I'm going to piss on their greater good to make life easy for a fucking traitor like you?'

This time Blake didn't try to hide his smirk and Liu didn't hold back with the spitting.

'Traitor? A word smothered in emotion,' Blake said. 'Does it serve to fully encapsulate all that I am, all of my motivations, my complete life potential? What does that word really mean to you?'

The numb sludge still bubbled around my head but the spark in the ember that makes me Con Maknazpy was burning back to life - no way was I about to play dumb word games with this asshole.

'What's the Chinese word for traitor, Liu?' I said. 'How much face does a traitor in China cost his family?'

Liu squeezed his palms together like he was sore from slapping me, or maybe he was getting ready to start over.

'You are a young man, Maknazpy,' Liu said. 'Yet you are old fashioned. You live like an unthinking animal in your war monger paradigm of the savage, brainwashed to remain paralyzed in the imperialist ghetto of the last century. But now you have a choice. We offer a choice.'

I preferred it when he pretended he hadn't much English but I understood enough of his bullshit to know my choice was either sell out America or be whacked by Beto. But why me? I wasn't like Jorginho, wasn't in a position to steer any useful intelligence to them, never would be. I was just muscle and Blake knew that. Why me?

'Yeah, well, in the United States even an unthinking animal like me has a vote, Liu,' I said. 'That's what we call Democracy.'

They both laughed, like I was an innocent child who had just blurted out some naive howler. Maybe I was still a little punchy and lightheaded but I couldn't see what was so funny.

'Laugh all you want,' I said. 'And maybe America isn't perfect but we are still the go-to guys when all you shitheads out there mess up and come crying for the United States to pull them out of a hole.'

They laughed louder, laughing at me, Blake nearly pissing himself.

'America takes the big hits so the rest of the world can sleep easy, pays for World Peace with our blood and guts,' I said. 'Like Sadam, like Bin Laden, like Korea, all that Arab Spring shit. If we hadn't manned up every time you foreign assholes brought trouble down on your own piss poor heads you would have been bombed back to the Stone Age by now. Why we don't just let you primitive peoples tear each other apart I don't know.'

Blake kept on sniggering until Liu's stern aura killed the laughing gas.

'This is the choice we bring to you,' Liu said. 'I realize that you are not responsible for your infantile prejudice. This is how you have been corrupted. We offer you the opportunity to open your eyes and see the world as it really is.'

I had already seen as pretty much of the world as I ever needed to see. I had seen men, women and children killed in Iraq and Afghanistan. In Turkey and Ireland. On my own streets in Yonkers and New York. Some of them I had killed myself. My eyes were already plenty open.

'You assume that your United States is the Superpower of the modern age, that it defines the modern age,' Liu rambled on. 'You should understand that this power is only a temporary blip on the long march of history. America is a savage and all-consuming power, yes? But it will burn out as quickly as a forest fire. It will burn out because it consists only of raw power, nothing else. It has no culture, no history, no tradition, no roots. It erupted as the bastard child of the dying European Imperialists, and will soon follow them to their incestuous and inevitable destruction.'

Did Blake really buy this crap? It seemed he did, a haze of ecstasy blossomed over his smug face as Liu punched out his lesson. The zeal of the convert, and all that.

'The seeds of America's fall were planted at its very beginning,' Liu said. 'The Imperialist's greed for power and glory. The impossible need for ever increasing resources; conquer and steal, rape and pillage, war and invasion. This way can never become permanent. Can you not see this thing? Your American world could only ever be temporary. This is the choice I offer to you now.'

Maybe it was the cotton wool sleeched through my skull, but I still couldn't make out what their offer was, unless it was the offer to listen to this Commie Red propaganda shit for ever.

'Yeah, sure!' I said. 'The rest of the world got you Chinese dead wrong right from the start, didn't we? Like, China is really the land of the free? All that free speech? Free newspapers, free bloggers, free assholes on twitter? You guys are all free, right? As long as you aren't tempted to think for yourselves. As long as you let the Commie Party rule every single part of your life. Yeah, I guess we Americans have got this freedom thing all wrong. Thanks for putting me straight, guys.'

A formal nod from Liu tossed the ball to Blake.

'We appreciate how difficult this is for you, Con,' Blake said. 'Now, I am by no means a political animal myself but even as a neutral observer I can see there is nothing "free" in the United States. It is a purely transactional society, everything is measured in terms of cost and everything has its price. Even those precious votes that oil your notion of Democracy.'

Blake selling himself as the good guy, the voice of reason, the light at the end of my tunnel.

'We could rename it "The United Corporations of America" and it would be more appropriate,' Blake reasoned. 'China, however, is a five thousand year old civilization. And that's the real difference, Con. China is a civilization. America is a business.'

Blake was pleased with himself, must have thought he was scoring big points with Liu.

'You of all people should know I'm not brainwashing material, Blake,' I said.

'No need,' Liu cut in. 'We give you a choice, you make your own mind up.' Then he rambled on with more of that Chinese civilization crap; people in China are happy, their economic power now matched their cultural riches, the future was theirs. America's power was strictly short term and could survive only so long as the world would tolerate its crushing and greedy intimidation. China nurtured its power through the harmony and respect its people shared with each other, one big happy family, all that shit.

'Which is more legitimate?' Liu posed at me. 'The illusion of your American "Democracy" or the reality of China's natural harmony?'

I knew my answer but didn't have the tools to shank their argument. My head throbbed a little but I was almost out of the smoke. Stall them for a few minutes more and then jump them, take Liu down quick and then tear Blake in half.

'Okay, okay, I get it!' I said. 'So just tell me straight what you want from me here. What's this choice you keep hinting at?'

Liu gave Blake the eye.

'The opportunity to start life afresh,' Blake said. 'The opportunity to finally get an insight into your true potential, to fulfill that radiant dormant promise. The opportunity to find out who you really are, to escape the limits of your default upbringing and to be true to yourself. Isn't that what being free should mean, Con? Can anything else really be freedom?'

Blake was a brilliant speaker; full of inspirational confidence and conviction, his delivery pitched at just the right tone of joyful energy that stopped short of righteous hysteria. Maybe I was brainwash material after all.

'I thought you told me one time that nobody knows who they really are?' I said. 'That me today is different from me yesterday and me tomorrow? Which me is it you're talking about here?'

Blake swallowed hard under Liu's searching gaze; this was good, a stab of uncertainty between the bad cop/bad cop combo, Liu wondering what the hell Blake could have meant by that, Blake anxious in case Liu would doubt his orthodoxy.

'I know who you are,' Blake recovered. 'At least I know the chemical interactions that drive your behavior. And, just in case you anticipate one of your explosive episodes, I have taken the liberty to ensure your brain chemistry is stable right now.'

My turn to be floored, like one of Liu's slaps.

'Just like I switched on your last frenzy,' Blake smirked. 'I hope you enjoyed that fish stew I prepared for you?'

That was a set-up? Yasmin feeding me the dope and Beto leaving the door open? Blake and Liu hovering to observe on the fringes until they had seen enough and flagged Thiago into action with the taser?

'Don't be alarmed, Con,' Blake said. 'You are an extraordinary individual and you ought to be recognized as such. Obviously, the elite classes in the United States haven't recognized you as anything more than an expendable resource; to be exploited, put in danger, to be sacrificed if convenient. Like all your friends and family. You deserve more than that.'

My head was almost back together, enough to know something was still missing, like one of those 3D puzzles my son would conjure up on a screen to rag me, laughing his scornful head off when I stumbled to the threshold of the solution only to be stumped by the last couple of pieces that wouldn't fit. Then he would always take extra delight in shifting and dragging the pieces to fill the gaps and make it whole again. But what if this was as good as it was going to get this time, my mind doctored by Blake so that the limbo was permanent, a gap scraped from my brain that I knew existed but could never prove?

'You deserve a better future, Cornelius,' Blake said. 'And I can promise you will get what you deserve. But you must make the choice.'

Panic started to fester and churn deep down in my gut. I must choose, but maybe they had already cooked my brain juices. What if Blake had it right? And the me today was different from the me of yesterday? Only Blake had fucked me up with some chemical shit to kill off the old me and boot up this new me?

Somewhere deep in my heart I carried a piece of each man I had ever killed, a dozen that I knew of for sure, maybe a few more. I owned that part of them and they existed now only in me, but that meant they owned a corresponding piece of me too, like a parasite tangled through your gut so that you can't be sure where the gut ends and the worm begins. It wasn't something I thought about all the time, but the burden was always within easy reach whenever I felt the need to punish myself. I always guessed it was nature's way of keeping that big wheel of life balanced; like I had aborted the physical being of those guys so I was sentenced to preserve whatever was left when their bodies were totalled.

What if Blake and Liu now owned a piece of me, that gap in my brain, whatever it was, and held it hostage as a marker for this so-called choice they liked to crucify me with? Maybe if Liu slapped his oven-fired hand across my face I would shake their shit out of my head. I swung my feet off the couch and planted my bare soles on the cold tiles, then pushed up and forward. The room cracked and keeled over to my left then ricocheted to the right before bouncing back into a twister that turned me inside out. Liu caught me as I wilted.

'Maknazpy! Stay alert!' Liu boomed into my ear. 'The choice is made. You come to China. You will assist Dr Blake in his research!'

I retched again, this time the red pellet of Yasmin's fish stew spilt out of my throat and splashed on the floor between Liu's shoes.

'Maknazpy! Hear me!' Liu ordered. 'Your father waits for you. You come to China. Your father is waiting!'

I froze, like my skull was about to explode, couldn't breathe, like my heart and lungs and guts would burst through my throat. Then everything started to melt away; Liu and Blake, the walls, the floor, my terror, all slipped away and I was drifting in a long dark tunnel, a bright light at the end, and my father's voice behind the light, calling me. I must have blacked out then, but I heard his voice, and he was waiting.

CHAPTER TWENTY-SEVEN

I blinked my eyes open this time to emerge from the only peaceful slumber I had experienced in years, like I had been released from a long tiresome illness so that I could breathe freely, as if my lungs had been released from a tight metal cage that I hadn't known was lashed around my chest. The bright light from the tunnel still shimmered a faint halo around my face and, for the first time in my memory, I wasn't steeling myself against the bad thing that was always waiting to pounce.

Then Yasmin sponged the warm cloth against my forehead and that fairytale world splintered like all the rest. I was in a different room, a bedroom, wedged into a queen sized mattress on a king sized bed frame. No sheets and no pillow cases, just a shabby goose down cover and a yellowed synthetic-filled pillow. Yasmin sat on the edge, to my right, to wash the vomit from my chin. There was another weight in the bed to my left. I turned my shoulders to see the back of a hunched figure with the cover pulled up to their neck. My hands were free, I could have gripped her neck and choked her, but her slow smooth movements said she knew she was safe. I reached for her shoulder to lever myself into a sitting position, she clasped my elbow and hauled me up. The kid Zheng was lying beside me, tapping hell out of the tablet he cradled under the cover.

'This is Mr Zheng's room,' Yasmin said.

I angled over his shoulder to see what he was typing, he hugged the screen close to his nose and worked his long fingers at a ridiculous speed, rows of little green men being skittled down before they could conquer Zheng's world. I lay back on the pillow and raked my fingers through my scalp, noticed the line of needle marks peppered along my inner arm.

'Looks like this is your room, for your work,' I said.

Yasmin rolled her eyebrows in a 'whatever' gesture and slapped the cloth around my neck.

'Tell Beto he did real good,' I said. 'I mean, I know you are a lying treacherous whore so I wouldn't have fallen for any play you made on your own, but Beto acted his part well, really had me going there for a while, thought I was home and free.'

She mopped the cloth around me some more before dropping it to the floor and squeezing her hands over her face and eyes.

'I am sorry,' she said. 'But you want too much. I live in this real world, I know what is possible for me. Your American world of dreams will not feed my children or keep them safe. I am sorry, but dreams do not come true just because you really, really want them to.'

I took her wrists and pulled her hands away from her face. She shifted her weight to pull away from me but I dragged her back and clasped her wrists tight against my chest and she allowed her face to nest against my neck.

'It is not possible,' she said.

Zheng's tablet trumpeted a fanfare and he punched the air in victory, another galactic tribute to his genius. Yasmin pushed herself up and scooped the cloth off the floor in a swift movement that took her to the door without looking back.

'It is not possible,' she said. 'Try telling this to yourself, Con Maknazpy, it is not possible but life must go on.'

She made to rush out but when she pulled the door open Blake was blocking her way. He stepped back and bowed his head to her like the gentleman he was, then quietly slipped into the space she had just vacated at my side.

'Feeling better now, Con?' he said. I could feel his smug self-righteous confidence, it oozed out of his pores and glowed a protective shell around him. 'I've given you a little something to help you cope with the shock.'

Zheng pulled the cover right over his head to make an isolation capsule for him and his universe. His bony feet strayed against my thigh and he recoiled across the bed as if he had taken ten thousand volts up his ass.

'It's okay, Con,' Blake said. 'Zheng doesn't understand English, we can speak freely now.' Like he wasn't speaking freely in front of Liu? 'As I said earlier, I have absolutely no interest in politics or nationalist sabre rattling shit. I am a scientist, first and last, and my only duty is to progressing science and to doing something useful for all the pathetic quasi-sapient creatures that can just about qualify as human on this little planet of ours. As it turns out right now our work can best be advanced in the People's Republic of China.' Blake wrinkled his nose and pulled back from me, some tincture of vomit had escaped Yasmin's wash down. 'That's just the way it is, Maknazpy, no point in beating ourselves up about it, that's the way it is, as Elvis might say.'

'Elvis?' I said. 'Is he in China too?'

Blake sneered his deep silver nostrils at me, stood up to smooth down his pants, and methodically paced out a figure of eight on the narrow space; one foot placed in front of the other as if he was walking a crazy looped plank.

'I know how you must be feeling about your old man,' he said. 'Truly, I do know, you can trust me on that one for sure.' He stopped his balancing act and swivelled to face me. 'So you really had no idea your father was still alive?'

No, why would I have any ideas about him? He had never figured in my life, except maybe as some sort of ghost that I could only ever see in my own mind when I was in trouble. He was about as much a part of me as that head shaped crater was a part of Zheng's pillow, the clue that somebody had been there once but was now long gone, leaving a scum of hair grease and a yellow ring of sweat.

'Fuck him!' I said. 'If he was on fire I wouldn't piss on him. You want to know what difference it makes to me if he is alive? Exactly zero, that's what.'

Zheng's excited gameplay was irritating me now, I swung my elbow into his back and he squirmed further down the bed.

'Okay, Cornelius, okay,' Blake said. 'Take it easy. You protest too much. You know your father has always been with you, even when he wasn't.'

'What happened to your science head?' I said. 'That crap sounds a lot like mumbo jumbo religious shit to me.'

'Sometimes our science catches up with the crazy hogwash and we find that there was actually something in the mumbo jumbo all along,' Blake said. 'Mostly just co-incidence, of course, but I'm too much of a science head to automatically deny an old wife her tales.'

'What are you telling me?' I said. 'The truth is my psycho episodes are really my father taking over my head?'

Blake ran his index finger along his crescent scar, as if he was still surprised to find such a violent blemish on his urbane features.

'Truth is such a clumsy word,' he said. 'I can't tell you what the truth in your head is. Only you know what it feels like when you experience one of your seizures.'

He looked like he should have been back in the Oyster Bar, sipping fizzy Saratoga water and waiting for his Naked Cowboys to be served.

'All I can do is perform empirical observations of your behavior,' he said. 'At this point I believe it is safe to state that there is a pattern; your father, yourself, your son. With appropriate observation I am confident we will be able to infer a causal connection.'

'What happens then? Will you cure my son?'

'Cure is also a clumsy word,' Blake said. 'However, if we can establish a causal connection then we will hopefully be in the business of prediction.'

'How long before you get a cure?' I said.

He shrugged and combed his fingers through his hair, like he was trying to weed out the silver strands that had appeared since that first time I met him.

'One step at a time, Con, one step at a time,' he said. 'I don't make rash promises, as you know, but I can say this with certainty: the only place we are ever going to secure anything that you might recognize as a cure is in China. I gave it my best shot in the United States but the establishment weren't buying it. It's China or bust.'

Zheng hissed and coiled under the cover. Another cosmic home run. I pictured the tablet rammed down his throat.

'I can't do it, Blake,' I said. 'I can't go live in China. You might strong arm me on to a plane but you won't keep me there.'

'What will it feel like to see your father again?' Blake said.

How would I know? My father had only ever been a shadow, no difference now between my buried memories of a real man and the daydreams I had conjured when I was a lonely kid to fill in the blanks. Now I knew he was never really there at all, just a cold star, all the bright life and light burnt out of him, wasted somewhere else, on somebody else, nothing left for me, a false moon in perpetual orbit out of my reach.

'He still speaks about you, you know,' Blake said. 'He was confronted with a difficult choice but he chose to follow his conscience. His only regret is that he had to leave you behind.'

I thought I had dumped those old images and feelings but Blake's intimate tones somehow stirred them to crank through my head again. Blake didn't create the taste and touch of those emotions, they were always there deep in my chest waiting to be unzipped back to life, but the needle marks on my arm said Blake had pumped some shit spinning through my veins. I didn't have to believe my old man was still alive, or that he was in China, or even that I was ever more than a minor inconvenience that temporarily messed with his own life. No, I had survived this far by stoking my cold-blooded gift for killing belief and attachment to anything and just about anybody, and I wasn't about to surrender now to whatever feel good cocktail Blake had spiked into me.

'Nobody came out of Vietnam unscathed, Con,' Blake slithered on. 'Your father was only a kid when he went over, eighteen years old. "The War against the Americans to Save the Nation", that's what Mr Charlie called it. That's what your father calls it now.'

Not enough, yeah he had seen some action, but that wasn't enough.

I had been to war, had a comrade's guts splashed across my face, recovered a child's hand from a shit filled drain, killed a man in the desert with my bare hands, slotted others at a distance. None of it made me feel good but no way was any of it enough to turn me into a traitor.

'He stood out even in that charnel house inferno,' Blake said. 'Too good to waste in peace time, they soon had other work for him. Some of those guys were so freaked out by our defeat in Indo-China that they were sure the Communist hordes would soon be marching up Pennsylvania Avenue. They weren't going to let it happen again, not in our backyard. That's why your father ended up in Nicaragua.'

Another flashback, two dark men in our apartment one night drinking beer and smoking strong cigarettes. My father chasing me back to bed when I went to piss and sneak a look at them. All three of them laughing at me, wise cracking in words I didn't understand then laughing even louder because I didn't understand. They could have been jeering at me in any language but I guess I always knew it was Latino.

'If the suits hadn't been so paranoid about the Reds abroad your father might have figured on their radar a little earlier. Nicaragua, Salvador, Honduras, Colombia; they thought the attack dog was on a tight leash. Until a CIA asset inside the Cuban Direccion de Inteligencia nailed him in a photo. Your old man was running a session in the DI's training facility outside Havana, Camp Mantanzas.'

Even if this was all true, even if only a fraction of it, what made Blake think it would be enough to convert me? Did he think I shared some weird genetic mutation that marked me as a turncoat?

'So you are wondering how your father got from Cuba to China, right?'

No, I was wondering what poison Blake had poured into me. I was still a little dizzy, my legs were weak and I had a weird shake going on in my fingers, my eyes couldn't focus properly and my heart pumped like it was going to split in two.

'That old guy you met, that old bum?' Blake arched his eyebrows. 'He told you about Macau, didn't he? The old Portuguese Empire in China? Well, they wanted their part of Africa too, just like all the other European Empire-builders. Modern day Angola was Portuguese territory in Africa until an uprising right here in Lisbon deposed the old Imperialist regime in 1974. Only that's when the real fighting started down there, between rival factions of the liberation movement, you know how that usually goes. Anyway, nobody at home had the stomach for any more Walter Cronkite exposés on how Americans weren't actually invincible after all, and the Soviets didn't want to get bogged down in Africa either, so we each sponsored a war by proxy. White South Africa didn't need any coaxing from us, and the Russians had their willing acolytes. Looked like our side was going to come out victorious too, until the Cubans came down heavy.'

Zheng moved in the bed. We had both forgotten about him and watched now as he slipped across the floor to charge up his gaming tablet from a socket on the other side of the room. Blake stood aside to let him pass, Zheng squinted to check the charging was in progress then smooched back past Blake and into the bed.

'Why did old Luis have to die?' I said. 'He knew nothing about nobody. He was a danger to nobody.'

Blake held his hands out in a gesture of innocence.

'I didn't know anything about that,' he said. 'But sometimes we don't need to know the reason behind things. There are local matters, things we can't begin to understand from our cultural crow's nest. Best not to dwell too long on other people's business, Con, and it is particularly inadvisable to start taking these details too personally.'

'Who did it?' I asked. 'Beto? Did Liu send that fat bastard Beto to nail that old man?'

Blake shrugged. It wasn't his business.

'Do you want to know what happened to your father or not?'

I shrugged to say I didn't much care either way but Blake knew too much about me to buy that one.

'The turning point in Angola happened in '88, the battle for Cuito Cuanavale. South African Defence Forces were all set to finally nail the Angolan army, the Russians had their own problems at home to deal with, it was all over. Then Castro sent in his elite battle groups to whip some South African ass. Your father was there with the Black Wasps, Cuban Navy Seals. You still got his Silver Star in a box somewhere? You can add the Cuban Medal for the Defence of Cuito Cuanavale to his collection, hung around his neck by old Fidel himself.'

I had my own clear memory from 1988. It was August 10th - my tenth birthday, a party in Ferdy's apartment, Mrs McErlane's lavish hospitality, all the neighborhood kids squeezed around the table. Ferdy's father rolled in from work in the middle of it, a few scoops of beer on his way home, started clowning and firing us kids into hyper party mode. Later on, when we were all leaving, he pulled me aside and slipped me $20, told me my dad would be proud of me and it was just a pity the old man couldn't be there, and if I grew up to be half the man my father was, well, then the whole neighborhood would be proud of me too. Mr McErlane still had his soft Armagh brogue and his voice was warm and kind but his words sparked a burning wave of shame that flushed up my neck and face. Mrs McErlane tugged me away from him and kissed me hard on each cheek before ushering me out the door to catch up with my pals. I heard the sharp rebuke she fired at him when we were all outside, and I waited until our gang had moved down McLean Avenue before drifting away on my own. I think that's when I realized my father's infrequent visits home were over for good and he would never be coming back. I didn't even try to hold back the tears, was angry and hurt because I didn't know what I had done wrong, what was so bad about me that made him abandon me without a second thought? I tore up the $20, and beat on two Italian kids that were hanging about outside the apartment, waiting for their dad.

'Why Angola?' I said. 'What's Africa to do with him?'

'Why Viet Nam? Why anywhere?' Blake said. 'Anyway, turned out that Africa had plenty to do with him. Your father was part of a small group of Special Forces Castro left behind when the foreign powers withdrew. The internal struggle between the Angolan power blocs continued right through the nineties, and that's when your father first made contact with Comrade Liu.'

Zheng tensed beside me in the bed at the mention of Liu, pricked a reaction out of him even though the name was drowned in a sea of English.

'Angola is a rich country,' Blake said. 'Only after Libya and Nigeria in terms of African oil production. Then there is timber, coffee, diamonds, all manner of wealth creating resources. The only problem was that thirty years of civil war had left the place on its knees. No infrastructure to speak of; roads, power, schools, hospitals. But the Capitalist monetary system elite were quite prepared to offer loans, of course. Why wouldn't they be with all those natural resources as collateral?'

I could feel Zheng still tapping an imaginary gaming tablet under the bed cover. I was working my fists under the cover too, trying to get some feeling buzzed around my muscles, dredge back the strength I was going to need. I wondered if Zheng could sense my movements just as I could feel his.

'But they fucked up as usual,' Blake rambled. 'The western banks thought they had Angola over the proverbial oil barrel, thought the dumb Third World natives were good for exorbitant interest repayments, financing and refinancing bad debt against the country's future. When the civil war finally ran out of steam Beijing stepped up to the plate; long term loans, low interest, paid in oil. Something like $10 billion invested in actually developing the country, without screwing them for the quick buck payback.'

This sounded familiar, like the rants Ferdy used to launch into about Iraq: we fought the war, sacrificed 4,500 American lives, 30,000 wounded, and puked up $2 Trillion for the privilege. What really lit his fire though was the aftermath. I had to drag him off a guy one night, a bleeding heart Liberal mouthing off that the whole thing was a set up by George W and his Petro-Chemical buddies to get their blood stained mitts on all that Arab black gold. Ferdy nearly twisted the poor guy's head off his neck, had him pinned against the wall screaming into his petrified face that the Chinese were stealing all the Iraqi oil that should have been ours. We had done all the dirty work, taken the hits, slushed our dollars into the desert sand, turned our young men into cold-eyed killers and then left them high and dry when they were tossed back into civilian life. That much Ferdy could take, war was war, but then we had betrayed our fallen comrades by standing by while the Chinese strolled in to clinch their dirty deals with the very Iraqis we had put on their pedestal – fuck it, we had created the pedestal.

'Your father had earned the respect of many in the Angolan leadership by this time,' Blake said. 'He played no small part in creating the environment that enabled Colonel Liu and his Comrades to establish the rewarding commercial and cultural ties that are bringing Angola and China ever closer.'

'And how did he do that?' I said. 'Whack anyone that might get awkward about it?'

Blake rocked a dismissive shake of his head.

'Those days are long behind your father now, Con,' he lectured. 'As they should be for you too. He is a respected figure over there, something he could never have achieved in the United States, no matter what service he volunteered, no matter what sacrifices he made.'

'So where is my respected father, exactly? Where is over there?'

'Where? Why, he is in Macau, didn't I tell you that already?' Blake said. 'He resides in a rather fine apartment on Connaught Road, quite close to the Macau Jockey Club Member's Club House, of which he is an esteemed member and regular patron.'

'You're shitting me here, right?' I said. 'Connaught Road? How do fuck do they say that in Chinese?'

'You can ask your father when you see him,' Blake said. 'He speaks pretty good Cantonese and passable Mandarin, although I think he prefers to conduct his business in Macanese Portuguese.'

'Is it near the docks?' I said.

'Yes, quite convenient to the main ferry terminal. Why?'

I thought of Luis, his knife slicing through his friend's body before Luis slipped him into the harbor water.

'Nothing, it doesn't matter,' I said. 'You won't be able to keep me locked down there forever. I'm nobody's guinea pig, Blake. My old man can play that game if he likes but I am out.'

'Really? Even if it is the only hope for your own son to lead a normal life and thereby avoid the horrific excesses that both you and your father have endured and, indeed, have so often inflicted on others?' Blake said. 'I didn't figure you as being so selfish, Cornelius. You would sacrifice your son's future so readily?'

I hesitated, faltered under Blake's probing eyes, slipped too easily into my inferiority skin. I was about to blab something out when Zheng nudged me with his knee under the bed cover. I thought at first he had just accidentally bumped against me but then he did it again; a definite nudge against my thigh. I clammed up, rubbed my knuckles back and forth across my mouth, kept my eyes on the ceiling and away from Blake.

'I'll not pretend that there is no pressure of time on us all, Cornelius,' Blake said. 'You have seen for yourself that Colonel Liu is eager to proceed and, of course, it would be best for all concerned if we navigated our way out of here before Cora and her colleagues get too close. However, this has been a shock for you. I understand that, certainly I do, and perhaps you need a little more time to reflect on the whole affair. The little sedative I administered to you is still working its way through your system and you will feel much better after another good sleep. I'll leave you to rest now and think things over in peace but, please Cornelius, try to appreciate the bigger picture here. You can do that, can't you? At least consider the benefits to your immediate family? Counter—balanced by the inevitable distasteful consequences if you really find yourself unable to join our exciting venture?'

I nodded to get rid of him and off he went, still wrapped in his bubble of gung ho arrogance. The door thudded closed with a bang and the echo rolled and fizzled away before Zheng pulled the bed cover down and sat up to face me.

'Everything they tell you is a lie.' Zheng's English was almost perfect, accented like any young hustler on the make at a beach party over on the Hamptons. 'They will kill us all, and you will never see your son again.'

CHAPTER TWENTY-EIGHT

This looked like the same Zheng; bamboo-thin, angry red puberty pustules erupting on his neck, lips too thin and tight to stretch over his long gums and twisted teeth. It sure looked like the frantic punk kid who was shitting himself that first time when I charged the room and took them prisoner, who froze in terror when he saw the guard dead and leaking his guts on the stairs. The same puny frame that slumped so pathetically when Yasmin nailed him that time at the Almeida Terrace cliff house when Liu offered himself in sacrifice to set Zheng free. The same hyper fingers that clenched the knife to Yasmin's throat in the beach hut. He looked the same, but this was a different Zheng.

'They do not know I learn English,' he said. 'I exert my ten thousand hours face time on the web and they trust I will not learn English.'

So they took a kid when he was eight years old and pressure formed him to fit the exact tool size they needed. Force fed a strict diet of school, work, submission and obedience, and then more work: okay, most normal folks at home swallow that routine more or less and they figure that's just the standard entrance fee to a no-hassle life in a safe society; you are allocated your slot and you make the best of it without letting the side down. Young Zheng maybe had the extra burden of genius latched around his neck and the 24/7 squeeze was righteous payback for their expectation and his future privilege, but it takes real genius to thrive in that hothouse when you are secretly nurturing the rebel streak that makes you their most feared and hated enemy – the dreamer, with the balls to screw your genius and their system to grab a hold of your own selfish wants and pleasures and never let go.

'I will assist you to get free,' he said. 'You must take me to America also.'

This was the same Zheng, but a different Zheng to the panic kid everyone had always thought he was.

'You must get your strength back quickly. Comrade Blake sedated you with a general non-benzodiazepine hypnotic. You must recover quickly as this does not target your Amygdala hijack response.'

I pictured the discussion between Blake and Liu, with Zheng sitting dumb in the corner.

'The woman,' he said. 'You will use the woman to escape.'

Maybe his English wasn't as good as I figured.

'The assassin Beto will assist us also, but only if you take the woman away.'

Maybe he wasn't such a genius either.

'She is paralyzed with fear,' I said. 'And what makes you think Beto would risk his neck to help her or us?'

'Get up and walk off the effect of the sedative,' he said, and vaulted over my side of the bed to start hammering and shouting at the door. He was screaming away in Chinese and I started to think maybe I should break his neck before he could rustle up Liu and the heavy brigade. 'Hurry! Hurry!' he turned to order me. 'Get ready! They are coming!' I heaved my legs off the bed and steadied myself against the wall. I was weak, but at least the room had stopped spinning and I could more or less walk a straight line. Somebody was outside the door now, Portuguese shouting, Zheng still Chinese shouting. The door opened and Beto's great round skull towered over Zheng as if he was about to snap the kid genius' head off, but Zheng transferred to Portuguese and reeled off a list of instructions to the amiable assassin. Beto rocked back at first, as if Zheng had slapped him, then his face creased with the effort of deep concentration until his big inkhead started to nod, slowly at first, then built up steam to keep rhythm with Zheng's staccato delivery. Zheng finished with a flourish, slapping the bull-like shoulder and pumping a vigorous handshake to seal the deal. Beto slowly looked me up and down before throwing his characteristic winking nod and stepping backwards out into the darkness.

'Be ready! The woman will come now. You must be ready!' This other Zheng said must a lot. 'You must trust me,' he said, bringing into play all his experience of social interaction over the web with the other nerds. I was close enough to claw my hand into his windpipe and pin him to the wall.

'I don't trust you,' I said. 'The first sign that this is a set-up means you get your neck broke, understand?'

His eyes flickered the panic of the original Zheng for a moment, I trapped his swallow against my fingers.

'You must trust me,' he said. 'We have no-one else, only each other. I trust you. You trust me. Or else we die.'

★★★

Beto bundled Yasmin into the room and then lent his broad back against the door, his feet splayed wide apart and thumbs hitched behind his belt buckle. She looked older all of a sudden; limp and exhausted, the lush hair now dull and brittle, orange peel skin rough and scoured across her cheeks.

'This crazy plan is not possible,' she said. 'You think you can trick poor people to believe in you but it is not possible.'

I didn't exactly know how the plan would play right there and then but I did know the defeat in her voice had nothing to do with me. Maybe it started back in the Manguinhos favela in Rio when her mother settled for a pig to replace her father, racked up when her dreams of a medical career fizzled out under the callous neon of Lisbon pick-up joints, scorched deeper in her heart by each succeeding year of hopeless survival by submission. Her eyes were empty and dead but it was nothing to do with me.

Zheng started to drill her in Portuguese until I tapped him and told him to speak English only from here on in.

'You will drive,' he told her. 'Beto will lead us outside and tell you a safe house. You drive. Understand?'

She understood okay but wasn't thrilled about it. She screwed her eyes up to inspect me, as if she might discover in my face even a glimmer of a spark of hope that would permit her to fool herself into dreaming that this crazy plan hadn't already condemned her children to an even more cruel and miserable life. I was all out of pipe dreams myself right there and she seemed to suck some satisfaction out of that.

'I will drive,' Yasmin said. 'We will get my children and I will drive.'

Zheng was about to start mouthing more orders at her until I nudged him and he bowed his head to her and stepped back to let her follow Beto into the corridor. We were upstairs above the casino, four other rooms on this level, the stairway at the far end of this dark corridor. Beto moved quietly on his toes as if he remembered a time before he was a pain machine, when he was a skinny street kid in the favela, maybe nuts about soccer, dreaming himself a yellow and blue God like their famous guy Pelé that used to play for Cosmos in New Jersey. He stopped to press his ear against the second door from the stairway, held his hand up for us to wait, satisfied himself it was safe before waving us forward to the stairs. There was a dim blue light at the bottom, just enough to make out the dark outline of the doorway that led to the outside.

Beto stalled half way down the stairs and nodded for me to go ahead. He slipped a 9mm Heckler & Koch pistol into his hand and held it tight to his right thigh. This was it. I had no reason to trust him, or any of them, but the only way out was to pass him on these stairs. I edged forward, kept my hands low and ready to grab the gun off him, just at his shoulder now, Zheng pushing Yasmin close on my heels, no space, not good, no way I was giving Beto my back, coiled to take him down.

'Pare! Pare, man,' Beto hissed in my ear and clamped his free hand on my shoulder to stop me.

Somebody was moving about down there. The connecting door to the casino kitchen swung open and light spilled up the stairs to almost reach our feet. Laughter and whistling from the chef and pot washers, music flushed out from the casino speakers; Mambo Italiano, but not Dino or Rosemary Clooney this time. At least it sounded like Mambo Italiano until it twisted and curled in on itself before straightening out again into something like the Irish reels and jigs I used to hear in the McErlane apartment. A ripple of dizziness slushed around my head then, and Beto had to throw his arm around me to keep me upright.

'I'm fine,' I said. 'Just Blake's dope working its way out.'

I was close enough to taste his cool sweet breath in my mouth, and to feel the steady beat of his heart and the pure gaze of his eyes.

'Okay man?' Beto whispered, the anxiety fizzing out of his eyes stoked by his knowledge of how they tortured traitors.

A couple of deep breaths and my head steadied, the door ahead was open; two kitchen workers grabbing a midnight smoke, hanging at that blurred edge between looking like they were puffing smoke outside and yet not being so far out as to be soaked by the cold rain. Beto led the way, the workers cut their chatter and parted to let us pass. Two guys in their middle years, worn thin and haggard through hard work and long hours, kept their heads down to let Beto know they were seeing nothing. Beto pointed to a beat up Honda Civic parked close to the wall, Zheng's excitement forced him to break into a run until I growled at him to slow down. Beto caught up with Zheng and grabbed the front of his jacket so that only the kid's toes were scraping the ground. He levered his great tattooed head up against Zheng's brow and dealt a parting threat to the boy genius – it was Portuguese, but I knew it was a threat. He released Zheng with a curse and a shove that bounced the kid off the hood of the Civic. Beto turned to me then, I braced myself for action but he flung his arms around me in a farewell man hug.

'Be lucky amigo,' he sighed into my ear. 'But do not let the devil Princess trap you.'

Yasmin lent against me and gripped my elbow, he slapped me twice on my back and then turned to her. They looked at each other and then looked away, no words between them, she looked down at her shoes and he looked up to the sky above her head. He pulled out the car keys and thrust them into her hand, then swivelled around and strode towards the gates. Zheng got in back and I sat beside her, she waited until Beto had dragged the heavy gates open and we rolled over the rough ground. Yasmin kept her eyes straight ahead when it would have been easier to look at Beto as he held the gate. He shuttled around to my side and signalled for me to lower my window, she kept edging out towards the street, he jogged to keep up.

'Take this luck,' he said, and slapped the 9 mill in my palm like a relay racer passing the baton. She hit the gas and bumped us out into the street.

'Babaca!' she sneered at the rear view mirror. Whatever it was with Beto pumped the fight right back through her veins, let her slip the victim mask, kindle the bitterness and remember who she used to be, or might have been. She seemed a little younger right then; all fierce eyes and angry mouth, quick hands and tossing head. I looked back to see Beto standing rock solid in the middle of the desolate street, hands in pockets, head tilted slightly against the rain, like he was working out what he should have told her when he had the chance. I watched her snatch a last glimpse of him before we turned the corner.

'Babaca,' she whispered to herself.

PART III:
THE ART OF WAR
....

Bravery without forethought causes a man to fight blindly and desperately like a mad bull. Such an opponent must not be encountered with brute force, but may be lured into an ambush and slain.

Sun Tzu (544 BC – 496 BC)

CHAPTER TWENTY-NINE

Yasmin took it nice and steady through the streets, no need for any excitement, no need to attract any attention. Not that anybody looked like they would be interested in us; couples coming home or going out, pods of men bouncing from one bar to the next in expectation, single men out hunting for company, a group of middle-aged women celebrating a wedding or a divorce. This was downtown Lisbon and even on a chill wet February night there were still plenty enough tourists and Lisboetas to party into the early hours, and plenty enough nightspots to be their playground from Baixa and Chiado over to the rocking Bairro Alto.

She even kept her cool when a gaggle of drunken teen boys staggered across the street and made her stomp the brakes. A lifetime as a city driver had robbed her of whatever patience she may once have had but she even smiled politely when one of them, a small meringue-faced punk with red hair and even redder eyes, shouted at her in English, telling the whole street what he would fucking do to her if she fucking got out of the fucking car. An older couple coming down the street paused briefly to register the commotion but then idled along when they realized it was just another binge drinking Brit teen seeking attention.

The couple actually weren't so old themselves, about my age or thereabouts, and dallied along as if they hadn't a care in this world nor had any reason to worry about the next one either. I guessed they had been to a movie or a show and had enjoyed a satisfying meal in one of those funky restaurants in the Bairro, maybe sauntering along now for a drink in their favorite bar if they were locals, or looking for a bar to make their favorite if they were from out of town. I was jealous then, because that should have been me taking a carefree stroll like a normal person with Rose on my arm, or even Yasmin, or even anybody. But it wasn't me and it would never be me again because I couldn't figure on ever nailing down that empty carefree space in my head whether anybody was on my arm or not, not now and not in the future. And that was my burden right there, because how could I knowingly condemn anyone, Rose or Yasmin or whoever, to take my arm when I knew what was gnawing away in my head and what that did to me and would surely do to anybody that I was selfish enough to let get too close to me? The Brit kids targeted a couple of girls coming out of a bar down the street and swept after them, red eyes was sucked along in the riptide. Yasmin dipped a courteous nod as she revved past him. 'Babaca,' I murmured to myself.

★★★

Yasmin lived in the Santos neighborhood but hadn't been home since our incident with the fat cop and his mean machine sidekick. He knew her, and knew he could have tracked her down at the casino but Yasmin assured me that the cops had stayed away. That puzzled me a little, but it could be the casino had bought the privilege to be off limits to prowling cops of his rank. Even when everything is above board in a joint like that, and you can bet it never is, the clientele are apt to get a touch nervous when a uniform appears, and that is bad for everybody's business. It could have been that or maybe the fat guy had too many dirty secrets of his own to risk having Yasmin cornered. Either way, I wasn't prepared to gamble on the fat cop's incompetence or corruption so I told Yasmin to drive right on by her apartment block and to park two streets down.

Yasmin said a friend of hers, an old lady, guarded her kids at night when she was at work. She thought about that for a second and then said that the old lady wasn't her friend: she was a neighbor. She also came from a favela in Rio but had grown old along the Lisbon waterfront. The old woman would not accept any money from her but Yasmin did her little favors in return; like buying the stem ginger chocolate biscuits she enjoyed, always making extra feijoada black bean stew so that the old woman would have a hot meal, or bringing replacement bed linen or household items when she noticed something was worn or broken in the old woman's apartment. But they were not friends: they were neighbors, and this was how neighbors looked after each other.

There was a tiny bar pinned to the corner of the next street. I sent Yasmin over to phone the old woman and tell her to bring the kids out through the narrow alley at the back of the apartment. Yasmin was suspicious, afraid that we would take off and abandon her now that we were out of the casino, but I shoved her out and told her to hurry up. Zheng rotated his head like an owl to watch her go.

'We do not need the woman now,' he said. 'Drive away before she comes back.'

Beto's nine mill was in pristine condition, like it was out-of-the-box new and just begging for me to squeeze it into punchy life.

'Why did she help us? Why Beto?' I said. 'They both know the risk. What's in it for them?'

Zheng shifted back into the corner, uncomfortable with me toying the pistol in his direction.

'It was impossible to escape without using them,' he said. 'Forget about these two, they are not significant.'

I stretched back to tap the barrel off his knee, he recoiled and I could see the anxiety start to swell and churn behind his eyes.

'The woman was easy,' he said. 'I told her that Liu had decided she must come to China also. To be with you. Without her children for ever.'

Me and China without her kids? Yeah, I could see how that would motivate her. Zheng reclaimed some poise, smiled at how clever he was.

'Beto also,' he said. 'I tell him what he likes to hear.'

Turned out Beto liked to hear that Zheng had a handle on where poor Jorginho had stashed his Lebanese cash, that Zheng wanted out of Liu's Chinese paradise so he could grab some harmony of his own and that Zheng would cut Beto in on his action. Sure, that that all sounded fine, no surprises: except I didn't figure Beto to be the trusting type that would believe he would ever see or hear anything of Zheng again. Zheng didn't think so either.

'You do not understand these people,' he said. 'You only see the world through your own eyes. You do not see their feelings, their problems.'

And I needed a Chinese computer geek kid who had lived his blinkered life in a shoe-box to tell me that?

'No, I am not a computer geek,' he said. 'I see problems and I use my intelligence to solve problems. Each type of problem requires the suitable category of intelligence. I have complete access to all categories. You have limited access to only one or two categories. I understood Beto's significant problem and I offered him a solution. If I was a geek you would not be free now.'

I tickled the trigger, wondered if it had ever been squeezed in anger, raked the barrel along Zheng's shin and then screwed it tight against the side of his knee.

'There is an old Chinese proverb,' he said. 'Two women under one roof is war.'

'Here's an old American proverb for you, Zheng, quit talking crap or I'll blow your knee off!'

He swallowed deep like the Adam's Apple was lodged hard in his throat.

'That is Beto's problem,' he said. 'This Yasmin is Thiago's sister. She is the other woman.'

He gave me the look then that said I should know what he was talking about but it just didn't click.

'Now Beto will not share Thiago with her, the older sister always interfering with their lives. She is like his mother. You understand? And Thiago will be in Beto's debt because he saved Yasmin from a life as a slave in China. You understand?'

Yeah, it clicked, now I did understand. I had picked up that there was some sort of buzz between Yasmin and Beto right from the start but I had just put it together the wrong way.

'Beto hopes I shall send him Jorginho's money but he knows I will not,' he said. 'But now he has sent Yasmin out of Thiago's life. That is sufficient. That is his significant problem solved. Yasmin is not sent to China with you. She is not separated from her children. That is sufficient. That is her problem solved.'

'And what do you figure my significant problem is, Zheng? What would be sufficient to solve it, huh?'

He screwed up his nose like my problem was I had dogshit on my shoes, and his eyes bounced from side to side.

'You are on your own,' Zheng said. 'People you thought were friends have betrayed you, so you cannot be sure who is really your friend and who will betray you in future.'

A pretty good analysis.

'And how do you suggest solving that problem,' I said.

He shook his head, and the Adam's Apple wobbled under the tight skin.

'No, this is not your significant problem,' he decided. 'Your problem is something deep in your heart that you cannot escape and cannot control. This is something I do not have a solution for. That makes you unpredictable. And dangerous.'

'Everybody has something deep inside them. That's what makes them who they are,' I said. 'I'm not so different to anybody else.'

'Doctor Blake is convinced you are different in an interesting way,' he said. 'Comrade Liu is interested enough to provide a budget and research facilities.'

'Blake knows shit about me!'

Zheng shifted sideways to ease the pistol away from his knee, as if his slow movement would escape my notice.

'Doctor Blake was sure that you could not resist the urge to see your father, and to make your son's life easier,' Zheng said.

'See? He knows shit!'

'He knows that shit happens in your brain,' he said. 'And Comrade Liu knows that if this shit could be switched on and off when required that China would command some very special soldiers.'

'Yeah, you think so?' I said. 'Let me tell you, Zheng, no soldiers are so special that the Screaming Eagles out of Wyoming couldn't stick a nuclear payload up their ass! Somebody should tell Liu that; doesn't matter how many uniforms you can fill, the United States can always go up another level.'

Zheng twisted that schoolboy smile of his.

'Colonel Liu is sincere when he says that China seeks harmony with the community of nations,' he said. 'And the People's Liberation Army will be too strong to be challenged by foreign powers. There will be no war on an international scale.'

So, what did that mean? I didn't figure on Liu screwing a research budget just to play out Blake's guinea pig theories on his dime.

'China is changing,' Zheng said. 'There are still too many people living in the wrong places. This is wasteful, these people are not productive. China requires a growth rate of 7% - every year. These people will be more productive when the leaders move 250 million citizens to the correct places over the next ten or twenty years.'

He cracked that smug smile even wider, like he had forgotten what it felt like to have my fingers biting his throat.

'The People's Liberation Army will require a band of special soldiers to maintain harmony. In Hong Kong and other problem areas,' Zheng said. 'These are the special soldiers that Comrade Liu and his superiors will need to switch on and off when the time comes.'

I got it, they would need the type of soldiers who could rough ride over civilians without getting hung up on civil rights and all that shit. The type who could take an order. The type who didn't see people as people, just as a problem to be contained or neutralized. And 250 million people would bring a lot of problems. Especially when they are people who look like you, speak like you, think like you; they might even be you.

'Doctor Blake says you have the correct qualities,' he said. 'But you are still a wild thing, you cannot be controlled. He believes he can harness your great gift but create predictability. Special soldiers who can be switched on and off.'

'I thought you Chinese were already all brain washed,' I said.

'Brain washed? The Chinese people are too intelligent to be brain washed.' He looked genuinely surprised. 'Perhaps you are thinking of the Democratic People's Republic of Korea.'

'Is that north or south?' I said.

He made the sort of throat rumble that Liu would make: if he had spit in the car I might have shot him right there.

A shout jerked both our heads around to see Yasmin striding across the street, an old guy picking himself up off his knees outside the bar. She broke into a shuffled half run as she got closer, pulling the emerald dress up with one hand, clasping the anorak close to her chest with the other.

'We do not need the woman now,' Zheng said.

'You don't understand real people as much as you think you do, kid, but don't worry about it.' I tapped his knee with the gun metal for emphasis. 'I said I would take her to safety, didn't I?'

Zheng shrugged his shoulders up to his ears and twitched a sharp shake of his head, an image of young Con flashed through my head. He clicked his tongue and murmured something in Chinese, sounded like Con telling himself that I was indeed an asshole, just loud enough for me to hear him but quiet enough for me to pretend I hadn't heard. Yeah, so Zheng was a genius but he couldn't compute why I didn't just drive off and leave her and I wouldn't waste my breath explaining it to him because this kid was all take and no give - there was no way he could have had any idea what it meant to commit yourself to someone, especially when that someone had no commitment to you. But that was his problem, I said I would get her out of there and that's what I was going to do.

Anyway, I did need her. I was on the run in this strange city with no backup and no contacts. Colonel Liu might have cut his losses if it had only been about me but there was no way he was letting me walk off with Zheng as a trophy. The house with the dead Chinese guards would have been left clinically clean, Liu wouldn't leave any traces behind him, but it was only a matter of time or bad luck before the Portuguese police braced me for the butchery of old Luis, and I wasn't about to bet everything on Cora still being straight. No, if I was going to get myself out of there I would need somebody and Yasmin was all I had right then, and the fact that she didn't expect there to be any trust between us was fine too.

'Sometimes you've got to put yourself out there for other people, kid, even when there is no payback on offer. That's what makes us human,' I said. 'Otherwise we would be just like your computers, you know?'

Zheng whipped up a neckful of mucus and poked his head out to spit on the sidewalk, my finger twitched against the trigger but I snatched the pistol away and stowed it under my seat. I reached over and opened the driver's door for her. Yasmin jumped in and dragged a plume of sweet fresh air with her.

'You only bring trouble!' she blurted out. 'The policia are waiting outside my apartment. My life here is over.'

'Stop being a victim, Yasmin,' I said. 'Take your life in your own hands and make something happen yourself.'

'Fuck your white north American ass!' she shrieked.

Zheng cupped his hands over his mouth and nose in a half-assed attempt to stifle his snigger.

'You make something happen!' she shouted. 'You get us into the United States embassy or else I will tell the police all I know!'

'We aren't going to the embassy,' I said.

Now she clamped her hands over her face and Zheng quit his snickering.

'You'll be safe with me, don't worry about it,' I said. 'But I don't know what's waiting for us right now at the embassy. Like I said, it's time to stop being a victim.'

CHAPTER THIRTY

Yasmin hauled Zheng out of the back seat before dragging her kids in and mantling them under her jacket so that they were hidden except for two pairs of tired and anxious eyes. The little girl looked as if she was about ten years old, she struggled to press her mouth closer to her mother's ear and whispered an urgent demand. Yasmin shooshed her but the kid ignored it and revved up her complaint as if Zheng and I weren't there. Yasmin barked sharply at the girl but that only converted the complaint into a crying whinge. I took the driver's seat and Zheng slipped in beside me with his palms pressed tight against his ears. I was about to move off when the old woman shuffled to the window and thrust a few Euro notes and a religious medal on a thin chain towards Yasmin. The little girl snatched the silver medal to kiss it to her lips and her whimpering turned to whispered prayers. I pulled the car away from the sidewalk and we left the old woman making the sign of the cross after us.

I twisted the rear view mirror to get a better look at the street behind us. Nothing unusual so far: the two guys that the old woman had made as cops outside the apartment had disappeared; maybe bumming a late drink in a cop-friendly bar or shoving their faces with fried chicken in that joint down the street. I angled the mirror a little more so that I could keep one eye on Yasmin. She didn't notice or didn't care, flopped back in the seat with her head rolling from side to side, the kids secure under her wings.

But this was a different Yasmin. Still wearing the emerald sheath dress and the jangling jade earrings, but this was a different woman to the haughty empress rocking to the attention she demanded on the casino floor. She was exhausted and defeated, just about keeping it together to shield the little girl and the boy, who looked to be about twelve. This was a different Yasmin to the one I had fixed on bringing back home with me, maybe seeing how things would go. I knew now how things would go; she would be sucked dry by the wants and needs of these two vampire kids, slapping her way around Walmart and eating herself up from the inside because she wasn't a good enough mom, hoping they would turn out good but waiting for them to go bad, afraid to look them in the eye in case they saw her shame and disappointment. And, in the end, it would always be my fault. Everything that had screwed up her dreams would be my fault because I would be the only one still around. She hadn't graduated as a medical doctor, hadn't set up a clinic back in the favela, hadn't made a difference in her world. She had been raped and beaten, then exiled from everything she knew only to be raped and beaten some more. And when things turned sour in New York all that would be noosed around my neck. Just right there

I could see clearly that if this was a different Yasmin it was probably the real one, or as real as I was ever going to find in my lap.

The boy wriggled out of her clinging arm and reached forward to turn the mirror away from her. He hit me with a hate filled stare for a second before sitting back and snuggling under her anorak again. Yeah, I had a different Yasmin on my hands now, but the aggro in this boy's eyes was of the very same deep and pure hatred that his uncle Thiago carried so easily. I imagined Thiago back in Rio, working that stare before he sliced through the pig-man, the one who bought their mother with drink and stole Yasmin with his pig violence. And if the boy was the young Thiago in my eyes then I was surely the pig-man in his.

'What's your name, son?' I called in to him.

Yasmin jerked upright and pulled him closer to her breast.

'You do not need to know his name. You will never know him and he will never know you,' she said.

He was only a boy but I knew he was never going to be anybody's victim, and I would have to be careful around him, right then and for however long I was in her shadow.

'Sure, whatever you say,' I said. 'I'll just call him Little Thiago, okay?'

I could feel two pairs of furious eyes burning into the back of my head, and the little girl panting her innocent prayers.

★★★

Yasmin directed me towards Martim Moniz square; she knew two sisters who were working their way on a luxury yacht in the Caribbean and their mother hung out in a bar over there, with the key to their vacant apartment at her disposal. I pulled up on a corner outside a farmacia, opposite the Metro station, and told her to just get the key without any chit-chat, no mention of me and no mention of anything. She kicked up a fuss about leaving her kids with us as she went off to get the key but I told her to think of it as an incentive to hurry back.

We needed someplace to lie low for a while but I didn't much like this set-up. The working girls' mother knew where we would be should anybody ask her, or pay her, but I didn't have a second option. There wasn't a second seat in the milking shed, as Ferdy's old man used to say. Yasmin came back after a long twenty minutes with the key and 300 Euro notes that the working mother had insisted she take. That was a good sign, but this was still a weak link I didn't need.

I threaded the car though the tangled weave of narrow lanes until

Yasmin called stop and pointed to a set of steps squeezed into the thin gap between two houses. Just about wide enough for two people to pass, with a handrail running up the middle to help the old people conquer the steep gradient. Up twenty steps to a small rectangular space and then maybe ten or twelve more steps until the alleyway ended at a small archway which led to the street above. The apartment sat just above the flat rectangular space. The exterior was grim, all flaking paint and crumbling plasterwork, and I had to heave my shoulder against the swollen door to get into the hallway. Six post boxes on the wall, four strollers pitched under the stairway and the lingering scent of boiled vegetables – we weren't on our own.

Yasmin shuffled her kids up to the second floor in front of her and had the door open before Zheng and I caught up. Her daughter whooped with excitement: the gleaming white marble floors and walls inlaid with neat purple and black scrolled details, black leather and shining chrome furniture that looked like nobody had ever sat their cute ass on it, two oblong purple glass mirrored tables with matching heavy crystal draped with silk purple blooms. This must have looked like a wonderland princess' palace to the little girl. The Little Thiago wasn't impressed; he seethed quietly at his mother's elbow, arms folded and eyes smouldering.

I pulled the phone off the wall and kicked the socket to bits.

'Let's go, Yasmin,' I said. 'Bring your son. We have things to do.'

She started to resist until I held her wrist and pulled her close.

'Your daughter will be safer here with Zheng but that boy will only be safe if you keep him close and under control.'

★★★

Martim Moniz had a rougher edge when Yasmin first landed in Lisbon. She was installed in a filthy basement across from the Metro station, and whipped and raped until they judged she was broken and tame enough to parade the northern edge of the square.

'Thiago and the other Brasilian boys came later and cleaned this place up,' she said. 'Now tourists can walk here in safety without being robbed or hassled by whores and drug pushers.'

That Thiago was a real law abiding citizen and paid up humanitarian, the way her voice glowed his name.

Largo Martim Moniz isn't so much a square as a long rectangle, about the size of one of their soccer pitches, I guessed. A paved area with seats and street furniture, with a narrow ribbon of trees and shrubs as a boundary between the sidewalk and the open space. A nice place for a picnic in the summer maybe, and during the day; just not in the dark hours of a Lisbon working night. I followed a truck as it hissed and bumped its way around; three lanes of traffic, sometimes more when somebody got impatient with the driver in front. It was after 2 a.m. and the night time economy was in full flow, two or three guys posed to smoke at the steps that poked through the trees into the square every twenty meters or so, other shadows meandering across the paved area behind the thicket of shrubs; sometimes single figures, sometimes two or three and in a hurry, like time is money. I circled again, then pulled up at the parking space beside the farmacia where we had waited on Yasmin earlier.

'Tell those three guys we don't want to see this car again,' I said, and palmed the key to her. She gave me that funny look again. 'We need to ditch this car,' I said. They were high on something, maybe glue in the blue plastic bag the big one had clamped around his mouth and nose. The small one stood to take the key off her but then staggered sideways into the green recycling bin that looked like it had taken root in the empty space beside the stairs down to the Metro. Yasmin towered over the fat one and slapped the car key into his dirt ingrained palm. I looked back as we turned into Rua Palma, the three high boys were doing a Laurel and Hardy routine to get themselves into the car. I didn't expect Liu to have officially reported Beto's car to the police as being missing, but he would probably pay a few bucks on the quiet to find out where it was in the hope we would still be in it. He would draw a blank with those three.

Up Rua Palma now, back to the bar where Yasmin had found her generous friend. Another wide avenue, two lanes each way, separated by a pavement dotted with spindly trees. The Little Thiago had been simmering all night and wasn't about to calm down anytime soon. I kept a firm grip on his wrist, Yasmin cajoled him along with her arm around his neck, leaning into him to kiss the top of his head and stroke his face as we bundled him along. The bar was on the left hand side, it looked from the outside like it might be closed for the night but she laughed at me and said it would never close as long as men had money and men would always have money as long as Bar Trocadero was open. Another couple of bars were further up on the other side of the avenue.

'Two things you have to do now, Yasmin,' I said. 'Just two things and your kids will be safe. You do this and I'll take care of everything else, okay? You will never have to worry about your children again, understand?'

The boy twisted to get free from me but I held tight, she took his face in both her hands and whispered something into his ear, he pushed her away with his free hand but gave up his struggle for now.

'Go in there and make a call to the United States Embassy. Ask for Miss Cora Oneale. They'll say they never heard of her, right? You tell them the Chief of Mission in there knows her. Tell them to give Cora Oneale a message from Con Maknazpy. Tell her to call Con Maknazpy at the Trocadero Bar straight away. Tell them Maknazpy will be there for fifteen minutes, if Cora Oneale doesn't call in that time, Maknazpy disappears, okay?'

'She is the one you spoke to before,' Yasmin said. 'You do not trust her, so why do you think she will help us now?'

'Just do it, Yasmin. I have it covered. Cora will do whatever I tell her to because she has no choice. That's how this thing works, you can make people do whatever you want when they have no other choice. You understand that, don't you?'

'What else, Maknazpy? What is the other thing?'

'Get a cell phone off your friend. Then get a contact number for the Russian big shot around here. I figure your friend in there will know him, or know how to get his number. A Russian guy called Yakov, okay? Yakov, the Russian big guy in Lisbon.'

His name hit a nerve. Her black eyes widened and her voice quivered.

'Yakov? That filth? Why does an American call him?'

'It's like I said, Yasmin,' I tried what I hoped sounded like a soothing tone. 'That's how I make sure Cora has no other choice. Trust me on this one. I've got this thing all worked out. You and your kids are home and dry already, okay?'

'I hope you are smarter than you look, Con Maknazpy!' she said. 'This Yakov is a Russian wolf, you look like a dumb North American sheep!'

She pressed her mouth to the Little Thiago's face and drilled her orders into his head, shook her hair down her back, shot a look of pity or despair at me, then marched into the Trocadero, her head high, her shoulders straight. The kid said something to himself, like a curse at her for getting them into this mess.

'Don't worry, son,' I said. 'Everybody thinks I'm dumb, but I'm still here, still on my feet. We'll be okay, you'll see.'

He growled a Brasilian curse at me, sounded a lot like his mom.

CHAPTER THIRTY-ONE

The first bar was closed, although I could hear the drinking voices inside. The second one was also closed, but I hammered at the door until a balloon shaped man opened it. He looked me up and down, glanced at the kid and shrugged at me as he pulled the door wide and bowed with a flourish. 'Bar Rio welcomes you, Senhores!' The sight of an American man bringing a young Portuguese boy into a bar like that at that time of night raised a few wisecrack comments and quizzical looks amongst the dozen or so men at the bar, but they soon settled down and continued their animated soccer talk and easy drinking.

Yasmin was in the Trocadero a lot longer than I had expected, maybe twenty minutes before she appeared back under the streetlights. The balloon man protested when I opened the door and whistled to her, but seemed a little more relaxed about the whole thing when Yasmin breezed in to embrace the kid as only a mother would. I had the idea that he recognized her; and he sure wasn't fazed when she rejected the brandy label he was about to pour, quickly replacing that bottle on the counter and stepping up on a crate of cola so he could reach above to a bottle on the high shelf. 'Aguardente Velha Reserva', the label said. She scooped up the glass before the ice had finished tumbling and jerked it down her throat. Balloon man hovered, ready to pour again. The kid reached out to steady her wrist before she could knock the second drink back. Yasmin squeezed her eyes tight and drew a deep breath, then threw her head back to whistle out the tension. The kid took her elbow and guided her back to the table beside the door. The barman twisted his ball head into a grimace, like he was passing judgement on me or her, then turned away to re-enter the soccer debate.

'You were wrong!' She spit it at me like she had lost the family fortune on a slow horse I had tipped. 'Your Cora Oneale was there, she spoke to me straight away!' Yasmin was a little too loud, too strident. Her son stroked the back of her neck and whispered in her ear. She shrugged him off but the pulse at her right temple twitched like the skin was about to burst open and her trembling fingers rattled the ice in her glass.

'You gave Cora the message?' I said.

'Yes! Yes! I gave her the message.' She sucked the glass dry and motioned for the boy to get a refill. 'Your Cora said you are in trouble, big trouble. She said if I cared about you then I must help her.'

'Help her what?' I said.

'How would I know? I told her you mean nothing to me. Why would

I care about you? It is not my business to care.'

'But you gave her the message? You told Cora to phone the Trocadero?'

'Yes! I fucking told her!'

'What about Yakov? Did you get a number for him?'

She pulled out a cellphone and slapped it into my hand.

'I do everything you tell me!' Her plump tear burst over my wrist. 'I do everything and still you do nothing for me! You will slip away and leave us here to be eaten by these dogs! I knew this would happen!'

'I didn't tell you to drink too much, did I?' I said. 'How many drinks did you knock back in the Trocadero?'

She launched forward as if about to slap me but the kid appeared at her side and pushed her back into her seat. She swung around to grab the next brandy off him then cursed when she realized it was one of their blow your head off coffees that he thrust into her hand. She started to twist away but he held her elbow and cajoled her into taking a sip. She relented, and rested the edge of the cup against her lips as she funnelled the rich aroma through her nostrils. The kid rubbed her back, keeping his eyes locked on mine the whole time. I thought that maybe he was reaching out to me, hoped I would help him to help his mom. Or maybe the little prick was giving me the evil eye because he figured this was all my fault.

The new cellphone shivered into life, the screen flashing and shaking out Barry Manilow's Copacabana. I pressed it to my ear and huddled into the corner, beside the window and as far from the TV as I could go.

'Pindos do not talk about me in bars.'

This voice was a weapon, a swinging club with nails driven through the business end, the sort of voice that caused pants to be pissed.

'Just shut the fuck up and listen, asshole!' I said. 'I've got business with your boss in New York, okay? If you can't handle it then get to fuck off this phone and send me somebody who can.'

Silence then, except for the rattle in his throat, too much vodka and bad cigarettes.

'You think that little shit Moscow Alex is MY boss?' he tried to laugh. 'I'll rip his balls off and push them down his throat the next time I see the little American whore.'

Crap, that was all I needed, to be shanked on an ego trip between two macho Ivans. Still, this Yakov guy must have felt pretty comfortable with his own set up if he didn't mind bouncing Alex's name over the phone network.

'Whatever, man,' I said. 'Are you going to work with me on this thing or not?'

'Jorginho is with you now?' he asked.

'So, you've been talking to Alex, huh? Well yeah, I have Jorginho, and he is staying planked somewhere safe until I get some other business taken care of,' I said.

'Yes, this Chinese business, too spicy for you?' he rattled that laugh thing again. Yakov was still rasping in my ear when I scoped the first automobile glide past the Trocadero: an Audi SUV with blacked out windows driving slowly, but not too slowly, down the wide avenue, the driver just nipping the brakes as they floated past the Trocadero.

'That's right, Yakov,' I said. 'So can you handle this thing, or are you all mouth and no trousers like Moscow Alex says you are?' He stopped breathing in my ear, probably working that one out. 'I need a house; nice and quiet, no neighbors, no cops, no Russians: just a house, with a clean computer and a good web connection.'

'I know what you need,' he drawled. 'Where are you now?'

The second car rolled into view, another Audi SUV, coming up the avenue, past the Trocadero, slowed down, pulled in, right outside this window. I squeezed my face against the window, the first Audi was parked down below the Troc.

'We need a seven seater, food and accommodation for three adults and two kids. The number you're calling me from is withheld; text me a number to call you back on. Have a car ready in half an hour, wait in Largo Graca until I call.'

'Hmm, we have a problem,' he said. 'You like giving orders, I do not like taking orders.'

The third Audi flicked its headlights as it stopped outside the Trocadero.

'See you later, Yakov.'

'Yes, I will see you and the problem later,' he rumbled. 'But before you go, Mr All American Big Shot, you know Moscow Alex has never set foot in Moscow? Or any square centimeter of Russia?'

'Yeah? So what about it?'

'Oh, nothing, nothing,' Yakov mused. 'Except that he is a CIA apparatchik, you know that, don't you? Just like his dirty father before him.'

Yakov killed his cellphone. Yasmin was on her feet beside me now, coiled a hand around my neck and nuzzled against my cheek.

'I am sorry,' she whispered. 'I do what you say. I will make you happy.'

Her body trembled a sweet brew of perfume and brandy. The boy avoided my eyes, lowered his head and stared at his feet. This was another stab into his pride that he would store away to stoke his anger in the future. The jade earring scraped against the stubble of my unshaven chin. She had told me before, that time on the clifftop Almeida Terrace, that I shared Jorginho's flaw; too special to allow happiness. This wasn't the time to remind her.

'Don't worry about Yakov,' I said. 'And don't worry about making me happy, your children will be safe.'

I nodded to the kid, he unwrapped her from me and edged his mom to the seat. The balloon barman pretended to smear a dirty rag across an already clean table top behind me. I stepped around him to see out the window. The shadows inside the Audis emerged on to the sidewalk, clustered outside the Trocadero for a moment before filtering in. I flicked through the cellphone contacts until I found the Troc's number. The balloon man could fake his work no longer, and had to move away. I got the ringing tone and pressed into the corner again. A Portuguese voice answered, I told her to get me the American woman with the blond hair; background music and chatter, glasses clinking, a waiter whistling.

'Maknazpy! Where to fuck are you, you asshole!' Cora's brittle membrane was torn. 'You are coming in right now, understand!'

The tension in her voice knocked a chuckle out of me but this wasn't funny. It was like those times when Ferdy would giggle as he spoofed some girl in a bar that his name was Jimmy McCracken; I echoed his laugh without knowing why.

'McErlane didn't make it, Con,' her voice seared through my skull. 'Ferdia McErlane is dead and you are out there right now fucking about with your new girlfriend!' I felt myself shrinking; my whole being spinning and scrolling like a corkscrew right down into the deepest knot of my gut, my senses drained out of my brain like juice squeezed from a lemon, my skull a black vacuum, a hollow silence. And then I heard myself chuckling, louder now, bulging into a full blooded cackle.

'Maknazpy!' Cora was screaming in my ear. 'Did you hear what I just said? Ferdia McErlane is dead! You fucking went off and left him and now he is dead!'

I heard my laugh but it wasn't me, as if I was standing over there at the bar with the balloon listening to the other me laughing over here.

'Con! Talk to me here!' Cora's screech bounced around the numb space between my ears. 'You have got to come in right now! If Liu gets to you before I do the war is over, you understand? There won't be another chance. Where are you?'

A veil of clammy sweat seeped onto my brow and sluiced down my head to sting my eyes in a salty pickle. Cora prattled on but it was like her voice and her message were isolated in a panic room on the edge of my brain. The bar was silent, like they were all straining to hear the drama on a misfiring radio. Cora was drifting away from me now, her words as lightweight as a cold sales pitch or a wrong number, but these frozen faces before me had caught the whiff of death in the air around me and each one would hold their breath until it was confirmed that the honor of the death sentence had passed them by this time, again, and that none of them had landed the leading role.

'Cora, what about our arrangement?' I said. 'Has Gallogly's attorney got that guarantee of my immunity yet? Or the signed document that promises this woman and her kids will be taken care of?'

I heard Cora gasp, and then she was silent for ten seconds as she pulled herself back on track.

'Con, listen to me good, okay?' she said. 'You have to come in. This thing is too big for you! You are way over your head. Please, Con, please! You are in no position to force anyone into any agreement. You have no cards left to deal!'

'I've still got Jorginho, Cora. Gorgeous George Oliver, you want him back, don't you? Or should I hand him back to Colonel Liu and your friend Blake? How do you like them cards, huh, Cora?'

Cora was back in the saddle now, firing on all cylinders.

'What about your wife and son?' she implored. 'Can you forget Rose and your own son as easily as you seem to be dismissing Ferdia? Don't you care anymore if they are in danger? Are you so blinded by your new whore?'

She wouldn't understand: I wasn't going there.

'I don't think Rose and young Con ever were in danger, Cora. I think Moscow Alex had his orders, in line with you and all the rest. Just tell Gallogly to take Rose and young Con home now, okay? Their holiday is over, and he can't afford to miss anymore school.'

'I don't know what you are talking about, Maknazpy!' she said. 'If you know where Alex is holding Gallogly and your family why don't you say so? We'll have a team on it straight away.'

'They are your team, Cora. Or somebody's team. Just forget that crap and send them home. We have moved on now, and that shit doesn't wash anymore, okay?'

'Fuck you, Maknazpy! You are deranged right now, maybe you're in shock, I don't know, but I can tell you this – come in now or you will be dead before daybreak!'

I left her hanging there; only her half panted breathing in my ear, her heavies must have cleared the Trocadero.

'Con! Con fucking Maknazpy! Are you hearing me? Well hear this good, you son of a bitch! We have a wire on the Chinese. Liu has drafted in a team of their Falcons from Guangzhou. That's their Navy Seals, Maknazpy, and they aren't risking putting them on European soil unless it's a winner takes all deal, understand? They are already here. They are on your tail right now. They will eliminate you and George and everybody with you before daybreak. You are on your own out there. You have no chance against these people. Come in now and I'll do what I can for the woman, okay?'

I let her stew in the silent space between us, could almost taste her juiced tension on my tongue, feel her white knuckles strangling the other end of the line.

'I'll bring Jorginho in when I'm ready. A couple of days, no more than a week. You will have the arrangements ready, Cora, right?'

'You have lost it, Maknazpy,' she said it sadly.

'Just one thing, Cora. Is it true? About Ferdia? Don't bullshit me now, you know it won't make any difference.'

She sighed, a hard swallow like she was about to switch back to her work voice but then a sob escaped, a strangled moan from deep in her throat. She put the phone down.

They piled out of the Trocadero. Cora must have been the small figure in the middle of the black huddle of big men. The driver of the SUV outside this window stepped on to the pavement, looked around, then jumped back in and revved the Audi down to meet them.

Yasmin was about ready to freak out entirely. Balloon man gave me a dirty look as if he was entitled to an explanation of what the hell was going on in his bar and would call the cops if I he didn't get one.

'Give her a brandy, and hurry up about it,' I said. 'Then we are going out your back door and we were never in here, right?'

He thought about it for a second, then swung around to dash a brandy into a glass for her and bounced his eyes towards the back door for me. He had all the explanation he needed.

CHAPTER THIRTY-TWO

I sandbagged my mind against any thought of Ferdy, and homed in on Yasmin's stomp as we crisscrossed through dark lanes and back alleyways until we emerged at the sweeping crescent of Calcada do Monte; up that and Largo da Graça was a short walk down to the right. I pulled the cellphone and texted Yakov. A car passed by, then slowed down and stopped before the driver wrestled the headlights around to come back behind us. We were almost at Graça, I hauled Yasmin and the boy over to the ATM at the Banco Popular. We huddled around as if I was pulling out some cash, I cradled Beto's nine mill, the car slowed before turning left into Largo da Graça and disappearing. Probably nothing. The cellphone rattled in my pocket. Yasmin gripped my elbow.

'Yakov is an animal,' she said. 'Let us go to your Cora Oneale.'

I told her Yakov would be no problem. I told her to relax. I told her I had it covered. She wasn't listening, and I could taste the sick fear twisting through her gut and churning itself into a thick knot in her throat. This strong woman had been through hell and back since she was a kid, surviving the worst that the men who infested her life could throw at her, scratching and clawing her way out of one hellhole to another until she had risen above that scum to create some sort of normal life for her own kids. I knew that, so I knew Yasmin didn't scare easy, but the dread in her eyes reminded me of warriors I had known who would look death in the face and spit in its eye but who had fallen apart when confronted with that inhuman thing, call it evil or the devil or whatever, that thing we can't fight because we don't know what it is and we are afraid we might find out. I could feel her fear in the grip she screwed into my elbow, and it amplified the menace of the voice that crackled in my ear to say the car was waiting down beside the tram stop.

I knew where that was, right in front of the Pastelaria Estrela da Graça, where I had sat with Ferdy drinking coffee and eating custard tarts, listening to that grumpy old guy sing Luis' 'Barca Negro', waiting for Blake and Cora to really suck me into this shitstorm. If only we had finished our coffee and walked into the nearest Policia station we would probably be back home already. Ferdy would still be alive. This was my first 'if only', and it marked the start of my sentence to suck up all the Ferdy 'if onlys' that would hit me every day for the rest of my life. If only I had nailed that Chinese guard before he threw that fucking cleaver. If only I had taken him to the emergency room straight away. If only we had stayed at home. Yasmin's fear of Yakov was only the fear of an evil that might never happen. My evil had already happened, bouncing off me as usual to catch somebody close to me, only this time I had blinked my evil eye to catch the one closest of all. The black thunder started to pulse and throb through my brain but the hard grip of the nine mill was a comfort, like the smooth pebble Rosary Beads I used to play with when I was a kid, promising that deferred gratification that meant I could suck up this shit that choked me. This Yakov would be no problem.

★★★

The Hiace jerked against the sidewalk, side door open, a hand waving us in. I pulled back, needed to see who was in there. The Russian bark was enough, took off almost before we had piled in. Two granite fighting men juiced for action; the driver chewing gum, his partner sucking on a cigarette and pluming a no-breathe zone above our heads. Yasmin steered him back towards the apartment; too heavy on the gas, then stomping on the brake to scrape around the tight corners, his gum jaw synched to the frantic pedal action.

I was lost, corkscrewed into enough twists and tilts to scramble the direction in my head, started to think we were headed towards the waterfront but Yasmin read the confusion on my face and smoothed it away with a stroke of her soft palm. And then one sharp plunge through a gap that snapped the wing mirrors and we were back at the steps leading up to the apartment. The kid had the door half open when the driver shouted and kicked us forward again, the smoker yanked the boy in by his hair, Yasmin screamed, I saw the lights coming fast behind us and dragged the kid close to her.

We banged our way back through the too tight lane, slapped against the wall and shuddered on, the lights right behind us now. Smoking Ivan held two fingers up. 'Three cars,' he drawled. He was calm, like we were being pulled up for a parking violation. 'They want you back, big time.' The steep lane was a launching pad into the street above, we hit lift off for a second before the Hiace flopped back down on the smooth cobbles, the driver rammed into reverse and wedged the back end into the lane at an angle. The lights were right there, right in our faces, the boy pinned like a rabbit until Smoking Ivan grabbed his collar and pushed him into the front beside the driver. The only way out was through the front doors, Yasmin scrambled over and was running before I stumbled out after them.

The black Audi SUV locked its fender against the van to force a way clear but it was jammed tight and their tyres squealed and burnt until the two Ivans stepped in front of our van and cracked a few pistol shots through the front window so that the glass on the back doors exploded in a crystal shower across the hood of the Audi. The Ivans laughed, and trotted behind me, catching up with Yasmin and the kid before they reached the steps down to the apartment. Smoking Ivan periscoped his head around the corner, the driver reported into his phone, I huddled Yasmin and her kid close into a doorway.

'Go! Quick!' Smoking Ivan pushed Yasmin down the steps. She struggled with the lock, then fell through the door and screamed to her daughter. We waited outside the apartment, crouched on the small platform between the steps leading up and down. I pulled the pistol and held it down in front of me in a two handed grip, the driver saw it and nodded to Smoking Ivan; they both looked me up and down and then shrugged as if it was no problem, for now. Yasmin was in there too long; we were strung out here in this steep rat tunnel braced for the fire fight that Cora's people would ignite when they tried to take us. Smoking Ivan said something in Portuguese and ruffled Little Thiago's hair, making like he was so relaxed he could indulge in casual banter. The kid smacked Ivan's hand away and the big Russian snarled when he saw that poked a chuckle out of me. We both knew this wasn't the time to make anything of it but there was just something about the way he handled the kid I didn't like. The driver spread his free hand across Smoking Ivan's chest and gestured up the steps with his pistol, telling him to wise up and mind his business, but that didn't help; Ivan strained against the hand and tilted his head back to assert his alpha rights through his Russian eagle eyebrows. I didn't like that either, so stepped up to him, eyeball to eyeball. The kid got between us as well, but the spell was only broken when Yasmin came screaming down the stairs into the hallway, dragging the sobbing girl along by her wrist.

Zheng trailed after them, he had been asleep; hair spiked up the back of his head, laces undone, struggling to get his arm into his jacket. The two Ivans stepped back, like they had been zapped by a taser. They weren't expecting a Chinese guest, and we left them standing in their muttered confusion as I pulled Yasmin and the rest down the steps. We hit the bottom step and were on the street below as one of the Audis crashed back out of the lane to our right and swung around to face us. The Russians were at our side now; the driver took a hold of Zheng's shoulder, Smoking Ivan crouched into the firing position. The second Audi rammed backwards into the street in front of us, revved up behind the first one and then the back doors of both cars opened and dark shapes piled out to take up covering positions.

We all heard the heavy boots crashing down the steps above us, and the Ivans and I were still wrangling our fight or flight reflexes when Yasmin darted into the dark, her children tight under each arm. There was an opening to the left, maybe forty meters away on the other side of the street, more steps leading down and away to another street. We launched after her, Zheng lifted off his feet between me and the driver, Smoking Ivan right behind, one hand on Zheng's collar, the other targeting the pistol where the dark shapes must have been. The Audis roared forward, running feet behind them, American shouts echoed off the cobbles. They were gaining on us, almost to the point where Smoking Ivan would have no choice but to take somebody down, when a van charged at us from the other direction: the Americans stopped and took cover, we made the black gap of the lane, the van slid to a halt right behind us. I didn't look back, slapped Zheng forward, keep low and keep moving.

The crack of automatic fire raked above our heads, we all went down, Smoking Ivan squirmed beside me to find cover and a shooting position. The darkness below screamed into fury; two shooters down there striking sparks and spinning masonry out of the steps below us. Ivan looked at me, he wasn't being paid that much, shrugged an apology and came up on his knees with both hands in the air. The driver was a couple of steps below, did the same, murmured something in Portuguese to Yasmin. A voice yelled at us from above: Yasmin panted a sob, the girl shrieked, the kid howled out in joy.

Thiago had come for them.

CHAPTER THIRTY-THREE

Thiago called out to Yasmin, told her to stay down until it was safe. The figures down below jogged up to push me and Zheng and the two Russians back to the street. No uniforms; black boiler suits and ski hats over their faces – Liu's Chinese commandos. But it wasn't over yet. The SUV's pitched forward to heave the van back on its axles. Cora's people formed a pyramid of firing positions along the sidewalk. The Chinese snapped into their offensive line, like they had practiced a thousand times.

'Back off! This gentleman is a citizen of the United States of America! You have no jurisdiction here! Back off immediately!' A strong military voice, telling it straight, no fear, no problem. Not Cora, but I knew she was back there somewhere.

'Your agent has kidnapped a citizen of the People's Republic of China.' Colonel Liu, in full voice, full authority. 'Withdraw from this area before you incite an international incident.'

We knew nobody would blink, shooters on either side statues in the dark, a calm front hiding nothing except their buzz at finally getting a sniff at the real enemy. But we all knew the frantic calls were being made at the fringes; how do we get out of this? How far can we go? What happens if we take them out right now? Lights fluttered on in some houses, curtains lifted, a couple of doors chinked open. Something would have to give. I tugged Zheng's elbow and we stepped into a doorway. I rapped my knuckles against the door, somebody inside might be too curious to resist. A movement then at the back of the American line, was that Cora? Sirens in the night, not so far away. I tried the door again, no answer, no luck. Smoking Ivan hunkered down in front of us, the driver was working his cellphone good, where was Yakov? The two lines of shooters strained to the limit, itching to lay down some fire and claim the kill. The sirens were near, the blue lights spinning closer in the windows down below: then they were here, a Policia squad car arriving from each side in a pincer movement, only to find they were way, way out of their depth. The street cops were wise enough to keep their heads down and stay inside their prowlers; they cut the sirens, then only one signalled their authority with the bouncing blue light, until they too realized that they didn't really want to draw attention to themselves and reversed back the way they came, quietly, and in the dark.

Smoking Ivan sprung from the ground and smashed his boot through the door lock in one flowing movement. The driver was behind him and the four of us crashed into the hallway, then scrambled through the narrow kitchen and out the back door. Zheng was petrified but allowed himself to be hoisted along. Over the wall and into another yard, kicked in that back door and through the house, out the front and into the narrow lane where they had caught us. Kept running, picking Zheng up between us when he stumbled, kicking him on when he faltered.

Nobody chasing us; maybe too proud to flinch in the face off back there, maybe had a team ready to scoop us at the end of this lane. No sign of Yasmin or her kids either: I hoped they had slipped away and would somehow get themselves out of the nightmare I had dragged them into. At the end of the lane now, opened to a wider street, followed Smoking Ivan and kept running, Zheng out of breath, his legs weak. There was a car ahead, a big Merc Executive, idling, dipped headlights, the back door opened. I rammed Zheng in the back after the Ivans. A different driver, but another Russian, squinting into Zheng's face.

'I don't like Chinese!' Yakov said.

'He's better than Jorginho,' I said. 'If you want to make money.'

'I said you would be a problem,' Yakov said.

'Who do you like, Yakov?'

'I like Russians,' he said. 'If they are from Moscow, if they are from Zamoskvarechye.'

'Nobody from that shit hole is going to make you cash like Mr Zheng here,' I said.

Yakov grunted the big Merc away from the sidewalk.

Yakov didn't speak much. Smoking Ivan wedged into the front beside him and nervously rolled a throb of Russian patter in his ear, as if silence and Yakov weren't a good combination. From where I was sitting Yakov looked like a regular guy, nothing special; maybe a cab driver ticking off the miles to scratch off another repayment, another night shift closer to freedom and debt-heavy retirement. Only I knew there were no regular guys; not anywhere and for sure not among the sewer life I rubbed against.

'What did they tell you about your friend?' Yakov lounged his right arm and shoulder over his seat to tilt his ear towards me. 'You believe these lies?'

I had blanked Ferdy out so far, quarantined him in a bunker at the edge of my brain, suspended in limbo to let me pretend I could avoid the brick wall.

'McErlane knew too much,' Yakov drawled it like he was giving the low down on last night's ball game. 'He was never going home to your USA. That's why they sent him, so they could make sure he never came back.'

I screwed my eyes tight and squeezed my fists into my thighs, every sinew coiled to keep Ferdy back there in our otherworld.

'You too, Maknazpy,' Yakov said. 'You know what they did last year. They want you to disappear, my friend.'

Disappear? That sounded attractive right then. Release Ferdy from his cocoon in my soul and we could disappear together. Not yet.

'Sounds like you know too much American business, Comrade Yakov.'

He split a smile in his round face, looked like a fat creamy camembert just cracked by a cheesewire. Smoking Ivan crawled to copy the boss but Yakov hissed at him like he was an over familiar lapdog.

'Does our Chinese friend here know his business?' Yakov said. 'I really hope so.'

Zheng folded forward, propped his head on his hands to stare at his feet. I shifted sideways, watched Lisbon sink behind us as Yakov ramped the Merc up the Golden Gate bridging the dark waters. A hulking tanker squatted like a bully on the Tejo, a nimble launch ploughed a bright wake under its skirts, a dream train tripped its rhythm below our motor lane.

Barco Negro, a cross stuck on a rock, and your black sailboat dancing under the light. Not yet; I wouldn't let Ferdy go, wouldn't let him drift away, leaving me alone in the darkness. Not yet.

CHAPTER THIRTY-FOUR

The security gate was open. Yakov cursed at the car already planked at the side door to the house. He had told the idiot to park further up so he would have enough space to get in and close the gates. Smoking Ivan hopped out and shunted the other car up against the wall at the back, then jogged past to clank the gate behind us. I stepped out and guided Zheng by his elbow, he kept his head down, mumbling some gibberish like he was fielding a three way conversation by himself. I needed him sharp, hoped he wasn't retreating into some sort of nerd withdrawal. The house was a concrete cube with narrow windows and a stairway rippled along the side wall to another door up above. There was a dim light inside the door on the ground floor, the rest of the neighborhood in darkness except for some fluorescent lights twinkling through the trees behind the high wall across the road.

'No problem,' Yakov said. 'The Almada Naval College. They aren't looking for us.'

The idiot who hadn't parked the first car properly held the door open with all the mustered menace of a tough guy but then withered under Yakov's blast for his misdemeanor. We shuffled through the narrow hallway and tight kitchen into a lounge. A comfortable home, a tad shabby and worn but somebody actually lived here, not what I had expected; a family's scent ingrained on the walls and fibers, remnants of an oily stew on dishes and pots, clothes and shoes heaped on a chair.

'Can Zheng get on-line in this place?' I asked.

'Make yourself at home,' Yakov said. 'This we have to speak about.' He opened a door to reveal an adjoining room, held the handle long enough to read the expression on my face when I saw Yasmin with her kids folded around her, then slammed the door closed again and ushered me to sit on the threadbare armchair. 'I like to keep things nice and simple, Maknazpy. "Moscow" Alex told me you would bring Jorginho. That was simple. But you bring this Chinese and the Brazilian whore. This is not simple and it isn't nice. I don't like this.'

'That's your problem,' I said. 'There is business to be done here, you are either in or out but don't try to act the big guy, okay? If you don't want part of this thing then we'll just walk out that door right now. Got me?'

The three tough guys tightened their toughest scowls and waited for his word. Yakov hitched Zheng by the collar, dumped him in beside Yasmin and then dismissed the muscle with a flick of his chin towards the kitchen. Yakov hunkered down in front of me; bobbing slightly on the balls of his feet, elbows on his knees, strong fingers loosely interlocked.

'Just you and me, cowboy!' he said. 'Man to man, huh?'

He looked like a wrestler poised to propel himself into a move. I settled back in my chair, stretched my legs out so my toes nudged his ankles.

'In or out, Yakov? It's your call.'

'I am in, of course,' he said. 'But it is good business to know exactly what it is you are signing up for. And who else is in the game, you know?'

Yakov had big blue eyes, clear and steady. They could have looked honest and sincere in a different face, say one of those young Orthodox holy men with the wild beards and tall hats. In Yakov's face the big blue eyes were iced with cruelty, no wonder Yasmin thought he was a wolf.

'Zheng is good. He can handle this end,' I said. 'I have Jorginho some place safe. That's my insurance. Zheng does his part, then Jorginho does his. We're all happy and good to go. If I had just walked in here with Gorgeous George you guys could have cut my throat and carried on without me. That's what I call good business, Yakov. Not getting your throat cut is always good business.'

He rocked up and down on his toes, made him look like he was nodding approval.

'Why this Brazilian whore and her dirty kids?'

Something in his tone needled me, a hot tingle rolled up my neck and ears.

'Nothing personal, Maknazpy. Your business is your business, but these Brazilians are bad news. Believe me! Animals!' He scraped the fine stubble of his round head with his manicured fingers, then sprung up to stand above me. 'Maybe ten years ago, this one, yes, I remember when she first came here, ten years ago maybe. But now?' He twisted his flat face into a sour grimace, like he had just discovered shit on his bespoke Italian shoes. 'Take my advice, Maknazpy. Her brother is an animal. This one can only bring trouble.'

He expected me to react but I wasn't going to, not this time.

'Jorginho is in Cyprus,' I said. 'That's where all your Russian money is laundered, isn't it?'

That stumped him, I could see his brain ticking over, working out who to call in Cyprus to nail down Gorgeous George.

'Zheng does his part, Jorginho does his, we all take our cut and go our separate ways. Is that nice and simple enough for you, Yakov?'

'How long will it take?' he said. 'The Americans and Chinese are tearing this city apart. How long do you think I can keep you a secret?'

'That's your problem, Yakov,' I said. 'I'm sure you and your KGB comrades can handle it.'

'KGB!' Yakov belched a laugh and slapped his hands together. 'Don't you know the KGB is like your American Mafia? It doesn't exist anymore, Maknazpy, it doesn't exist!'

★★★

I woke with a jolt; unable to breathe and spinning down into a bottomless pit, the devil's fist down my throat squeezing my lungs and dragging me all the way to hell.

'It's okay, we are safe,' Yasmin's voice close in the dark room. Her hand stroked the back of my neck, I grabbed her wrist like it was the only anchor to save me from the evil that gripped my guts.

'You were afraid you were on your own?' Her mouth whispered in my ear, arms wrapped around my chest, holding me tight. 'I know this fear, it comes to me often in the night also.'

I crushed my face hard with my clenched fists and squirmed free from her embrace. A square room with two beds and a table in the corner. Her daughter's long hair breaking out from under the covers on the other bed, Zheng tapping a computer at the table, Yasmin kneeling behind me on this bed.

'You are sorry for your friend.' She clasped my ribs and hauled me back against her warmth, her softness. 'I know, a slice of your heart is lost with him and gone forever.' She nuzzled into my neck from behind, clawing the tension from my skin. 'But now you are free to be who you need to be.'

I slumped back into her strong arms, her smooth bare legs cradled me softly, her hot breath filled my mouth and smothered the terror in my throat. My panic retreated, the room settled, Zheng rattled the keyboard in his secret frenzy. And Yasmin's son braced against the door, hatred burning in his black eyes in the darkness.

★★★

Yasmin singing to herself, Zheng drumming the keyboard, a dull Atlantic morning ebbing through the cheap curtains, the little girl's hair still streaked against the pillow, the boy asleep in a chair. Yasmin stooped over a tiny hand basin in the corner, hair overflowing the sink like purple black seaweed in a stranded rock pool. Amy Winehouse:

Back to Black and I'm No Good; something tragic in her voice.

Zheng didn't move when I clapped my hand on his shoulder, as if nothing existed that wasn't framed in his screen.

'Can you contact Cora Oneale on this thing without being traced?' I said.

Zheng slowed down, fingers still tipping the keys but slower now.

'I could if I wanted,' he said. 'I do not want.'

I laced my hands around the back of this neck and squeezed slightly. He looked up at me with his long crooked teeth filling his open mouth as if he had a problem. Yakov tapped the door like a butler, breakfast ready, tea or coffee? I squeezed Zheng a little more and felt his shoulders shrug, he hit the keys again and a different screen pinged up.

Breakfast was hard black bread with a sort of soft salami, a sugary porridge dotted with red berries, and not so bad pancakes with butter and sour cream.

'Pyotr is a better chef than he is a gangster, no?' Yakov was in a good mood. 'Actually, he is a chef in one of my entertainment facilities. And none of us are gangsters.'

Pyotr shuffled about the small kitchen and attended our table like we were in some big time Moscow hotel. And maybe Yakov had a piece of that action at that, for all I knew.

'Zheng needs a better computer,' I said. 'He reckons that laptop is a pile of piss.'

Yakov almost choked on his pancake.

'I have 120 piles of piss just like that in a storeroom in Alverca,' he said. 'Top of the range, they cost me twenty grand. What more does he want?'

'That's what Zheng told me, it's crap, he needs a higher spec,' I said. 'Maybe you are a better KGB man than you are a gangster, Yakov, ever think of that?'

Yakov puffed out a dry smile, dipped his pancake into the porridge and wedged half of it into his mouth so that his right cheek mushroomed out of his face.

'Again, the KGB Maknazpy?' Yakov rattled his cup and spilt some tea, waved Pyotr away when he swooped to clean it up. 'You should be careful, cowboy. This life of lies and treachery is bad for your mental health. Soon you will imagine there are no normal people left, that everyone is as corrupt as you and your bosses.'

'Yeah? Funny you seem to know so much about it,' I said.

'I know shit about anything except my own business!' He splattered globules of the porridge pancake over the plate of black bread. 'But I know none of your shit happens by accident either. You know it too but you sell your soul to this liberal fascist brainwash. Glory hunters like you and Moscow Alex play their game, it makes you feel big, yes? Good for you, but don't complain when they betray you because, with all your lies, what future do you deserve?'

It wasn't the first time a top line carnivore like him had justified himself by making comparison to the regime I spilt blood for. I had meant to prepare a killer response after the last time some un-American desperado had thrown that in my face but I had never quite nailed it.

'You speak pretty good English for a Russian hood in Portugal, Comrade Yakov.'

'I ran a successful business in London for some years, English language was useful, you know? I also know German, Portuguese, and enough Spanish too,' he said. 'What about you, American Savior of the Civilized World? Or are you prepared to wait until the entire world speaks American? Maybe drone bomb any stubborn savage that speaks a different language?'

Zheng stuck his head around the door and gave me the nod. I rose from the table and called my thanks to Pyotr.

'You are welcome!' Yakov said. 'But just remember we run a results operation here, yes? With good results come reward. And bad results – well, you understand what that must mean, don't you?'

'Come, Comrade, drink your cup because you'll get no sup in eternity!' I bent low to laugh in his ear as I passed. 'You keep telling yourself your Red lies and we'll keep telling ours, okay?'

'As you wish!' he shouted after me. 'But you didn't get here by chance. You are in somebody's plans, Maknazpy. I hope they don't cut across ours and, for your sake, I hope you can tell the difference.'

I left a finger hanging for Yakov as I followed Zheng into the room. The Red Goon didn't know it but I was already thinking along the same lines as he was.

CHAPTER THIRTY-FIVE

Cora was spooked out. I knew she had heard me because she squawked like a scalded cat when I spoke into the mike on Zheng's piss laptop. I pressed my ear against the screen, could almost feel Cora at the other side numbed by my remote presence, spooked out.

'Cora, you heard me right the first time,' I said. 'I want to see Ferdy before you take him home. You fix it for me or you'll never see George Oliver or Zheng again.'

Zheng giggled into his fist like he had sat up the coolest schoolboy prank ever.

'You can walk in here any time, Con,' she said. 'That's what I have been trying to tell you all along.'

Cora was a quick thinker; always on her toes and first to recover and adapt. I guess I was a little intimidated when she first swayed into my life with that whole package; the looks, the confidence, the superiority, the natural order. It said more about me than her but she knew how to work me right from the start. She probably hit straight A's in her training at Anacostia-Bolling or Camp Peary or wherever but that was just an extra layer of lacquer on an already highly polished piece. Sooner or later, though, even that polish goes dull if you rub against it every day.

'Listen better, Cora!' I said. 'You don't tell me anything right now, okay? I'm telling you one more time. You fix it that I see Ferdia McErlane in private, no shadows, and then I disappear again until I am ready to come home.'

I would never conquer her cold intensity but I had learnt how to chip away at her armor, how to get under her skin.

'We'll need proof of life before we go any further with this, Maknazpy,' she said.

'Proof of what life? George Oliver? You sent me here to get him, right? I got him! That's your proof!'

'We think he would have made contact if he was safe. That hasn't happened. We need proof of life, proof that you can deliver.'

Comrade Yakov was smarter than me also but I was catching up.

'You are a liar, Cora!' I said. 'You were lying from the start and you're lying now. The reason you expected Gorgeous George Jorginho Fucking Oliver to be in contact is because he was in contact with you all along! Only now all of a sudden he's not in contact and you guys figure you really have lost him, isn't that it? You didn't send us here to bring him home! You had him embedded here as part of the deal, didn't you? He was the meat in the trap, like me and Ferdy! So who are you really after? Zheng? Liu? I think Zheng must be the bigger prize, Cora, but you aren't getting him unless you fix it so I see Ferdy one more time.'

'This line isn't secure, I can't continue this discussion right now,' she said. 'Although I can't help but notice you use the past tense when referring to the subject.'

'If I don't get to see Ferdy everything will be past tense, Cora, get me? Everybody and everything; Zheng, Liu, Blake, everybody! I'll flip them all into past tense!'

'You are getting yourself all worked up, Maknazpy,' she said. 'And you haven't even asked me about your wife and son.'

That was a slap in the face. I hadn't asked, they were mixed up in all the shit swirling around my head and I had forgotten them.

'They are fine right now,' Cora stuck it to me. 'Rose, Con and your friend Gallogly are all home safe.' She twisted the blade in my gut. 'Don't worry, Con, I'll tell them you were asking about them and that you will be home soon.' She laughed, sneered, to rub my face in it. 'We managed to get them home without your help. Your friends look after you, Maknazpy, so don't you feel it is time for you to help yourself?'

'You maybe brought them home, Cora, but we both know it was your people who took them away in the first place!'

'Never your fault, is it?' she snapped back. 'Always an excuse! Poor Con Maknazpy is always the victim! The poor guy pushed around by the high and mighty, right? Well it's time for you to take a look in the mirror, Maknazpy, and come back to me when you are ready to play by our rules, okay?'

'She has gone,' Zheng said. 'She has turned her machine off.'

Good, I was glad to get rid of her, she was starting to wear me down there for a minute. Nothing with Cora was ever straightforward but that just hadn't panned out the way I had imagined; I needed a couple of minutes to work it out, find another angle. Yasmin was singing again, a brighter tune this time, full of hope and joy, and washing her daughter's hair in the basin. The girl's silk black hair tumbled over the side like her mother's. And the son was right behind me, like he had been listening to me and Cora, pouting a scowl even more bitter than his usual sour face. I wasn't in the mood right then, and wondered if a smack in the mouth wouldn't give him something to moan about.

'Maknazpy!' Zheng called me back. A shadowy figure moved across his dark laptop screen. It was a room much like this one; curtains drawn, a dim cream light, a bed and a dresser against the wall. Maybe a hotel room, maybe not. The door from a bathroom opened and the figure came into view.

'I activated the camera in her laptop. She does not know we are watching her.'

Cora twisted the blood red towel over her breasts and flopped on the bed. Her wet hair looked darker and her bare back and legs seemed paler in this skewed view. I peeled Zheng away from the screen. Cora hit a number into her cellphone.

'He's still here ... Yes, Sir ... I'm pretty sure our man will show soon ... No problem, Sir ... I know how he thinks better than he does himself ... laughter ... No, Sir, I don't believe he has a clue ... laughter ... Yes, Sir, Whatever it takes ... He won't be a problem, it will be all over before he even suspects ... laughter'

Cora cut the cellphone and tossed it on the bed, yanked the towel with both hands and twirled it in front of her long coiled body like she was playing with a Mexican bullfighter's cape, spun into a neat pirouette and came out the other side wearing the towel as a turban. Zheng shoved past me, nearly knocked the laptop over. Cora posed in front of the camera, like the screen was her mirror; massaging her blond head with the red towel, singing to herself, swaying her hips, a slow seesaw bump and grind, uninhibited in the privacy of her room. And she was in better light now, the long naked body as honey brown and lithe as I had imagined, purring the afterglow of a wildcat's deep kill-slaked thirst. Her sweet voice a million miles from Johnny Cash, When The Man Comes Around – but poor Johnny never moved like that.

I always had Cora figured as too cool to ever indulge in such simple pleasures. And way too cute not to notice the tiny red light that said her laptop camera had been activated.

CHAPTER THIRTY-SIX

My father told me, back when I was a little kid and I thought he would be there forever, that one day fear would come along and grab me by the throat. He said it happened to everybody and it didn't matter how big a house you lived in or how smart you were: this fear was part of life like water and air and would ambush me some day, like the big black wolf with red eyes in the forest that sunk its teeth in the lamb's neck and carried it away from the sheep. He said if I was lucky it wouldn't come for a long time but, either way, I should start getting myself prepared for it – I guess I was about seven or eight years old then. He said the only thing to do was to accept it, embrace it even, and keep going because that's what a real man has to do: survive and keep strong for the others. Then the selfish cowardly bastard disappeared before I could find out who he thought the others were supposed to be. Turns out he was right. Okay, I had survived the highs and lows of combat more times than any normal man should, and I could even admit to myself that sometimes I maybe rode a little too high on that buzz: I was the wolf, but that do-or-die fear is where the deepest kicks are to be plundered, and my hero father was just as greedy for those blood thrills. No, he had something else in mind, and figured I would recognize that honest fear when the time came.

And so this was it. A metallic white door with an over-sized polished chrome handle. I was paralyzed, couldn't move, couldn't speak, couldn't reach out and open that door. Cora stepped forward and pulled the handle open. I saw the lower half of his body draped with a white sheet. She nudged me forward, I stalled, a claw nailing my throat, she grabbed my elbow and shouldered me into the room. The doorway was my threshold: once inside I couldn't avoid his church clay face, scorching my lungs and sucking the juice from my eyes. She heaved me towards him but I collapsed to my knees like a baby before I even made the table.

'He was a good man. A good American,' Cora kneaded her sympathy into my shoulder. 'I am sorry for your loss. He was your dear friend. I understand.'

She didn't understand. She thought I was crying for Ferdy. She thought my grief was for his life cut short, the vacuum, the mayhem and love that was supposed to flicker around his crazy orbit forever. No, even then, in the fucking tsunami stripping me bare, I knew why I was crying. For myself. Only myself, like my father before me.

Okay, Cora understood that Ferdy was gone and I was left here on my own, and understood that I would have to man up and get over it. But she didn't understand what Ferdy took with him. That idol under the shroud had made me exactly what I was now, had nipped and tucked my thoughts, had forged the hook that let me hang on his tails. Forget all Blake's shit about the amygdala and genetic abnormality and being somebody new every fucking day! Ferdy was the filter that docked me into the real world and whatever I was now only bounced back from his golden boy reflection. Yasmin said I was free now to be who I needed to be. Oh yeah? But who was that? Without Ferdy I was nobody, because without him I didn't exist. Not as me, not as Con fucking Maknazpy, not without my brother to let me pretend I lived a life.

So, I knew it now, there had never been an escape. Even when I was a happy little kid of seven or eight my old man could see that dark cloud waiting for me in the distance. He knew the lie to keep me sane in the meantime; the macho swagger, the false pride, sticking it to the man, trample the ghosts and don't look back. And he knew that someday the big lie would stab me in the back, leave me standing here guilty and ashamed to face the truth.

The truth, the fear, that nobody knows you are there, that you only exist in your own head, that you are alone, that you were a waste of space but it didn't matter anymore because you would be dead soon anyway. Cora and Yasmin and Blake didn't understand shit.

★★★

A blitz of Atlantic hail ripped through the tight alley and slapped me back to life. Cora hovered at arm's length, her four big guys hung back.

'Are you okay, Con?' Cora asked. 'You are looking kind of green there.'

I doubled up to let my guts burst out of my throat, Pyotr's red berries and all. I hung on to a drainpipe and it all erupted out of my system. Cora shuffled back, one of her heavies made a crack and the rest sniggered. They didn't have the look of her usual spooks, weren't the stern zealots juggling their Arabic dictionaries and hi-tech codes. They had the look of killers.

'It's a whole new ballgame now, Con.' Cora handed me a wet wipe. 'Ferdy has gone, your family are safe. You could join them by tomorrow morning.'

'I am going home!' I snapped at her. 'Just not yet. You get me a signed statement saying last year will never be hung on me and a green card for Yasmin and her kids. Then I'll come in and bring Zheng with me.'

'Yasmin? Is that her real name or her professional one?'

The black bread bulged out and splashed over her shoes. Ruby red heels matching the blood red earrings and beaded necklace. Not the cream soft leather brogues.

'People get burned out in this game,' she murmured. 'You have to know when to quit. You have changed, Con. I think you are going soft. It happens. If you don't get out now you will be a danger to yourself and your friends. Whatever their real names are.'

Cora being the smart ass again, trying to work me as usual. Soft? Maybe. Changed? I wished. Maybe Blake had spiked some shit into my fucked up head and changed something. Maybe I had wised up. I wouldn't know, only somebody else could tell me that but I wouldn't be asking Cora's opinion anyway.

'Miss Oneale, Ma'am!' The closest one pressed his earpiece tighter. 'Incoming! Two automobiles, thirty seconds!'

Cora grabbed my collar and pushed me up the hill; one of the killer guards followed, the other three faced down the hill, slotted into doorways, no pasaran. The lane narrowed up ahead, cluttered with garbage cans and dumped white goods, could see ahead for about twenty five meters before it gouged a sharp turn to the right. I was in front, Cora tick tacking behind until she stumbled to fling the red heels into a mini dumpster. The guard hung about five meters behind. Cora caught up with me as I reached the turn, pulled my arm back so she could lean around the corner first. Clear, keep going, the lane twisted down to a set of steps, then emptied out onto another street. The sharp crack of gunfire bouncing around the lane back behind us, three warning shots, then a pause. Cora in control overdrive through earpiece and wrist-mike, fielding frantic reports, dealing back her calm instruction, switching to relay our status to base in composed staccato, conducting the three-parter in cool harmony. We were at the steps, traffic thunder close, the busy avenue an escape. A three second burst of automatic fire, not ours, then another. Rapid fire pistol shots, our three guys still in the game. Cora on point, stockinged feet slapping against the wet steps, ear and mouth working the scene, no problem.

'A support vehicle will be here in two minutes to pick us up, Maknazpy, so just hang tight!'

The guard pressed close behind me, Cora mouthing into her mike. A bus pumped its air-brakes and zoned us off from the rest of the avenue. The guard was a good pro but sweating on the comrades left behind, I jerked his wrist forward with my right hand and dragged his shoulder back with my left, felt his balance shift and swept his ankles with my left foot. He hit the concrete with a thump, I drop lunged a punch into his solar plexus and swallowed his stale early morning breath. Cora spun in reflex but I stooped low and flipped her ankles forward and up, her shoulders snapped back and she crashed down on the guard.

'Getting picked up wasn't part of our deal, Cora. I'll be in touch.'

The bus lumbered into the traffic, I surfed around the back of it, felt the hot fumes in my face and kept moving, dodging trucks and cars to get to the other side of the street. Police sirens were homing in from all directions but the drivers here didn't care, too busy cramming forward to funnel into the roundabout fifty meters ahead. There was some sort of city park on the other side of the roundabout. I ran towards it, no need to blend in, just get to cover and then work out the next move. The shooting had stopped. Police vehicles ploughed an opening through the meshed traffic ahead. Cora needed to get her men extracted quick and wouldn't hunt me now.

A statue of some big time Portuguese sailor pinned the middle of the roundabout. I skipped up the three steps of the plinth and hunkered down against the cold stone. I was breathing hard, needed some oxygen in my lungs before my next sprint into the park. A policia car scraped past, the driver too hyped up about getting through that fucking traffic snarl to even notice me. I guessed that's what it was to be a statue; standing there in prime view for so long that people stopped seeing you. That's what I needed now. This guy was Pedro Álvares Cabral. Some piss artist had sprayed all over the sandstone block in red metallic glitter paint. Something about Brasília! The gates to the city park were right in front of me, a couple more deep breaths and I'd be good to go. I tilted my head back to pierce through the blanket of traffic fumes and filled my chest with a revved up cocktail of cold air and sour exhaust. The heavens above ripped apart: a straight line demarcation between dark brooding clouds and deep blue winter sky. A seagull squawked on old Pedro's head. I took my chance and launched out into the traffic.

The cops had cordoned off the road ahead, the two lane roundabout sprouted extra channels that meant nobody was going anywhere soon. Fender to fender, I criss-crossed through, almost at the park gate when I saw them. A big black SUV, Beto driving, Thiago riding shotgun. Maybe Cora had called it good, I was becoming a danger to myself, I should have nailed them before they got anywhere close. Now they saw me too, but the assholes were hemmed in tight by a truck on each side and couldn't get their doors opened. They struggled as if rattling and shaking against the side of a ten tonne truck was going to make any difference. I retraced my steps to laugh straight in their red Brazilian faces, gave them both a big wave with a finger each as the flourished finale.

Then I could see they weren't on their own. Blake poked his head in between them from the back seat. I gave him a special double barrelled finger salute. A policia van pushed and scraped its way forward until it lodged in the car levee, the blue light spinning and bouncing off Álvares Cabral's statue. I backed towards the park gate, keeping my eye on the SUV, picked out Liu's shape at the back left window, looking like he was inconveniently late for a dental appointment.

I was at the gate and the helpless fuckers were never going to catch me now. I stopped. The hairs on my neck prickled. My chest felt empty, like my heart was in the back of my head pulsing and throbbing that black force field through my skull. I doubled back behind them and came out to their right. Another figure beside Liu. A solid big man. I edged along the side of a Lisboa Empresas truck to get closer. Gray hair scorched in tight to his skull. An old man but still strong. My black energy spinning, gathering force, ready for lift off. A weathered tan face with a fine two day white stubble, close enough now to pick out the patchwork of red scar tissue imprinted over the brown and white face. He cocked his head to the side as if assessing me, ticking off my weaknesses and shortcomings, confirming his judgement of my deficiencies and flaws. He was the big black wolf with red eyes. He was my father.

CHAPTER THIRTY-SEVEN

Yakov went off-the-scale ballistic. I was a fucking CIA mudilo, an American blya, a dirty khui. He hammered his fist on the table and screamed spit in my face. Yasmin huddled her kids in the corner. Zheng ladled code into the machine, waited, picked the bones out of the response and ladled some more.

'I'm back now, Yakov, so what's your problem?'

Yakov wasn't in the habit of talking around issues. He preferred a more direct approach to problem solving. But he needed me almost as much as I needed him, so the showdown could wait.

Zheng was ready to roll his first dice. Yakov pulled a brown envelope out of an inside jacket pocket and presented it to me with all due ceremony. I ripped it open and pulled out the single sheet. Expensive heavy cream paper with twenty rows of neatly hand printed numbers and letters.

'You are certain this one knows what he is doing?' Yakov said.

I slipped the sheet to Zheng and ushered Yakov towards the other room.

'The kid doesn't need an audience right now, Yakov,' I said. 'You certain you can organize your crews?'

'It all works and we are all happy,' he said. 'Or nothing works and some of us will be very unhappy.'

I closed the door after him and pulled a chair over beside Zheng. He was already pouring the numbers in, on a different level now, hot for the chase: searching out the significant problems and zapping them like the little green men in his game.

'How long?' I asked.

He ignored the pointless question, immersed in his parallel universe and on a roll. I settled back, this would be a long day and I really needed to be busy, needed to banish the ghosts humping on my shoulder and whispering in my ear that I had failed them.

'Jorginho had talent,' Zheng said. 'He left his code behind but locked it with a key that made it invisible. The white hats think his Fifth Code was never completed. They think the Red Protocol is an orphan.'

'So it's looking good?' I prompted.

He didn't hear me, kept plugging away at the tangle of code shuffling up the screen, knocking it down and reshaping it to fit the patterns in his head.

A long thirty minutes. 'I thought you said you were good to go?' I said. Blanked out. Yasmin fixed up dinner with Pyotr. Zheng gulped down a pot of coffee. Yakov sulked in his room. I was struggling to keep a lid on the pressure steaming in my own head, really didn't need the extra tension brooding in this cell. Another hour. 'How much longer?' Even Zheng was uptight. 'If you insist on interrupting I will finish and you can take over!'

Another hour and I was about to break out. 'It is done!' Zheng pulled a wicked smile and applauded his victory with a polite Chinese hand clap. 'Just over six million dollar. I have already settled my share. Tell me again how to split your three million.'

Yasmin was at my shoulder now, flanked on either side by her kids.

'Two million in the name of Rose Maknazpy. Five hundred grand to John Gallogly. Five hundred grand to Yasmin here.'

Zheng juggled the banks on his screen. Places I had never heard of before; Nauru, Aruba, Antigua. Others were familiar from the movies; Grand Cayman, Liechtenstein, Monaco. He switched to Chinese characters for Singapore and Hong Kong, back to English for the British Channel Islands, Israel and Dubai. He picked out a private bank in Sao Paulo for Yasmin. And Jorginho's favorite was there – Cyprus, the Russian Laundromat.

'It is leaving Beirut now,' Zheng said. 'I have set the sequence to be actioned automatically. The funds will be available in the end banks in two weeks.'

She cried out, on her knees, hands clamped over her face to stem the heavy panting.

'What have you done? They will kill us all for sure! Why did you do this thing to my poor children?'

'And Yakov can't trace it, right?' I said.

Zheng smirked. 'Yes, the Russians will see what I have done. It is the Russian network I am using. Their banks, their shell companies, their subsidiary trading partners. But it will be too late by then. The money will be gone. It is the Russian bus, Jorginho was the mechanic, but I am the driver!'

Yasmin didn't hear him, too deep in her misery to care, pulling the little girl close and crying into her long black hair. But the little girl wasn't listening to Yasmin either, because her brother was at her other side, hand cupped over her ear, buzzing the news to her. Yasmin wailed, and the little girl's face transformed from her usual nervous anxiety to a dazzling bright smile of beauty.

'You said you would save us but you have killed us! You don't know these Russian savages! They will kill us all!'

I disentangled Yasmin from her daughter and led her over to the bed. The little girl skipped and hopped around her brother and even he almost cracked a smile.

'Yasmin, listen to me, okay? This is part of the deal. It is all agreed. This is just step one. Me and Zheng get this first, then Yakov's Russians get what they want. It's a business deal. We all get what we want then we go our separate ways. End of story.'

'I can't believe this thing!' Her tears and snot and slobber ebbed in dark patches across my chest. 'Why would the Russian pigs allow this? Why would you do this for me? This doesn't happen in real life. This is not fair! You make false hope for my children, it is not fair on them!'

I cupped her chin and lifted her face up, dabbed her eyes with the edge of the sheet, caressed her face as tenderly as I could. But the truth was I didn't need her shit right then; I had things on my own mind, things to keep under control, things to finish.

'It's time to start believing, Yasmin. Time for you to forget the hard life and start giving your kids some hope, hear what I'm saying?'

She buried her face in my neck to sob out all the years of hurt and disappointment.

'Don't worry about the Russians. They figure to get ten times what we're getting out of this. That's a lot of black bread and vodka, right?'

I waved the kids over to take her off me, the boy gripped her tightly to squeeze the trembling out of her, the girl patted her shoulder with one hand while still hopping and skipping around her brother. She stopped me in my tracks for a moment, and I couldn't help smiling myself. With her brilliant eyes and flashing teeth she was the picture of beautiful innocence, like her mom must have been once. I had deserted that world long ago, and it was too late for Yasmin also, but her daughter's joyous face was a reminder that there was another world outside our vicious jungle. That sort of reminder was worth five hundred grand of anybody's money.

CHAPTER THIRTY-EIGHT

Cora was majorly pissed at me. Two of her guys had stopped slugs from Liu's scalp-hunters to let us escape. They weren't hurt bad, would be back in action after a spell of rehab and partying, but Cora carried the responsibility for what might have been and so blamed me for what was.

'No wonder your wife left you, you cretin! How did she tolerate you for so long?'

I held the phone at arm's length while she got it out of her system.

'Cora baby, aren't you blaming the victim here instead of the aggressor? Anyway, what progress with our arrangements? This Zheng kid is a real shit hot operator. I've seen him in action. You can't afford to let him slip through your fingers.'

She paused, I could hear her deliberate deep breaths. That's it, Cora, let it all out and get back to business.

'We can't speak over the phone, Maknazpy. Meet me at the statue in Praço do Comércio tomorrow at noon.'

'Sure, I'll be there, Cora. But I think you'll find we call it Terreiro do Paço here in Lisboa.'

Cora didn't like it when I laughed at her.

'Just be there, you adolescent shithead!'

It was much like the day we met Yasmin here. Cold and bright, a sharp breeze off the Tejo, clusters of tourists blown away by the city sights and going around in circles. Only I was on my own this time. I thought I might feel different after I had seen his dead face but I didn't. I was still caught between numb acceptance and wishful denial. I took up position in the corner where he had stood.

A couple of hours before Cora's crew might start sniffing around, probably up there right now going through the briefing torment. You do this then she does that then you do this other thing. And two of her team were down, that meant they would be light or the replacements would be briefed to bored death.

Yakov would be holding a screaming inquest back at the house too. Pyotr had surprised me when I climbed on the hood of the car to get over the wall, I had to get back down and persuade him Yakov's bad tempered screaming was the lesser of two evils. Anyway, Zheng was about ready for step two so Yakov should be plenty busy getting his end of it in motion without freaking out over my business.

A tourist ambled towards me with one of those small plastic coated maps. Didn't he see those two cops standing doing nothing on the other side of the statue? I made out I was from Denmark, didn't speak English. He sensed something wasn't right and backed off quickly, not likely that he was Danish himself, probably guessed I was a junkie. That's the good thing about cold mornings like this, you can bury your head in a hood and nobody's going to think anything of it. The tourist was over in a small huddle of his companions. I didn't like the way he pointed and nodded towards me. Time to move on.

I retraced Yasmin's footsteps down Martinho Da Arcada and Rua Alfandega, made as if I was waiting for a bus, everybody else with their head down going about their business, too busy to notice me. And that's how I had approached this whole trip. I had come with my head down to get the job done and get home again. It wasn't my business to think. Maybe it was too late but I had plenty to think about now; Ferdy stretched out under a white sheet, my hero father come to town, Jorginho's black magic siphoning petrol dollars from Beirut through a Russian pipeline. Yakov saying I was always in somebody's plan. Yasmin saying I was free to be who I needed to be. Three million dollars to keep me cool now, maybe a bullet at the end to keep me sweet forever.

Somebody else told me one time that there are no accidents and everything happens for a reason. Some important big guy up there in the sky had everything covered and I should just hang on for the ride because a little guy like me shouldn't hope to understand his important big sky reason. Keep my head down and mind my business, that's the only way the world could work. So how come my asshole father had made himself into such a big shot? Not by playing to their rules, that was for sure. So maybe Yasmin was right. All I had to do was be a bigger asshole than the competition. Why not? They always said I was my father's son, after all.

★★★

I left the Praço down below and headed up to Alfama. It wasn't just my paranoia that said the policia were more visible than usual. I almost slammed straight into two of them at that big chapel on the corner but managed to hop on the yellow tram before they had time to get a look at me. My heart pumped a little harder as we bumped closer to the castle, and I pulled the hood down over my face and turned to concentrate on the back window as a creepy little geek panned around all the passengers with his iPad. Thanks to him I didn't see the patrol car slung across the sidewalk until it was too late. The cop balanced on the second step of the tram to give us the once over but retreated quickly when geek boy stood up to catch him in all his glory. We jolted forward again, and I jumped off at the next corner.

A cleft between two houses disguised another tight alley twisting into the heart of Alfama. It was cold and dark in here, a black cat froze when the echo of my steps filled the empty space and then slinked into a hole in the wall when I got too close. I felt good in here, like I had discovered an abandoned cave and I would never have to see anybody ever again unless I wanted to. But right now, more than anything, I wanted to see Cora.

★★★

It took me a while but I found it in the end, and it looked the same now as it did that night I sat here with Ferdy and old Luis drinking beer and sharing the plump sardines. No reason why it should have been any different, of course, just that nagging voice that whispers people and places are being disrespectful when they don't mark the traumatic milestones in your life. But life goes on, and the boy I sent to pick up Cora could have been one of the kids rollicking around Luis' ankles as he trawled us far back into his own youth in Portuguese China.

The kid left Cora standing at the tree outside the bar and sprinted to the edge of the square to snatch the other ten Euro I owed him, swore she was on her own before I flipped him the note, then disappeared.

'Your cat and mouse games are absolutely idiotic!' she fizzed. 'I could have had you picked up any time I wanted. You know that.'

The same girl slid a glass of the same foaming red beer across the table. Sagres Bohemia. Cora plucked her sunglasses from the bridge of her nose to wipe the raindrops away, ignored the girl, then refused even a coffee. The girl took the insult as it was intended.

'Tell me about George Oliver, Cora. All the stuff about Jorginho the Genius you left out before.'

A mist of perspiration on her upper lip, maybe the exertion of chasing the nimble boy up all those steps.

'Like what? It was an easy pick up job but you fucked it up so George and McErlane end up dead? What else can I say?'

She was rattled now, big time.

'Like why did you send him in here in the first place?' I said. 'Forget the bullshit about him disappearing on his vacation. I know he was in contact with you all along. You gave that one up already when the contact stopped.'

'You give up things yourself, Maknazpy. Like seeing Zheng in shit hot action? What action? Against the United States? What action have you facilitated Zheng to deploy against us?'

Good, a nudge to remember she was smarter than I was, needed to take this easy and not overplay my hand.

'Ask him yourself when I bring him in,' I said. 'If I bring him in, that is. If you make those arrangements I asked for.'

The girl came back out to ask if everything was okay. Cora crossed her right leg over her left knee and sunk down in her seat, and her leg swinging up and down caused the table to rock and my beer vibrated along the edge of the glass. Or else she was double checking whether I really was one of the Americanos that sat here with Luis the night he was stabbed in the back.

'Your girlfriend and her children can be accommodated. That has been approved. Any sort of official statement on your involvement in last year's business is impossible. I told you it would be and it is. You'll have to accept our goodwill on trust.'

I sipped my beer, nodded for her to continue.

'You will bring in Zheng immediately, today, and you will be debriefed on the whole sorry episode. Bottom line is you need to play ball, Maknazpy, and you need to play now. Otherwise you will be classified as an enemy of the United States. Last chance saloon.'

'Why interrogate me?' I said. 'I know shit about anything.
All I know for sure is you played me and Ferdy like a couple of toy soldiers. Anything else is guesswork.'

She shrugged her shoulders and fingered her sunglasses. I lunged forward and pinned her right wrist down to the table with my left and clamped my right over her swinging knee. The sunglasses tumbled from her face and landed among the wet tree roots under the table.

'But I'll tell you what my best guess is right now, Cora. George Jorginho fucking Oliver was sent here as bait to lure Zheng and or Liu. Next guess is that wasn't enough. Some fuckhead at home thought we were missing a trick, right? Thought we could manufacture a crisis here that would draw some other big shot out. So me and Ferdy were the secondary bait. But you didn't think we needed to know that because guys like us are just pieces of worthless shit.
And when things got fucked up Blake did show himself, right? So did you already know Blake was a traitor or was it one of those fucking games people like you get off on in your scenario planning fantasy fests? And you expect me to accept your goodwill on some shit called trust?'

Cora whipped down her right heel into my left ankle and twisted her wrist free.

'Then it's a pity you let Ferdia McErlane be mortally wounded, isn't it, Maknazpy? He knew the strategy! Didn't he trust you enough to share it with you? Is that why you let him die?'

The fury surged through my head like an earthquake, I grabbed her throat and cracked her head down on the table, the glass fell to the ground and I started to swing the bottle above my head to smash it into her face. But I stopped. With the bottle in mid-swing something switched in my head and the rage froze. I saw Ferdy's gaping skull, saw my father's wolf red eyes, saw Yasmin's daughter with her angelic smile, and I froze. I set the bottle on the ground at my feet and lifted her shoulders off the table.

'I said you were going soft, didn't I?' Cora slotted me with her unblinking gaze. 'Maybe the softer you get, the smarter you get.' She cracked a smile, and fanned my shame even further. 'And maybe things were a little more complicated than you needed to know but we can't predict everything with certainty.' Smoothed her hair behind her ears and slipped her sunglasses back on. 'I hoped for Liu and Blake but didn't predict your father. Now he is here it's a bonus shot we can't refuse.'

My stupid face reflected in her shades. She gripped my collar and dragged me over the table.

'Your father, Maknazpy! Your father the big Commie hero! We sure as Christ aren't going home without him so this would be a real bad time for you to become that problem we talked about! Understand? You like to prove you're still on the team? Or do I report back that you're still Daddy's little boy with your piss-the-pants nightmares and panic attacks?'

The ingrained nightmare squirmed from head to gut like a bucket of flesh eating worms.

'What do you want from me?' I said.

'The trouble last year? We didn't get them all, Con. A lot of the ringleaders at home? Sure! But those neo-con fanatics were set up. This time we bring it full circle.'

'What do you want, Cora?'

'The guarantee you need about that mess is possible if you do your duty on this thing,' she said.

'What do you want?'

'I fucking want Zheng, Liu and Blake! Help us bring them all in.

Bring your father back to face American justice. Get back on the team and bring in Con fucking Maknazpy Senior!'

'What about my son? What about the treatment from Blake?'

Cora pulled on the edge of her blouse to wipe the sunglasses again.

'Sometimes things don't work out the way we would like in an ideal world, Con. That's unfortunate but, like I said, we can't predict everything. You know how it is.'

Yeah, I knew: the important big guy was still up in the sky and all I could do was to hang in there for the ride. I suppose I knew all along that's all there is for the small guy.

CHAPTER THIRTY-NINE

Yakov heaped a mountain of coarse sugar into his tiny coffee cup. I downed the bitter tar in two mouthfuls. No mention of my latest vanishing trick, he knew when to pick a fight. Pyotr offered a refill, his right eye peeping out through the purple and black swelling.

'Tell Zheng there better be no stupid mistakes,' Yakov said. 'No excuses! For any of us!' More sugar spooned. 'You ever see a Colombian Necktie? They cut your throat and pluck your tongue out through the hole. If your Chinese fucks up I will shoot myself. I advise you to do the same.'

'The kid knows what he is doing,' I said. 'It's your side that might be the problem.'

'No problem. Our management system is first class. You would be amazed if you knew some of the projects we have delivered.'

'Not on this scale,' I said. 'Not in so many countries at once.'

'No problem!' Yakov beamed, but a Colombian Necktie would be a problem on that thick red neck of his, and on mine too. Zheng's walk better be as good as his talk.

★★★

Zheng had been glued to the computer for days. Nobody had seen him leave that chair even to go to the bathroom. The room reeked like a septic armpit, some sort of gas billowed around but it sure wasn't oxygen and Yasmin and the kids refused to sleep in there anymore. His feet massaged the coffee and food debris into the cheap carpet. His teeth glowed yellow and a weedy beard spiked through his deathmask skin. Yakov gave me a look and stroked his throat in reflex. I cracked the narrow window open but the fresh air stalled on the outside. A mangy tee-shirt hung off Zheng but he twitched his imaginary cuffs as if he was a diva conductor on a podium about to deliver his masterpiece. My own throat thought a long thick snake was squeezing it like a tube of toothpaste.

'It is done!' Zheng proclaimed. 'They can commence!'

Yakov pulled a couple of chairs and we nested down like the Super Bowl had started without us.

And Zheng was already in the game, picking up the pieces from Jorginho's false start. He said Jorginho was like one of those top class engineers that work pitside on the Formula One circuit, knew how everything worked and how to tweak performance by that extra millioneth of a millimeter, and maybe was a even a pretty good driver with it. But Zheng was the real deal, the World Champion of Champions, the enigma who could forge that product of engineering genius into high art, who could take a machine and make it fly. That's what Zheng said anyway, and he was the only one in the cockpit so me and Yakov sat tight and resisted the temptation to choke the bullshit out of him and ram his face through the screen.

Jorginho had played out a trial run last year and Yakov said it had worked out pretty good. Moscow Alex was the captain of that particular ship but Yakov had worked his end of it here in Portugal. It turns out old Gorgeous George never quite lost his taste for the high risk numbers game, and while he was sniffing around the bowels of the Arab financial carcass, on the taxpayers' dime, he hit on a guaranteed winner. His old bosses, at least any that hadn't already been permanently retired, smelt blood but wanted to see him prove it first.

So, with Moscow Alex as the go-to logistics man, George had cracked open a credit card processing outfit in the outsourced silicon trough of India. Not a bank, not the daunting shell of a place where they take your money and with their cold greedy manners assure you that your pennies are safe. No, this was a humble back office function that some management guru rationalized so that it was separate from your real bank. The place maybe processing cards for a thousand different banks without any account holder knowing they exist. The place with no name, where you will never see or hear or speak to a human being because that's not what they do. All they do is process your credit and debit cards; set up numbers, match credit card numbers to bank account numbers, all that backroom stuff you think your own bank is doing.

Jorginho got in there, maybe using his government issue computer, and hit on half a dozen pre-paid debit cards. Pre-paid cards with a set limit of five hundred dollars. The sort of cards that somebody without a decent credit rating score can stuff in their wallet if they can scrape up the $500 in advance. The sort of cards where you pay the bill before you even get the card, never mind get a chance to blow it on 24/7 online gambling, porn and Ebay. Now these cards were from a big British bank, and most people would take the name as some sort of guarantee that the card is good but that was irrelevant anyway because they are pre-paid so it is like somebody holding out $500 in their greasy palm.

'Okay,' the bosses said to George, 'smart boy, six card numbers with $500 riding on each. How many of these cards can you crack open?' Gorgeous George laughed. 'That's it,' he said. 'Six cards are all I need.' The bosses thought maybe Jorginho had finally crashed into the madness that awaited all weirdos like him. 'Six cards? $3,000?' George had the balls now to laugh in their faces. 'Six cards, sure. But unlimited cash!'

Because the genius part of Jorginho's scam was that a couple of clicks on his keyboard turned those $500 cards into unlimited cards. Instead of hitting an ATM for the bare $500 and then throwing the spent card in the garbage, a guy could keep plugging away with that card all day, as long as the ATM had cash in it, as long as there were ATM's to be hit.

It sounded too good to be true but all thieves are eternal optimists so the dark market got to work. Cranking out the magnetic stripe with George's magic numbers was the easiest part. Ten crews in five cities around the world had a card each. Manhattan, London, Tokyo, Paris and Lisbon. They harvested over 1,000 ATM's in a single day. Withdrew close on two million dollars. Hard cash, straight from the machines into sports bags and back packs. Not even a real victim, and no tight fisted miser to notice the cash flooding out of their stash and cry wolf half way through the feast. No pepper spray, no alarms, no cops, no problem. Some of it maybe went missing between the crews pulling it out and handing it over to the middle management, but that is inevitable and factored in.

Then Jorginho fucked it all up by mixing business with business. Yakov said Jorginho's fifty grand share was planked in Lisbon with that old uncle or whatever that died in Sao Vicente but somebody held a pillow over the old man's face before Jorginho got back over here to collect. Probably my Brazilian friends, Yakov suggested, or the Chinese. Definitely not any of the Lisbon Russians that knew the cash was in a bag under the old man's bed, so Yakov said.

'Your Jorginho is a crazy man,' Yakov said. 'Thought he was the US fucking Marines! Straight to me from the airport shouting and giving orders with his bad Portuguese and loud American mouth! Moscow Alex this! Moscow Alex that! Fuck your Moscow Alex I told him! I knew then he was CIA also, just like your fucking Moscow Alex!'

George was crazy okay, but not the kind of crazy Yakov meant. He was genius crazy and knew it, knew he was outside the ordinary rules, knew the worker bees were there to be twisted to serve his higher purpose.

'I almost shut his big mouth for good except we needed him for this thing. Gambling with money he didn't have, always dangerous. More and more he went to the Chinese to gamble, even more dangerous. Gambling and whoring with other people's money, other people's women.'

Maybe Cora's bosses started to get jumpy around about then. It wouldn't have surprised me if Gorgeous George had worked Miss Cora so that the whole Chinese thing was set to happen here, where his bonus cash was stashed, with more in the pipeline.

'So, you tell me he is safe in Cyprus?' he said.

Yasmin was leaning against the doorframe, arms folded, stroking the back of her right calf with her left foot. Yakov twisted in his seat to unroll a cold grin towards her.

'Don't you think poor Jorginho is missing his friends where he is now, Yasmin?'

It was the first time he had said her name but the way he used it said there was something between them once. Maybe long ago, and maybe long finished, but he screwed the meaning into her name so even I could pick up that vibe. Yasmin shrugged herself upright and slouched off the way a sleek bored cat might. Yakov celebrated a malicious chuckle to make sure I got the undercurrent that lapped between them and his eyes challenged me to ask.

'He is in Cyprus if we need him but Zheng here looks like he can manage fine without the arrogant prick,' I said.

Yakov was running some sort of assessment of me through his head, looked like he was about to pronounce his judgement then decided to let it go, for now.

'And nobody needs an arrogant prick, do they?' he rattled out a comradely laugh, with slaps on the back to match.

★★★

'Two million from the Japanese dogs already!' Zheng shrieked with excitement on the hour mark.

Ten crews were operating in Japan, three in a crew and a floating back up man to record each crew's turnover. The cards were from the First Arab Emirates Bank of Abu Dhabi, at least that's where the cracked card numbers came from. Originally pre-paid debit cards with $300 on the slate, they now swished through Japanese ATM's at a rate of one withdrawal every three minutes and were on course to cream seven million dollars before the day's work was done.

'I do not trust Japanese,' Yakov growled.

Yakov didn't trust anybody, but Tokyo was always going to be the biggest earner in this project because Japanese banks allowed up to ten grand to be pulled from their machines in any one transaction.

'Make sure you keep an accurate record,' Yakov reminded Zheng.

That was the upgrade Zheng brought to Jorginho's business model: the ability to track each individual transaction; where, when, who. There was a back up guy keeping a tally, but any crew thinking they could slip a few grand down their trousers would soon find a strong Russian arm down those pants to rip their balls off.

Yakov and his bosses didn't work on trust, but the banks did. With all their seamless high tech security, the Tokyo banks trusted that each withdrawal was approved by the First Arab Emirates. The Emirates had the water tight systems to allow their trust in the card processor to keep the cards to their pre-paid limit. The card processor trusted that its bunker in the United States couldn't be breached.

'How is the famous Moscow Alex performing?' Yakov mused. Zheng juggled the pop-out screens and pulled New York up. 'Slow. Only a hundred grand. Americans are lazy!'

The numbers started to merge and wriggle before my eyes after another hour. Paris, 500 grand. London, 800. Hong Kong, two million. LA, one million. Chicago, one million. Zheng could have been calling the runners and riders at Belmont Park. Frankfurt and Berlin neck and neck on the outside, Munich coming strong on the rails. Boston pulling away from Zurich, San Francisco losing ground to Miami. Over $10 million after three hours, not even half way round the course yet.

Once the rhythm settled down Yakov regularly stepped outside to wrangle his own crew; lieutenants reporting back, all word of mouth and silent running, a cop associate helpfully pulling the wire on the Lisbon CCTV network, a bank official overseeing the restocking of all ATM's. Yakov had the franchise for Lisbon, Porto and Braga, with a minority interest across the Spanish border to Madrid and down to Seville and on to the sun coast of Malaga. Some other lucky bastards from Ukraine had the golden goose of Barcelona but Yakov hadn't completely abandoned his ambition to elbow the sitting tenants out of his way to that high table.

Sydney and Melbourne making a late surge now. Singapore and Hong Kong on fire, but Tokyo still clear of the pack. Five hours, over $25 million and looking good.

'We have a problem!' Zheng waved to Yakov. 'Birmingham, Britain. No withdrawals for over thirty minutes.'

Yakov switched to focus overdrive. He gripped the back of Zheng's neck and loomed over the screen, made Zheng itemize the Birmingham sequence; how many withdrawals so far, how much, how many per minute, what distance had they travelled, where should the next ATM be. Zheng had it all at his fingertips and reeled it off as quickly as he could because Yakov's own fingertips were clawing deeper and deeper into the kid's neck. Yakov pulled out his iPhone and started the chain reaction in Russian despite the communication lock-down.

'Keep your eyes on Birmingham, Zheng! Tell me immediately if they surface!'

He bolted out of the room and shouted commands to Smoking Ivan and the rest. Zheng looked tired all of a sudden, as if he had been squatting in front of that screen for days without a break. Yasmin appeared with a jug of scalding coffee and he downed three cups without a breath. She left him the jug and pulled me over to the bed.

'He will kill us when Zheng is finished. We must get out now. Leave Zheng behind if he is too heavy with greed to leave.'

Over her shoulder, I could see the coffee had re-booted Zheng's mojo: he wouldn't be prised away from that screen anytime soon.

'That isn't going to happen. They don't want to lose an asset like Zheng. They want him in the United States so they can do this again, or something like this. That means he is safe. They know he isn't getting there without me. That makes me safe. And that makes you and the kids safe. Don't worry about it, I have it all covered.'

She squeezed her body tight against me, and her arms were strong, but that tremble thing was still going on deep in her bones. I stroked her arms and shoulders, gave her my full attention this time without looking for an escape first. Shit! She was crying again, heavy sobs escaping like electric shocks up her spine. I smoothed her hair behind her ears, tickled the little jade teardrop. She panted a couple of deep breaths and pulled away to wipe her tears.

'What about your wife and son in North America?'

I was about to tell her I had that covered also but Yakov burst back into the room.

'How much in total so far, Zheng?'

Zheng pulled out all the pop-up screens like spinning plates and updated his numbers through a currency converter. Yakov slapped the back of his head and barked at him to hurry up.

'Almost $30 million.'

'Anything less than $50 million and you lose that eight million we gifted you from Beirut!'

Eight million? Not six, like three for Zheng and three for me? Zheng shrunk closer to the screen, fingers scrabbling like a New Orleans card mechanic. I shouldered Yakov to the side and hammered a punch right between Zheng's shoulder blades: he fell in a heap and took the computer screen with him. Yakov looked at me as if I had flipped my lid. You've seen nothing yet pal, I said to myself. Yakov lifted the screen and set it up on the table like he was fixing an exhibit in an art gallery.

'What's happening in Britland?' I said.

'A dickhead was too lazy to empty the bag between withdrawals as instructed. He stuffed fifty grand into a bag that would only hold twenty. The fucking thing split open in the street and a mob of English hooligans jumped all over him. He got away but lost most of the cash.'

'What happens now? Call it off?'

'No way! It will be at least tomorrow before the idiots work out what we are doing. Maybe a week! We keep going as planned everywhere else. The dickhead from Leningrad that lost the money won't talk even if they catch him. You have my word on that much!'

'Leningrad? Where's that?'

'Leningrad was a good enough name when my grandfather sacrificed his life for victory against the fascists there in 1944. It will always be a good enough name for me.'

'Who was your boss in the KGB? Stalin?'

Yakov hauled Zheng up by the collar and shoved him into the seat. The kid was still doubled up in pain, Yakov slapped him around the head.

'Unlike the CIA, the KGB no longer exists. Ask your Moscow Alex and his treacherous fuckhead father! Or ask your blond American lady that you have been slipping off to meet in secret. She knows all about it! Ask her!'

★★★

Zheng wrapped it up at just after five in the morning. Los Angeles was seven hours behind, our crews there clocked off at 10 pm leaving lines of punters scratching their heads at finding so many ATM's with no cash to dispense. Tokyo nine hours ahead; 2 pm and downtown ATM's already out of service.

'Over fifty million,' Zheng reported. 'Almost fifty-three.'

Yakov had already filed his best guess reports and hadn't been too far out. He used my shoulder to lever his ass off the seat and stretched a hoarse yawn from deep in his gut, patted Zheng on the head and left the two of us in the room.

'What happens now?' Zheng said.

'They launder the cash,' I said. 'Buy jewelry, gold, Rolex by the dozen, all the stuff that is easily transferred back to cash, no traces, no questions asked.'

'I am not a fool! I know how it works!' he pouted. 'I mean what happens with us? How do I get to America?'

Smoking Ivan and three others burst through the door and had Zheng hoisted above their shoulders before he knew what was happening. I pulled Beto's pistol and stuck it under Smoking Ivan's chin. Yasmin heard the commotion and ran in to scream louder than Zheng. Yakov stuck his head around the door.

'Take it easy!' he growled. 'Too much noise in here. The neighbors will complain to the authorities!'

'Tell them to put the kid down!' I ordered Yakov. 'He stays with me unless you want a big problem on your hands right now!'

'Of course! How else will we get him to America?' Yakov laughed. 'But we already have a big problem! A big stinking problem that soap and hot water will fix! Take the dog out of here!'

Zheng disappeared down the hallway, his shouts drowned by their laughter echoing up from the bathroom.

CHAPTER FORTY

Cora said we would be invisible in the suite waiting for us on Avenida Combatentes because Americans often stayed at this hotel. The US Embassy was just around the corner in Avenida das Forcas Armadas, nobody would notice us. Yasmin didn't much like that idea, thought armed protection should be ready at the front gates to admit us and then put the embassy into lockdown, and she sulked in the dark at the back of the minibus, staring out over the Rio Tejo as we crossed back into Lisbon.

Yakov sat up front, working his phone and keeping Smoking Ivan nervous. Zheng was on his own, in front of me, all spruced up in the new suit, shirt and tie that Yakov had picked out for him. He looked like a kid on his way to his first job interview, but a lot more comfortable than he was a few hours earlier when Yakov had ordered Pyotr to burn Zheng's clothes, stick a torch up the kid's ass and then pour a heavy duty laxative down his throat so that he couldn't smuggle out any confidential info – Yakov's idea of risk management.

'I will leave you now, Maknazpy,' Yakov said. 'Let us hope everything goes well. That Beirut money can be transferred out of those bank accounts as easily as they were transferred in.'

Smoking Ivan pulled off the motorway and doubled back to a parking lot squatting beneath one of the huge 'H' shaped trusses that held the bridge up. Yakov opened the door to hop out but then turned as if he had just remembered something. He cupped his hands around Zheng's skinny cheeks and growled like a playful bear, then pulled out two fifty-dollar bills and flicked one to each child. 'Some American money for your new life,' he said, like he was their old Russian uncle. Yasmin held her stony stare but then a slight nod was the signal for the kids to scoop up the notes.

'Good luck to you, Yasmin,' Yakov said. 'I hope you have better luck in America. Don't let that old anger eat you up inside.'

Yasmin stared out the side window.

'No problem, Yakov,' I said. 'Everything will go just fine. When I say I'll do something, I do it. Watch this space.'

Yakov shouted something to me but he was drowned out by the train rattling over the bridge above our heads. He slammed the door and flopped into the waiting BMW saloon. Smoking Ivan puffed out his relief and waited until the beemer's tail lights disappeared before nosing the minibus to the parking lot gate.

'I will drop you close to the hotel. A short walk. Be ready to get out.'

That wasn't the plan. I eased Beto's nine mill on to my lap.

'Fuck Yakov!' Ivan shouted back to me. 'What if the policia or your American spooks are waiting there to attack me? You see Yakov taking the risk? You think I am so stupid?'

If he hadn't been such a smart ass he might have avoided the risk right in front of him. A flatbed truck rammed across the exit, black figures emerging from the darkness behind and the street in front. Smoking Ivan reached under his seat.

'Take it easy, Ivan!' I screamed at him. 'Don't force them to make the call!'

Ivan came back up gripping a pistol and launched out into the darkness. Two rapid shots, Ivan bounced off the minibus. A figure stepped forward, a single shot. Zheng freaked out, started to clamber over the seat to get to the door, I grabbed his collar and pulled him down. This wasn't the plan either, I held Zheng down with one hand and had the pistol ready in the other. The front and back doors opened in unison. Ski masks and black boiler suits. I hoped for a second that Cora had sprung a new plan on me. Yasmin and her kids thrown to the floor. Zheng punched in the face and out cold, concussion or fainted. I was pinned to the floor with an automatic screwed into my ear. Yasmin silent beside me but the despair in her face promised she would never be so stupid again. We jolted forward to the street, the two in front laughing when they realized the bump was Smoking Ivan's legs crunching under the back wheel. Liu's Falcons. At least now I wouldn't need to sweat about luring my father into Cora's ambush.

★★★

We were in a factory, looked like the despatch section, cardboard boxes and crates lined the walls like a library; Chinese writing mostly, then Portuguese, English and German. The Falcons moved us around with minimum fuss as if we were just parcels for delivery, except for poor Zheng: each one of them landed a slap or kick on his sharp bones as they passed by, but I guess nobody likes a traitor.

A steel stairway led to an office overlooking the factory floor. The lead guy had Yasmin and Zheng sit on boxes in the corner and motioned for me to go up. On my own, no gun in my back or hands above my head. I just sauntered up there like I was going to see the foreman. I suppose that's what he was, in a way.

'It's good to see you, son!' My father gathered me in his arms and hugged my feet off the floor. 'I know you are pissed off at me, I understand that, but things aren't as bad as they look.' He set me back on the floor and held me at arm's length to inspect me up and down.

'Look at you! I'm proud of you, son. Even though I wasn't there for you in person I was always thinking about you. I know this is hard for you to understand but I'll do anything to make it right for you.'

'What to fuck are you talking about!' I shouted in his face. 'Make it fucking right? I ought to break your yellow fucking neck, you cowardly bastard!'

He had tears in his eyes and did nothing to hide them, like he was trying hard to prove how sincere he was.

'I didn't care that you weren't there, you piece of shit! I was glad you were dead! We all had better lives because we thought you were dead! My only regret is that you've turned up now and I have to look at your ugly pathetic face!'

He was dead. The big man that held my hand and made the world safe was dead. Just like the happy little kid I used to be died long ago, so did the father I used to have. This faded old man with his gray hair and loose skin was a different animal. Just because he shared memories with my real father didn't mean it was still him.

'I'm sorry, Con. I really am. I didn't mean for things to work out like that. We can't make things right just because we really want to.'

The red fury started to spin around my skull. I pictured my hands around his throat choking the pretender out of my old man's body.

'And I know you've gone through the same hell with your own son,' he said. 'I thought if I stayed away then you would have a chance to be different. Dr Blake knows what makes us like this. That's why we have to do this. For your own son.'

Footsteps clanged up the steps behind me. Blake looking at us like his fingers were almost touching that Nobel Prize, Liu looking like we weren't really human beings at all.

CHAPTER FORTY-ONE

Now it was business time. He had purged his guilt with the prodigal father routine, now he was ready for the main act.

'Just humor me, okay? Again, what happened to George Oliver?'

I told him, although I don't know why I indulged his pompous assumption that he could expect an answer. Maybe it suited me to deflect from the conversation I really needed to have with him. And yes, I was sure that was how it happened. How many times was he going to ask?

'What did George Oliver reveal when you tortured him in that cellar?' he said. 'About America's dirty war against Iran and Syria?'

Torture? I slapped him around a little because he decided to be a smart ass, he deserved it, that's not torture.

He got up to check there was no-one outside the door. Liu had lost his cool earlier when the old man said he would speak to me on his own. They stood toe to toe screaming at each other until my father lifted Liu by the collar and pushed him outside.

'Do you ever think about what you are doing, son? I mean, do you ever wonder if it is right? Are you doing the right thing?'

Right or wrong wasn't so simple. If there was ever the luxury of making a choice then, sure, who wouldn't be the good guy? Most times the situation doesn't give you a choice, there's nothing to think about except to survive first and come out on top second. Somebody up above has already made all the real choices.

'You are a man now, son. You need to take responsibility for your own actions instead of letting yourself be blown all over the place like a leaf in a storm. You need a sense of purpose in your life.'

The asshole was about thirty years late with the fatherly advice, for what it was worth. I made a mental note never to sound like that when my turn came to pass the wisdom on to young Con.

'You know when I first started to question what I was doing?' he said. 'Thirty years ago I hit Nicaragua with a brand new manual on psychological operations and the brainwash that democracy meant freedom. Except democracy down there had bitten us in the ass and elected what we called an anti-American Communist dictator. We operated the rebels out of Honduras using Noriega's drug money from Panama and a slush fund from Washington. We invented terror, perfected it.'

'I remember,' I said. 'You brought two of your red friends to the apartment one night when I was a kid. They laughed at me and you laughed with them.'

He sat on the edge of the table and reached for my hand. I pulled it away and folded my arms.

'They weren't friends, and they sure as fuck weren't red either,' he said.

His voice now didn't square with the voice I had carried in my head since I was a kid. He was older, sure, and had lived with foreigners for thirty years but it was more than that. He had changed, either that or I had been straining to hear somebody else's voice for all these years.

'So, George Oliver told you he was part of a special unit established to target banks in Beirut that Iran and Syria use to circumvent America's illegal financial embargo?'

I didn't think they could trace the money route Zheng had used, so the cash for Rose and young Con should be safe, but I wasn't giving him any help on it.

'It's not the first time America has thrown its financial weight around to intimidate the international community,' he said. 'We targeted Iran back then in the eighties also. And our enemy's enemy was our friend, so Mister Saddam Hussein Abd al-Majid al-Tikriti in Iraq was our flavor of the month, and we propped up his torture regime to fight our war against Iran. Just like we kindly donated the military and financial muscle for Mister Osama Bin-Laden to fight the Russians in Afghanistan.'

'It's a crazy world,' I said. 'Suck it up and move on.'

'Right about then I decided I wasn't going to suck it up anymore,' he said. 'You've heard of Irangate, right?'

'Sure,' I said. 'Redford and Hoffman, Deep Throat and all that shit.'

He stood behind me now with his hands on my shoulders; he squeezed and his hands were still strong, still a heavy weight.

'We had just about squeezed the fight out of Iran. Their economy was in freefall, they couldn't buy food to feed their people, arms to defend themselves. So, they captured some Americans and held them hostage.'

I remembered the panic and outrage around McLean Avenue at the time. The dead weight now on my shoulders had disappeared again, and I made a story up for the kids on the block that he was one of those hostages. He was a hero and would free everybody and bring them all home.

'I was still perfecting the terrorist manual in Honduras at the time,' he said. 'We broke just about every national and international law in the book. We sold arms to Iran as a ransom for the hostages. Then we breached any remaining international conventions by diverting the hostage money to buy arms for the fascist murderers we employed to attack the democratically elected Government of Nicaragua.'

'Like I said, it's a crazy world. It saved the American hostages, didn't it?'

He let go of my shoulders, knelt down in front of me and tried to take my hands again. I kept my arms folded tight.

'Those weren't my red friends, as you have been brainwashed to call them, I brought to our apartment that night,' he said. 'Those were two of the most savage and cruel torturers the Contra fascists had. They were part of the delegation we brought to the United States to rig that whole filthy set-up. I was told to baby sit them while the leaders talked business.'

I remembered their cigar smoke and hard brown faces. That's what I had always pictured a Cubano Commie to look like; not Fidel or Ché, but those two laughing killers.

'And you are surprised Iran still resists American dictatorship even now?' he said. 'Illegal sanctions to starve them into surrender?'

'Why did you bring them into our home?' I said. 'Why did you let them laugh at me? Why did you laugh with them?'

'I don't know.' He shook his big gray head and screwed his fists into his skull - the same way I did when I was under pressure. 'I was told to do it, so I did it. Just like everything else. Except I started to feel ashamed of myself. I grew so ashamed that I knew I couldn't keep going that way.'

He had tears in his eyes again. I couldn't remember him ever crying at anything when I was child but now he seemed ready to spout at any moment. I unfolded my arms and wiped tears off his cheeks.

'I started to think about a lot of things, son. Maybe I was right, maybe wrong, but I changed my life and went a different way.'

'You left me behind,' I said.

'I met up again with those two fascist murderers a couple of years later,' he said. 'I dropped both of them myself. A bullet in the back of each savage head.'

'Was it worth it?' I asked.

'Who knows?' he said. 'I've been lucky enough to live most of my life following a belief system. I never could have done that in America, wouldn't have been admitted to those circles.'

'You drafted me in to be an altar boy at St Barney's,' I said. 'Wasn't that enough of a belief system for you?'

'I have been very fortunate, son. Even though it meant many personal sacrifices, I have been fortunate. I wanted to change my life and I managed to do that. Mostly because I met a great man in Angola, back in the nineties. He has done great things for China, and therefore great things for the world. He saw something in me, I'm still not sure what, and took me under his wing. If this business has provided them with an easy way to attack him through me then, no, it wasn't worth it.'

'I fucking meant was leaving me behind worth it, you prick!'

He got up and walked around the room, hands behind his back.

'You still say Colonel Liu killed George Oliver?'

I couldn't be assed answering that one again.

'You know, a lot of shit happens in this dirty world we are in,' he said. 'How do you know anything Oliver told you was true?'

'From my experience I can safely say that none of the shit any of you drop on me is true,' I said. 'But it doesn't matter, because we move on and then nothing ever matters again. Either somebody looks back on it and makes that false thing suddenly become true, or it is wiped clean completely so that it never existed. Jorginho's dead so his truth doesn't matter.'

'I know why you are here, son.'

I laughed at him. 'Pity you weren't around for the last thirty years or so, then, isn't it?'

'Oliver's unit weren't only stealing money from those banks,' he said. 'America's proxy wars don't come any cheaper than they did thirty years ago, you know. Your Jorginho was redirecting millions of dollars to the so-called Syrian rebels, to the Jihadis and Al Qaeda. Anti-aircraft and anti-tank weapons supplied from Qatar and Saudi Arabia. How long do you reckon before those are turned on American troops?'

Standing above me now, he seemed a little more like my real father, and I felt a little more like the kid he had abandoned.

'It's not my problem anymore,' I said.

'Nothing was ever your problem, was it?' he said. 'Well, it's going to be somebody's problem. It's going to be my problem. Because George Oliver was about to go public on America's dirty tricks in Syria. The international community was about to discover the latest installment of America's corrupt program to manipulate and dominate the free world from an agent at the heart of the deception.'

He scraped his fists along his skull again.

'Nobody would have believed a con artist like Jorginho anyway,' I said. 'They would have made him out to be a fantasist. They would have demeaned him so that nobody would take him seriously anyhow.'

'Maybe so, but you have covered their tracks now,' he said. 'Your enterprise to satisfy your personal greed means you have made it easy for them. Nothing to do with them. Any independent body tracing what happened will find gangsters working with the Russian Mafia. What they did before will be buried in that mess.'

Jorginho should have said something. I slapped him about because he was shooting his big mouth off. It wasn't torture; he knew that, he was from our streets, he knew I couldn't let him give me his smart lip. He should have known that and come clean with me.

'Then you turn up and Oliver is dead, son.'

'Well I fucking never killed him! Go ask Liu about it!'

'Colonel Liu reports that you killed George Oliver in that house on the clifftop before you tried to escape.'

'Zheng was there! He saw it happen!'

'Comrade Zheng corroborates Colonel Liu's account,' he said. 'You murdered Oliver and tried to escape along the cliffs but Colonel Liu managed to capture you.'

'That's bullshit! Zheng is a weak bastard who will say anything Liu tells him to! Ask Yasmin! She was there. She knows the whole story.'

More tears in his eyes.

'Your lady friend has confirmed Colonel Liu's account also.'

'So what?' I said. 'It makes no difference to me anyway, I won't be stuck in fucking China. The only truth that matters is that I'll escape and be back home in Yonkers before you even know I'm gone.'

The metal stairs outside rattled under the heavy boots running towards us. Both his big hands smeared the tears across his cheeks.

'It's not so simple, son,' he said. 'Colonel Liu has already submitted his report stating you murdered our three soldiers in that house as an act of terrorism. Your murder of George Oliver is reported as an act of espionage against the People's Republic of China.'

'Liu can go fuck himself,' I said.

'I thought I was helping you,' he said. 'But I was always a millstone around your neck.'

Liu kicked the door open and six of his Falcons flanked in beside him.

'So what happens now, dad?'

'Espionage and terrorism resulting in death means the death penalty in China,' Liu said.

My father's tears caused me to cry. Liu pumped himself up like he was about to address the massed faithful from the rostrum on Tian'anmen Square on the Big Red Holiday.

'Death by lethal injection for all foreign spies and traitors!'

CHAPTER FORTY-TWO

Liu left us up there in the office, with a bowl of green tea and a pot of noodles. The phone line and net connection hung out of the wall. I considered trying to put it back together but who was there to call? My old man said Liu had been tipped off that our minibus was coming over the bridge but Liu didn't say who had made that call. I knew it wasn't Yakov or Cora. The Tsars of Yakov's empire needed Zheng safely wedged in the United States so that they could put him to work in the future. The Tsars of Cora's empire would bleed him for every drop of info he had on Chinese cyber skills, and then chain him to a keyboard. I knitted the wires back together but the lines were dead.

'I'm not going to China!' I said. 'Liu has got eight ninjas out there that I counted. At some point we'll only be covered by maybe three or four of them. I say we stay ready and take our shot when it comes and see what happens.'

He sat quietly with his eyes closed and his hands resting lightly on his knees, palms upturned. I scooped up a pile of papers off the desk and threw them in his face.

'I don't know about that, son.'

'You don't know? What? So the great Con Maknazpy, my hero father, really did turn yellow?'

He gathered the papers and smoothed them back into a neat pile on the desk.

'I owe a lot of people a lot of gratitude,' he said. 'I don't know if I can indulge my selfish needs to jeopardize their position.'

'What about my fucking position you selfish old bastard!'

Footsteps on the metal stairs, Yasmin ushered the boy and girl in and calmly closed the door behind her.

'I am sorry, Con,' she said. 'I have no choice. I must go with you to China but Colonel Liu says my children can stay here if I agree to tell his story.'

She looked like shit, and I was glad.

'At least she is playing it straight,' I said. 'She is selling me out to save her children. Fair enough. What's your excuse again, old man? You don't want to embarrass some dickheads back in China?'

He pulled an office chair across for Yasmin to sit on, made a big deal of smacking the dust away and adjusting the back rest to make it comfortable for her. A real gentleman.

'I said I don't know yet, son. I don't know if this is just Liu twisting the situation to his own advantage or if there is a bigger picture I am not aware of.'

'Liu's picture sees me as a terrorist getting needled with a one way ticket to the great paddy field in the sky,' I said. 'That's me we're talking about here! You're son, remember? What fucking picture is bigger than that?'

He said he would do his best but some things were more important than our personal feelings. He knew the arrangement was that we were to ship tonight to the Angolan port of Lobito. A regular shipping container fixed up with a mobile air conditioner, beds, a small gas cooker and a chemical toilet would keep us away from the crew, but they wouldn't want to know anyway. We would be there the day after tomorrow, exchanging a cargo of engine parts for cotton and beeswax. The upgraded airfield in Lobito was close by, and we would be in Beijing the next morning.

When I pushed him on it, his best guess was that Liu's ambition had overtaken the original plan. He knew George Jorginho Oliver had been the original target, but that plan had been simply to have Zheng learn all he could about Jorginho's dirty work in Beirut against Iran and Syria. Jorginho would school Zheng in the Red Protocol and the code he was known to be working on. In return, Jorginho would be granted confidential banking facilities in Macau to stash his dark market winnings. Then Jorginho would go back to the US to continue his ascent as a cyberspy, but, once compromised, he was always going to be easy meat for any future assignments. Then Blake suggested that I would also be a willing guinea pig in his brain study. That was how the plan stood when Liu left Beijing before Christmas.

'Liu doesn't strike me as some sort of reckless maverick making plans on the hoof,' I said. 'You sure this wasn't all set up from the beginning?'

The old man laughed, and a little stab of joy pulsed through my veins.

'The Colonel is an old school diplomat with five thousand years of intrigue as an artform to fall back on. "Dim our light and thrive in the shadow", that's how he works.'

'But he's double crossing you, right?' I said. 'I thought you guys were all about harmony and all that shit.'

'Reaching harmony is a struggle,' he said. 'And a long haul. We have twenty-five leaders on the Politburo, elections to a higher rank in 2017 and the top job up for grabs in 2022. Liu has been sponsored to his current position by one of those twenty-five, just as I have been lucky enough to receive the support of my own mentor.'

'And? Your guy loses face if his American pet project is packed home in disgrace?'

'He took a lot of risks to support me, was warned many times it was a bad move, but he stuck with me. If my son turns up now as an American spy terrorist murdering Chinese soldier heroes, it reflects badly on him, on his judgement. Especially if my American spy son has been diverting cash to buy arms for fascist terrorists, just like I did myself thirty years ago. I'd say Liu has marched ahead in the harmony struggle, wouldn't you?'

'Fuck him! It's the other side of the world and none of my business!'

He looked me over, then turned his eyes to the floor. I remembered that look. He was disappointed in me but trying hard not to show it.

'How long before they take me away?' Yasmin asked him.

'The ship sails at midnight,' he said. 'But it's not all over, I still have friends in Angola, my friends have friends. Liu's faction aren't welcome there. It's not all over yet.'

The three of them clung together like it was the end of the world, Yasmin and the little girl choking in their tears and deep throated howls. The boy crushed them together with frantic strength but didn't cry, just locked that hate stare on me as if it was all my fault. There was nothing much to say to them, it was the end of their world.

CHAPTER FORTY-THREE

Liu stood at the bottom of the steps and shouted a long spiel up to my father. Two of the black masked ninjas were primed outside the office door to ease the old man down the stairs. Just the two of them in a tight space, and fenced in by the metal safety rail. I pressed close to my father's shoulder but he turned and eased me back with a stroke of his rough red hand.

'Take it softly,' he said. 'A dead hero is no use to anyone, understand? Liu says my people have ordered him to stand down until they speak to me. Wait here, I'll be back in a few minutes.'

I reached for his hand to pull him back but he patted me away and disappeared down the steps. Something drained out of my chest and twisted in my gut.

'Your father thinks only of his new family in China!' Yasmin kicked the chair over. 'Liu told me this. He has a boy and girl studying medicine at university in Macau.'

His new family? It never occurred to me that he could have started over after he left me.

'His important friends pay for this. They pay for his family's rich life. He does not care about you! He only cares about the shame of his powerful friends and saving his real family's good life!'

She was in my face and I couldn't think straight. What was she saying? He was down there now selling me out so he could still be the big guy in the Macau Jockey Club? I was a threat to the new paradise he had wormed his way into?

The kid shook us apart. He shoved Yasmin away and flipped the chair up on the desk. A thin skylight plugged into the slope of the ceiling. He yanked it open and squeezed his head into the night air until Yasmin threw her arms around his knees and pulled him back. She wouldn't let him go, Liu had pledged to hand them both over to Thiago as her pay off for backing Liu's script of my crimes and my father's guilt. I hooked my fingers around the sill and hauled up to the opening. Barely more than a hand's width, it was all I could do to stick my nose out, no way was my big head getting through. The kid could just about make it, though. The girl for sure. As far as I could see, this roof joined to the main depot roof a few meters away, and that ran for maybe forty meters before it ended just short of the link wire fence that separated this yard with the next. There were lights on over there, trucks shuffling around that yard, and a gang of workers near our fence.

'You trust Liu to do that?' I said. 'The boy could easily drop on to the fence and get over.' The little girl looked up at me with her big black eyes. 'She could sit tight up there until help arrives.'

Yasmin stepped up on the chair and chinned up for a look herself. She nudged against me and the heat of her body was like a furnace, like the pressure steaming up inside her would combust into a fireball. She looked along the roof and over to the fence, looked back at the boy then measured up the gap between roof and fence. She was going to go for it until she looked down at her daughter's big black eyes. Okay, I couldn't blame her.

I was looking where to put my feet to get down when it started. Headlights pulled up at the gate to our yard, Chinese shouting down below and black shapes running to take covering positions. The gate opened and four vehicles rolled in slowly, crunched over the potholes and drew up in close formation thirty meters from the main door. There was stillness then, just the headlights and the exhausts pumping into the darkness down there, and the heat of Yasmin's body beside me.

Somebody stepped out from our building and approached the vehicles; three figures in pyramid formation, Liu at the head and two shadows tagging along behind. Liu stopped halfway. Doors opened in the vehicles and at least ten figures slipped into rehearsed positions. She was in front. The heavy jacket gave her a man's shape and a skullcap hid most of her blond hair but it could only be Cora.

Nobody moved until they had all picked out their targets and locked a field of fire, then Cora strolled forward, looking pretty cool about the whole thing until they met and she mangled an awkward hand shaking gesture, even tried a clumsy bow. They exchanged a couple of words and then Liu turned and waved somebody forward from the depot. Two of the Falcon ninja's jogged forward, carrying a stretcher between them. My father was on it; strapped down but looked like he was bombed out anyway.

That meant there were only two or three of them left inside. I edged out to the top of the stairs. There was nobody around but the main doors were out of my sight. A few steps down and I could see the whole layout below. Two soldiers crouched in firing positions at the door covering Liu and the stretcher bearers, another room with a light on to my right, at the opposite end from the doors. I vaulted over the stairway railing and crouched towards the room, somebody was moving inside. I launched through the door and knocked him down, stuck my knee in his back and pinned his head against the wall. It was Doctor fucking Blake.

'I am truly sorry about this, Mr Maknazpy. Liu changed the plan. I was not consulted. I am sorry.'

I smacked Blake's head off the wall, just enough to knock the bullshit out.

'It was that night of the stand off, when you escaped with the Russians.' I slapped his glasses off to spin across the floor. 'There was urgent diplomatic chatter between Beijing and Washington that night. They came to an accommodation. I was not consulted. I'm not even political.'

Somebody was moving in the dark across the floor outside. I grabbed Blake's ankles and wedged him against the door to this room.

'Somebody doesn't want you back in the United States, Maknazpy.'

I twisted his right hand up his spine, the hand that was so precise with injections and Naked Cowboys, and cranked the manicured fingers back until they snapped. Blake would have screamed if I hadn't lodged a heavy duty stapler halfway down his throat, and I thought he might pass out, so I gripped his oiled hair and rammed his glowing face against the wall a couple of times.

'There is a bloc within Beijing that has a major problem with the Russians, they favor a pragmatic alliance between China and the United States on certain issues. Your father's patron is one of the old guard antagonistic to the US. These are matters of politics that don't concern me. I am a man of science!'

'Remember you told me nobody really knows what goes on inside somebody else's head? And that other shit? We can't conceptualize how reality is perceived by other people? I'm pretty sure I know what's going on in your head right now, Blake! And you can tell me what's real when I split your skull apart just as easy as you open your oysters and I spill your brain out on this floor!'

'Why? I have nothing to do with all this! I am a scientist! How will causing me harm advance your position?'

I was going to tell him that sometimes bad things just happen and they don't need justification, before or after, but there was a crash outside and Yasmin screamed down to me. I kicked Blake a couple of times until his eyes rolled loose in his head and then made a run for the stairs.

Yasmin had seen it coming, a truck from the yard next door steamed over the fence and the gang of workers piled through the gap, workers carrying AK47's. Two more trucks fired through the gate now and rammed into the rearguard American vehicle, figures spilled out, shooting wildly, running for cover. The Americans were sandwiched between Liu's Falcons in front and the raiding party behind; one of Cora's guys called it, took down the Falcon on the right flank and led the charge to take over that covering position behind the row of big trucks parked along the fence on that side. Two of them grabbed Cora and hauled her over there. The old man's stretcher lay dumped in no man's land. Liu was already back in the depot, ran out to help drag the wounded Falcon to cover. The workers from the next yard pressed forward along the wall of the depot, they must have been exposed out there but they were laying down heavy fire towards Liu's men, grenades flashed down below at the doors, Liu was cut off from the depot and ran to join the Americans with three of his men.

Yasmin was switched on now; no panic, no tears. She helped me hike the girl up through the skylight and on to the roof. I boosted the boy up, told him to take the girl to the far side of the roof and stay there until it was safe.

'There are three or four of Liu's men down these stairs between us and your kids,' I said. 'You ready to go for it?'

'Is it not better to wait here until it is over?' she said.

'No! It's never better to wait and hope,' I said. 'We'll make it happen ourselves. That's what our Faugh a Ballagh thing means. You ready?'

I took a quick look to see what was happening. My father hadn't moved, strapped tight to his stretcher. Liu and his guys that were caught outside were embedded with Cora's Americans over to the right, in good positions among the heavy trucks. The wild truckers who had rammed the gate had them pinned down from the top of the yard, and some of the AK47 workmen from the next yard had them pinned down from this end, near the depot building. The real firefight was going on below us, as the remainder of Liu's Falcons fought to keep the rest of the AK47's out of the building.

We dodged down the steps and into Blake's room. He was curled up in a ball, vomit down his dapper shirt and the wrinkle in Yasmin's nose said he had shit his pants. A door at the back opened to a narrow corridor, three other offices and into the canteen at the end, a heavy padlock on the fire door, a small window above the cooking area. I smashed a chair through the glass and shouldered Yasmin's ass up there, cut my wrist squeezing out after her. A storage enclosure for garbage and utilities backed by a five meter high cinder block wall iced with razor wire. I pulled Yasmin behind me to the right, to bring us out behind the shooters attacking the door and closer to the gap in the fence they had ploughed with the truck.

There was a lull in the shooting. The Portuguese authorities must have been alerted by now but what could they do about it? Mobilize their army? Whatever, the attackers would get one quick crack at this because the combined killing power of the teamed up Chinese and American group would roll over them once they had regrouped and Liu agreed tactics with Cora's team leader. If we could get through the fence to the next yard I would find a secure observation point until the chance appeared to reach my father and her kids.

We slipped around the corner, kept going along the end wall, reached the second corner, the gap in the fence was maybe forty meters away across the open yard.

'Do I run side to side to miss the bullets?' she said.

I pushed her forward and screamed in her ear. 'Forget that shit! Just keep your head down and run like fuck!' She sprung forward but fell in a heap straight away, a black shape moved on the ground, I jumped on him and wrapped my biceps around his neck.

'Stop! Stop! It is me! I made your breakfast!'

Fuck! It was Pyotr, with his bum fluff beard and sensitive eyes.

'My uncle told me to watch his back but I didn't see you coming. I am sorry.'

Yakov? Where was he?

'We came from this side. The others were late, my uncle said we would do it ourselves.'

What others? Who were they?

'It is Thiago of course!' Yasmin said. 'The Brasilian boys would never let these animals take me!'

A twister of crossfire forced the Brazilians back, Liu with his act together, a dump truck revved out from their position under cover from the Falcons still in the building. It rammed up against the door and the Americans and Chinese kept the firestorm going as they retreated inside. That was the chance, I grabbed Pyotr by the shoulder and hauled him across the yard. The kid was shit scared but kept going even though his legs buckled under the weight of the stretcher.

'Your father is dead!' Yasmin said.

He sure looked dead; head hung at an angle, mouth open, tongue hanging out, a ghost's complexion and sunken eyes. But his chest bubbled with shallow breathing and there was a slow faint pulse. Whatever Blake had pumped into him would probably wear off, nothing to be done about it now.

'Pyotr, think you can make it over to the gap in the fence and take her with you?'

'But my uncle told me to watch his back.'

'I've got his back here, Pyotr. You rather face the Chinese killer squad now than Yakov's bad temper later?'

'Give me the Chinese any day!'

We both laughed at that but Yasmin wasn't in the mood.

'I am not going nowhere!' she said. 'Thiago is here. He will save my children!'

Pyotr's AK was against the wall where he had dumped it. It was an old one, old like it had been handled plenty, not like it had been long time in storage. Pyotr assured me it worked okay; Yakov bought them for $40 each from a source in the Congo – probably the same ones he sold into Africa for $100 ten years ago.

Cora and Liu were locked down inside the building now, Yakov and Thiago forced back to cover on either side of the doorway. I pushed Pyotr in front, told him to give plenty of warning that we were friendlies.

'Yakov! It's like I always say, thank Christ for the KGfuckingB!'

'We have big plans for Zheng in your USA,' Yakov laughed back. 'We aren't giving up on him so easy. And the KGB doesn't exist, you asshole!'

Sirens in the distance wailed their warning that the mainstream world couldn't stand back forever and pretend we weren't here. The cops unlucky enough to get the call probably hoped their racket would let us all merge back into the shadows before they got here, but we would have to get this wrapped up quick before they blocked the exit roads.

'So what's your objective here?' I said. 'You want Zheng, right? What about Thiago's Brazilians? What are they doing here?'

'I told him his sister was going on a one way trip to China,' Yakov said. 'Plus I waved some cash under his nose.'

Some of them would never see the cash; at least four Brazilians were down and two or three Russians – one of them certainly dead, a clean head shot. Yakov had six men standing plus Pyotr, we left three to help the Brazilians keep the pressure up at the front and took three to get in through the canteen window. I told Pyotr to sit on Yasmin if she tried to make it over to Thiago's position. Yakov's men covered the ground like a well-oiled fireteam, all synchronized movement and telepathic co-ordination.

'You sure train your gangsters well in Russia, Yakov.'

'These were all Spetsnaz fighting terrorism in Chechnya until they realized the government at home were the real gangsters. Stand back and learn.'

The point man was in the window almost before the blast from the stun grenade had receded, the other two followed like they were attached by elastic and snapped back into formation before I could heave Yakov's flat head through the gap. They forced their turtle formation into the corridor, scuttled forward to the first room, kicked the door in — empty. Hit the second one as two of Liu's Falcons burst into the space in front of us: the short explosion of sound and fury, the adrenaline buzz of seeing your life or death spinning before you like a flip of a coin, the fear that this might be the first and last time you choke. In the room, Zheng cuffed to a pipe, Yakov ripped the radiator off the wall and we dragged Zheng out between us. Two Russians down, one dead, one hit bad on his pelvis and upper arm, only saved by his body armor. Yakov thrust Zheng into my arms and went back to help drag the wounded Spetsnaz out of the corridor. The Chinese were both down but still just about breathing: Yakov stepped forward and finished then both off, tapped each of them twice in the head.

Back outside and the policia massed outside the gates; five squad cars blocking the exit, more coming and no doubt some sort of tactical unit already scrambled. The Russians trailed their wounded over to the next yard through the gap in the fence. I held on to Yasmin and waited by the stretcher. More policia stacked up outside, then split to let three unmarked cars nose to the front. The shooting from inside stopped, somebody must be talking, duty supervisors on three continents freaked out and begging PR for an escape route. Then somebody inside the depot hit the switch for the yard spotlights to blink into blinding life.

Thiago's crew were caught between the depot in front and the cops outside, so made a run across the open ground to our side. The movement must have spooked the Chinese and Americans inside because they launched out to rescue their wounded before the Brazilians could roll over them. A ceasefire; the Brazilians running, Chinese and Americans scooping up wounded and dead, cops watching at a safe distance. Thiago was out front leading the way, four or five behind him but Beto wasn't one of them, the big lunkhead must have been too easy a shooting target for this sort of game.

Yasmin saw the boy first, leaning around the building at the far side then running after Thiago, pulling the girl along behind. She screamed at him to go back, they had come down off the roof on the wrong side, go back and hide, go back until it was over. They kept on coming, trailing about thirty meters behind Thiago but closing on the Americans huddled around a wounded comrade on the ground. Thiago couldn't hear Yasmin but waved and waved as he ran like he had found her back in the old favela. The kids startled the American group and one of them spun around with his MAC-10 at waist height. Yasmin screamed, the scene tripped on in slow motion; the kids running, the guy spinning, the MAC-10 levelling out.

He fired. Yasmin saw it happen before her eyes and her scream died in her throat. The kids were five meters from the shooter, if he was the hotshot he was supposed to be he should have seen they were only kids — but he couldn't stop himself. The little girl froze, her nails clawed into the boy's arm. The boy turned to shield her, he saw the gun fire and tried to save her. Thiago jerked his head just as the MAC-10 broke the ceasefire, heard my scream and followed my eyes. The kids didn't move, stood there like petrified statues, because Beto dived his slow running hulk in front of them, took the blast full square on the chest and staggered backwards, arms out wide, making himself big, taking the hits but staying strong on his feet.

Yasmin broke free from me and ran to her children. The gates opened and policia blue lights nervously advanced into the yard. Thiago was already nursing Beto's head on his lap when I reached them. The yard was cleared now of the American and Chinese dead and wounded. Frothy blood foamed out of Beto's chest as Thiago whispered in his ear. Yasmin smothered the little girl's face against her breast, the boy broke free and stood next to Thiago. Beto cracked a smile with his eyes, gestured for me to come closer and took the boy's hand in his.

'This is my man Bebeto!' Beto rasped. 'He will do good in your América do Norte. Look after him! I will need my man Bebeto to look after his uncle Thiago when I am gone.'

Thiago howled and clamped his arms tightly around Beto so that blood spurted from the great chest in little red fountains. Bebeto smoothed his hand over the back of Thiago's head but didn't cry. Yakov was at my side now, cellphone pressed to his ear as he tugged my sleeve.

'Maknazpy, I've bought five minutes before the police start their work.'

The boy helped me to guide Yasmin and his sister away and we followed Yakov towards the gap in the fence. Yasmin stopped when we were halfway there and jogged back to Thiago. Beto's smiling eyes were glass holes into his black inked head. Yasmin hugged her crying little brother until I yelled at her to hurry up, then she pressed a firm kiss on Beto's lips and a slow, gentle kiss and prayer on each of his dead eyes. The little girl clasped her brother's hand, the boy's face twisted under the pain of loss and, maybe for the first time in his young hard life, tears surged and rippled along his eyelashes. He was still weeping softly as Yakov was waved through the police cordon and we turned back to the city. Still weeping, but still able to fix me the bitter look that said it was all my fault.

CHAPTER FORTY-FOUR

Yakov's house from outside the security gate reminded me of a municipal building – maybe a library or a small museum. From the back it looked a lot like a health club - three cubes of brick and glass welded together to overlook a fifteen meter pool and hot tub. He guided me around the six bathrooms, the terraces fringing the four bedrooms on the third floor, the hi-tech kitchen, and then insisted I worked the touchscreen in the master bedroom which controlled his 'smart' house. The tour grand finale was in the basement gym and bar which shared a full length glass wall with the adjoining pool.

'Once a man sips this life it is impossible to go back to the ordinary world,' he said. 'You can enjoy a life like this yourself, Maknazpy, or you can permit them to keep using you until they either kill you themselves or leave you abandoned in some dirty hellhole nobody has ever heard of.'

'Thanks, Yakov,' I said. 'You make it sound like I have lots of choices here. Never thought of the Russian Mafia as a career option before.'

The lights flickered behind the bar as Yakov plucked the props for his next act; Tanqueray No. TEN, peach vermouth, two grapefruits and a lime.

'You can laugh now but, believe me, you are at the crossroads of your life, Mr Maknazpy.'

His big hands pulped the grapefruit dry, then nimbly scraped the lime skin.

'You sound like my old man,' I said. 'What's next? A lecture on ethics and morals?'

Yakov pulled down two crystal sherry glasses. He noticed something on one of them and held it up to the light like it was a chalice, checked for lipmarks around the rim and frowned at the blemish before smashing it against the wall. He rooted around for an acceptable glass, then poured and stirred with an artist's exaggerated concentration.

'If you were Russian you would know there is supposed to be a difference between ethics and morals,' he said. 'Me? I don't believe in that shit. We make it up as we go along. We all do, not just people like you and me, but everybody; governments, religions, the man in the street, even the Party. People like us are just more honest about it.'

He flicked a dash of clear syrup and placed the glasses on the bar like they might explode in our faces if he didn't do it slowly and carefully.

'No ice? No cocktail umbrellas?'

'Fucking barbarian!'

Yakov's cocktail was fine, though a bit sickly sweet for my taste.

'You have plenty of choices,' he said. 'But Zheng isn't one of them. You will get him placed in America. That is what we business people call a non-negotiable, a deal breaker. Of course, after that, your life is your own, my friend, go back to your gray little world if you wish.'

As if my life ever had been my own. As if there was a gray little world back there somewhere waiting on me.

'And be quick about it. We have our friends in the Lisbon authorities but the Chinese and Americans can shout louder than us, and higher up the food chain. Especially the Chinese. I have been promised two days. So far, the Portuguese military have been kept on a leash. If they are set free then our war is over, believe me. So, two days! After that, the situation becomes dangerous – for some more than others, understand?'

'Where is Zheng right now?'

'Not here and you don't need to know where he is. You make the arrangements and I will bring him.'

I gestured for another drink and Yakov started his flick and dash routine to prepare a masterpiece. I hopped off the bar stool when his back was turned and headed back upstairs.

'American asshole!' Yakov shouted after me.

Pyotr was in the lounge watching breakfast TV with a gang of Yakov's 'helpers' – not the Spetsnaz guys, just ordinary wannabe Mafia. I went up to the third floor. Yasmin and her children were in the first bedroom. They were asleep, or pretending to be asleep, so I backtracked quietly and eased the door closed behind me. My father was in the next room. Yakov had roused a friendly doctor to have a look at him. Nothing to worry about, he told me, probably a common sedative and the old man would be fine after it had worked its way out of his system.

I tiptoed over and sat on the end of the bed. His gray head stemmed out like a meaty Chinese mushroom from the goose down pillows and Egyptian cotton sheets. The doctor had said I didn't need to worry about him. I wasn't worried. There were deep emotions spinning around in that quiet room okay but I couldn't pin any single one down to satisfy myself that I understood how I felt.

'Nobody at home thought I was dead,' he chirped from under the sheets. 'It made it more convenient all around to pretend I didn't exist anymore.'

'Yeah? Well nobody ever told me that.'

'You? It was especially convenient for you, son. It meant you could grant yourself permission to blame all your weaknesses on me. All the hurt you caused was actually my fault, wasn't it? The pain? The brutality? The killings? You weren't really to blame for any of it. Disappearing was the best thing I ever did for you, and the most convenient.'

I stood up and rubbed my fists along my skull, walked around in a circle, sat down again, got up and stood over him.

'What about the brain shit?' I said. 'That came from somewhere. Blake might be a traitor but he knows his science! I have you to thank for that, haven't I?'

He sat up in the bed and scraped his hands up and down his face. He looked old.

'When is the last time you had one of your brain blow-outs?' he said.

When? I couldn't remember, that's the fucking point, you lose control and some other part of you takes over until you snap out of it later on and it is too late.

'I haven't experienced one in nearly thirty years,' he said. 'And if the reports I read were anywhere near accurate, it affected me far worse than it did you.'

Why? Did the Chinese have some cure, is that what Blake was getting at?

'I started taking responsibility for my own actions, that's why,' he said. 'I realized it wasn't enough to say I couldn't help it. I decided it would stop. I made it stop.'

Great, like if I really, really want something then I can really, really have it.

'Sounds a lot like you still believe in the great American Dream there, fella!' I said. 'So why don't you decide we can forget about all this Chinese crap and go home?'

He swung his legs out of the bed and pulled himself to his feet. His pants and vest looked like the ones I remembered him wearing when I was a kid – or was that another trick of memory?

'Because being grown up means it isn't all about me,' he said. 'If it has been decided that the greater good is to be progressed by my exile then it is my duty and honor to comply.'

'Greater good progressed? What to fuck does that even mean?'

'It means Pipelineistan!' Yakov backheeled the door closed and swaggered past me with two crystal sherry glasses. He ignored me and handed a Speedbird to my father.

'Your father will progress the greater good by his loyalty. By not disrupting Pipelineistan even though he is privately against it, apparently. If only we still had loyalty like that in Russia! Ah, I would still be in Moscow!'

'What to fuck is Pipelineistan?' I said.

My father gave me one of his blank looks, partly blank but not quite enough to hide his disapproval. My memory wasn't so bad after all.

'Where do we start?' Yakov said. 'Well, let's start with the capitalist west's fear of Russia. America's strategic imperative to destabilize Moscow. Is that where you would start, Mr Maknazpy Senior?'

My father sipped the cocktail and took in the luxury of Yakov's guest room.

'Well, let's see,' Yakov tongued his drink and licked his lips. 'If Russia turned off its gas pipelines today western Europe would collapse tomorrow. Russian gas keeps the Germans warm, and all the little countries as well. Agreed?' He looked to my father, still the blank look, but enjoying the Speedbird. 'But this does not follow the American agenda. How can they enjoy the perfect capitalist market when the Russians have their finger on the power switch? Now, if only Washington could install their Arab proxy states as the source for gas and oil to the west and paralyze Russian supplies, wouldn't the world be a better place? Follow me so far?' I followed, it sounded like the paranoid crap Ferdy used to recite about Iraqi oil after he had a few drinks. 'Qatar and the Saudis – fanatic Islamists still living in the Middle Ages but lots of oil and gas, yes? If only they could replace Russia then all America's dreams would come true! Ah, but you know the problem, don't you?'

I was still tired after last night's fun, and I wished I had taken that second Speedbird after all.

'Jorginho's target was the Lebanese banking system, wasn't it? Which juggles the finances of Iran and Syria, right?'

Sure, and Zheng had just juggled eight million dollars out to create the perfect capitalist market for us.

'Iraq, Iran, Syria, Lebannon, Palestine. What do they have in common? No, not that America and your Israeli subjects have tried to eliminate them. No, the problem is that Syria is at the crossroads of Pipelineistan, like it has been at the centre of that world for centuries, and blocks your pet Arabs from connecting to the great anti-Russia project. Worse than that, an Islamic pipeline across the Mediterranean from Libya and

Egypt through Syria to Iraq and Iran would mean defeat for America's war in the east that you have been waging since Pearl Harbor!'

Pearl Harbor? Wait a minute, Yakov, you lost me on that one. And what to fuck has any of it to do with China anyway?

'The Chinese? They will do what they always do. Lead others to fight their wars for them and then step in and take the rewards for themselves afterwards. Like they did after the west sabotaged the Soviet Union, taking the oil from the old Soviet States in the south. Like they have already the lion's share of Iraqi oil.' Yeah, that was the Ferdy McErlane history lesson as well. 'They have already bought Gwadar off Pakistan and deepened the port so they can extend the Islamic pipeline to China.'

Gwadar? Where's that? Some other Arab hot spot waiting to erupt?

'Gwadar is a deepsea port at the mouth of the Persian Gulf. When Americans want something they provoke a war and invade but when the Chinese want something they pay for it. They are happy to pay billions, Pakistan is happy to accept. Without Gwadar, Chinese oil supplies are vulnerable, they must ship it 20,000 kilometers through seas they don't control. With Gwadar they have a direct pipeline overland to their own borders. What does that tell you?'

It didn't tell me anything but my brain started to hurt and I really could have handled another drink.

'It tells me the Americans are fools!' Yakov said. 'The Chinese are making it known that there is a split in the Politburo, yes? One faction are said to be reformists, dynamic modernists with a pragmatic strategy. They want to work close to the American agenda and screw Russia! They say they will abandon Russian supplies and only trade oil and gas with the old Soviet States like Kazakhstan and Turkmenistan. This faction will back the Americans to block the Islamic pipeline and instead will push the Arab supply lines through Syria to join with Turkey and screw Russia again. The other faction are supposed to be old school anti-imperialists. They say screw the Americans! They say take the Islamic pipeline to China through Gwadar, buy Russian supplies through Siberia and say they will block the Saudis and Qatar from going through Syria. Is that a fair report, sir?'

The old man was back between the Egyptian thousand thread count cotton, nuzzling into the goose down pillow, like the sedative was still stalling through his veins.

'From what we are supposed to believe, Colonel Liu is with the reformers and Mr Maknazpy Senior is with the old guard. Are you getting the picture now? Pipelineistan is another Chinese war without a war. And the Americans might believe this shit about a split between two factions but we Russians wised up to how they play their game hundreds of years ago. Understand now? Any more questions?'

My father buzzed an easy snore.

'May I have another drink down in the bar, please?' I asked.

CHAPTER FORTY-FIVE

'I need Zheng if we are going to pull this off,' I said.

Yakov's face almost touched the cutting board as he sliced the lemon into leaf-thin strips.

'I will get him into the United States but I need to put him to work first,' I said.

'What about your father?' Yakov said. 'Will he be a problem?'

My father had always been a problem, and always the source of all my problems, no matter how smart he was at deflecting his guilt back on me.

'We will see what the Americans say,' I said. 'We might get a little extra leverage if they want him so bad.'

Yakov wiped his lemon juice fingers on his shirt before scrolling the recipe on his iPad.

'Hmm, I think they want him because the Chinese have made them think they want him,' Yakov said. 'But not our problem as long as you don't start that Irish sentimental shit, okay?'

'No problem,' I said. 'You must be thinking of somebody else.'

'Pyotr will bring him,' he said. 'But you must sort it out by tomorrow, understand? After that, we will cut our losses.'

He lobbed a lemon in the air and swung his knife at it but, instead of splitting in half, the lemon bounced over the counter and spun around the floor at my feet. I picked it up and tossed it back to him.

'It'll be done when it's done,' I said. 'But tell me, how come the take from the Syrian bank was eight million? Who said so? Why not eighty million?'

Yakov shrugged and cut savagely through the lemon.

'I don't know! That's what I was told. It was only to pay-off you and Zheng, not my business. Maybe somebody worked out that was the maximum that could be moved without raising the alarm and putting our own ATM thing under pressure.'

'Who told you?' I said.

He shrugged again, like he hadn't a care in the world and my questions were so boring he could hardly bother himself to answer.

'I don't fucking know who,' he said. 'All the arrangements were made in New York, ask them when you get back there.'

★★★

Zheng didn't look up when Pyotr led me into the dark room. I pulled the curtains back and opened the window. He sat curled up in black track pants and a child's T-shirt with a faded mutant ninja turtle print. The suit was gone. His feet were bare. He looked like he had been down a hole for a year.

'You can still get to Cora's laptop, right?' I said.

His hands shook and his teeth chattered. I took his face in my hands and made him look at me.

'Zheng! Get me Cora! Don't let them trace you, okay?'

He tapped at the keyboard as if he hadn't seen one before and had to search out each key. Pyotr made an 'O' with his lips and sucked air through his teeth. I rubbed the back of Zheng's neck and squeezed his shoulders. He started to warm up, the memory muscle in his fingers kick started back to life before his brain could catch up. I nodded for Pyotr to leave us. Zheng raked the spit from deep in his gut and splattered it over his shoulder – he was back in the saddle.

Cora looked like she had been down the same hole as Zheng. Greasy hair flopped over most of her face so that the camera accentuated the black bags under her red eyes and the angry rash under her chin.

'It looks like I've been drafted to the other team, Cora,' I said. 'So where do you guys want to take it from here? Nailing my old man for something he did way back in history is a higher priority than bringing in Liu or Zheng? Who had that great idea?'

Cora pressed her hands together and touched her fingertips to her lips. She closed her eyes and looked like she was in prayer.

'That's your problem right there, Con. You aren't a team player. You play by your own rules. I don't have that luxury. I don't have that arrogance. I follow orders. I don't play God.'

'So what are your orders now?' I said. 'You don't have my father, don't have Zheng, and you lost Jorginho. Your team doesn't have much to show for all its trouble, so what now?'

She reached to cover the camera but I could still see movement in the shadows at the edge of the screen. She wasn't in her bedroom, looked more like an office, maybe a control center. She wasn't on her own.

'The original plan was good but you fucked it up, Maknazpy,' she said. 'Circumstances changed, so we reacted in the best interests of the United States. That doesn't give you a free pass to betray your country now.'

I rocked back with laughter, even Zheng smiled.

'I have come a long way since that childish crap meant anything, Cora, so you go get your orders for this new circumstance, okay? Or maybe me and Zheng and my old man will take a trip to China after all. Or maybe Moscow, how would that fit with your orders?'

Zheng jumped like I had pumped an electric shock up his ass, I motioned to him to take it easy and listen.

'Moscow? What's in Moscow for you, Maknazpy?' she said.

'Pipelineistan, Cora! Maybe Pipelineistan is in Moscow!'

'What are you on, Maknazpy?' Her voice strained to stay strong. 'Where did you pick up that nerd conspiracy garbage? Your gangster friend Yakov?'

'Maybe so, Cora, maybe so,' I said. 'But I think we would get quite a hearing in Moscow right now, don't you? I think they would pay big time for our insight into Jorginho's Fourth Code and financing the Syrian rebel Jihadis, and your deals with the Chinese to cover it up. How would that go down in the United Nations or wherever to fuck they score points on that shit?'

She covered the camera and mike for a few seconds.

'Fine! You go right ahead with that! In fact we would be delighted if you did! Seeing as how those funds were bouncing back and forward between bank accounts linked to our Russian friends. Yeah, it would be a lot of fun to see how Moscow handles that little number. Like where does the Russian black economy stop and the government begin? Try again, Maknazpy! The Russians are the last people on earth who would want to shine a light on that particular business!'

'Okay, Cora, not the Russians then, you win, but there's always somebody out there waiting to take a crack at America,' I said. 'It won't be so hard to sign somebody up on an anti-American ticket.'

'You don't care about America, Con, that's fine also!' That brittle tone when she liked to demean me. 'What about the innocent civilians at the raw end? The children? The chemical weapons? Don't you care about any of that?'

'I care plenty, Cora,' I said. 'There's just nothing a little guy like me can do about it. All I can do is look out for myself and hope you big guys have a plan. But when your plan includes screwing me over then I need to care plenty about that too.'

Somebody whispered to her and she glanced off camera.

'So what's your bottom line here, Maknazpy? What do you want from us?'

'Zheng used the Russian Mafia banking network to liberate those funds from the bank in Syria. Somebody in New York made that happen.' I said.

More whispers and anxious glances.

'I don't have a fucking clue what you are talking about, Maknazpy, except that we do know millions of dollars have been stolen from ATM's all over the United States! Care to explain yourself?'

'Don't know anything about ATM's, but somebody in New York fixed it so Zheng could help himself to the Syrian money, Cora. You can tell me who it was later, when I check in to find out our travel arrangements. That's travel for a party of four adults and two children. And a guarantee to make me out of bounds forever. And my Dad also, he gets a free pass as well.'

I nodded Zheng to cut the line. Sorry about that, Cora, but Yakov's sanctuary would expire soon, and I had arrangements of my own to make.

CHAPTER FORTY-SIX

Yakov said it was a shit idea. He had already pulled in all the favors he had banked with the Portuguese big hats over the years. I had to buy twenty grand's worth of favor from my own share before he agreed.

'Two good men dead and four wounded,' he said. 'That means I have a responsibility to their families, now and forever. You think I should go looking for more trouble?'

He was the sort of man that wouldn't have been persuaded unless he had secretly wanted to be, and my twenty grand to buy the address from a nervous cop was enough to let him indulge his appetite for revenge. And he maybe thought the interest on my twenty would mushroom by the time I paid it over, but that would be another story. So we rolled up nice and easy at the corner of Rua São Domingos á Lapa and Rua das Praças, just me and Yakov in the Range Rover and Pyotr behind driving three new young guys from Moscow – The Noviciates, Yakov called them.

Twenty grand was the finder's fee for pinning Liu and Blake in one of the new apartments a few meters down Rua das Praças. They had protection but our cop couldn't say for sure how many. He did know at least two of the Falcons were killed in last night's action, and some more wounded, but the Chinese embassy denied any knowledge and had bolted a very tight lid on the details. Portuguese cops were on high alert and their surveillance teams had reported Chinese medical personnel coming and going since last night. And all sorts of other people also, people who had never been seen at the embassy before now charged in there like they had big time business to do. Anyway, Portuguese security around the embassy was highly visible, the law being seen to be done, and the Chinese knew better than to insult their hosts by having Liu and his Falcons walk out of there like they owned the place. Better to plank Liu and his party somewhere low-key from where they could make their exit without putting the Portuguese on the spot.

Yakov's cop said government suits were even tasked to secure a refuge suitable for Liu until it was time to go, and somebody was up there late last night preparing the empty place for their arrival. It was a good call, whoever made it. São Domingos rumbles down a steep hill towards the Tejo. Yakov said the Chinese embassy was a few blocks away and Liu could slip down to the docks for a boat to Angola in a couple of minutes.

'This won't be so easy,' Yakov said. 'I should have brought my old comrades, the young boys they send from Moscow these days are more like fucking Americans than Russians!'

'No offense taken,' I said. 'I take it your old comrades are KGB also?'

'Fuck you and your KGB! The KGB fucking sold the Soviet Union to the highest bidder!' He breathed through his nose like an angry buffalo and shifted in his seat to wave Pyotr to be ready. 'If you must know, I served the people for over twenty years in the Intelligence Directorate of the Soviet Army – the GRU of the General Staff. Ask your father to look me up in his files sometime. Our paths maybe crossed, I was stuck over there in Havana for three years in the 1980's listening to the mindless babble that passes for American communications.'

'You were a fucking spy in Cuba also?'

'How is the St Regis Washington these days? Only two blocks from the White House and always an excellent cocktail! Let's just say I was a well travelled young man back then, before the world went fucking mad.'

'So what happened?'

'What? You mean what happened to me or what happened to the world? I don't think you could understand either thing, Maknazpy, they have you blinkered like a race horse. That's not such a bad thing in our present situation though but, please, shut the fuck up and let's do this thing!'

The policia car crept up Rua Praças, stalled at the lip of the junction to flash their signal to us, and accelerated away down São Domingos. My twenty grand had bought us five minutes before the replacement policia surveillance would trundle into place. Yakov lugged the Range Rover around as if it responded to his brute strength rather than the steering column and jammed it into reverse down Rua das Praças. Pyotr was already half way down the next street so that he could block Praças from the opposite end.

'We want Blake alive, right?' I said. 'Let's keep our cool in here and get the job done with minimum force, okay?'

'What, you are a Peacenik all of a sudden?' Yakov rolled his eyes and snorted a laugh, jumped out and hauled the bag from the trunk; two M4's, the Close Quarters model with the shorter barrel, and four M84 Flashbangs – I didn't ask where the major upgrade since last night came from. Pyotr stayed with the automobiles while the three young Russians tripped along at Yakov's heel.

Liu and Blake were on the third floor at the end of the corridor. Yakov was maybe twenty years older than me but he took off up the stairwell like a man half his age. I told him to save his breath for when he got up there but I guess he was making some sort of point to me and the young guys about the hard Russian and soft American.

He was hanging over the banister gasping for breath when I reached the third floor. If our information was good, the apartment directly opposite this stair exit had been commandeered by Portuguese security. That was a headache because the last thing we needed was for some Portuguese cop or military people to get in our way. So far, the security and sovereignty implications for the Government of what was spilling out on the Lisbon streets would be so horrendous that the authorities needed to keep the whole thing locked down from public view. They could probably just about cope with the pressure from Washington and wherever to manage the fallout while we were only scalping each other, but once their own uniformed guys start carrying the coffins of their comrades all bets are off.

Yakov placed one of the Moscow boys at the top of the stairs and the other two outside the Portuguese door. Liu's room was about thirty meters down this corridor. I favored the stealth option but Yakov pumped his lungs for a spell and then took off again, bumping me aside and hitting Liu's door with more of his ass than his shoulder and stumbling into the tight hallway. I threw my flashbang in and yanked him back into the corridor. The floor shook beneath our feet, it was like forked lightning bouncing around a tin can in there. My head was still rocking when Yakov stepped in to throw another one, came out holding three fingers up.

He went in first, smacked the Falcon on the temple with the butt of his M4 and again on the back of his neck as he went down. Blake was on his knees in the middle of the room, head in his hands and spewing his guts up. Liu squatted behind the sofa with his hands clamped over his ears. Yakov kept them covered, I booted open the bedroom door - clear, bathroom - clear. Back inside, cuffed the Falcon, grabbed Blake by the back of the neck and hauled him to his feet. Yakov nodded at Liu.

'Leave him!' I yelled. 'Blake is the one we want. Let's go!'

I pushed Blake into the corridor and whacked an open hand slap around his ear to keep him moving. A shot cracked behind me, then another, Yakov backed out of the apartment and caught up with me.

'I can't hear! He shouted in my face. 'I thought you said nail him!'

Up ahead, the Moscow boys had screwed up. The guard we had left at the top of the stairs was pulling the other two out of the Portuguese security apartment. I kept moving with Blake, Yakov stopped to kick and thump them to their feet and then corral them to the stairway. Blake stumbled on the stairs and twisted his ankle as I dragged him on, Yakov kicked him from behind and he fell the last four or five steps to the bottom. Pyotr took his other arm and helped me plug him into the Rover's trunk.

'Change of plan!' Yakov shouted close to my face, our ears still numb. 'The stupid bastards ran in before the stun grenades detonated! Four SIS inside – Portuguese CIA! They raised the alarm, we'll never make it back to Restelo in this car!'

The M84 Flashbang has a standard detonation gap of 2.3 seconds. How green could they be? 'That twenty grand I owe you?' I said. 'Take it out of their wages!'

'Did you never make mistakes when you were young?' Yakov shouted. 'Do not worry, if I have to offload this Range Rover and lose money on it, they will pay for that. However, your twenty grand plus interest still stands, my friend. But no extra charge for taking care of Colonel Liu for you.'

Somehow I reckoned Liu had been a personal touch, and if I had read Yakov better I could have saved myself twenty grand, plus interest.

CHAPTER FORTY-SEVEN

The cops sitting outside Yakov's cube house in Restelo made no fuss when we rolled back in a different vehicle. One raised his hand in casual salute as Yakov waited for the security gates to creak open, the other one buried his head in his newspaper and the cloud of cigarette smoke. Blake's casual veneer had been scraped off long ago, and he was way outside his comfort zone by the time Pyotr and the others dragged him down to the basement gym.

'You are a man of science, Blake, isn't that what you always tell me?' I said. 'No politics, no patriotism, no dogma. You are above all that crap. Science is above it. All the Joe Sixpacks like me should be grateful but we're not but you don't give a shit anyway because you live in a different world, right?'

Blake's eyes twitched and stared, a lot like the white rats he kept in his lab. Yakov's stale testosterone and sweat would ooze out of the floor and walls no matter how much the cleaning lady scrubbed and polished but now another scent blossomed in the tight space – Blake's fear.

'You know how this goes, Blake!' I squeezed the fingers I had snapped last night. 'Bin all that shit about being a new person every day and not knowing what you know and what you don't know. Just know this – if I don't hear what I need to hear, you won't have to worry about who you are ever again.'

I cranked an extra twist and he started to black out so I slapped him around the ear, his eyes ricocheted around his head and he slumped forward like a corpse.

'Heart attack!' Pyotr said.

I slapped his other ear, no reflex.

'Just shit scared,' I said. 'Keep an eye on him until Zheng is ready.'

I left them and headed through the bar for the stairs. Yakov had his iPad propped against the ice bucket to follow another cocktail recipe, he grunted without looking up.

'We cut our losses tomorrow, Maknazpy, mid-day tomorrow.'

I kept going, up to Yasmin's room, the kids flopped in front of the plasma screen stretched across the wall, Yasmin leaning over the balcony railing, lilting Barco Negro and looking like she might take a tailspin into the pool below.

'Yasmin, what did you mean that time you said Jorginho was too special to permit happiness,' I said. 'What was it about him that made you think that?'

She bent further away from me, hanging over the balcony and staring down at the tiny birds nipping the surface of the heated pool. I tugged her elbow to bring her back to this world.

'He was like you,' she said. 'He said one thing but meant another. Like this was a toy Jorginho and the real one was somewhere else, watching the fun and laughing at the fools who believed they knew the true Jorginho.'

'What did he say about New York?' I said. 'What about people? He must have told you what a big shot he was, all the VIP's he knew?'

She turned away like she was breaking free from an old skin, arced her back and stretched her arms high to the blue sky, then scooped her hair into thick black ropes to be twisted and pulled into a crazy mess.

'He only spoke about himself,' she said. 'Even when he wasn't talking about himself that was what he was thinking. About what he would do with all his money and what he would do with me when he took me to New York. The same things you say. Then we found him in the house in Sintra and he looked through me as if I wasn't there. That was the real Jorginho. I saw it in his eyes that this was the real one, but too late for me.'

'This lady can't tell you anything you don't already know.' My father slid back the glass door to the balcony. 'You dug this hole for yourself, you can't expect Yasmin to pull you out.'

He was still in his pants and vest; 50 degrees and he was flapping about in his bare feet.

'More chance of help from her than from you,' I said.

'I'll help where I can,' he said. 'That has always been my position. And I'll be honest. I think that's what you resent most of all, son – that I was honest, not that I abandoned you. I think you found it difficult to incorporate my honesty into your self-serving worldview.'

He looked old here in the late winter daylight, old in his pants and vest. I wondered if his bullshit was an early sign of dementia and if my genes were predestined to unravel when I got to his age.

'So what about Jorginho?' I said. 'What did Blake tell you and Liu about George Oliver?'

He shrugged and the bull chested man of my memory looked withered in his discolored vest.

'You know that already also,' he said. 'George Oliver was gifted with a remarkable capacity for logical reasoning and an exceptional mental energy.'

'Yeah, very interesting, but who gave him the key to the Russian Mafia's banking network?'

'Do you really not know?' The disappointed look on his face again. 'He worked for the CIA, didn't he?'

'I don't know who the fuck he worked for!' I said. 'Why would Liu break his neck if he was so useful?'

'Say what you like about Colonel Liu but he is a loyal and dedicated servant of the people,' he said. 'Whatever the reason, it certainly wasn't for any personal gain or vindictive motive.'

'Was dedicated. Was loyal. Yakov put him to bed about an hour ago.'

My father's face wavered and then held its composure in a rock solid grip. But his eyes pulsed an anxiety that nobody else would recognize, thirty years later and I knew I was still the only one in the world who could have picked it up.

'Why would Yakov do that anyway?' My claws were tearing him apart and I wouldn't let go now. 'Yakov was Russian Military Intelligence, you know, GRU? Think that has something to do with it?'

He rallied, cleared his throat to buy time and rubbed his eyes like he was still affected by Blake's sedative.

'Yakov is nothing more than a criminal, a voracious gangster,' he said. 'Anybody can say they were GRU, doesn't mean you have to believe them.'

'I believe him,' I said. 'But okay, say he wasn't GRU, why the risky hit on Liu when the Portuguese intelligence service were sitting next door?'

'Who knows?' Another vest shrug. 'Don't waste your time searching for a reason. When you step outside civilization the barbarians don't need excuses.'

Yasmin coughed and flicked her eyes to the glass door. Pyotr was standing there, straining to hear our conversation above the cartoon racket on the plasma, but opened the door then as if he had just arrived.

'Zheng is ready,' he reported. 'My uncle says you should come now.'

★★★

The resilience of youth and arrogance crackled out of Zheng's new suit as he reclaimed his pedestal. Yakov had splashed out on a silk number, cobalt blue, and somebody must even have taken Zheng's measurements. Ankle boots and a purple leather string tie. Zheng was the real man about town, one more day before he hit his Manhattan nirvana; all the girls he wanted, an American apartment, and recognition as the Alpha Geek.

Blake stumbled like a zombie and sagged into his seat. The big wheel had turned, Blake was pitched to the opposite end of the scale from Zheng and had defeat stamped all over his face. Maybe this was the new Dr Blake for today.

Cora was waiting, and I let her wait some more until Zheng had mapped out the audience – trailing back to Salt Lake City, Maryland, Virginia and, maybe even without American invitation, Cheltenham in England.

'We all want to finish this and go home,' I said. 'I hope we can do it the easy way.'

'We lost good Americans last night,' Cora said with all the solemnity they had rehearsed into her. 'The security of the United States remains paramount. We don't play ball when American lives are at stake.'

She kept her eyes fixed on the laptop camera, no sideways glances or distractions, but I knew she had company.

'I'm an American life. So was Ferdia McErlane, so was George Oliver,' I said. 'Maybe we were the wrong sort of American lives and don't count, but we can end this chat now and I'll talk to Moscow instead, how about that?'

No hesitation or pause for instructions.

'Good luck with that, Maknazpy!' She gloated, and touched a finger to the tiny ear-piece. 'If you think our Russian friends will welcome international scrutiny of the role their business and political elite play in global cyber-crime and money laundering, then go right ahead!'

I nudged Zheng and he pulled a file up on a pop-out screen.

'Have a look at this file in front of you,' I said. 'Rock solid proof that the United States plundered legitimate bank reserves in Beirut, Lebannon, of fifty million dollars and filtered these funds through Israel and Saudi Arabia to supply arms to known terrorist groups in Syria and other regions. This data confirms the process began in late 2010, at least six months before violence began, and two years before any allegations of chemical weapons being employed.'

Silence at the other end, Cora squinting to read the file and reconcile it to what she knew as the truth. She looked up then, off camera, needed a prompt, maybe this was true and she had been fed bullshit.

'This is absurd!' she said. 'Even the most superficial audit of the authentic transactions will place the trail from Beirut through bank accounts to Russia and Ukraine!'

'The proof is in front of your eyes,' I said. 'Enough proof for Moscow to expose the United States as being responsible for engineering the war in Syria: part of America's quest for global domination and its ongoing campaign to sabotage the Russian Federation – or something like that.'

Panic at the other end, Zheng almost purring, the connection to England died.

'The Guardian in London, the New York Times and The Washington Post. Who else is on the UN Security Council anyway? The Xinhua News Agency, Al Jazerra and TASS will have it on-line in minutes. Germany, France and Brazil are still pissed off at us since the last exposure of US spying on their governments, aren't they? Let's see how good your spin doctors are at clawing their way back to the high moral ground after this.'

The camera on her laptop was covered, the mike muffled, they were in meltdown over there.

Pyotr hammered up the stairs shouting in Russian to Yakov.

'The policia outside say they have orders to pull back and stay back,' Yakov said. 'The Americans are coming.'

Zheng's screen froze, he pushed me away and went into overdrive.

'They try to hack this machine!' Zheng laughed. 'Their technicians thought I was in Moldova but I have changed it to Odessa.'

'Cora knows exactly where we are,' I said. 'And who is in here with us.'

'The technicians can only work with what they see!' Zheng was having a lot of fun. 'She tells them we are here but I show them we are in Odessa. What can they do?'

'You better stop them coming through those fucking gates!' Yakov said. 'If they try to take my house I will fill the pool with their blood!'

I knew he would, and that the situation would quickly spin out of control.

'Zheng! Get fucking Cora back here now!'

The kid was as calm as if he was changing the fuse on that plasma screen, smiling to himself and basking in his bubble of glory. I started to think he was showboating the whole thing for maximum effect, taking it to the edge so he would be an even greater hero when he pulled it back.

'Cora! Tell your people to stand down!' I said. 'Your attack dogs can't win this time. If you force us to the next level then we are talking a crisis like Irangate, like Watergate! You think that is in the best interests of the United States?'

I could hear them charging towards us like a train, rubber burning to a stop, engines revving outside the gate.

'We can handle it,' Cora bounced back. 'If the United States has to stand alone for the truth then let the chips fall, Maknazpy, let them fall.'

'Listen to yourself, Cora. That is bullshit. You are spewing out the same old depressing crap that got us into this shit.'

I tapped Zheng's arm, he started again.

'Another file, Cora. Details of the scrambled credit cards used to skim over fifty million dollars from ATM's all over the world. This is proof that the biggest credit card scam in history was part of the 'arms to rebels' scandal. Originated in the United States, ripened in Israel, delivered from Qatar and Saudi Arabia. It all ends up in the same corrupt pot; arms to Jihadi rebels in Syria, Libya, Somalia, Yemen. These are the American fingerprints all over the blood stained pot.'

They fumbled through the impenetrable mesh of IP Addresses and numbers, bank accounts and withdrawals. Zheng had cooked it up so the information looked good. Cora and whoever was in her ear couldn't make the call on whether it was true or not: there was always the possibility, the likelihood, that some other guardians of National Security had created this little empire of justified means.

'You want to play the end game right now?' I said. 'Go right ahead, let the dogs off the leash and I'll launch both these files in a heartbeat. Think you've got the firepower to block them in Odessa?'

Cora stepped back from the camera, huddled with three or four other figures, somebody relaying messages like a trackside bookie.

'How do we make this go away, Maknazpy?'

Her voice was still pumped with aggression, like she was in control, like she was calling the shots, like she could demean me at will.

'One more file, Cora. Just for insurance.'

Zheng was proudest of this one, would hawk it around all his new colleagues when he got over there.

'Encrypted communication between Joint Base Anacostia-Bolling in D.C. and Colonel Hu Lui, Chinese Military Intelligence, Seventh Bureau. You can see here, the named Case Officer of the Defense Intelligence Agency is openly colluding with Colonel Liu to present false information against the Russian Federation.'

'Fucking bullshit, Maknazpy!'

'You want it to go away, Cora? Take the easy way. You know what I need.'

Silence at the other end.

'And Cora, remember to tell your friends there that I'm a good American also – just like Ferdy McErlane was.'

CHAPTER FORTY-EIGHT

The call came in as darkness settled over the rooftops.

"I can confirm that residency visas have been approved for Miss Yasmin Azevedo and her two children."

Still a soft liquid Donegal voice despite forty plus years in his Bronx law firm.

'I also have in my possession a statement that confirms the US Department of Justice is aware of no outstanding matters as of this date of unlawful activity concerning Cornelius Maknazpy jnr., and foresees no circumstance whereby it would be in the interests of the United States of America to investigate, advance or prosecute any legal action in relation to any such matters which may come to light in future. As regards Cornelius Maknazpy snr., the statement likewise confirms that it will not be in the interests of the US to seek prosecution pertaining to certain historic events.'

'Is that good enough, Mr Ward?' I said.

'It is good,' Mr Ward said. 'It is authorized and duly witnessed by two notable signatories, both of whom occupy high office in the Department of Justice. I won't mention their names over the telephone but you can be assured that they will not be over-ruled. Your NYPD friends Dart and McAnespie also witnessed it, for reasons I am not acquainted with. It is very good.'

'Is Jack Gallogly there with you now?'

'He is not,' Mr Ward said. 'I am advised that your party should be prepared to leave tonight. Your transport will collect you at 8 pm.'

'And that's it? They can't backtrack on it?'

'Backtrack? If they try it I'll screw the dickheads so far into the ground they'll need a fucking periscope on top of a bastarding elevator to ever see daylight again. Tell your father I was asking about him. Tell him not to be a stranger when he gets home. Good luck, son.'

So that was it. A clean slate. Two million in the bank for Rose and young Con. No more looking over my shoulder waiting on the bullet. Free to go home and start a new life. It felt good but it should have felt better.

The engines outside throttled up, headlights on, doors slamming, bumping off the sidewalk, and they were gone. I found my father beside the pool as their red brake lights vanished into the dark. He knelt on a mat in the shadows, outside the crucible of blue light suspended over the water, praying or meditating or whatever they do in Macau.

'A few minutes a day to purge my brain of all the white noise that infests this modern world,' he said.

I told him Gallogly's attorney had confirmed the deal. He could forget about Nicaragua and Salvador and Cuba and all his twisted betrayals of the United States; it was time to go home.

'I got it all wrong when you were a child,' he said. 'I thought you had to be tough to survive. That was all wrong.'

I told him he should get ready, Cora's people would be here soon to transport us to the airport.

'Don't be afraid of the dark, son,' he said. 'Let your demon free, look it in the eye and spit in its face. When the devils burn out you'll find your true spirit. It's there, son, I always saw it in you, it was always there.'

'Old man Ward said you should look him up,' I said.

'Try it when you are alone some time,' he said. 'Just shut all the crap out and let your mind heal itself.'

A car pulled up outside the gates. The policia taking up their post again.

'I remember Hughie Ward, one of the smartest when we were young, but you know your smoke and mirrors trick is strictly a short term fix?' he said.

I knew.

'Zheng's first job over there will be to dismantle that 'proof' you blindsided them with,' he said. 'Then they will be free to come after you, after all of us'

I said I knew. I always knew.

★★★

Pyotr rattled the pots and slammed the cupboard doors like any good chef. A barrel load of paella to prepare and somebody had swiped his saffron. Yakov indulged Pyotr's tantrum and his own ego, ruffling his nephew's hair and making mocking eyes over his shoulder to the audience of Noviciates who were careful to laugh at the boss's good humor without risking payback from his lightweight, but influential, sister's son. Yasmin ignored Yakov's ruckus and the eyes of the young guys checking her out, kept her head down to chop the onions and red peppers in the corner.

'Bring Zheng down to the pool,' I whispered. 'Yakov doesn't need to know.'

'How do I bring him?'

The jade ear-ring teased my lips.

'However you like,' I said. 'But keep it quiet.'

★★★

The water in the hot tub was cold. A black mold dotted the underside of the cover and a skin of slimy green algae held the water still. One of the young guys brought drinks to the cops outside the gate; coffee first, then Yakov's latest cocktail experiment. The security gates clicked behind him and he strolled around the back to the kitchen, spinning the tray on two fingers like a circus juggler. He must have been inside when the lights in the pool area dimmed to a twilight glow.

Zheng was still on a high. New clothes, secret millions in the bank, Jorginho's old gig waiting for him, his own apartment, a red Italian sportster, and everybody would know he was the best. And the girls, that's what kept him spiked during thousands of hours of keystroke frustration - screen stalking websluts and smut talking teens. All those American girls, and him with his sportster and millions and an apartment. And this one, she had pinned him down to the floor back in the house on the cliff. Now she knew who he really was.

The lights blinked off, just the blue haze over the pool. He let Yasmin direct him, pinching himself to stay cool but clutching his arm around her shoulder in case she would disappear in a puff of smoke or change her mind. She ducked out from under his right arm and bobbed up again under his left, trailed his left hand over her shoulders and clutched it tight above her breast. Somebody switched on a light on the third floor terrace, Juicy J Bouncing It all over the neighborhood on Yakov's industrial scale sound system, nobody would complain.

Yasmin lanquished her ass against the curved Swedish timber of the tub and pulled him close, the kid looked as if he would faint or throw up and she had to take his face in her hands to steady him.

'I love you' he croaked,

She giggled, and I whipped his ankles in the air and plunged his head and shoulders into the cold tub. I pinned him against the side, pressing his head down and shanking his right arm up his back. Twenty seconds, pulled his head clear of the water, he choked and panicked, coughing and spluttering so much he couldn't breathe. I forced him under again. Fifteen seconds. Jerked his head up.

'You did good work,' I said. 'I have all the guarantees I wanted and I'm going home. Now I'm going to drown you like the rat you are and take back the rest of the cash.'

Down, twenty seconds, he came up half drowned.

'I'll ask you once. Why did Liu kill Jorginho?'

Zheng tried to cough words out but his throat was full of water. I stood back and thumped him between the shoulder blades, then braced his nose and mouth over the water. Yasmin stuck her nails into his left wrist and locked it tight against his side.

'Hurry up, Zheng! You were there! You heard Jorginho's big mouth! Liu still thought you didn't understand English! What did they say before Liu broke his neck!'

He was crying and croaking, tried to struggle but couldn't move, heaved and emptied his stomach, the disgusting blue mess of Yakov's cocktail recipe rank in the air and water.

Grabbed his hair and put him under. Thirty seconds, in case he was counting. Yasmin shook my shoulder, a worried look on her face. Dragged him up, coughing and choking.

'Jorginho was talking to the Americans! Even before you came! I saw it over the network. I told Comrade Liu when you locked us in that house!'

Liu killed Jorginho because of that? Even though he had the key to all that Flame and Red Protocol shit? I ducked him under, he was getting weak, hardly struggling at all. Out again.

'Comrade Liu was mad, kicking and beating George Oliver in that hole you put us in,' Zheng wheezed. 'Oliver got mad too, he did not respect the Colonel. Jorginho said he knew that Comrade Liu was speaking to the Americans at the same time. He said Colonel Liu was a traitor to China and Jorginho would tell the whole world about it.'

I could picture that scene; Jorginho firing off his smart ass mouth, Liu banging crap out of him, George with his 'fuck you!' attitude, not knowing when to stop, until Liu stopped him for good. I straightened Zheng up, he held on to the hot tub and spewed the filthy water over our feet.

'So who was Liu talking to?' I said. 'Who were the Americans Liu was working with?'

'Who? I don't know who. Jorginho did not say who. How could I know?'

The tremor fizzed up my neck like a low voltage electric shock. I strained against it, tried to push it back. Deep breaths, keep control, breathe: but still the black cloud pumped at the base of my skull, heart rocking in my chest and the scent of death pulped in my throat. 'Con! Con! Stop! Stop it! You are killing him!' Yasmin's screams spun around my ears but I couldn't connect her voice to my mind and the hands around Zheng's throat. His tongue bursting out of his mouth, twisted and grotesque, his eyes sizzling out of his face, trying to escape. 'Please! Stop!' Yasmin crying in my ear but I wasn't there now, it wasn't me, the red pressure in my brain spat me out and sucked the other me in for the kill. Ferdy killed, Luis killed. The little black boat in the moonlight and these fingers before me grinding the last drop of blood and air from his lying tongue.

He hit me from behind, a heavy punch on the back of my neck that rocked right down to my knees. Then he harnessed his arms around my biceps, wrestling me away from Zheng but I couldn't let go and Zheng stumbled and took all three of us down. Yasmin dived on top of me, her knees thudding into my chest and forcing me back, my father wrangled me on to my stomach, my head wedged against the hot tub slick with Zheng's sick and the mucous water. He held me still, quiet and calm in my ear, until I surrendered to his father's strength. Because he was still strong, and still my father.

CHAPTER FORTY-NINE

Nausea licked the pain burning its way through the centre of my head. I gripped the sides of the table and screwed my eyes tight until the spinning stopped. Yasmin's daughter brought a glass of iced water from the kitchen and her neat trembling hands shamed me. No need for words between them, the girl withered under Yasmin's bad vibes like an inverse sponge, shrinking in body and spirit as fear and tension bloomed around her, as if she was somehow to blame for some untold sin. I tried to rekindle the beautiful smile but her tight lips quivered and her mother snapped at her to go. My shakes splashed the water over my pants until I latched my mouth to the glass and choked back the drink. Yasmin buzzed with a callous scorn, coiled and ready to spring my apology down my throat.

'Cora will be here soon,' I said. 'I need to go see Blake.'

Yakov came to meet me at the bottom of the stairs when he heard my footsteps above. Four men formed a wedge of ruthless muscle behind him; the Spetsnaz were back.

'How come you whacked Liu?' I said.

Yakov rose up on the first step, realized he only reached my chest and brushed past to look down at me from the third step.

'Because I didn't like the way he looked at me, okay?' he blustered loud, finger stabbing down into my chest. 'Why? What's it to you, Maknazpy?'

'Fine,' I said. 'I'll see what Blake has to say about it, maybe he'll feel like fixing a better deal for himself before Cora's people get here.'

'Be my guest!' He carved a sweeping gesture with his hand and the Spetsnaz parted below me. 'But keep away from our young friend Zheng. We have invested big time and money in this kid, he will be an asset to our business model in America. Keep your hands off him.'

The Spetsnaz breathed a bubble of half digested vodka and antiseptic wound dressing. The oldest one, smaller and more evil than the rest, bumped his shoulder into me as I passed. They laughed, like any clutch of bonehead corner boys, but I ignored it and headed down to the basement gym, with Yakov cranking up the big joke as I turned the corner. Pyotr was down below, mopping the small hallway at the bottom of the stairs between gym and bar. He straightened up when he saw me, gathered his mop and bucket, and backed into the bar.

He had already washed the gym floor, I could follow the wet mop tracks around Blake's feet and the fumes from his bleach and ammonia mixture stung the back of my raw throat. The air extractor rumbled and churned high on the wall above Blake but it would never purify this atmosphere because the respected Doctor James Blake, Professor of Systems Neuroscience and distinguished Member of the National Academy of Sciences, lay slumped in a chair with his neck screwed off his shoulders.

The head dangled down to his lap, stretched as if it was only the pampered skin of his neck determined to claim it for the body. No black scuffle marks on the gym floor from Blake's fine Italian shoes, and I doubted Pyotr's mop would have removed the last desperate gouging of a choking man. And this didn't look like asphyxia over a panicked last few moments when the damaged spinal cord fails the breathing function and leaves you to drown. No, strong arms had locked around Blake's head, tearing apart the spinal cord the way Yakov pulped limes for his cocktails. The bladder and bowels had surrendered but Pyotr had only mopped the floor. The taut neck was still warm and the eyes cold but I could imagine them still receiving inkspots of light and shadow and shuffling them around until they realized the deadend couldn't be avoided. Just like Jorginho back on the cliffs. Strong arms, but quick and precise; practiced, skilful even, but not Liu this time.

Back upstairs, Yakov holding court out on the terrace under a blanket of rough smoke and Russian chatter.

'First Liu, then Blake?' I said. 'You keeping something quiet, Yakov?'

Somebody mimicked me in Russian and they all cracked up, but the older evil one snatched a quick look at Yakov's face, just to be sure.

'Blake? Who said that was me?' Yakov bared his teeth, almost like a smile. 'I thought it was you, Maknazpy! Right after you tried to snap young Zheng's neck off at the pool. Just like you did for Jorginho. It looks like you have something to hide, my friend.'

I left them there and ran up to the bedroom. I trailed Yasmin off the bed and pulled the mattress up. Her face said I was a wild animal that might attack her children at any minute.

'Where's the gun I left here?' I said.

She shook her head and moved backwards like she wanted to get away but was afraid to turn her back on me. I grabbed her elbow and steered her out to the balcony where my old man was playing cards with her kids. I planted her down at the table and gave him the nod to follow me in.

'Blake's dead! What did he and Liu have on Yakov?' I said. 'Is Yakov working with the Chinese also?'

My father linked his hands behind his head and stretched out on the bed. He looked up at the ceiling as if he had scribbled the answer up there but couldn't find it now when he needed it.

'Are you saying Yakov killed him?' he said.

'Who to fuck else would it be! You think I did it?'

He found his spot on the ceiling and homed in on it, like he was preparing for an interrogation.

'You lost it out there with Zheng,' he said. 'You would have finished him off if I hadn't stopped you. Liu was pretty adamant that you did George Oliver. You sure you know what you're doing, or exactly what you have done?'

I had already told him I hadn't touched Jorginho, Yasmin would say the same now she was free, and he still tried to rattle me about it? This empty old man in front of me didn't know the first thing about me, and anything he did know was about a lost little boy who didn't exist anymore.

'What about this faction shit in China?' I said. 'You think Liu and his faction were working with America?'

He kept his eyes on that spot.

'Colonel Liu was no traitor,' he said. 'Whoever he was working with, I know he was no traitor.'

'Okay, so how about the other side?' I said. 'Maybe there is another American traitor, like Blake, somebody working for the Chinese. Who would that be?'

The old man swung his legs around and pushed himself upright.

'Things often happen for no reason, son, or they have a reason that you couldn't understand. Just let this mess go. Take this girl and her children and go home. That's all the reason you need right now.'

'Yakov says this stuff about you being sacrificed to the US is bullshit,' I said. 'He says Liu wouldn't have handed you over to Cora unless your Chinese bosses had a job they needed done in the US. A job to do and you the best man to do it.'

'Yeah? And you listen to Yakov now?' He dismissed me with a wave of his hand and made for the balcony. 'Go home, make your peace with your family or this girl or whoever. Make your peace and let your mind heal itself.'

'I can do that,' I said. 'Like a friend of yours said, I can let the poison be my cure.'

He stopped at the doorway and half turned like he had something to say, but changed his mind and slid the glass door closed between us.

Then the four of them sat around the little table out there, flipping cards and laughing in the cold night air. They laughed at his funny Portuguese from Macau; the weird words and sounds that were and weren't Portuguese at the same time. They laughed at the faces and goofy card tricks he pulled. Even Yasmin laughed, and even her angry son Bebeto. I frisked down my thin layer of memory searching for a time the old man joked and cracked like that with me. A sad blank. They were outside but it felt like I was the one on the outside looking in, and their laughing made me feel maybe it was my fault.

Pyotr opened the bedroom door and then stood back in the hallway.

'My uncle says the Americans are on their way. It is time to go.'

Yakov was in his office on the ground floor, feet up on his too big desk and almost horizontal on the executive buffalo hide swivel chair. Zheng flinched when Pyotr pulled a chair over for me and I slapped the geek genius' back.

'Just so we all understand each other before you fly off to the land of the free,' Yakov chuckled. 'We have made a big investment in Mr Zheng. We do not want to have any worries about what happens when he gets over there.'

Zheng rubbed the back of his neck as if it was still sore, probably trying to make some sort of point but I ignored it.

'We have been very generous,' Yakov rambled. 'Eight million dollars, a lot of money, but it is just the start for you, Mr Zheng. So, you can work for the Americans, no problem, this will be good for us also. But do not forget who you really work for! We will make it easy for you, of course. And I don't have to tell you what will happen if you disappoint us, or even think you can ever forget about us?'

Zheng shook his head, nodded his head, shook his head. Yakov called Pyotr, waited until he had led the kid out, then scraped his feet off the desk and swung around to me.

'He is a good kid, this one,' he said. 'Good for business, good for the future, no problems.'

He opened a cupboard in his desk and pulled out a bell-shaped brandy decanter with a long neck, and two heavy glasses. The crazy celtic swirls and loops stood out like veins in the crystal, like reading the Book of Kells by Braille.

'My wife brought these from her holiday in Ireland,' he said. 'When she was still talking to me.'

The brandy slid out of the top drawer – Armenian cognac.

'They asked me if you will be a problem, Maknazpy.' He gulped a good mouthful of cognac. 'I said no, we have an arrangement, and you are too smart to be a problem.' Another suck to empty the glass. 'Was I stupid to be so positive? I am not permitted to make such mistakes, as you know.'

'No mistake,' I said. 'We have an arrangement. I keep my word.'

He poured again, more this time, enough for three people in one glass.

'Good! So you will forget all this nonsense and stop acting like a frustrated cop?'

'My best friend died here,' I said.

'We have all lost comrades, I know what this means – but what do you hope to do about it now? Your comrade died in action, you killed the man who did it, so what else is there?'

'Somebody brought us over here, Yakov, like two frisky pups chasing a bone. Maybe to flush out Blake or Liu, I don't know. Used us to hide their looting of Beirut banks to arm the rebels in Syria. Maybe it was to take Zheng, or maybe my father. Some of them are dead and that's too bad, but Ferdia McErlane died in my arms out here. I'll forget the rest of it but not that. Just like McErlane wouldn't walk away if it had been me taken down. So, are we going to have a problem here?'

He reached forward with the cognac, I refused by placing my hand over the glass but he tugged my wrist away and slushed in enough to choke a hard drinking donkey.

'What about your father? Will he be a problem?'

'Not my problem!' I said. 'He's not my responsibility, this isn't a 'buy one get one free' deal.'

'Somebody brought you here, you say.' Yakov planted his feet wide apart and used the desk to lever himself out of the executive chair. 'What if the strings were made in Beijing? What if the Americans were wearing their usual aggressive blindfold. What if the strings were pulled from Macau?'

'I don't give a shit where it came from,' I said. 'I'll follow it to wherever it leads, and Ferdy McErlane will have his revenge. Wherever it leads, Yakov.' I knocked back the cognac in three burning swallows. 'But you sound like you're leading up to bad news here, so just spit it out, I can take it.'

'All news is bad for somebody,' he said. 'We don't know what the Americans wanted but it would have been something simple, that's the only way they can work. Wham Bam, Thank You, Ma'am!' He made like he was a gunslinger pulling a fast draw and smacking the hammer on a 45. 'The Chinese have their own way of thinking, a way that you

Americans will never understand. Even Russians find them difficult.'

'You mean we don't have the right education?'

'Something like that,' he said. 'But take my advice, complete our arrangement as soon as you get home and before you get lost in a Chinese maze. You will keep your millions from Beirut, we won't come after it. We will have Zheng where we need him and you will be free. You and Yasmin.'

'I said I would do it.'

'Good! And you never know, sometimes those Chinese strings are all tied up together. You pull the right string for us, you might trap the trigger finger you are looking for attached to the end of it. But a warning, my friend, we didn't touch Blake, so if you didn't either, then who did?'

PART IV:
THE CROCK OF GOLD

The life of the dead is placed in the memory of the living

Marcus Cicero (106 BC – 43 BC)

CHAPTER FIFTY

New York, March 18th - Gallogly cruised along the Montauk Highway like he was treating me to a midnight picnic on an East Hampton beach. One headlight dead so we blinded oncoming traffic with full beam but, other than that, his Merc SUV wasn't out of place on this road; Southampton, Water Mill and Bridgehampton, a St Patrick's Day leprechaun and Irish Tricolor grotesque in Wainscott, the town of East Hampton, East Hampton village – Gallogly didn't need directions.

'You sure you can trust this woman?' he said.

'She'll be there, Jack,' I said, but resisted the snipe that I used to think I could trust Rose.

Between the East Hampton Golf Club and the South Fork Country Club, Gallogly found the lane and then the track, 'PRIVATE -DEAD END' - an ordinary gate, the track slipped into the bushes, a dark roof sketched against the glow of distant lights.

'You know I'm not into waiting on the sidelines,' he said. 'Let me come with you.'

I wriggled into the plastic forensic suit and wrestled with the latex gloves.

'Sorry, Jack. Only have one suit,' I said. 'Anyway, I need you to be ready with the car. No longer than twenty minutes. I'll give three flashes with the torch on my way back.'

'Fuck that! Young Con took it real bad about Ferdy. How do you think I'll feel if I have to tell him we've lost you as well?'

'He'll be okay. He has you and Rose, hasn't he?' I said, but knew instantly that didn't sound the way I meant it to. 'Listen, Jack, I mean it, he is lucky to have you. He is better off with you. And don't worry, I don't figure on getting lost.'

The big meathead clamped his fat sausage fingers on my shoulder, started to say something but choked up and turned his face away. I reached under his seat for the clean SIG 250, gave him a friendly Ferdy-slap on his gorilla thigh.

'Don't worry about it, brother,' I said. 'This one's for McErlane.'

Out and over the gate, kept to the rough track, through the bushes, the house planted square in the hollow below. All dark at the front, but the outside spots splashed their daylight right across the back – the barbecue pit, the dining area, the lawns. Not good in a shining white forensic suit. I fucking told her to make sure all the outside lights were knocked off. At least she had left the back door open, into the kitchen, tensed for the alarm to spring – nothing, just music from up above. Moved through the lounge to the stairs. They were up there, 'Not a Bad Thing' bouncing out of speakers the size of a small car; too loud, they didn't hear this bad thing coming right at them behind a SIG 250.

I booted in the bedroom door, he sprung out of the four-poster like a rat disturbed at a carcass and grabbed at a bedside drawer. He was quick, just not quick enough this time, I gouged my knee into the back of his neck and sunk the pistol into his fat cheek.

'Hi Alex! I told you I would come looking for you, didn't I?' I said. 'And Yakov sends his compliments. He said to make sure you knew he was thinking about you.'

'You're making a big mistake here, you fucking asshole!' Moscow Alex shouted in his $30,000 fees a year prep school voice, not his rough Russian voice. 'You are way over your head! Way over! Back off now you won't get hurt. Your fucking retard son won't get hurt!'

He was saying all the wrong things but, this time, there were no right things. I screwed the SIG tight into his ear like I was Blake looking for a brain in there. Alex tried again.

'Look, I've got cash here! Two mill at least! Take it all and you'll never see me again, Maknazpy! Two million dollars and walk!'

'I can't hear you over this shit music you're assaulting my head with, Alex!' I shouted into his face. 'How much did you say?'

The music cut out, a green silk kimono came floating over the thick shag carpet.

'Where to fuck were you?' Yasmin screamed at me. 'How long did you think I could hide in the bathroom?'

I laughed, but Moscow Alex didn't see the funny side of it. He was sweating like a Turkish wrestler's jockstrap, beads of sweat plumping up to quiver the thick gray and black hair that sprouted over his back and shoulders in coarse handfuls. I smacked his head off the floor a couple of times to give him something to think about then dragged him up by the hair. He stood there in front of us in all his red sweaty glory, a trickle of blood from his nose and fear in his eyes. Yasmin cursed something Brazilian and turned her face away. And he wasn't a pretty sight - his back was as hairy as a fucked mountain goat but his front was as smooth as a baby's ass. His chest, legs, even his balls, all waxed red and bare.

'Two million, Alex? How much do you say Ferdia McErlane's life was worth? Or the old guy Luis? If you say you have two mill I reckon that means you have twenty stashed away somewhere real secret – especially after our ATM gig.'

I should have heard them coming - they crashed down both doors at once; wood splintering, glass smashing, came charging up the stairs like a whirlwind. She looked at me in panic, shook her head, buried her face in the long fingers. I trailed Alex back to a corner and held him tight in front of me with his neck trapped in the crook of my elbow, the SIG rammed up under his chin. They stopped outside on the landing.

'Maknazpy! Stand down! We'll take it from here!'

Yasmin stared at me and pointed to the door. Yeah, Yasmin, I heard her, I heard Cora demeaning me. The hit squad came in first, all bullet proof armor and bad attitude. They swarmed up close to pin me against the corner. One of them stepped forward and jerked his MP7 into my face.

'I wouldn't do that if I were you, soldier!' My father's voice, black behind Cora in the doorway. 'Take it easy, son! Breathe deep and take it easy!' It wouldn't have been the first time I had heard his voice when he wasn't there – but he was there, right in front of me, with Cora and another dark shape. Cora pulled the dogs back then stepped aside to allow my father and the figure to advance. My father, and Cora's anvil-headed boss – still a dark shape, still all outline and no features.

'You know what we need right now, Alex,' Cora said.

Only my necklock kept Alex's sweaty body upright; steam rising from his shoulders like he was a racehorse, his guts rumbling and squeaking like he was about to explode. I pushed him away from me and he landed on his knees before the Anvil Head.

'Put some pants on this guy, for Christ's sake!' A voice to ring sparks off iron. 'Take him down to the basement!'

They smothered over Alex like rats, found track bottoms to pull over his hairy ass and boosted him out the door. I started after them but Cora placed her hand on my chest and eased me back. The Anvil nodded to my father and told Cora it was okay.

'Mr Maknazpy has made the journey this far, he deserves to know how it turns out. Besides, he is such a fucking pain in the ass that we can't afford to leave him curious.'

The basement was more than a basement; Cora hit the light switch and a series of fluorescent tubes flickered and spurted in sequence to push the room further and further back, far beyond the footprint of the house, stretching maybe half way across the lawns above. Somebody whistled, somebody cursed under their breath, but they were all as stunned as I was.

A row of glass cabinets stocked with oil paintings, climate controlled and meticulously catalogued, some in ornate gilt frames, some stretched across board, some rolled up in tubes. The next section looked like it had been shopfitted straight out of the Diamond District down on West 47th Street, rows of cabinets holding velvet lined drawers sparkling with diamonds of every shape and color. Then small bags brimmed with stones; from tiny pin-heads to the size of my thumbnail, rough and uncut – Blood Diamonds, my father said. Then cabinets and drawers so full of watches and antique jewelry that gold and silver clattered to the tiled floor when we opened the doors. Further down, rows of antique pieces – sculpted chairs, ornate tables, ridiculously high chiming clocks, writing desks, even a four poster like the one I had kicked Alex's hairy naked butt out of.

On the right hand side there was a wall safe, not quite big enough to walk into but not far off it. A shabby desk and plastic office chair squeezed against the wall; in-trays stacked high with paperwork, red and green folders bulging with notes, receipts, valuations and certificates – some of them probably even genuine. A heavy duty green plastic garden garbage bag wedged under the desk, Cora tugged it and thick wads of cash spilled across the floor. More cash stashed in the desk drawers; not sorted and counted, just heaps of loose notes shoved and crammed like somebody had become bored and had put the job off until later.

They held Moscow Alex in front of the safe. He keyed the password without a struggle, like he was relieved it was all over. Cora folded herself into the safe and funneled the contents out to the floor; bags of cash, jewelry, diamonds and other gems, and passports, credit cards, driver licenses, share and stock certificates, authorizations and ID cards. Cora stood back and shook her head, gestured to show the safe was empty. A slap to Alex's cheek was enough, he pointed to the desk, they kicked it over and found the floor safe beneath the tiles, the key taped underneath the desk.

Cora had better luck this time, dipped her fingers in and fished out a computer hard drive. They set a laptop on the desk and Cora plugged in a drive adapter. The tech side ready to go, the guard dogs retreated out of the basement trailing Alex along by handfuls of his hairy red blubber. They edged Yasmin away from the door, left me as a spectator beside my father.

'What did Yakov know about this?' he said.

What did Yakov know about what? What was this? And what to fuck was he doing here?

'Syria wasn't the only troubled region where insurgents received illegal funding from the United States,' he said. 'You think that crap in Kiev just happens spontaneously? Think the Russians aren't pretty much pinned down right now between Ukraine and their own Ultra-Nationalists and imported Jihadis right across their southern flank. Suicide bombs on buses? Black Widow attacks on Volgograd? Ask your friend Yakov about Russia's own Pipelineistan. Their gas is piped through Ukraine, through Crimea. Ask Yakov about Chechyna, Dagestan, Ingushetia, Ossetia. Let's see how things pan out in Ukraine. Okay, so Moscow has muscled in on Crimea – but that's going to stay a real pain in the Kremlin's ass no matter how many tanks they roll in there!'

'Jorgingho siphoned off Beirut funds to Chechen suicide bombers also?'

'He didn't,' he said. 'Those funds were scraped up elsewhere, he shouldn't even have known about it but he found out somehow. Knew Alex here held the keys to that enterprise and knew the damage exposure would do. He thought he knew how much his silence was worth. He mis-calculated, make sure you learn from his mistake.'

'Are you ready, sir?' The metallic voice inflected an invite to perch on Cora's shoulder as she flashed the numbers across the monitor. SWIFT, IBAN and RTN codes clicked up the screen like Zheng's little green aliens eating away borders to spew mayhem and anarchy. A few thousand here, a few million there – neat rows of marching dollars, Saudi riyals, Israeli shekels. Cora highlighted a worksheet, scrutinized it, keyed back to cross-reference, forward again, ran a finger under the code.

'Here, BIC code is MO, ten million: here, BIC code US, ten mill. Both paid to banks in Qatar, then dispersed in small transfers to banks all over the place; Turkey, Pakistan, Turkmenistan, Bulgaria, Armenia, Ireland, Latvia, all over the fucking place.'

'What's that mean?' I said.

'Every country has its own BIC code,' Cora sighed. 'US is the US. MO is Macau.'

Anvil Head had seen enough, whistled for the guard dogs to come bouncing in again; one had a heavy duty power drill, another two shuffled a metal basin with four large flasks rattling at the bottom.

'You are satisfied, Sir? As agreed?'

Cora extracted the hard drive from the adapter and placed it on the floor at their feet as if it was a sacred tribal offering. They even paused in silence for a few moments like there was an accepted ritual to be observed, like the piece of crap radiated some divine energy to bond them in spiritual communion – and maybe it did, maybe that was no more absurd than any of their other bullshit codes and beliefs.

The drill deafened us in that narrow cave. He couldn't bite into the disk casing at first and the drill bit skidded over the surface like seven cats scraping a blackboard. That didn't sit easy with the guy's elite swagger, especially in front of that audience, and he cursed the fucking thing to hell and lip-synched at another one to hold it steady. They worked it between them and pretty soon he had five holes punched through the metal. My father shook his head, so they gouged a couple more. The basin was still sheathed in its new plastic packaging, they scrambled that off and tipped the contents of the flasks to swirl a toxic tide three fingers deep. The drill guy held up the blitzed hard drive like he was a warrior priest then slipped it into the holy acid font. I flashed back to Blake, and Pyotr's bucket of fumes in Yakov's gym.

Whatever it was, it drove us all back, except for my father and the Anvil Head, neither wanting to lose face. I took my father's shoulder and backed him away.

'Ferdy McErlane died for this?' I spit in his ear. 'So you could fucking slip in here to decommission a Russian time bomb?'

'No, Con, Ferdy McErlane died because you screwed up. You failed him. Not me, not anyone else, just you. So now suck it up and get on with your life.'

He felt my fingers biting into his shoulder.

'I told you to stop wasting your time expecting to find a reason for everything,' he said. 'Things happen, people react, plans change. Get over it!' The angry authentic voice from my childhood, but then he softened his tone. 'I went to Portugal for you, like I said, and that's all you need to know, okay? That's when Colonel Liu discovered this situation. I am here to prevent an escalation.'

The poison cloud mushroomed up against the ceiling and snaked down the walls to ambush us from behind. We moved towards the open doorway, he kept his eyes on the basin.

'The United States partners China to sponsor terrorism against Russia?' I said. 'And you make it sound like you've earned the Nobel fucking Peace Prize?'

He shrugged. 'Sometimes we work with Russia, sometimes the US and Russia both join against us. So what?'

'Okay, okay, I get it,' I said. 'But you haven't come all this way just to witness Cora destroying the evidence, have you?'

'Why are you here, son?' He turned that look on me, the one that I couldn't stand up against. Yeah, this was part of my deal with Yakov, three million dollars and more to come from Zheng, but nobody said anything about financing kamikaze Chechens and Ukrainian Ultras.

'How come Moscow Alex is screwing the Russians?' I said.

'He is a criminal thug like your Yakov,' he said. 'And he hates Russia! Isn't that why Yakov sent you here?'

'Like you hate America,' I said.

He turned away and took the face mask Anvil Head offered. The drill guy covered his own face as he gripped the remains of the hard drive with a pair of tongs and lifted it clear of the basin. My father bent over to get a closer look; inspected the mangled drive, checked it was the original and not a plant, peered into the toxic pool. That was it: he was satisfied. Anvil Head shook his hand in a curt formality and wheeled away to the exit. The hit squad relaxed, somebody clowning, chat about going for a beer and a golf trip at the weekend. Only Cora was still tense: the angry rash under her chin stood out in this harsh light and up close I could see it had spread across her neck and up the side of her face so that her make-up couldn't mask it.

'Let's get you upstairs to get dressed, Alex,' my father said.

The goon holding Alex had taken off his helmet and balaclava, stood there casually scratching the heavy jaw that made him look like a gorilla, as if he had been pumped with way too much testosterone when he was a kid. Alex was one of the defeated, maybe had been fighting against it all his loser life despite his father's blood money. He fell in place between me and my father like he had been rehearsing this drill since prep school. Cora touched my wrist as we steered him to the stairs but I brushed her away and told Yasmin to wait, we would be back in a few minutes.

It couldn't have even been five minutes before I followed my father down but they had all disappeared, only Cora left waiting on us, making sure the lights were turned off.

'What happens if there are copies of that Chechen stuff?' I said. 'What will the Russians do when they get proof China and America have been paying for a war against them?'

'We have just killed the proof,' Cora said. 'And that was the copy.'

'Who had the original?' I said.

'Blake,' my father said.

'Doctor Blake?'

'Sure, Doctor Blake!' Cora smirked. 'What other fucking Blake was there?'

Cora gripped my arm again but this time it was urgent, she flicked her eyes over my shoulder, Yasmin had come out of the bathroom and was jogging up the stairs.

'Yasmin! Stop! Don't go up there!' I yelled after her.

'Seu babaca!' she jeered. 'My bag is up here. I am not leaving it for this hairy pig!'

I jumped up the first three steps and scrambled after her but she had gathered the green dress up and the bare brown legs skipped away faster than I could match. She was in the room before I could reach her. I stood at the door, she burst out with the bag clutched to her breast and bumped past me to run down the stairs again. I closed the door to Alex's bedroom and followed her down. Cora had moved to the front door and held it open for us.

'Where'd he go?' I said.

Cora looked at me like I was speaking Russian backwards.

'My father? Where did he go?'

She screwed her eyes tight and pouted her lips like she was working out how best to demean me.

'Your father? Wasn't he buried in the jungle somewhere in Honduras in 1988? That's what it says in his file. What can I tell you?'

'So, you're saying my memory is playing tricks again, right?' I said. 'Like, things are only real if you say so?'

'On my payscale? I'm just a messenger around here!' Cora barked a rough cackle. 'But listen good - you're back on the team, you're untouchable now, and you've banked a few million dollars that we don't want to know about. You tell me what's real!'

Up close, Cora was damaged; black rings under her eyes, the shiver in her voice and fingertips, and the whisper of creeping decay on her sour breath.

'What about Ferdy?' I said. 'You think this was worth it? Worth losing him?'

She turned her back on me and stepped out into the darkness. 'You got what you wanted, and we have fulfilled our obligations,' she called over her shoulder. 'I'm sure we won't ever need to remind you of yours.'

Yasmin spread her hand against my chest and eased me back into the light of the doorway as Cora merged into the blackness, just the blond hair pulsing a trail until the darkness reclaimed her, and we were on our own.

'Do not be afraid!' Yasmin said. 'If your friend was with you now he would tell you your Irish prayer - Va a Balla!'

She was right, Ferdy's reckless voice ricocheted around my skull.

'Faugh a Ballagh, bother, Faugh a Ballagh!'

★★★

Gallogly was angry.

'I thought you were fucked!' he shouted in my face. 'They jumped me! I thought for sure they would nut me!'

'Sorry Jack,' I said. 'They knew we were coming, they were waiting for us.'

He made his red face purple by grating the scabby skin with his rough fingernails. 'And? What happened? Are we good to go?' I nodded for him to drive, he looked back at Yasmin using the hem of her green dress to wipe something off her seat, like she suspected Gallogly had spray-scented a marker while we were gone. 'Is she okay?'

'Yeah, we're okay, Jack,' I said. 'They got what they wanted in the end, so we are all okay now. The ones who are still alive got everything they wanted.'

Gallogly turned back towards East Hampton village, we could see the convoy of red lights ahead, snaking back to wherever they came from. He studied Yasmin in the mirror when he thought I wasn't watching, probably composing his report for Rose, about the wild woman from Brazil with the thousand yard stare and blood on her hands, humming a weird song.

'You sure she's okay?' he said. 'That fucking racket sounds like a banshee's wail!'

'It's a song about a dead guy,' I said. 'She knows his spirit sticks with her so he never dies as long as she keeps loving him.'

'Yeah?' He reached over to hit me a mighty slap on my thigh. 'Maybe she saw a ghost back there or something?'

Maybe she did, because the ghosts we all carry with us really aren't so hard to see, we just need to stop and look around. And Yasmin had seen the same thing as I had before I closed the door on Moscow Alex's bedroom; Alex face down on the floor, drowning in his own blood, the heavy knife wedged deep between his shoulder blades and pinning a bright holiday postcard to his fat hairy back –

'Greetings from Atlantic Beach, Rhode Island!'

Printed in Germany
by Amazon Distribution
GmbH, Leipzig